KT-514-529

04985056

MURDER IN THE QUEEN'S WARDROBE

A selection of previous titles by Kathy Lynn Emerson

The Face Down series

FACE DOWN ACROSS THE WESTERN SEA
FACE DOWN BELOW THE BANQUETING HOUSE
FACE DOWN BESIDE ST. ANNE'S WELL
FACE DOWN O'ER THE BORDER

Diana Spaulding Mysteries

DEADLIER THAN THE PEN
FATAL AS A FALLEN WOMAN
NO MORTAL REASON
LETHAL LEGEND

The Tudor Court series
(written as Kate Emerson)

THE PLEASURE PALACE
BETWEEN TWO QUEENS
BY ROYAL DECREE
AT THE KING'S PLEASURE
THE KING'S DAMSEL
ROYAL INHERITANCE

The Mistress Jaffrey Mysteries

MURDER IN THE QUEEN'S WARDROBE *

* *available from Severn House*

MURDER IN THE QUEEN'S WARDROBE

A Mistress Jaffrey Mystery

Kathy Lynn Emerson

This first world edition published 2014
in Great Britain and the USA 2015 by
SEVERN HOUSE PUBLISHERS LTD of
19 Cedar Road, Sutton, Surrey, England, SM2 5DA.
Trade paperback edition first published
in Great Britain and the USA 2015 by
SEVERN HOUSE PUBLISHERS LTD.

Copyright © 2014 by Kathy Lynn Emerson

All rights reserved.
The moral right of the author has been asserted.

Emerson, Kathy Lynn author.
  Murder in the queen's wardrobe.
  1. Women spies–Fiction. 2. Ladies-in-waiting–Fiction.
  3. Murder–Investigation–Fiction. 4. Great Britain–
  History–Elizabeth, 1558-1603–Fiction. 5. Spy stories.
  I. Title
  813.6-dc23

ISBN-13: 978-0-7278-8459-6 (cased)
ISBN-13: 978-1-84751-560-5 (trade paper)
ISBN-13: 978-1-78010-608-3 (e-book)

Except where actual historical events and characters are being
described for the storyline of this novel, all situations in this
publication are fictitious and any resemblance to living persons
is purely coincidental.

All Severn House titles are printed on acid-free paper.

Severn House Publishers support The Forest Stewardship Council™ [FSC™],
the leading international forest certification organisation. All our titles that
are printed on FSC certified paper carry the FSC logo.

Typeset by Palimpsest Book Production Ltd.,
Falkirk, Stirlingshire, Scotland.
Printed and bound in Great Britain by
TJ International, Padstow, Cornwall

One

The crowd, more than two hundred strong, roared with laughter as the man in motley and his little dog capered across the boards used to construct the makeshift stage in the inn-yard of the Horse's Head. To fill the interlude between acts, the jester danced and sang and called out rude remarks to the audience.

Two tiers of galleries ran around three sides of the yard. On the lower, seated only inches above the player's head, a woman wearing a visor that concealed most of her face took as much delight in the merriment as any groundling. Such low humor, sprinkled with risqué puns and suggestive antics, was exceeding improper entertainment for a young gentlewoman. It was for precisely this reason that Mistress Rosamond Jaffrey found it so amusing.

Despite the ban on performances within London's walls, Rosamond had seen a half dozen plays in recent months. She had not yet visited the Curtain or the Theatre. To reach them she would have had to travel some distance north of the city, beyond Bishopsgate and past the muster ground and archery butts in Finsbury Fields and into Shoreditch. But she had been to the purpose-built playhouse in Newington Butts, a mile or so to the south, and this was the third play she had seen performed at the Horse's Head on St Margaret's Hill in Southwark.

The inn was small and hospitable and located conveniently close to the house Rosamond had purchased when she came into her inheritance. Despite the proximity, she was certain the innkeeper had no idea who she was. She did not rely upon the visor alone to conceal her true age and appearance, and she was vigilant both when she walked to the inn and going home again. Only once had anyone tried to follow her. It had been child's play to lose the fellow.

If she'd had a choice, she'd have taken the additional precaution of attending plays alone. Maids and grooms might be invisible to their masters, but other servants had no difficulty remembering what they looked like. Rosamond's maid had a distinctly foreign appearance, making her easier to recognize than most.

Women in the audience, especially seated in the galleries, were not an unusual sight when players plied their trade. Some, like Rosamond, had servants near at hand. Others sat next to a husband or some other respectable male relative. These were merchants' wives and daughters. Rosamond felt certain she was the only gentlewoman present.

At the other extreme were the whores. Any female who attended without an escort, especially if she dressed to catch the eye, was understood to be one of the so-called 'Winchester geese', women who earned their living in the Bankside brothels. On the surface, they did not look much different from other women Rosamond knew. It was their bold behavior and rich apparel – in clear violation of the sumptuary laws – that gave them away.

If she did not wish to be mistaken for one of them, Rosamond was obliged to suffer the company of both a maid and a groom. The necessity galled her, and made it more difficult to conceal her identity. Even the most loyal retainers were inclined to boast about their employers, and not all servants were devoted to their masters and mistresses. At an early age, living in a variety of households, Rosamond herself had learned how to worm secrets out of the stable boys, cooks, and laundresses. She'd also developed a facility for making the upper servants forget she was in the room, a ploy that allowed her to overhear what they talked about among themselves. When she'd set up her own household, she'd chosen her staff with great care.

Charles, her groom, was conveniently mute. He was also blessed with an unremarkable appearance, big enough to deter unwelcome interest in his mistress but not so muscular that he stood out in a crowd. He was a trifle slow-witted, although he understood Rosamond's instructions well enough. He could be trusted to pay their admission fee to the gatherer stationed at the entrance to the inn-yard and seemed to enjoy watching the players' antics almost as much as his employer did.

Rosamond had no doubt at all about her maidservant's loyalty. Melka's devotion belonged, first and foremost, to Rosamond's mother. She'd been sent to spy on Rosamond, as well as to serve her. That said, Rosamond knew that the older woman would die before she'd let any harm come to the girl she'd helped raise. The added advantage was that Melka, although she understood English and could parrot back entire conversations, did not like to give voice to her own thoughts in the language of her adopted country.

The host at the Horse's Head had never heard either Melka or Charles speak and he'd never seen Rosamond's face. Only the weight of her purse was of any interest to him. The lady in the visor could afford the best his inn had to offer. On this late November day in the year of our Lord fifteen hundred and eighty-two, during the twenty-fifth year of the reign of Queen Elizabeth, she had paid extra to sit on a padded bench on the balcony outside one of the inn's best chambers. A small wooden table at her elbow held a bowl of hazelnuts and a jug of raspes, a wine made from raspberries.

A charcoal brazier, well worth the extra penny it had cost, gave off welcome warmth and helped dispel the late afternoon chill. Rosamond edged her leather-booted feet a little nearer to the heat and rearranged her fur-lined cloak to defend against errant breezes. Out of the corner of her eye, she saw Melka sidle closer, pick up the bowl, and begin to shell the remaining hazelnuts, thus giving herself an excuse to linger in proximity to the brazier.

A flurry of catcalls drew Rosamond's attention back to the activity in the inn-yard below. The stage, no more than a series of broad planks laid across a dozen or more hogsheads of beer, swayed alarmingly as a player mounted it. For a moment, it appeared that the poor fellow would tumble backward onto the unforgiving cobblestones, but he righted himself in the nick of time. Red-faced, he ignored the laughter and taunts of the crowd and began his monologue.

Rosamond leaned forward, propping her elbows on the railing so that she could rest her chin on her folded arms. The people who had paid a penny apiece to stand and watch the action on the stage were almost as amusing as the play itself. In less than a minute, Rosamond spotted a cutpurse at work. She admired his dexterity as he snipped the silk points attaching a small velvet bag to the belt of an overweight merchant in a dark green gown. To Rosamond's mind, the fat man had no one but himself to blame for being robbed. Anyone with sense kept valuables out of sight.

The coins Rosamond carried with her were secure within a pocket sewn to the inside of her skirt and accessible only through a placket hidden in its folds. She wore both gown and cloak over that garment, making the money almost as difficult for her to reach as it would be for a thief.

Once the boy playing Dame Christian Cunstance appeared, the action on the stage moved apace. There were cheers when Dame

Cunstance boxed the ears of her suitor. He'd courted the widow not for herself but because she had a marriage portion of a thousand pounds.

Rosamond cheered and stamped her feet in approval when the widow rallied her three waiting women and a brawl ensued. Every player in Lord Howard's company took part, milling about and whacking one another, landing kicks and blows with such enthusiasm that one of the boards flew up and sent a boy in woman's garments somersaulting into the audience. Rosamond laughed so hard that tears came into her eyes. She had to unhook her visor and reach beneath it with a handkerchief to wipe them away.

When the play was over, it was Rosamond's practice to remain seated and wait until everyone else had left the inn-yard before descending by way of the outer stair and slipping out through the entry passage. To keep darkness at bay as sunset neared, the inn's servants brought out torches to light the cressets beside the stage. These illuminated the entire inn-yard – spectators, stage, stables, and warehouses – but left the galleries in shadow. Like most inns, the Horse's Head was long and narrow, its yards stretching back from the street. There was room for shops between them – more concealment, should she need it – before she stepped out into the open.

This was the time when servants were most useful. Just in case their presence was not sufficient, Rosamond put one gloved hand on the dagger concealed in its purpose-built sheath in the lining of her cloak. She had learned caution at an early age.

Once clear of the inn, she and her escort walked briskly down St Margaret's Hill toward London Bridge, relying upon the sheer number of people still out and about to deter unwanted attention. The broad thoroughfare known as Long Southwark was crowded with the last rush of travelers leaving the city and the press of local folk heading home to sup or to the nearest alehouse for a drink. The Bridge Gate was about to be closed for the night.

In daylight, Rosamond did not hesitate to walk anywhere, even unescorted, but she was not fool enough to go about unprotected after dark. Keeping her hood drawn close about her face to further conceal her features, she hurried past two of the great inns of Southwark, the Tabard and the George, before stopping at a third, the White Hart, where she'd left her henchmen.

She paid them well. The instant she came into sight, two burly fellows chosen for their strength and their ability to keep their mouths shut, rose from a bench beneath a shade tree and fell into step behind Rosamond, Melka, and Charles. No one bothered them as they continued on their way. No one appeared to be following them, either.

Rosamond had to walk nearly as far as the Bridge Gate with its gruesome adornments – the severed heads of traitors, left to rot on iron spikes above the stone gateway – before she reached the street that would lead her home. By the light of lanterns set out by householders, the close-crowded buildings on the bridge rose up, dim and spectral. Beyond them, on the opposite side of the Thames, was London itself. In full daylight, dozens of church spires gleamed against the sky, towering over three- and four-story buildings. At night, lights winked here and there like fireflies, only hinting at the thousands of people living cheek by jowl in the chief city of the realm. Just before Rosamond turned east to plunge rapidly downhill into Bermondsey, she glanced at the far shore, her eyes drawn to the thick, ancient walls of the Tower of London. Even at night, they stood out.

The village of Bermondsey was separate and distinct from the borough of Southwark. Once it had been a popular spot for churchmen and noblemen to build houses. In more recent times, it had fallen out of favor. The fashionable location these days was to the west of the city, along the highway known as the Strand. Many of the unwanted estates on the south side of the Thames had thus become available for purchase by members of the gentry and wealthy merchants. Rosamond had acquired Willow House at a good price, complete with gardens and outbuildings. Strangely, there were no willow trees. The nearest Rosamond had seen grew along the path that ran beside the river.

Dismissing her escort in the courtyard, secure in the knowledge that she was safe in her own home, Rosamond hurried inside. Parts of her disguise had begun to itch, and she was hungry despite having gorged herself on hazelnuts.

'Fetch bread and cheese and bring them to me in my chamber,' she ordered, tossing her cloak, knife and all, to Melka.

By the time Rosamond reached the gallery, she had divested herself of her gloves and the silk visor and had tugged off the coarse black wig that had further concealed her true appearance. Hairpins pinged, landing on the wide wooden planks when she crossed the long, narrow room that led to her bedchamber. She sighed with relief as she scattered the last of them and masses of her own thick, dark brown hair tumbled down her back. It was almost long enough to sit upon and heavy when it was all piled atop her head. Her steps slowed as she gave her scalp a vigorous rubbing.

One hand dropped from head to jaw to pick at a large, hairy mole. She'd been too generous with her glue pot. It refused to come loose. Rosamond stopped three-quarters of the way across the gallery to dig in with her fingernails. The appliance clung stubbornly to the skin beneath. Even after she managed to pry it away, a sticky patch remained behind. Impatient, she scraped at it, giving herself a small scratch on her chin. It stung, but was scarce worth fussing over. Moving forward again, Rosamond reached up under her stomacher to remove the padding she'd used to complete the illusion of of a heavy-set older woman.

Her hand stilled when the tiniest of sounds reached her. She was not alone after all.

In a single motion, Rosamond stopped, stooped, and withdrew the second small, sharp knife she was accustomed to carry, this one sheathed in her right boot. It felt solid and reassuring, fitting her hand for size and weight. She had practiced with it, both stabbing and throwing. Thus armed, she advanced another step. There! A foot shuffled off to her left in one of the window alcoves.

Two

Only candles lit the gallery, flickering eerily and giving off the faint smell of beeswax. The light was insufficient to make out the features in the painted faces in the portraits that lined the walls or the details on the shields displayed between them. There was no furniture, since the purpose of the room was to provide a space for exercise in inclement weather, but each window was set deep enough into the thick walls to accommodate a stone bench. Squinting, Rosamond at last discerned the figure of a seated man in an alcove.

'Come out where I can see you,' she ordered, pleased when her voice emerged strong and steady.

Instead of obeying her, he clapped his hands together once, then twice, then faster, as the spectators at the play had done. The applause continued until Rosamond lost her temper, plucked a candle from one of the wall sconces, and strode near enough to the presumptuous fellow to recognize him.

It had been nearly two years since they'd last met. His hair and beard were a bit more grizzled than she remembered, but otherwise he looked the same. In build he was short and stocky, with broad shoulders and intelligent dark brown eyes. His doublet was richly embroidered and he wore a hat in the latest fashion. He was a good deal older than Rosamond, having passed his fiftieth year. Mayhap that was why he did not appear in the least intimidated by the deadly little blade in her hand.

She lowered the knife.

'Most women would have run screaming from the room at their first glimpse of an intruder,' Master Nicholas Baldwin observed. He remained seated, anchored to the window seat by the immense gray and white striped feline across his lap.

'That thought never crossed my mind.'

'You barely thought at all.'

Baldwin idly stroked Watling, named after Watling Street, the old Roman road where Rosamond had found the cat as a kitten. The man's short, thick fingers skimmed over the animal's fur with a gentle touch and then shifted to scratch behind Watling's one whole ear.

The other was crimped, damaged in some long-ago battle. For a moment, the only sound in the gallery was the cat's loud, ragged purr.

To herself, Rosamond conceded that she had acted impulsively. But was that not all to the good if taking action staved off unreasoning terror? The point was moot in any case. She had no reason to be afraid of Master Baldwin. A London merchant wealthy enough to own manors in both Northamptonshire and Kent, he had been in and out of her life so often when she was a girl that she'd come to think of him as an honorary uncle. As she had with all her kin, she'd severed her connection to him shortly after she'd come into her inheritance.

Belatedly, she was struck by a terrible thought. 'Is someone—?'

'No one is dead, or even ill.' He continued to pet the cat.

Relief rapidly turned to annoyance. She glared at him. 'Why, then, are you here?'

Affecting disinterest in his answer, Rosamond tipped her candle to make a puddle of wax on the wide window sill and fixed the taper to the spot. Since there was no longer any need for the small dagger she still held in the other hand, she slid the blade back into its sheath. Beneath the soft, supple leather of her boot it made only a slight bulge.

Baldwin watched her in silence, making no response to her question. Once both Rosamond's hands were free, she curled them into fists, rested them on her hips, and directed a fulminating glare in his direction.

'Were you the one who tried to follow me home from the Horse's Head?'

The hand stroking the cat stilled. 'I was not. Nor did I send anyone else to do so. I have known where to find you for some time.'

'I suppose you badgered my servants into letting you in.' She'd have a few words to say to them for not warning her of his presence.

'I assure you, I did not.'

His calm demeanor fed her irritation. 'Then how did you reach my privy gallery? You should have been left to cool your heels in some deserted antechamber, if my gatekeeper allowed you to come inside at all.'

'He did not. I let myself in.'

That casual statement required a moment to digest. Baldwin's presence, and the apparent ease of his entry, made a mockery of her belief that she was safe in her own home. 'How?'

'Over the hedge. In through an unlatched window on the ground floor. Up the servants' stairs. It was not difficult for me to pass unseen.'

'But why go to all that trouble? You could have come in through the front like an ordinary visitor.'

She'd have spoken with him if he had . . . eventually. At the least, she'd have been better prepared to deal with the conflicting emotions evoked by seeing him again. Aware she was clenching and unclenching her fists, Rosamond flattened her palms across the front of her stomacher to stop their nervous movements.

Baldwin hesitated before he answered. 'I thought it best that we speak in private.'

'Why?' she asked again.

He shifted his gaze to the bulge of padding at her waistline and then to the discarded wig and the hairpins she'd scattered in her wake. 'Had I seen you anywhere but here, I would never have recognized you.'

'That was the idea, and you have not answered my question.'

His slow smile rivaled Watling's for satisfaction.

Rosamond blinked at him and then, from one heartbeat to the next, realized that they were no longer speaking English. He'd made that remark about not recognizing her in Russian, the language of Muscovy. Without thinking, she had answered him in the same tongue.

They had played this game when she was a girl. In common with Nick Baldwin, Rosamond had a facility for languages. She had learned French from a Frenchwoman, Polish from Melka, her mother's Polish-born maidservant, and Russian from Baldwin himself. He had mastered the foreign tongue as a young man, when he'd spent time in Kholmogory, Vologda, Moscow and Narva as a stipendiary for London's Muscovy Company.

Rosamond bit back the spate of questions filling her mind. She would not give him the satisfaction of hearing her beg for answers. She was proud of her self-control. Not by a single tap of the foot would she betray her impatience. She'd make him think she no longer cared to know why he'd invaded her home.

'Admirable restraint.' Baldwin's comment was just loud enough for her to hear.

The wretched man knew her far too well! Of a sudden, Rosamond wanted to hit him. Hard. To stay the impulse, she thrust both hands behind her back and clasped them tight. Baldwin's gaze tracked the movement. She had the uncomfortable feeling that he knew exactly what she had been thinking.

'Sit down, Rosamond,' he said. 'I have a delicate matter to put before you.'

After a brief struggle, curiosity won out over pique. The narrow window seat curved in a half circle. She seated herself so that she faced him and reached across the short distance between them to tickle Watling under the chin. As she did so, the faint scent of sandalwood reached her from Baldwin's clothing, exotic and yet familiar. It stirred pleasant memories of hearth and home, kith and kin. She repressed them and willed herself to concentrate on the present. A delicate matter, he had said. *More* than delicate, else he'd have come to her openly and in daylight.

'Delicate?' she inquired aloud. 'Or secret?'

'Both.'

Rosamond's interest quickened. She'd found life a trifle dull of late, and with winter coming on there would be even less to amuse her. 'Explain, if you please.'

'It has to do, as you will already have guessed, with Muscovy. In the middle of September an emissary from Tsar Ivan the Fourth arrived in England, one Feodor Andreevitch Pissemsky.'

'What an unfortunate name!' At his repressive look she swallowed the urge to laugh.

'He was allowed a formal audience with the queen earlier this month, at which he presented Her Majesty with dozens of sable furs, but he has not, thus far, been given any opportunity to discuss the business that brought him to England. In particular, he has not been allowed to broach the subject of a marriage alliance between the tsar and an English princess.'

'There are no English princesses.' It was rude to interrupt, but Rosamond had already used up her store of patience for the week.

'True enough.'

Baldwin leaned back against the window. At first glance, the pose appeared casual, but when Rosamond looked more closely she saw the truth. Tiny lines of tension bracketed his mouth and wrinkled his forehead. The hand resting on Watling's back had gone stiff. The cat twitched in reaction but remained where he was.

'The queen has a number of unmarried female cousins, but it is Lady Mary Hastings Pissemsky means to ask for. Although she is the earl of Huntingdon's youngest sister, it is the queen who will decide whether or not she weds. Her courtship is likely to take on ever greater importance during negotiations on other matters.'

Rosamond supposed that the Muscovy Company wanted new trade concessions from the tsar, but she did not see what that had to do with her. 'I have met a few members of the nobility,' she said in a cautious voice, 'but not the earl or his sister.'

Baldwin avoided her eyes. 'That can be remedied. In truth, Lady Mary is in need of a waiting gentlewoman.'

Rosamond reared back, offended. 'Are you asking me to take that position? I am no one's servant!'

Watling, startled, dug his back claws into Baldwin's thigh and abandoned his perch. The merchant's startled curse left the feline unmoved. With a dismissive flick of the tail, he stalked away.

'I am tempted to follow my cat's example,' Rosamond said.

Baldwin fixed her with a stern look. 'We only ask that you *pretend* to serve Lady Mary while Pissemsky is in England.'

'We?'

He hesitated. 'Certain interested parties.'

'Do they have names?' Her voice was so sweet it could have been used to make candied fruit.

Demeanor solemn, he said, 'It will be safer for you not to know them.'

Rosamond huffed out an exasperated breath. 'Master Baldwin, you must speak plain if you wish my cooperation. You have just asked me to become an intelligence gatherer.'

She knew better than most people what that meant. All of the queen's most trusted advisors employed spies. Both her late father, Sir Robert Appleton, and her stepfather, Sir Walter Pendennis, had been intelligencers in their day, charged with uncovering plots against the Crown. They'd worked both abroad and at home and had even spied on each other, an aspect of the business that left Rosamond with a bad taste in her mouth.

Seeing her reaction, Baldwin leaned closer. 'England needs your help. It would be most helpful to queen and country to have someone trustworthy in that household.'

'I have no experience as a spy, nor any great desire to acquire it.'

He smiled at that, but refrained from reminding her of certain childhood escapades. 'You are uniquely qualified for this assignment,' he said instead. 'Trained as a gentlewoman. Clever. Able to read and write. And you understand enough of the Russian language to be able to follow a conversation conducted in that tongue, should you happen to be nearby when one occurs.'

'And what difference will that make if you already know that Lady Mary is to be courted by the tsar's representative?'

'Mayhap none at all. I have no way of knowing if your presence in Lady Mary's entourage will prove helpful or not, but it could.'

'I have grown accustomed to being accountable to no one but myself. I enjoy my independence and am loath to give up so much as one moment of freedom, especially if it means being at someone else's beck and call. Besides, what makes you think I would be acceptable to Lady Mary?'

'You are a young married gentlewoman with respectable family connections and thus ideally suited to enter the service of a noblewoman.'

'Have you forgotten the details, Master Baldwin? Neither my marriage nor the circumstances surrounding my birth will withstand close scrutiny.' There was no delicate way to explain the latter – she was Sir Robert Appleton's bastard daughter.

'If you agree, you will enter the household on the recommendation of the wife of the earl of Sussex, your good neighbor here in Bermondsey. You *have* met Lady Sussex.'

'Once only. I would be surprised if she remembers me. Besides, her husband is seriously ill, dying of consumption, and she rarely leaves his bedside.'

'And that is precisely why she was chosen to vouch for you. That and the family connection.'

Genealogy was not among Rosamond's interests, but even she knew that Lady Sussex had been born Frances Sidney. A moment's thought brought her to Sir Henry Sidney, Frances's brother, who had married Mary Dudley, and thus to Mary Dudley's sister, Katherine, who was the wife of the earl of Huntingdon and sister-in-law of Lady Mary Hastings.

'Even supposing that no one questions my background or sends to Lady Sussex for further confirmation, I can see little point to this scheme. Nothing of importance is likely to be said in the presence of a waiting gentlewoman.'

'Lady Mary will go to court for Yuletide,' Baldwin said.

For a moment, Rosamond was tempted. She had never visited any of the royal palaces and she'd only seen Queen Elizabeth once, from a distance, passing by on the royal barge as she traveled between Greenwich and Whitehall. The festivities marking Christmas, New Year's Day, and Twelfth Night would be spectacular – plays and tournaments, masques and dancing. But she would not be an honored guest at such entertainments. She would be an upper servant, relegated to the background. She might even have to wear livery. Rosamond scowled. A disguise she chose for herself was one thing. Being forced to abandon her finery for plain, sad-colored garments was quite another. She had to repress a shudder at the thought.

'No. Find someone else.'

Baldwin shifted uneasily on the hard stone seat. 'If I cannot call upon your love of country and the chance to spend time at court does not appeal to you, perhaps you will reconsider for a different reason.'

'Do you mean to offer me a bribe?' The thought made her chuckle.

'Would that sway you?' He sounded skeptical, as well he might.

'I do much doubt it.' Rosamond already possessed more wealth in lands and annuities than she could spend in an entire lifetime. 'But I should like to hear how much your master is willing to offer.'

'I serve no master.' Baldwin bristled visibly.

'Then you owe no one your loyalty. Tell me who sent you here. Was it Sir Francis Walsingham?'

From her stepfather, Rosamond knew that the queen's principal secretary controlled a goodly number of intelligence gatherers. Of all the powerful men at court, he was also the most likely to have heard of her existence and be aware of the particular skills she could bring to the assignment. She was poised to repeat her demand for a name when the expression on Baldwin's face gave her pause. He looked like a man torn between two choices, neither of them palatable.

'Walsingham is known to use coercion as well as bribery to persuade people to cooperate with him,' Rosamond said in a thoughtful voice. 'With what does he think he can threaten me?' She'd done nothing illegal. Not that she knew of. Then again, mayhap Baldwin was the one who was being coerced.

'What I have to tell you is meant to provide incentive.'

'Then why do you hesitate?'

'I am loath to worry you without cause. I can only speculate at this point. My worst fears may never be realized.'

She folded her arms across her chest and fixed him with an implacable look. 'Go on.'

'It is as yet unclear how much depends upon sending Lady Mary to the tsar.'

'You have told me that there are other negotiations ongoing. I can but suppose it is your connection to the Muscovy Company that has caused you to become involved in this affair. But you have already made a goodly fortune trading in foreign parts. Failure to win new concessions from the tsar is not likely to ruin you.'

'I will be blunt, Rosamond. If the talks that are about to begin fail entirely, every Englishman now in Muscovy will be in mortal danger. Tsar Ivan is called 'the Terrible' by allies and enemies alike for good reason. If sufficiently provoked, he would not hesitate to massacre every foreigner now living in his realm.'

Rosamond frowned. 'You can scarce expect me to feel responsible for those lives. You have already admitted that there may be no advantage at all to placing me in Lady Mary's household.'

'Rob Jaffrey is in Muscovy.'

Halfway to her feet, Rosamond froze. 'What?'

'Your estranged husband is in Muscovy and is unlikely to leave until after the tsar's ambassador returns with his report.'

She dropped back onto the window seat with a thump. 'That is not possible. Rob is at Cambridge.'

Baldwin shook his head. 'He sailed for St Nicholas on the first of June.'

Rosamond did not need Baldwin to put the pieces together for her. If Rob was in Muscovy and the tsar struck out at all Englishmen, Rob would be among his victims. He could die a horrible death.

Numb with shock and dread, she struggled to accept the possibility that her presence in the household of Lady Mary Hastings might somehow avert that disastrous outcome. The idea seemed preposterous. And yet, how could she refuse to help if there was even the slightest chance that she could make a significant contribution to keeping Rob alive?

'When we first agreed to live apart, it was so that Rob could finish his studies at Cambridge.' Her voice was unsteady. She gave a nervous laugh. 'It must have been a great disappointment to everyone when he left without taking his degree. No doubt his mother blames me.'

'He promised to return to his studies next year. Had he not, I'd never have given him passage on one of my ships.'

Rosamond turned accusing eyes his way. '*You* sent him to Muscovy? How could you do such a thing if there is so much danger there?'

Baldwin held both hands up in front of him, palms out. 'There is no *certainty* that his life is in jeopardy. Only the *risk* is real. It decreases in proportion to England's success in dealing with the Russian ambassador.'

In an abrupt movement, Rosamond sprang to her feet. She needed to put a little distance between herself and Nick Baldwin. She stood alone, hugging herself. All warmth – and there had not been much to start with – seemed to have been leeched out of the gallery.

Even though she was a few months younger than Rob, Rosamond had always taken the lead, both in the schoolroom and in childhood games. One memory after another flooded into her mind, all of them sweet. *Rob* had been sweet. They'd been sixteen when she suggested that they run away together and be married. He'd made a token protest, but she had soon overcome his qualms. To get her own way, she had used the fact that he loved her against him.

For two years and more, Rosamond had avoided dwelling upon how badly she had managed that part of her life. All's well that ends well, she'd told herself. But it had not ended well for everyone. Marrying Rob Jaffrey had been a surpassing selfish thing to do.

At the time, Rosamond had been trying to avoid marriage to a man her mother had chosen for her. Although she'd known full well that she could not be forced to wed any man against her will, she had grown tired of Eleanor Pendennis's endless schemes to find her a 'suitable' husband. Determined to put an end to them, she'd decided upon marriage to her childhood playmate as the means to solve all her problems.

In part, her plan had succeeded. True to his word, Rob had relinquished all claim to Rosamond's father's fortune. He could have kept it for himself. Under the law, as soon as a woman wed, her husband gained control of everything that had previously belonged to her. In the event, however, the legalities of Rosamond's financial situation had turned out to be more complicated than she had supposed. Months of wrangling had ensued before she'd gotten her way. Once she was her own mistress, wealthy and independent, she'd chosen to ignore the fact that she was saddled with a husband in a union only death could undo.

Her breath hitched in something suspiciously like a sob.

She had not wanted Rob to live with her in this house, but neither did she want him to die.

'Did you hear me, Rosamond?' Baldwin came up behind her. Head cocked, he eyed her with a peculiar expression on his deeply tanned face. 'I asked if Rob's presence in Muscovy has changed your mind.'

'Why should it when you cannot promise me that my presence in Lady Mary's household will be enough to keep him safe?'

'I cannot offer you proof of that, no. But I do believe that it will help. If negotiations go smoothly, the tsar will have no cause for anger.'

'And you still refuse to tell me who wants to make use of me?'

'You do not need that knowledge to play your part.'

Rosamond gave a derisive snort. She'd heard similar logic before. It had never impressed her. Still, Master Baldwin was an honest man. As much as she hated being manipulated, she looked into his eyes and saw the truth in them. He feared for Rob's life.

Before Rob Jaffrey had become her husband, he had been one of her dearest friends. Rosamond could not bear the thought of losing him. 'How soon must I give you my answer?'

'Pissemsky cannot be put off past the middle of December. You should enter Lady Mary's service before he meets with the queen's advisors and the representatives of the Muscovy Company.'

'Then I have a bit more than three weeks to decide.'

'Far less than that, I fear. To keep from arousing suspicion, you should join Lady Mary's household as soon as may be.'

Rosamond plucked at the silk ribbons decorating her stomacher. The padding made it bulge a good three inches in front of her. She was comfortable with this – disguising herself so that she might flout convention. What Baldwin proposed was far different. It was not a game. Failure to play her part well could have terrible consequences.

He waited for her decision with no overt sign of impatience. Did he guess that her mind was already set? If Rob's life was in danger, she had no choice. On the other hand, she had learned the hard way that it was unwise to make any lasting commitment on the spur of the moment.

'Come back in two days, Master Baldwin,' she said. 'I will give you my answer then.'

Three

'Did she agree?' asked Sir Francis Walsingham.

'Not yet.'

By the light of a crescent moon and the waterman's lantern, Nick had been rowed some six miles from Southwark to the water stairs at Barn Elms. Walsingham's modest gabled country house sat in a formal garden full of flower beds and fruit trees on the south bank of the Thames in Surrey, conveniently close to Richmond Palace. Despite the late hour, the queen's principal secretary was still hard at work in his library, where books ranged from tomes on philosophy and religion to lighter fare dealing with exploration and music. Letters from diplomats and from agents in a dozen different countries littered his desk, along with the half-finished missive he'd been composing when Nick arrived.

'Are you certain she is the best choice?' Nick asked.

'Have we any other?' For Walsingham, this was loquacious. He did not believe in sharing information without good reason.

Nick had been through the arguments in his head a dozen times already. There was no female in England so well suited for the role Walsingham had in mind. Rosamond might not be fluent in the Russian language, but she had a working knowledge of it, enough to understand most of what she overheard and to remember any words she could not interpret on her own. Further, she had learned something of codes and ciphers from her stepfather, Sir Walter Pendennis.

The counts against her could be overlooked. She was the bastard daughter of a knight and had married the son of two of her late father's servants, but she was still of suitable birth to serve as a noble-woman's waiting gentlewoman. That she was wealthy in her own right, should it become known, was unlikely to raise any eyebrows. Most young women would leap at the chance to spend time at Court, even if it meant accepting a subservient position.

Walsingham set aside his pen and put the top back on the inkpot. As was his custom, he was dressed in somber hues with a prepon-derance of black and had added little in the way of ornamentation.

Even when he attended upon the queen, he limited the size of his white ruff and was content to wear only a single jewel, a pendant containing a likeness of Her Majesty. He regarded Nick with his customary intense, disconcerting stare, the kind of scrutiny that could make a man confess even when he had done nothing wrong.

'Did you tell her of the danger to her husband?'

'I did. It was plain to me that she cares for him, despite the fact that they live apart. She promised to give me her decision in two days' time.'

'Friday, when I must return to court.' Walsingham considered for a moment, running one hand over his neatly trimmed beard. Once as dark as his doublet, it had in the last few years acquired flecks of silver. 'The queen intends to remain at Windsor Castle through Yuletide. Lady Mary will join Her Majesty there in mid-December. At present, Lady Mary is at Chelsea Manor. Take Mistress Jaffrey there.'

He added a few more terse instructions, confident that Rosamond would fall in with his plans. Nick did not contradict him. Few men did.

Mr Secretary Walsingham was a formidable figure, both in the political power he wielded and in the image he showed the world. He worked tirelessly to protect queen and country, making no secret of his intention to thwart treasonous plots by any means necessary. He saw such plots everywhere. What scheme he expected to uncover during negotiations for a treaty with Muscovy, Nick had no idea. He comforted himself with the hope that Walsingham was merely being cautious.

'She is to use Griffith Potter, clerk of the Great Wardrobe, as an intermediary should she have information to pass on,' Walsingham said. 'Arrange a meeting between them on your way to Chelsea. Potter can be found in the Queen's Wardrobe of Robes at Whitehall.'

Nick frowned. Whitehall Palace, in the city of Westminster, was a goodly distance from Windsor Castle. Having no pressing business at court, Potter would likely remain at his post, in which case he'd be no help at all to Rosamond if she found herself in trouble.

'Mayhap I should take lodgings in Windsor during Yuletide,' Nick suggested, 'to provide a second layer of support.'

'There is no reason to suppose she will require one. She is to do no more than keep her eyes open and her ears stretched. If she has need to speak with Potter, she can send word to the Wardrobe of Robes.'

'I have known Rosamond since she was a small child. Trouble has a way of finding her.'

Walsingham dismissed Nick's concern with an impatient gesture. 'Your part in this will be done once you deliver Mistress Jaffrey to Chelsea. You would do well to go and rusticate at your manor in Kent for a time. I would not take it amiss if you decided to stay there until the Russian delegation has left England.'

He had already picked up his pen when Nick moved closer and flattened his palms on the desk. 'I have a certain interest in the affairs of the Muscovy Company myself, not to mention a business to run in London. One of my ships—'

'Stay in the city if you must, but do not meddle further in this matter. Nothing good can come to you or yours if you interfere.'

Walsingham had not raised his voice, but his tone carried an unspoken threat that chilled Nick's blood and had him straightening and taking a rapid step back. He nodded to show he understood.

Although it galled him to capitulate, he could not escape the fact that English lives were at stake. Compared to the danger in Muscovy, the risk to Rosamond Jaffrey was small.

The rules of hospitality dictated that Walsingham offer Nick a bed for the night. Nick accepted only because it was already so late that he was unlikely to find a boatman to row him into the city. Dismissed from the great man's presence, he was taken to a small guest chamber with a comfortable bed but he slept poorly.

He kept racking his brain to think of more he could do. He felt responsible for Rob Jaffrey's position of imminent peril, and not just because he'd given the lad passage to Muscovy. Rob's desire to travel, as well as Rosamond's fluency in the Russian language, had both grown out of the long winter evenings Nick had spent entertaining the children at Leigh Abbey with tales of his adventures in the land of the tsars.

First light found Nick breaking his fast with bread and ale. He was on his way back to London within an hour of rising. Once there, he went straight to the large stone building he owned in Billingsgate.

Close to Billingsgate Harbor, the largest inlet east of London Bridge, the warehouse was situated hard by the Customs House and the former parish church of St Botolph, now secularized and divided up into lodgings. The lower levels were filled with trade goods but on the top floor several large rooms had been converted into living quarters. They were comfortably furnished and staffed by a couple, Arthur and Maud Saunders, who had come to London from Candlethorpe, Nick's estate in Northamptonshire.

He scarce had time to take off his cloak before Saunders pressed a letter into his hand. A blob of red sealing wax held it closed, impressed with a signet ring showing the crest of an apple pierced through with an arrow. His first thought was that it had come from Sir Robert Appleton's widow in Kent, his neighbor and dear friend. While Mistress Saunders fussed over him, supplying a beaker of mulled ale and bustling off to prepare something for him to eat, Nick broke the seal and unfolded the letter.

The page was blank.

A smile tugged at the corners of his mouth. He had been wrong. The message was from Sir Robert Appleton's daughter – Rosamond. Trust the wench to make a complicated situation more so! He wondered if she'd used alum mixed with white garlic juice or relied upon garlic juice alone. Onion juice was another possibility. Rosamond would doubtless know of several ways to produce invisible ink.

He sniffed cautiously and his smile widened into a grin. She'd used lemon juice. That meant all he had to do was hold the page above the wavering flame of the candle on his table. In seconds, the few lines Rosamond had written – in Latin, to show off her learning – appeared as if by magic. The letters were brown against the lighter color of the paper.

The essence of the message was just as clear. Rosamond agreed to enter Lady Mary's service. Nick would have felt relief had she not added a request. No, make that a demand. She wished to take up her new duties at once. She expected him to wait upon her without delay.

Nick lowered the paper into the flame. Once it caught fire, he watched it burn until only the corner he held between thumb and index finger was still intact. He dropped the tiny remnant onto the floor and ground it under his heel.

Hands clasped behind his back, Nick went to stand in front of the mullioned windows that overlooked the Thames. His gaze slipped past the ships at anchor in the middle of the wide river to the houses and shops of Bermondsey on the far side. He could not pick out

Rosamond's property from this vantage point, but he did have an excellent view of the ferry that ran from Pickleherring Stairs to the Tower. It had just set out on one of its regular runs.

The sight reminded him that he had much to do and little time in which to do it. Taking his ale with him, he descended a steep flight of steps to the counting house from which he ran his business. His private chamber at the back was a small, cluttered room. Its single window looked out over the same view he'd just left behind in his lodgings.

A ferry would not do to transport Mistress Rosamond Jaffrey, nor would a wherry. He'd have to hire a small barge and the men to row it. There were other arrangements to make, as well. No matter how quickly he completed them, there was no hope Rosamond could leave Bermondsey for Chelsea any sooner than the following morning.

Seating himself at his writing table, Nick selected a quill from the assortment he kept sharpened and ready. When he had dipped it into one of the two slender pewter inkwells that were souvenirs of his long-ago sojourn in Persia, he made a list and then added projections for expenditures. He frowned when he totaled them.

What did you expect? he asked himself. *Few men grow rich in the queen's service!*

Once he'd carefully sprinkled sand from a decorative little sandbox onto the pages to keep the wet ink from smearing, Nick rose and turned to face the paneled wall behind his writing table. While narrow laths ran around the interior of the room to serve as letter racks, here a carved wooden shelf had pride of place. Three items sat upon it. Two wooden boxes hasped with steel contained his most important papers. Next to them was a round moneybox. A pomander ball scented with cloves hung nearby, mitigating most of the stink that rose from the Thames when the tide was low.

Nick counted out coins sufficient for his purpose and transferred them to the leather purse attached to his belt. He tucked his list inside, too. While it was true that he could send one of his servants to run errands for him, that was sure to arouse their curiosity. He thought it best to do everything himself.

He left the warehouse a few minutes later, on foot and alone. His first stop was the place of business of the local goods carrier, there to arrange for a cart to transport Rosamond's belongings from her house to the river stairs. Conveniently, he was now but a stone's throw from a certain building in Seething Lane – the center of Sir Francis Walsingham's network of intelligence gatherers. Nick paused to study the large, fair dwelling before entering. He could not help but wonder if it was significant that it had been the London headquarters of the Muscovy Company before being sold to Sir Francis two years earlier.

Four

From the frozen surface of the Moscow River, Rob Jaffrey stared up at the thick brick wall of the castle that loomed over the city. He'd been told it was up to sixty feet high in some places and that one of the towers soared to two hundred feet. He could well believe it. Situated on a hilly terrace, triangular in shape and surrounded by water, it was far larger than the Tower of London. In faith, it was bigger than some entire English cities! The tsar's palace was located inside those walls, as were nine churches and a cathedral. Mayhap more than one. The architecture ranged from the mundane to the fanciful.

Rob thought it a great pity that he'd never be allowed inside to see these wonders at close range. The Muscovy Company's agents had made it plain that with the exception of individuals who were of use to him – physicians, apothecaries, astrologers, engineers, and artisans – Tsar Ivan had no use for foreigners. Casual visitors to the castle called the Kremlin were further discouraged by cannon on the parapets, not to mention drawbridges and the defenses mounted in towers, blockhouses, and barbicans.

The alluring scents of cinnamon and nutmeg diverted Rob's attention. In late autumn, the merchants who at other times of the year set up their collapsible trading stalls in one of the squares within the city, moved out onto the ice. Rob had heard that the Thames sometimes froze solid at London, but he'd never seen this phenomenon. It did not do so every year, and most certainly not in November. The occurrence was, in truth, so rare that each time it happened it was celebrated by holding a frost fair. In Moscow, daily bazaars on the frozen surface of the river were an ordinary annual event.

The merchants' stalls were arranged in neat rows, one row for each kind of item. Rob followed his nose to find the baker selling gingerbread and made himself understood well enough to walk away with an ample portion. He had only a few words of Russian, but he had always found that smiles and gestures went a long way towards communicating what he wanted.

As he ate, he wandered down one row and up another admiring such diverse wares as caftans and smocks, pelts of red fox and sable, bone for buttons, and fine warm boots of soft leather. He thought it a great pity that the leather had been tanned with birch-bark. This practice resulted in a dark color and a strange smell. The latter had given rise to the English expression 'ranker than Muscovy leather'.

Rob paused to examine a lynx fur, debating whether or not to buy it as a gift for Rosamond. He decided to put off the purchase for a few more months and save his roubles. He would not be leaving Russia until summer.

Travel by sea was hazardous in winter and there was no easy route overland to England. The Muscovy fleet customarily left London in May or June and reached St Nicholas in about a month. The ships stayed long enough to load cargoes of wax, tallow, hemp, train oil produced from seals, furs, and sometimes live bears for the bear-baiting ring at Paris Garden. They sailed for home at some point between the end of June and the middle of August. In good weather, they reached port in six weeks. In bad . . . he did not want to think about *more* than two months at sea!

Abruptly, Rob came to the end of the rows and saw what was displayed beyond. There was no slaughterhouse smell to warn him he'd reached the butchers of Moscow, nor had he ever seen such a sight as now met his startled gaze. A small herd of cows stood on the ice, and another beyond it of pigs . . . except that they were no longer living, breathing animals. Each one had been skinned and frozen whole. It stood on its feet in that condition, awaiting a buyer.

'Now there's something you don't see in London,' Rob said under his breath.

At his elbow, a woman drew in a sharp breath and seized his forearm with a clawlike grip. In a whisper, she asked, 'Are you English?'

Rob turned to find a small, haggard-looking woman peering up at him with desperation in her eyes. 'I am,' he said.

'You must help me. They will not let me go home.'

'Who will not?'

'We cannot talk here.' She cast a fearful look over her shoulder and started walking, never loosening her grip on his arm.

Confused but intrigued, Rob let her lead him off the ice and away from the river. He quickly lost all sense of direction. Three strong walls circled the city, one within the other with streets lying between. The houses all looked the same, built foursquare without any lime or stone. They had low doorways and high thresholds and little casement windows. Moss was pressed into chinks and seams to keep out the cold.

The woman hustled him along a fir-tree pavement. She didn't speak another word but her agitation was so great that Rob felt obliged to go with her. She was plainly English and plainly in trouble. How could he not try to help her?

She slowed her steps as she approached the great square to the northeast of the castle. 'There,' she said, pointing to a circular wooden dais with a stone balustrade. It stood just opposite the gate that led into the Kremlin.

'For speakers?' Rob guessed. In London, clergymen and others addressed the public in the open area beside St Paul's.

'Public addresses, yes. And public executions. That is where they will kill me if they catch me trying to escape from Muscovy.'

'Surely not!' Shock had him speaking too loudly.

She clapped her free hand over his mouth.

Seizing her fingers, he pried them away from his face, pulling free of her grip on his arm at the same time. 'Who are you?'

He was careful to whisper. If this woman was at risk of being arrested and executed, then anyone who helped her was also in danger.

'I am Jane Bomelius.'

This meant nothing to Rob, except that the surname was not English. Jane was though. He was certain of it. Born in London, too, unless his ears deceived him.

'I expected you to run away when you learned who I am.' She sounded surprised.

'I am not going anywhere until you tell me why you need my help. Mayhap not even then. Is it safe to talk here?'

'No.'

She stared at him for a long time before she said anything more, giving him ample opportunity to change his mind. Instead he studied her person. She was younger than he'd first thought. A kerchief covered her hair, but the few strands showing beneath it were untouched by gray. The lines in her face came from worry, not age. The fur-lined cloak she wore had once been exceeding fine. Now it was patched and worn. Her gloves, too, had seen better days. The fingers were much mended.

'We can go back to England House,' he suggested, referring to the dwelling in Moscow that the tsar had granted, rent free, to the Muscovy Company.

'No! They will not help me there.'

'But they are your countrymen.' How could they not take pity on an Englishwoman far from home? 'Surely they will offer aid.'

Her bitter laugh silenced him. When she set off at a trot, he followed her.

They walked for a long time. He'd been told the city stretched for more than five miles along the banks of the river, with a circumference of some twelve miles. It was home to more than 50,000 people. They reached the outskirts, then moved beyond, but not so far as to encounter the soldiers who guarded the roads leading into Moscow.

The hovel she brought him to was in a section of shabby buildings. Instead of a sturdy wall for protection, an earthen rampart surrounded them. From the threshold of the dwelling, Rob could glimpse the nearest of several semi-fortified monasteries that ringed the city. He wondered if it was one of the ones that housed a permanent garrison but he did not ask.

A cart rumbled past, empty now that it had delivered its load of grain to market. Before it was allowed to return to the countryside, it would be stopped at a checkpoint and examined for contraband.

'Come inside.' The hissed command held an urgency he could not ignore.

The interior boasted neither heat nor light until she stirred the fire to life. Then the one small room heated quickly. Rob picked out her few poor possessions in the shadows. A battered cypress chest held pride of place next to a straw pallet heaped with blankets. The only other furnishings of note were three wooden boxes.

'Where are we?' he asked.

'They call this area Zemlygorod – Earthen Town. It is home to laborers who work in the mills along the Yauza River or do menial tasks in the armament plant or pull carts. The women scrounge for mushrooms in the forests beyond the monastery.'

'Is that how you survive?'

She nodded. 'I am invisible here. Safe. But a prisoner all the same. I dare not leave.' Tears filled her eyes. 'My husband lived at court once. He was honored by the tsar. We were wealthy. I had a new-built house in Belygorod, where courtiers and rich merchants and even some of the lesser nobility live.'

White Town, Rob translated. He'd heard of it. 'Your husband – what did he do at court?'

She sat on one of the boxes and gestured for him to do likewise. She did not offer him refreshment. He doubted she had any food to spare. Then he listened with rapt attention as she told her tale.

'I married a native of Westphalia, Eligius Bomelius. He had come to London to practice medicine after taking his degree at Cambridge. He had a good reputation as both a physician and an astrologer, and many wealthy clients, until the College of Physicians brought charges against him for practicing without a license. That was when he decided we should try our luck in Muscovy. We traveled in the entourage of a Russian ambassador returning to his homeland and my husband was taken into the tsar's household. For six years, all was well. I bore two children. Eligius amassed a great fortune and sent most of it, by way of England, to be invested in his native city of Wesel.'

Mistress Bomelius stared at her gloved hands, tightly clasped in her lap. Still huddled in her ragged cloak, she was a pitiful sight. There were no children now. Rob knew without asking that they had died. The great fortune, if it ever existed outside of her imagination, was now far out of her reach.

'What happened to your husband?'

'He was charged with treason and tortured.' She gave a soft sob at the memory, wrapping her arms around herself and rocking back and forth, struggling for control. After a moment, she drew in a ragged breath and added, 'He died in the tsar's dungeon.'

There was more to the story. Rob wanted to ask for details, but he could not bring himself to badger this poor widow with questions.

'The tsar is mad,' she whispered. 'He has no good reason to keep me here, but he will not let me leave.'

'The queen's envoy in Moscow—'

'He will do nothing.' Contempt underscored her words. 'He is too afraid for his own skin.'

'Then what do you think I can do?'

She leaned forward, once again seizing his arm in a bruising grip. 'When you leave Moscow you can smuggle me out hidden in one of your trunks.' The second hand joined the first, nails digging in even through his thick padded sleeve. 'I beg you, sir. You are my only hope.'

'I . . . I will do what I can.' Rob was well aware that if he was caught helping her escape, he'd be the one in prison and facing torture. 'Are you certain you will not come with me now to the headquarters of the English merchants?'

'They will not let me in. They will not dare. Tsar Ivan's condition for giving the Muscovy Company a house was that they keep a Russian housekeeper and two Russian servants. My presence there would be reported within hours. Then you'd all suffer for your charity.'

Rob did not want to believe her. He wanted to think she was exaggerating the danger, but it was clear she believed what she was saying.

'You must tell no one of our encounter,' she insisted as he took his leave of her. Then she begged him once again to take her with him when he left Moscow.

'I will do all I can to help you,' he repeated.

Deeply troubled, Rob walked back into the city proper. As he passed the spacious yards and gardens attached to many of the houses, he felt the contrast to Mistress Bomelius's dwelling all the more keenly. The plan to hide her in his baggage train was passing foolish but, by the time he reached England House, a fine, large stone building in the Zaryadie, on the east side of the Kremlin, he was determined to do *something* to aid her.

Five

Rosamond greeted Master Nicholas Baldwin in the great hall of Willow House, having been given warning of his arrival by her servants the moment he set foot on her property. 'I was ready yesterday,' she announced.

Her trunks, boxes, and capcases had been packed and waiting for two days while she'd been left to chafe at the inexplicable delay, confined to her own house lest Baldwin arrive while she was away.

'Arrangements had to be made.' He sent a quizzical look her way. 'Why are you in such a rush now? You lacked any enthusiasm for the idea at first.'

'The sooner I join Lady Mary's household, the sooner I can come home again.'

Melka bustled into the hall, bundled in a cloak with the hood drawn up over her head to shield her non-English features.

'My tiring maid. I assume there will be no difficulty about bringing her with me?'

Baldwin spared the older woman a single, disinterested glance. 'You are expected to have a servant.'

Rosamond had hoped, but had not been certain, that Master Baldwin had never set eyes on Melka when she was in the service of Rosamond's mother. Servants were part of the background in a gentle or noble household, much like the furniture, and Melka had been more invisible than most. Before coming to Rosamond, she had spent most of her time in the kitchen or in Eleanor Pendennis's bedchamber, waiting hand and foot on a mistress who had lost the use of her legs in an accident many years before.

Rosamond was unsure why she'd thought Master Baldwin might object to Melka accompanying her on this mission. Mayhap it was because Melka herself so heartily disapproved of what Rosamond was about to do. She had overheard the last part of the conversation between Rosamond and Baldwin in the gallery. When she could not dissuade her mistress, she'd insisted upon going with her to Lady Mary's household. For her own reasons, Rosamond was in favor of this plan.

'We are bound for Chelsea Manor,' Baldwin announced. 'I have hired a small row-barge for the journey and arranged for a cart to transport your baggage as far as Pepper Alley Stairs.'

'A good choice,' said Rosamond. 'We will walk the short distance from Bermondsey into Southwark rather than bother with horses or a litter.'

Pepper Alley Stairs was the nearest landing place on the Thames from which they could safely embark for destinations upriver. Other water stairs were closer, but Rosamond had never seen the sense in shooting London Bridge, not even when the tide was low enough to allow for safe passage. To board a fragile wooden craft and try to thread it through the formidable stone arches at high tide was madness. Although she considered herself to be daring, she was not a fool.

They set out on foot a short time later. There had been rain the previous night, flooding some of the low-lying areas of the village. Rosamond wrinkled her nose at the smell. She liked her house and Bermondsey was convenient to London, but this was its one disadvantage. Buildings located too close to the riverbank were perpetually damp and in addition to being swampy, the area was home to all the noisome but necessary trades unwelcome within the city – leather-working, blacksmithing, dyeing, and brewing. On most days it was possible to ignore the stink in the air, but not when clouds hung low in a colorless sky and kept the mingled odors close to the ground. Then, like fingers of fog, they crept closer and closer, bent on engulfing everything in their path.

It seemed a good omen that, by the time the boatmen launched their barge out onto the Thames, the day had become a trifle less overcast. Streaks of sunlight appeared in the sky, giving promise of more to come. Although the water was icy and full of floating objects Rosamond thought it best not to identify, the tidal river was more calm than choppy. In the hands of skilled rowers, the barge glided smoothly over the surface.

Rosamond and her escort sat on the padded bench provided for passengers. She had an excellent view of the Southwark shore, dominated by a series of whitewashed walls. They were alehouses and each was painted with a sign so large that it could be distinguished from the London side of the river. Rosamond recognized most of these symbols. Animals were popular – swan, crane, and hart. There was even an elephant. A little farther along they passed the Barge, the Bell, the Cross Keys, and the Cardinal's Hat. She could not help but smile at the sign for the latter. The representation bore a remarkable resemblance to a man's yard – appropriate, since it was an open secret that most of these alehouses were also brothels.

'The tide is in our favor,' Baldwin said. 'It will not take us long to reach Chelsea. However, we have one stop to make first.'

'Where?' Rosamond shifted her gaze to the north side of the Thames.

They were just passing the former monastery of Blackfriars, now carved up into private lodgings. One of them belonged to her stepfather. There was also an indoor playhouse featuring performances by a company of children.

The old city wall rose up just beyond this enclave, and soon after they passed the point marking the start of the Strand, the highway that connected London to the separate city of Westminster. The grand houses built along it showed their best faces to the river. Many of them boasted extensive gardens and terraces leading down to private water gates.

'Whitehall Stairs,' Baldwin said in answer to her question.

'The royal palace? Why?' She was certain it was not to meet the queen.

Baldwin nodded toward the rowers, a silent reminder that anything they said could be overheard. 'All will be explained once we arrive.'

The swift-moving row-barge was fast approaching the bend in the river that marked the start of Westminster. As soon as it rounded the turn, Rosamond had a clear view of Whitehall, Westminster Abbey, and the old palace of Westminster. On the opposite side of the river, Southwark had given way to Lambeth and the Archbishop of Canterbury's palace rose up on that shore in a princely splendor of its own.

Rosamond watched in brooding silence as the barge drew closer to Whitehall Stairs. Guards patrolled all the entrances to Whitehall Palace, even when the queen was not in residence, but they did not demand more than a brief explanation before allowing Baldwin and Rosamond to disembark. Melka remained on board with the rowers.

'The sergeant porter's quarters,' Baldwin explained as he ushered her inside a set of lodgings above the water gate. 'We can be private here.'

A man rose from a chair beside a table. While he'd waited, he'd helped himself to a generous share of the cheese and ale set out on the table for them.

'This is Master Griffith Potter, clerk of the Great Wardrobe,' Baldwin said. 'Potter, meet Mistress Jaffrey.'

Potter looked her over from head to toe in an assessing manner Rosamond found offensive. She asserted herself by moving closer to him and could not help but feel a trifle superior when she saw that she was taller than he by at least two inches. He had to crane his neck to meet her eyes. In addition to being small of stature, he had a heavily pockmarked face. His hair, cut short, was nearly concealed by his bonnet so that Rosamond could not see its color. That made it difficult to guess his age, but he was well past the first flush of youth.

'If you have anything to report,' Baldwin said, pulling her attention back to him, 'you are to do so verbally to this gentleman. Master Potter is assigned to the Queen's Wardrobe of Robes, housed here at Whitehall.'

'I thought the queen's gowns were kept in the Tower.'

'Some are.' Potter's voice was gruff and his cold, gray gaze held barely suppressed resentment. 'And also in the Great Wardrobe in London where most of the queen's clothing is made. There are also livery tailoring workshops on the premises. When you go to court, Mistress Jaffrey, you will see many of those who serve our gracious queen wearing black velvet coats or coats of green marble cloth guarded with russet velvet. More senior officials are issued gowns of damask guarded with black lucca velvet and furred with—'

'Must I wear livery, too?' Rosamond interrupted. The possibility had crossed her mind when Baldwin first proposed his scheme but she had dismissed it as unlikely.

Perceiving her alarm, Baldwin laughed. 'Have no fear. As one of Lady Mary's waiting gentlewomen you will wear your own clothing.'

'It is no small matter!'

'It is of little consequence compared to more important concerns,' Potter cut in. 'This is a mistake, Baldwin. A frivolous woman is worse than useless.'

'And of what use are you to me, Master Potter, if you work here at Whitehall and I am at Chelsea?'

It was Baldwin who replied. 'Before Lady Mary goes to court for Yuletide, she will visit the Wardrobe of Robes.'

'Why?'

'Queen Elizabeth enjoys presenting her old gowns to ladies she favors,' Potter said. 'Her Majesty has a great many of them.'

'Gowns or ladies?'

Baldwin's lips twitched in appreciation of Rosamond's wit but Potter's condescending attitude remained unchanged. 'Both. Moreover, ladies of the court are permitted to order clothing for themselves from the royal tailors by private commission. For that reason, if you have need to speak with me, it should not be difficult to arrange a meeting.'

'Everything has been well thought out in advance,' Baldwin assured her.

Beset by a sudden vision of herself as a puppet, her every action controlled by some unseen hand, Rosamond did not find his words at all comforting, nor did she sense that Baldwin truly believed what he was telling her.

'Should you discover anything worthy of my attention, you are to deliver your report in person and verbally.' Potter's sneer made it plain he doubted she would.

'Do not write anything down.' The stern look Baldwin sent her told Rosamond he was thinking of the invisible ink she had used in her message to him.

The smile Rosamond bestowed upon both men was heavy with false sweetness. 'During the past two days, I have been considering certain elements of the stories my stepfather told me about his years as a spy.'

She did not like being dictated to, nor did she relish the idea that Griffith Potter saw her as a brainless female who would ultimately fail in her assignment. She would have him know she was not entirely without knowledge of intelligence gathering. Although he busied himself cutting another wedge of cheese, the tilt of his head assured her that his ear was cocked in her direction.

'There are many ways to convey written messages in secret. Since I am to communicate with a clerk of the wardrobe, I could write on Holland cloth, use the cloth to line a damaged garment, and send the garment to the Wardrobe of Robes with a request that it be repaired.'

Stone-faced, Potter repeated Baldwin's warning that she was to write nothing down.

'Not even to send word that Lady Mary requires a new garment?'

'That much is permitted.' Baldwin sounded as if the words were choking him . . . or as if he was trying not to laugh.

'Mayhap it would be best to devise a code using colors,' Rosamond said brightly, not at all deterred by their lack of enthusiasm. 'If I am to send an order for clothing for Lady Mary in any case, then why not indicate the level of urgency my real message entails? Red could signal extreme importance. And for something of a middling nature, why not make reference to the shade called Dead Spaniard. That is a pale, grayish tan color,' she added in an aside to Master Baldwin.

'No codes.' Potter snapped out the words. 'No ciphers.'

'And no invisible ink.' Baldwin took her arm. 'We must be on our way. The primary purpose of this meeting was to assure that you would know each other on sight when next you meet.'

'Oh, never fear. I will remember Mistress Jaffrey.'

Rosamond ignored the sneer in his voice and bade him a polite farewell.

Six

'What a petty little man,' Rosamond muttered when they were back on the barge. 'I wonder if he will trouble to pass on any information I do give him.'

'He will obey his orders.' Of that much, if naught else, Nick felt confident.

'At least you credit me with possessing a mind.'

'How could I not? I have visited your schoolroom.'

She'd been given a remarkable education, equal to that received by any gentleman's male heir. Susanna Appleton, who had fostered her late husband's by-blow for much of Rosamond's childhood, believed girls were every bit as clever as boys and likely more so. Her own abilities were proof of that. There was no woman Nick admired more.

Mollified by his response, Rosamond made another attempt to worm information out of him. She had guessed that Sir Francis Walsingham was behind her placement in the household of Lady Mary Hastings but Nick steadfastly refused to confirm it.

'How does Lady Mary feel about being married off to a foreign prince?' she asked.

'I have no way of knowing that, Rosamond.'

'Does her brother the earl approve? I know little about him.'

'Nor do I. He spends most of his time in the north, where he is the queen's Lord Lieutenant.'

'Is that where Lady Mary has been living?'

Nick had no idea. He let his silence answer for him.

'What of Lady Huntingdon? Is she one of the queen's ladies?'

Again, Nick did not know. 'I have naught to do with the royal court,' he confessed. 'London merchants hear of it when the queen grants one of her courtiers a license to import or export goods. We have a good idea which noblemen are in debt to the moneylenders. We know that some men – Walsingham, Lord Burghley, the earl of Leicester – hold positions of power. But otherwise?' He lifted both hands in a gesture of helplessness. 'I am as ignorant as you are, Rosamond.'

Her scowl made him smile. She liked to think she knew everything.

Chelsea was only a bit more than two miles upriver from Westminster. Rosamond continued to pepper him with low-voiced questions the entire way. What did Lady Mary look like? How old was she? Who else lived in the household? How large was it? How soon did he think they would leave for the royal court?

Unable to give her any answers, Nick felt a deep sense of relief upon sighting Chelsea Manor. 'There,' he said, pointing. 'That is where Lady Mary currently resides.'

The house, a mansion built of rose-colored brick, was set back from the riverbank. Tall chimneys rose up from its roof. Dozens of glazed windows glistened in the noonday sun. As they approached, he could see that a long pathway ran north from a gatehouse, passing between two large walled courts before terminating at a second gate that gave onto a terrace.

A barge was already tied up at the foot of Chelsea Manor's water stairs. As their smaller craft pulled alongside, he took note of the crest emblazoned on the hull. Badges bearing the same design – the bear and ragged staff – also appeared on the livery of the oarsmen.

'Whose device is that?' Rosamond asked.

This time he was able to answer her. 'It belongs to the earl of Leicester, the queen's favorite courtier. It is not all that surprising to find him here. Lady Huntingdon is his youngest sister.'

'Robert Dudley,' Rosamond murmured.

'Do you know him?' Nick thought it unlikely, but with Rosamond one never knew.

She shook her head. 'Leicester knew my father many years ago.'

As soon as they stepped ashore, the Huntingdon servants swarmed aboard the barge to collect Rosamond's bags and boxes. She ignored them. Without hesitation, she ascended the water stairs, crossed a grassy strip well planted with trees, and approached the gatehouse. Nick, following a few steps behind, heard her announce in a clear, carrying voice that Lady Mary's new waiting gentlewoman had arrived.

Seven

Rosamond fidgeted as Melka brushed her clothing to remove the grime it had collected during the journey from Bermondsey to Chelsea. Second thoughts had tormented her from the moment Master Baldwin left her in the hands of an upper servant and beat a hasty retreat. He had been so reluctant to answer her questions that she had to wonder if what little he *had* told her was true. As a child, she had trusted him implicitly, but that was no guarantee of his honesty. Had he misled her when he'd said that Rob would be in danger if negotiations in England did not go well?

Not for the first time, Rosamond regretted burning so many bridges when she started her new life in Bermondsey. A letter to her stepfather, or to her foster mother, would have answered many of her questions. She doubted either would reply to her now, not after she had behaved so abominably to them both.

With a sigh, she abandoned all thought of appealing directly to her family. Still, her mother and Sir Walter Pendennis, her mother's husband, might hear something of her situation from another source. Rosamond slanted a sideways glance at Melka. She'd never been able to discover how her maidservant communicated with her former mistress in Cornwall, but she was certain that Melka did so. All Rosamond needed to do was confide in her.

Another sigh escaped her. She'd never been one for sharing her secrets. She'd wait, she decided. After all, she had no compelling reason to doubt Master Baldwin's story. Perhaps this was only a case of wishful thinking – she did not want the danger to Rob to be real.

Assume Master Baldwin told you the truth, she ordered herself. If there was any chance she might discover something while in this household that would help keep her estranged husband safe, she had to do her best to find it.

Melka adjusted Rosamond's coif and stepped back, indicating that her mistress was now presentable. She could not put off her first meeting with Lady Mary Hastings any longer.

'You will busy yourself unpacking while I am gone, Melka.'

When she received no answer, Rosamond sent a questioning look at her maidservant. Melka returned one of her own, prompting Rosamond to survey the tiny, dismal chamber she'd been assigned. It contained a bed, a three-legged stool, and a small table. Her trunks and boxes filled nearly all the remaining space. There was no wardrobe chest for her clothes, nor was there a cupboard to hold the rest of her belongings.

'How lowering,' she murmured. She had forgotten that she was not a guest in this house but rather an upper servant. She supposed she should be grateful she had not been housed in a dormitory and made to share a bed with another of the waiting gentlewomen.

Leaving Melka to her own devices, Rosamond went in search of her new mistress. She took the opportunity to explore the house, committing its layout to memory. She had poked her head into most of the rooms before anyone – an officious, liveried manservant – asked her what she was doing.

'I was attempting to locate Lady Mary when I became lost,' she said in a meek voice.

'This way, mistress.'

He led her to the long gallery, a chamber she'd taken care to avoid when she'd heard feminine laughter issuing from it. As she'd rightly guessed, it was occupied by Lady Mary and Lady Huntingdon and several other women of the household.

'Your new waiting gentlewoman, Lady Mary,' the serving man announced, addressing a tall, slender woman in a richly embroidered gown.

Rosamond approached with a smile on her face, bobbing a perfunctory curtsey to show respect for Lady Mary's superior social status.

The noblewoman looked at her down a long, straight nose, examining Rosamond the same way she might have stared at a strange but as yet unidentified insect.

Rosamond stared back. Lady Mary was older than she'd expected and excessively plain. Her large, widely spaced cornflower blue eyes were her best feature. She had pale, almost translucent skin and hair that was a washed-out shade of yellow that did nothing to enhance her appearance.

'I do not see why I need *another* waiting gentlewoman,' Lady Mary said.

Although Rosamond had not been expecting a warm

reception, the chill of this one was colder than the icy waters of the Thames.

Lady Huntingdon sent her sister-in-law a tight-lipped, reproving glance. She had been a beauty in her day and still had a certain plump prettiness. For a noblewoman, she dressed plainly, wearing only a few ornaments, although the broach pinned to her bosom was valuable enough to have fed a yeoman's family for a year.

'When you are at court,' Lady Huntingdon said to her sister-in-law, 'you must be seen to be a person of consequence. You are, after all, a near cousin to the queen.'

Rosamond expected the countess to say more, perhaps even refer to Lady Mary's future status as tsarina of Muscovy. Not just a queen, as Rosamond understood it, but more akin to an empress. Instead, Lady Huntingdon appeared to be exhibiting caution in the presence of a newcomer to the household.

Rosamond was not much interested in political machinations, but it was no secret that Queen Elizabeth, who was nearly fifty years old, was unlikely ever to marry or have children. Since no one wanted her closest relative, the captive queen of Scots, to succeed to the throne when Elizabeth Tudor died, some of the queen's advisors had put forward the earl of Huntingdon, Lady Mary's brother, as the most logical heir apparent.

The connection was not all that close. The day after Baldwin made his proposal, Rosamond had made it her business to find out how Lady Mary came by her royal blood. She'd sent one of her servants to the nearest bookseller. He'd returned with a pamphlet advocating Huntingdon's succession and detailing the earl's descent from that infamous duke of Clarence who had been, so legend claimed, drowned in a butt of Malmsey wine while a prisoner in the Tower of London. Huntingdon and his sister were Clarence's great-grandchildren while Queen Elizabeth was the great-granddaughter of his brother, King Edward IV.

The relationship did not make Lady Mary a princess. In truth, she had no title at all. She was only *Lady* Mary because her father, like her brother, had been an earl. Why, then, was she such a haughty piece? Rosamond's eyes narrowed. Did that secretive little smile playing about Lady Mary's lips mean she was thinking of the proposed marriage alliance with Muscovy? Rosamond supposed that might be reason enough to revel in a sense of self-importance.

'Our dear kinswoman, the countess of Sussex, recommended this young woman to you,' Lady Huntingdon said. 'With the earl so ill, she can no longer keep her herself.'

'Then I suppose I must take her.' For the first time, Lady Mary deigned to address Rosamond directly: 'What is your name?'

Swallowing her annoyance at the future tsarina's disdainful manner, Rosamond kept the bright smile on her face and answered, 'Rosamond Jaffrey, my lady.'

'Do you play a musical instrument, Rose?'

The arbitrary shortening of her name put an end to the forced smile. It was just as well. Rosamond's cheek muscles had begun to ache. 'The lute,' she replied, and in honesty added, 'But only a little.'

She'd been taught the rudiments, but she was as likely to get her fingers tangled in the strings as she was to produce a recognizable melody. She was even less proficient at singing.

'Can you read?'

Thinking that it might prove useful to be perceived as amiable but stupid, Rosamond did not reveal the full extent of her education. 'Only a little,' she said again, and hoped that everyone in the household, especially Lady Mary, would underestimate her intelligence.

Without troubling to lower her voice, Lady Mary turned to her sister-in-law. 'If I must take a stranger into my service, must she be a dullard?'

Instead of answering, Lady Huntingdon gestured toward three gentlewomen seated close together on a padded bench in front of one of the long windows at the far end of the gallery. 'Will you join the others, Rosamond? They will instruct you in your duties.'

After making another halfhearted obeisance, Rosamond turned her back on her new mistress and walked, feet dragging, toward the window seat. A large embroidery frame had been set up in front of it. Rosamond hoped it held nothing too elaborate. Needlework was no more one of her talents than music was. Since she had never had any inclination to practice either, she had made little progress beyond an amateur's first clumsy attempts.

Even before she seated herself on a stool next to the embroidery frame and reached for a needle, she saw that she had been right to be concerned. The design was exceeding complex. The simple cross stitch Rosamond *had* managed to master would never suffice.

Three pairs of eyes bored into her as she ran her fingers over a selection of embroidery silks. 'I am not accustomed to such quality,' she said in an apologetic whisper. 'How fine these are.'

No one said a word.

She tried again. 'I am Rosamond Jaffrey. Lady Mary has kindly taken me into her household.'

'There was nothing kind about it,' said one of the three gentle-women, a horse-faced female a little older than Rosamond.

Her gaze followed Lady Mary and Lady Huntingdon as the two noblewomen left the gallery. Neither of the others spoke until the sound of their footsteps died away.

'I am Elizabeth Farnham,' said the taller of the three. 'Bess.' She nodded toward the woman who had already spoken. 'That is Anne Morgan, called Nan, and this is Margaret Ellerker – Madge.'

Madge, pink-cheeked and dimpled, offered a nod of acknow-ledgement but said nothing.

'You have joined us at a good time,' said Nan. 'We are to spend Yuletide at court.'

'Is that unusual?' Rosamond asked, still dithering over how to begin stitching without revealing her shocking inadequacies as a needlewoman.

'Perhaps not, but it will be my first visit there.' Nan offered a few helpful suggestions concerning the needlework and then returned to her theme. 'There are courtiers at court, you see – wealthy, unmarried young men, some of them with titles.'

'It is Nan's greatest desire to marry a man with money,' Bess said. 'He need not be young.'

Nan's laugh was good-natured. 'It is no sin to have ambition and my ambition is to be rich.'

'And yet you waste time befriending people who do not have two farthings to rub together.' Madge shook her head, but whether with disapproval or in simple disbelief, Rosamond could not tell. 'That bald man who was wont to call on you when we were still in Leicestershire will never amount to anything.'

'Do not be so certain of that.' Nan continued to stitch as she talked. Her fingers flew, plying her needle with a skill Rosamond envied. 'I believe in being friendly to everyone because you never know who will end up in a position to do you a good turn at some point in the future.'

'A reasonable philosophy.' Rosamond admired Nan's forthright attitude and plain speaking.

'Where are you from, Rosamond?' Bess asked. 'I was born in Leicestershire. Madge comes from Yorkshire, and Nan was raised, for the most part, in Herefordshire.'

'I was born in London and have lived in Lancashire, Kent and Cornwall, with a brief stay in Derbyshire,' Rosamond said before she remembered that she was supposed to have been in service with the countess of Sussex. To avoid further questions about the places she had lived and when she had lived there, she added, 'I have a husband. He is traveling on the Continent.'

Madge's hand froze in mid-air, her needle poised above the embroidery frame. She gave Rosamond a sharp look. 'He is not a Papist in exile, is he?'

'Not at all. He just likes to visit new places.'

'And prefers to leave you behind?' The pity in Bess's voice was impossible to miss.

'Has he abandoned you?' The blunt question came from Nan.

'He . . . we . . . that is, I—'

'No need to confess all,' Bess interrupted her. 'If the wretch cannot provide you with a house and servants of your own, you are better off here with us.'

'I have a friend who has gone abroad to make his fortune,' Nan said. 'Mayhap your husband will come home a rich man, too.'

'That is devoutly to be wished for.' Rosamond applied herself to her embroidery, hoping she had not already said too much. Although she was curious about her new companions, she could not ask too many questions lest they expect to have their curiosity satisfied in return.

The rest of the day passed with interminable slowness. The embroidery was tedious and the conversation ranged from the trivial to the overly pious. This was, to Rosamond's dismay, a *religious* household.

At Willow House, praying was perfunctory at best and often neglected. At Chelsea Manor, the entire household was required to attend both morning and evening prayers. Lady Huntingdon's chaplain, Augustus Treadwell, was a long-winded fellow. He droned on and on, but the gist of what he preached could be summed up with few words: he was against anything that might contain the slightest hint of enjoyment.

Rosamond was dizzy with fatigue by the time evening prayers ended and she was free to seek her bed. Only then did she discover that she would have to share her tiny room with her maid.

'Truckle bed,' Melka said as she helped Rosamond undress.

Rosamond sighed deeply. She could endure Melka's company, and the other waiting gentlewomen were pleasant enough, but she envisioned an endless procession of long, dull days looming ahead of her.

Any sacrifice, she reminded herself, was worthwhile if it preserved Rob's life. Holding on to that virtuous thought, she crawled under the covers . . . only to discover that the mattress was lumpy and the sheets were damp.

Eight

It had been a week since Rob Jaffrey first encountered Jane Bomelius. He'd seen her twice since, each time taking with him small contributions to make her strained circumstances more palatable. The first gift had been of food, the second of clothing.

Despite her conviction that no one at England House would lift a finger to help her, Rob had only been waiting for the right moment to call attention to her situation. That evening, in the comfort of the main hall, close to the warmth emanating from the ornate fireplace, he decided the time had come. Only his closest associates were present, most of the men currently in residence being elsewhere.

Toby Wharton, a jovial fellow with a bushy yellow beard who was Nick Baldwin's man in Muscovy, had challenged Egidius Crew, longtime employee of the Muscovy Company, most often used as an interpreter, to a game of Hazard. While they wagered and threw the dice, the remaining member of their circle, Harry Vaughan, busied himself polishing the brass barrel of his wheel-lock pistol to a brilliant shine. He'd fired it earlier in the day, killing a rat in one of the large storerooms at England House.

A stipendiary with the Muscovy Company, Vaughan had been in Russia a year longer than Rob. As tall as Crew, Vaughan had a more muscular build. His black hair was in marked contrast to Crew's receding hairline. For some reason, women found the combination of that dark hair, sapphire blue eyes, and a clean-shaven countenance surpassing attractive. Rob had seen stolid matrons turn their heads to watch Vaughan walk past.

'I met an Englishwoman on one of my rambles,' Rob said in what he hoped was a casual manner. 'She asked my help to travel home.'

Toby lifted one pale eyebrow, a trick Rob had tried to master without success. 'An Englishwoman? They are rarer than hen's teeth in this part of the world.'

'A comely wench, is she?' Crew's bright, curious green eyes sparkled in the firelight. He threw the dice, grimacing when they did not fall as he'd hoped.

'She is a respectable widow,' Rob corrected him. 'Her name is Jane Bomelius. She—'

Vaughan looked up from loading his pistol to shoot Rob an incredulous look. 'By Saint Basil's holy beard! Have you run mad?'

His reaction made Rob scowl. The scowl deepened when he took note of the concerned frown on Wharton's face. Ten years Rob's senior, he had been known to the younger man for most of his life.

Wharton exchanged a look with Crew and then asked, 'Did the widow tell you *how* her husband lost his life?'

'She said he died in prison, but—'

'His crime was treason,' Crew said.

'Was he guilty?'

'As sin.'

Wharton nodded in agreement. 'It must have been five or six years ago now. Bomelius disguised himself as one of his own servants and traveled into territory controlled by Polish troops. English ships were in port there, but since Muscovy and Poland were at war and he was in the tsar's employ, he was arrested and charged with intriguing with the enemy.'

'How could he be such a fool? He left his family behind in Moscow – children, a pretty wife.'

'So she is pretty!' Vaughan's leer was so offensive that Rob ducked his head and drank deeply from the cup of mead he'd only sipped from throughout the evening. At once he regretted it. The cloying aftertaste of honey and spices had him fighting not to gag.

'He was put to the rack,' Wharton said. 'Then he was tied to a stake and the fire lit beneath him.'

Rob's stomach twisted. To be burnt at the stake was a punishment usually reserved for heretics and those who murdered their masters. Or for wives who killed their husbands. 'Did his widow lie, then, when she said he died in prison?'

'Not at all.' Vaughan did not look up from returning his gun to its purpose-built, velvet-lined wooden case. 'He wasn't burnt to *death*, you see, just roasted sufficient to make sure he'd spend the remainder of his life in agony. I've heard that he survived for a long, long time.'

'No one should have to endure such torture,' Rob said, 'and what call has the tsar to punish the poor widow? She exists in the most dire poverty. And she is *English*. How can we abandon her to her fate, no matter what her husband did?'

Crew rolled his eyes heavenward. 'God save us from boys who still believe in chivalry!'

Vaughan snorted. Even Wharton looked as if he agreed with Crew's sentiment.

'What if she were your widow?' Rob demanded. As if to underscore what had happened to Bomelius, a log crackled loudly in the fireplace as it was consumed by the flames. A downdraft sent wood smoke drifting into the chamber.

'Since I have no wife, it is difficult to imagine having a widow.' Crew toyed with the neglected dice, a fine pair carved from ivory.

'And my queen of hearts,' Vaughan said without looking up, 'the woman I mean to marry one day, has too much ambition to ever put a foot wrong.'

'Queen of hearts?' The reference was odd enough to momentarily distract Rob from the plight of Jane Bomelius. 'Why do you call her that?'

'Have you never seen the likenesses of royalty painted on playing cards? One such has a most excellent portrait of Queen Anne Boleyn as the queen of hearts and King Henry as the king.'

'So your beloved is a dark-haired siren, as Queen Anne is said to have been?' Wharton seemed genuinely curious.

'She is no great beauty, but she does treat me royally.' The self-satisfied smirk on Vaughan's face nearly as offensive as his leer.

Crew shook the dice and made his cast. Satisfied with the result, he slanted his gaze toward Vaughan. 'Did this queen of hearts encourage you to take a post in Muscovy?'

'She did, the clever girl. Fortunes to be made, she said, and she was right.'

'What a great pity she did not come with you. That knack for never putting a foot wrong would serve you in good stead.'

There seemed to be a deeper meaning in his words. Rob frowned, trying to puzzle it out. He supposed Crew meant that Vaughan was engaged in private trading. This practice was strictly forbidden by the Muscovy Company but, since the company had no way to enforce the policy, most Englishmen in Russia dabbled in this lucrative sideline, some with considerable success.

'I am a passing clever fellow,' Vaughan boasted. 'I need no advice from a mere female, even one so clever as she, to make my fortune in this benighted land.' So saying, he picked up his gun case and left the hall.

Wharton took his last turn with the dice and lost. The money wagered on the outcome changed hands.

'A round of pass-dice?' Crew suggested, looking at Rob.

He shook his head. 'I have no spare coins to risk.'

Instead, he sat by the fire, lost in thought, for some time. He was dimly aware of comings and goings as the hour grew later. By the time Toby Wharton stepped up beside him and dropped a heavy hand on his shoulder, everyone else had gone to bed.

'You think too much, lad.' Wharton drew another stool across the tiled floor so he could sit and offered Rob one of the cloves he always carried with him.

Absently, Rob took the dried, unopened flower bud and popped it into his mouth. As he chewed, its sweet, pungent flavor was released, something like nutmeg but stronger, or mayhap more like cinnamon, only not so hot. In any case, Wharton swore by the imported spice as a way to sweeten the breath and promote digestion and had taught Rob how to chew lightly for a few minutes and then tuck the clove into his cheek. Nestled there, its goodness could be made to last an entire day.

Wharton was already sucking on his own clove. Its scent overpowered the smell of the Russe wine he'd been drinking while he diced.

'Is there no way to help Mistress Bomelius?' Rob asked.

'Not as long as the tsar wishes to keep her here.'

'I doubt he even remembers she exists, let alone that she is still in Moscow. Tsar Ivan must have weightier matters on his mind than one lone Englishwoman.'

'I'd not be so sure of that. You know he dispatched an ambassador with the fleet when it left for England in August. I have it on good authority that his orders were to fetch back an English princess to marry old Ivan.'

Startled, Rob looked away from the dying fire. 'But the tsar already has a wife. She gave birth to his son only a few weeks ago.'

'He already has *two* wives. He sent the other one to a convent. Word is that he'll do the same with the current tsarina, if it will seal an alliance with Elizabeth of England.'

'How do you know all this?' Rob asked. 'The last I heard, you were not part of Tsar Ivan's intimate circle.'

Wharton chuckled. 'Nor would I want to be. But there is one Englishman who is, a physician named Robert Jacobi. He was sent here some time ago by our beloved queen herself. Jacobi was a regular visitor to England House before he left to serve as the ambassador's interpreter on his visit to England.'

Stirring the fire with a poker, Rob only half listened as Wharton rambled on, but he interrupted the other man when Wharton started talking about someone he called 'Lady Mary'.

'Who is she when she's at home? Ow!' Knuckles rapped against the side of the head were not particularly painful, but Wharton's blow caught Rob by surprise. 'What was that for?'

'Disrespect. The woman the tsar wants to marry is the earl of Huntingdon's sister and a cousin to the queen.'

'How was I to know? Come to think of it, how do you? Jacobi again?' Rob abandoned the poker and gave Wharton his full attention.

'It was Jacobi who suggested her name to the tsar in the first place, or so he claims. The good doctor is something of a braggart. To hear him tell it, he's been promoting this match nearly as long as he's been in Muscovy. I cannot fathom why.' He shook his head. 'For myself, I pity any poor woman who falls into Ivan's hands.'

'Then help me help Mistress Bomelius.'

Wharton sighed. 'The tsar is not to be trifled with, not on any account. He reacts badly to being thwarted and tends to take out his frustration on innocent bystanders.'

At Rob's disbelieving look, Wharton abandoned his seat and returned to the table where he'd left a beaker of wine and his cup. Spitting out his clove, he refilled the cup and drank half the contents in one gulp. 'Let me tell you a little story. Four years ago, when I first arrived in Moscow, Russia was at war with Poland over territory they both claimed in Livonia. When Ivan got word that Polotsk had fallen to the Polish army, he took swift and merciless revenge on those he imagined were his enemies. He dressed a thousand gunners all in black and sent them into the suburb of Moscow inhabited by Dutch and Livonian merchants. His henchmen's orders were to strip naked every person they found there, to rape every woman, regardless of her age, and to rob every house. They took it upon themselves to also burn two protestant churches to the ground.'

'I do not understand. The tsar was angry at Poland, and by extension at the Livonians. That much I follow. But why did he attack the Dutch?'

'Because he is a madman. And because he could. A few of the

victims who managed to escape came here to England House. It was a near thing we weren't subjected to similar treatment just for harboring them. Listen well, my friend. We are none of us truly safe in Muscovy. Not ever. But we stay a little safer when we take care not to do anything to provoke imperial wrath. Take my advice. Forget you ever met Mistress Bomelius. No one less powerful than Queen Elizabeth herself can win that poor woman's freedom. Come to think of it, I am not at all certain Her Majesty's intervention would succeed. Not if old Ivan's in a bad mood.'

This time when Toby drank, draining his cup, Rob reached for his abandoned goblet, still half full of mead. He fumbled with the clove, which seemed to have adhered itself to the inside of his cheek, but once it was out, he followed suit. The result was a pleasant buzz that helped him fall asleep that night . . . and a pounding headache all the next day.

Nine

From an upper window, Rosamond Jaffrey watched a richly dressed young woman disembark at Chelsea Manor's water stairs. Unless she was much mistaken, the trim on her cloak was sable, expensive to import and somewhat rare in England. For her to wear it was also, Rosamond suspected, in violation of the sumptuary laws, although she doubted there was much danger of an arrest. A great many illegal things managed to flourish when one had the wherewithal to pay for them.

'Who is she?' Rosamond directed the question to Nan Morgan, who had gone out of her way to be friendly during the week and a half she had been at Chelsea. The other two waiting gentlewomen – pretty, excessively pious Madge Ellerker and tall, awkward Bess Farnham – had shown more interest in hemming shirts for the poor and discussing the much finer garments they would soon see, and perhaps wear, at court.

'That is Mistress Frances Howard, age sixteen, the middle daughter of Lord Howard of Effingham.'

As Rosamond watched, Mistress Frances rushed toward the house with the boundless energy of a puppy. She was followed at a more sedate pace by at least a dozen servants.

'I have seen Lord Howard's Men perform,' Rosamond said. 'They are a most excellent company of players.'

'You will see better at court. That is where our young visitor is bound. She stops here for the night on her way to Windsor.'

'I would have thought an earl's daughter would be received by the queen before the child of a mere baron.'

Nan chuckled. 'There are special circumstances. Lady Howard is one of the queen's gentlewomen of the privy chamber. She is also Her Majesty's cousin and dear friend. The oldest of the Howard daughters, Elizabeth, is already at court as a maid of honor. Mistress Frances goes to Windsor to spend time with her mother and sister as much as to join in the Yuletide festivities.'

'You speak as if you know her well.'

Nan's smile was complacent. 'And so I do. I came to Lady Mary from the Howard family seat in Surrey. I was sent there by my family to learn the ways of the nobility and spent several years in service to the Howards.'

Just as she had once been dispatched to the household of an earl's daughter in Derbyshire, Rosamond thought. It was a common enough practice, but not one of which she approved. No one ever asked the young girl in question where she wanted to live.

Rosamond welcomed the break in the monotony of life at Chelsea. Never in her life had she spent so much time sitting with other women, sewing or embroidering while being read to from 'improving' books. The usual reader was Lady Huntingdon's humorless chaplain, the same one who conducted prayers twice a day and preached long, tiresome sermons on Sunday.

In most households, games of chance using cards or dice or both enlivened the evenings, but the earl of Huntingdon disapproved of gambling and had forbidden the practice among his womenfolk. Dancing was permitted, since it was considered healthful exercise, but under Lady Mary's leadership it was little more than that. Three sad-faced musicians produced staid and uninspiring sounds to accompany the dance steps, dealing a fatal blow to any pleasure Rosamond might have derived from the pastime.

Frances Howard was more than a breath of fresh air, she was a gale-force wind, blowing away the cobwebs and setting the dust motes swirling. High-spirited and dynamic, the dark-haired young woman not only chattered incessantly, regaling her listeners with stories of previous visits she had made to her mother and older sister at court but, after supper, she announced she intended to stage an impromptu masque.

Lady Mary tried to object, but the younger woman was unstoppable. Frances Howard insisted that, having spent considerable time with her father's players, she knew just how to put together a production. With blithe indifference to social standing, she assigned parts. She made Nan, for whom she seemed to have a special affection, a king's wayward daughter and Bess was her stalwart suitor. Rosamond found herself portraying a nearsighted goddess who could not tell one mortal from another. The story made little sense and the performers were pitifully inexperienced. Bess kept tripping over her own feet, shod in oversized shoes borrowed from a groom. That she also wore the fellow's clothing, the garments so loose on her that they flapped, became the source of great amusement. By the time they took their bows, even Lady Mary was smiling.

The next morning, the young noblewoman continued on her way to Windsor and life resumed its normal routine at Chelsea Manor.

'Why did you leave the Howard household?' Rosamond whispered to Nan.

Seated in a wooden box chair without even a cushion under his bony rump, the chaplain, Augustus Treadwell, read to them from *Commentaries of the divine, John Calvin, upon the prophet Daniel.* Each section consisted of two or three verses from the prophet followed by Calvin's long-winded explanation, more verses, more exposition and finally a prayer composed by Calvin. Rosamond found it difficult to keep from yawning.

'There was no place for me with Lady Howard,' Nan whispered back. 'Lively as Mistress Frances is, I had no desire to remain in the country. Lady Howard recommended me to Lady Huntingdon so that I might better my chances of serving at court.'

A glance at Treadwell assured Rosamond that he was too entranced by the sound of his own raspy voice to pay attention to his captive audience. 'I do not see that this is much improvement.'

Nan glanced up from her stitches with an impish grin. 'Had I known I'd spend most of the next year in Leicestershire, I might have remained in Surrey. I made the mistake of assuming that Lady Mary would soon be called to court.'

'Why?'

Madge shushed them. Rolling her eyes toward the chaplain, she whispered, 'Do him the courtesy of listening.'

Nan indulged in some eye-rolling of her own when Madge returned her attention to her needlework, but she lapsed into silence and Rosamond was not curious enough to pursue the matter. Everyone knew Lady Mary was related to the queen, reason enough to suppose she would spend time in her majesty's company.

One tedious day after another passed in similar fashion. Rosamond's skill with a needle did not improve, and she spent far too much time weaving fantasies to amuse herself. Subjected to the droning of Doctor Treadwell for more hours than she wished to count, she made a study of his features, taking note of his long, reddish-brown hair, his hawk nose, and the way his watery blue eyes had to squint when he read to them. He was short-sighted, she decided. Thin and of medium height, no more than thirty years old, she supposed he was toothsome in an aesthetic sort of way, although his type held no appeal for her. Nor did she find his strong evangelical leanings attractive, but she took note of the admiration in Madge's gaze when she looked at the chaplain and wondered if there was a wedding for the two of them in their future.

She shared this thought with Melka in the privacy of their bedchamber.

Melka, busy with a clothes brush, made no comment.

'I have yet to hear anyone mention the plans being made for Lady Mary after she goes to court.' Rosamond sat on the bed in her night rail, legs folded beneath her in tailor fashion, a book of poetry, open but unread, balanced on her knees. 'No one has said a word about Muscovy or the tsar. I cannot believe that Lady Mary's courtship is such a closely guarded secret that not a single member of her own household knows a thing about it. I wonder if her tiring maid has any inkling of what is afoot. I have only glimpsed the girl once or twice. She keeps herself well in the background, as a proper maid-servant should.'

'Beatrice Unton,' Melka said without looking up from her labors. 'Ticey.'

Rosamond grinned. 'Have you, by chance, become friendly with this Ticey Unton?'

'Haughty,' Melka said.

The unexpected comment had Rosamond swiveling her head in her maidservant's direction. 'Lady Mary is. Do you mean that Ticey is, too?'

To illustrate, Melka repeated, verbatim, an exchange between Ticey and one of the grooms, a young man who'd shown an interest in the tiring maid. Melka was a skilled mimic, capturing both voices to perfection and leaving Rosamond in no doubt about Ticey's high opinion of herself.

'I wonder – does she put on airs because she knows about the tsar? Do you think you could convince her to confide in you?'

A snort was Melka's only reply, but Rosamond understood. The servants at Chelsea Manor, in common with those Melka had encountered elsewhere, were wary of anyone who was not English.

With a sigh, Rosamond tossed aside her book and crawled under the covers, hoping sleep would come quickly. If something did not happen soon to relieve the monotony of her days, she feared she would go mad with boredom!

Ten

Dressed in their finest garments, skirts held out by cone-shaped farthingales, Lady Mary Hastings, her four waiting gentlewomen, and her tiring maid crowded onto the Huntingdon barge. When it promptly sank lower in the water, Rosamond wondered if it was wise to have so many people on board at once.

The livery-clad rowers seemed unconcerned. Why should they be? If the vessel capsized, they would be able to swim ashore. Only those encased in whalebone and yards of heavy brocade, velvet, and wool would sink straight to the bottom of the Thames.

Word had finally come to Chelsea Manor. The queen had authorized Lady Mary to visit the Wardrobe of Robes at Whitehall. She was to select one of Her Majesty's own gowns to be altered to fit her. Today they would travel downriver on the morning tide and Lady Mary would spend as many hours as necessary trying on fabulous creations of satin, silk, and brocade.

Rosamond had a slightly different agenda planned for herself. She intended to locate Master Griffith Potter, clerk of the Great Wardrobe. Somehow, she must find occasion to speak with him alone. She had no news to impart, but she did have questions. This time, she was determined to receive answers.

The water journey to Whitehall passed uneventfully. From Whitehall stairs, their party passed through the palace gardens and into the palace. They encountered a goodly number of people, mostly tailors and other artisans and yeomen of the wardrobe, but in a storeroom filled with bolts of fabric, they came upon a man who was not a tailor or a clerk. By his dress, he was a gentleman. The elaborate bonnet he wore had likely cost more than a pair of coach horses.

He swept into a ground-glancing bow. 'Sir Jerome Bowes at your service, my lady.'

Flattered, Lady Mary at once forgave the effrontery of this unorthodox introduction. Rosamond was less impressed. Bowes had considerable charm and exerted it with a will, but there was something forced about his manner.

She seemed to be the only one among the women to notice.

Lady Mary lapped up his compliments like a cat offered cream and he made himself agreeable to the rest of her party with a word and a smile for each of the waiting gentlewomen. He even bent down and kissed Nan's fingertips. Rosamond kept her hands tightly clasped in front of her.

As a group, they moved on into the room where the queen's excess gowns were kept. Giddy as small children turned loose from their nurse's supervision, Lady Mary's gentlewomen fluttered this way and that making admiring noises. Rosamond stood still and stared. Lady Mary faced a daunting task if she was to make her selection in one day. There had to be at least a hundred gowns for her to choose from, each more gloriously decorated than the last.

Eager to begin, the noblewoman called for Ticey, her tiring maid, to help her remove her cloak and the elaborate gown she already wore over her kirtle. Sir Jerome's admiring gaze swept over Lady Mary's garments. Skirt, bodice and sleeves were all of imported brocade embroidered with flowers and birds. The attached ruff and cuffs were of finest lawn.

He talked a great deal of frivolous nonsense, Rosamond thought. It was well enough for Lady Mary and her women to chatter of velvets and silks, but it seemed to her that a man who was even now calling himself a 'rough soldier', albeit in a jovial, self-deprecating manner, should have more important matters on his mind than the latest fashion in doublets.

'May you have both pleasure and good fortune in your hunt for treasure, Lady Mary,' Bowes said with another bow. 'I will look forward to meeting you again when you come to court, and all your lovely ladies, too.'

Bess had temporarily vanished behind the mass of clothing, but Bowes tipped his hat to Rosamond, grinned at Nan, and winked at Madge. A nervous giggle escaped the latter before she could control it. Her cheeks, normally pink, flashed to bright red.

Rosamond wondered why Bowes had been in the Wardrobe of Robes at all. She felt certain the queen had not offered to give *him* any of her unwanted clothing!

From somewhere in the depths of the storeroom came a cry of delight. A moment later, Bess reappeared carrying a heavy crimson brocade gown decorated with gold thread. 'You must try on this one, my lady! The color is called Bristol red and it is accounted the most pleasant of shades.'

In her eagerness to present her prize, she stumbled and would have dropped the queen's gown if Madge had not been there to catch her elbow. Together they brought it forward, draped over their arms, for Lady Mary to inspect.

Other gowns followed. Even Rosamond found herself caught up in the excitement of the hunt. She took her time examining the exquisite creations before offering her selection. At the same time, she considered how easy it would be to disappear into this forest of clothing. Each in their turn, Bess, Nan, and Madge did vanish for a time. When they were in sight, they were so engrossed in debating which colors and fabrics most flattered their mistress that they paid no attention to anything else.

So it was that none of them noticed when Rosamond slipped out of the room.

By her reckoning, more than two hours had passed since their arrival at the Wardrobe of Robes. That was longer than she'd intended to wait to seek out Griffith Potter. On the other hand, by now there had been time enough for him to hear that Lady Mary and her women were in the building. If the fellow had any sense, he would be lurking nearby, keeping an eye out for her.

He was not.

Rosamond had considered this problem in advance. She saw no need for secrecy, not so long as she had a believable reason to ask for Potter's whereabouts. She stopped the first person she saw.

'I am looking for Griffith Potter,' she said in her most autocratic voice. 'Do you know where he is?'

'Ask Ralph Gargrave,' the man answered. 'I saw him speaking with Potter only a short time ago.' He pointed the way, giving terse directions.

A few minutes later, Rosamond located a bald man seated at a long work table. He looked up with a frown. 'Are you lost, mistress?'

'Oh, is it forbidden for me to be here?' She added a little trill of laughter to the end of the question. 'I do not mean to cause trouble for anyone. Truly. I am Mistress Jaffrey. I came with Lady Mary Hastings. She – well, I am sure you know why she is here.'

'Ralph Gargrave, yeoman of the robes, at your service, mistress.' He half rose from his stool. 'Shall I escort you back to Lady Mary?'

'Oh! Well! That is most kind of you, but in truth I wish to speak with Master Griffith Potter.' At his startled look, she favored him with a smile meant to convey wide-eyed innocence. 'His cousin is married to my husband's sister and she asked me to extend her greetings, should I chance to encounter him here.'

The claim of kinship worked as smoothly as a key in a lock. The bald man resumed his seat, but he did not know where Potter was. 'It has been an hour or more since I last saw him, mistress.' He picked up a heavily embroidered pair of gloves and held them close to his nose.

Taken aback, Rosamond eyed the other items on the table. It was piled high with an assortment of garments, everything from sleeves and headdresses to shifts made of the finest cambric. 'What is it you do here in the Wardrobe of Robes? This is a most peculiar collection of accessories.' She removed one of her own gloves to finger the exquisite lace edging on a pair of cuffs.

He spoke sharply. 'I would not touch that if I were you.'

She jerked her hand away. 'Why not?'

'It could be poisoned.' His craggy face split into a grin. 'I cannot tell, you see, until I have examined it.'

'Poison?'

'Poison. Precautions must be taken to make certain no poison contaminates any apparel that touches the queen's person.'

For the first time, Rosamond noticed that he wore sturdy canvas gauntlets to protect his hands. A heavy leather apron covered him from neck to knees.

'I examine every gift of clothing presented to the queen, whether she is ever likely to wear it or not.'

Rosamond heard the note of pride in his voice. 'Her Majesty is fortunate to have such a loyal servant. Do you often find dangerous substances?'

'Often enough to keep me vigilant,' he said with a laugh. 'And I have work to do. Can you find your way back to Lady Mary?'

'I can, but are you certain you have no idea where Master Potter is?'

Another employee of the Wardrobe of Robes, passing by at that moment, overheard her question. 'Try the last storeroom at the end of this passage,' he suggested. 'Potter is wont to take his midday meal there, apart from the rest of us.'

'My thanks, good sir.'

He nodded and kept walking, intent upon some task of his own.

Rosamond bade Master Gargrave farewell and made her way down the long, dimly lit corridor until she came to the last door.

Since it stood open, she went in. At first glance, there did not appear to be anyone within.

'Master Potter?'

So faint she almost missed it, someone whispered, 'Help me.'

Every sense alert, Rosamond moved deeper into the storeroom. It was filled with bales and boxes, many of them stacked so high that she could not see over them. A low moan gave her a direction for her search, but it still took a few minutes to find its source.

Griffith Potter lay sprawled on his back, his eyes open and staring and his mouth slack. All around him were the remnants of his meal. Bread, meat, cheese, and a cup that had once contained ale had fallen from the top of the barrel he had been using as a makeshift table.

Rosamond knelt beside him, speaking his name. The smell of vomit made her wrinkle her nose but she forced herself to ignore it. His face, beaded with sweat, was suffused with red.

When she touched his cheek, his whole body twitched. Then his eyes shifted her way and seemed to focus on her face. His pupils were so widely dilated that hardly any color showed.

'You,' he whispered in a hoarse croak.

Recognition? Or accusation? Rosamond could not tell. His lips moved. She bent closer, straining to hear.

'Attack,' he gasped.

She reared back onto her heels. 'You were attacked?'

She looked for blood and found none. Nor were there bruises on what she could see of his skin. If there was a wound, mayhap from a cudgel, it must be on the back of his skull.

Belatedly, she thought of her own safety and swiveled her head, trying to peer into every corner, nook and cranny. Her right hand hovered close to the knife in her boot, but nowhere did she catch sight of even a hint of movement, nor did she hear the shuffle of feet or the swish of fabric that might mean Potter's assailant was hiding somewhere in the storeroom.

The only sound was Potter's labored breathing.

Rosamond looked again at the fallen man. The red had faded from his face and neck. Now his skin was tinged with blue. The sight set alarm bells ringing. She scrambled to her feet and ran back into the corridor.

'Master Gargrave!' she called to the man at the work table. 'I need help! Master Potter has been injured.'

It was close enough to the truth.

Ralph Gargrave responded swiftly, but he was not fast enough. In the short time she had been absent, there had been a subtle change in Potter's condition. Rosamond stared at his motionless form in dismay. She did not need Gargrave to tell her that Griffith Potter had stopped breathing.

He bent over the dead man, shaking his head all the while he searched for any sign of life. He knelt, joints creaking, to examine the body at closer range. Removing the heavy gauntlets, he touched Potter's face with his bare hand, then held two fingers under the other man's nose to determine if there was any stirring of breath. Finding none, he gently closed the dead man's staring eyes.

Rosamond could not tear her gaze away from Potter's face. How could this have happened in the queen's own palace and in the selfsame rooms where so much care was taken to keep Her Majesty safe from poison?

The bald man bowed his head. Rosamond thought he must be praying. After a moment, he stood and turned to face her. 'Likely choked on a bit of meat.'

'What?' She could not believe what she was hearing. She had expected Gargrave to find Potter's sudden death as suspicious as she did.

Gargrave pointed to the scattered food. 'He was a loutish fellow, always gulping down what he ate, as if he was afraid someone would take it away from him.'

Words of protest trembled on Rosamond's lips. She bit them back. Anything she said would only bring trouble down on her own head. If the attack on Potter had something to do with his work as an intelligence gatherer, the last thing she should do was admit that she knew he'd led a secret life as a spy.

'An unfortunate accident,' Gargrave said.

Rosamond shook her head to clear it. Surely Potter's last word – attack – made nonsense of Gargrave's conclusion. Unless she had misunderstood. Was it only because she'd had poison on her mind, the result of talking to Gargrave about his duties in the Wardrobe of Robes, that she'd been so quick to see Potter's death as a murder?

Gargrave was trained to look for harmful substances. It seemed impossible he would overlook evidence of poison. And yet, the more Rosamond tried to convince herself she was mistaken, the more her instincts told her she had not been.

'Leave this to me, mistress,' Gargrave said. 'Come away now. Time to rejoin the other gentlewomen.'

Rosamond allowed him to lead her out of the storeroom. She wished she could take a sample of the spilled food with her to test on an animal, the tried and true method of detecting poison, but to attempt to retrieve any of it would focus unwelcome attention on herself.

'Never you worry, mistress,' her escort said. 'I'll say it was me that found him. There's nothing you can tell the coroner that I cannot, and were it known you were in that storeroom alone with him, there might be unfortunate speculation.'

That he meant speculation about her reputation was not Rosamond's first thought. After her stepfather had retired to quiet rustication in his native Cornwall, the queen had appointed him a justice of the peace. Rosamond had often heard him talk about the crimes he encountered while fulfilling his duties for the Crown. According to Sir Walter Pendennis, the person who sounded the hue and cry after discovering a body was looked at most closely . . . as a suspect. She had been with Potter just before he breathed his last. If anyone else thought he had been poisoned, she'd be the one suspected of administering it.

'Why are you protecting me?' The question popped out of her mouth before she could stop it.

Gargrave's avuncular smile eased her mind. 'You took the time to stop and talk with me, mistress, and saw the value in what I do.'

'You risk your life every day in the queen's service,' Rosamond said slowly.

Searching for poisons, an inner voice screamed. Why had he not seen what she had?

As if embarrassed by her praise, Gargrave ducked his head and avoided meeting her eyes. His modesty seemed genuine. His next words sounded sincere: 'Leave everything to me, mistress. No one will bother you about this unfortunate event. Go on in, now, and be of good cheer.'

He gave her a gentle shove toward the room where the others were still helping Lady Mary try on gowns. They took no more notice of Rosamond's return than they had of her departure.

Loud chatter and louder laughter rose up to engulf her as she moved deeper into the chamber. Of a sudden, her body began to tremble violently. She backed up in haste until she could lean against a wall. She felt weak as a newborn kitten, no longer able to stand upright on her own.

She'd held herself together during the crisis. Now that it was past, the implications of Potter's sudden death bombarded her. She heard again his last word – attack.

Recognizing Rosamond, he'd tried to tell her what had happened. He had been the victim of an attack, although not in the conventional sense. Poison had been the weapon used. She was certain of it. Moreover, she knew it was her responsibility to report her observations to . . . someone.

Unable to decide what to do, Rosamond did nothing. The man she'd been told to use as a conduit for messages was the man who now lay dead, murdered in the queen's wardrobe. She barely moved until Lady Mary, having at last made her choice, called her ladies together in preparation for leaving Whitehall.

Rosamond followed after the others, her mind still spinning. She'd barely known Griffith Potter and she hadn't much liked the man, but she'd been the only one with him at the end. He'd entrusted her with his dying message. She wanted to deliver it, but how could she? No one had seen fit to tell her the name of Potter's employer.

By the time she boarded the Huntingdon barge for the return trip to Chelsea, Rosamond's swirling thoughts had given her a raging headache. The possibility that the barge might capsize from the weight of so many passengers did not trouble her in the least. In truth, she took a certain dark amusement from the thought of drowning. That would be one way to resolve her dilemma!

Eleven

Damn all spy masters for their love of secrecy! What harm would it have done to give her the name of the man who had recruited her?

Rosamond stood at her window, staring at the distant spires of London. As soon as the Huntingdon barge had docked at Chelsea, she had used her headache as an excuse to retreat to her bedchamber. She had until supper to decide what to do next.

If it was Sir Francis Walsingham, the queen's principal secretary, who had sent her to Lady Mary, she could send word direct to him. But what if her guess was wrong? Did she dare take that risk? To do so might put an end to her intelligence gathering and, worse, increase the danger to Rob.

Walsingham seemed the most logical person to have sent her to Chelsea, but he could just as easily have a different agenda. What if he was the one who wanted the negotiations with Muscovy to fail? More men than Griffith Potter might die if that were the case, Rob Jaffrey among them.

Rosamond crossed to the bed and flung herself down full length atop the coverlet. She buried her face in the feather-stuffed pillow, cutting off sound and light. The quiet darkness failed to soothe her. She had been brought up to believe that murder must not go unpunished. She had to report what Potter had said and what she suspected about his death.

That was easier said than done.

The moment she spoke the word 'murder' there would be consequences. At the least, she'd be dismissed from Lady Mary's service for going off on her own to meet with a man. They were strict about such things in this household. Her lie about being kin to Potter would not hold up under scrutiny. Worse, any justice of the peace worth his commission would at once suspect Rosamond herself of the crime. Her hand crept to her throat, as if she could feel the rough hemp of a hangman's noose already settling around it.

The local authorities would not do, whoever they might be. She had no idea if a royal palace had its own magistrates or if the matter fell under the jurisdiction of the city of Westminster. It scarce mattered. If she was to tell her story at all, it had to be to someone who knew her. Someone who would believe in her innocence. Someone who would not betray her secrets.

Uncomfortable on the lumpy mattress, Rosamond rolled onto her back. Now there was a hardened clump of wool stuffing poking into her shoulder. With a sigh, she sat up, holding her still aching head in her hands.

The most obvious solution was to ask for help from her stepfather, Sir Walter Pendennis, but it would take weeks for a message to reach Cornwall at this time of year. Besides, what could she say that would make him forgive her and offer his assistance, especially when she was loath to write down anything specific about her foray into intelligence gathering? In truth, did she dare write to him at all? A letter could easily go astray. Even a missive written in invisible ink might come back to haunt her.

Wrapping one hand around the bedpost, Rosamond hauled herself to her feet. Perhaps there was another way to reach Sir Walter. She could send one of his own men to him with a verbal message. It would still take weeks to get a response, but at least she'd have done *something*.

Her stepfather had kept his old lodgings in Blackfriars, leaving one or two trusted servants in residence. All she had to do was slip away from Chelsea and hail a wherry to take her there.

Rosamond banged her forehead against the bedpost. Her plan was not so brilliant after all. It was one thing to disappear from a storeroom at Whitehall for less than an hour and quite another to go haring off to London, a journey that would take the best part of a morning or afternoon. To go at night was out of the question. She'd be taken for a whore by the watch and thrown into the nearest gaol.

Let it be, she told herself. *Let them rule Potter's death an accident.*

She flopped back onto the bed just as Melka entered the chamber. She carried a goblet, steam rising like a mist from within it – a healing herbal posset by the smell.

'How did you know I had a headache?' Rosamond snapped at her, taking out her frustration on her long-suffering maidservant.

Melka snorted, as if to remind Rosamond that servants always knew everything.

'You do not know as much as you think you do!' Rosamond sat up and grabbed the goblet. The contents tasted bitter but the effect was almost immediate. The pounding in her head eased. She felt less edgy.

Despite a strong urge to confide in Melka, Rosamond cautioned herself to resist. Melka would carry the tale to—

Cursing herself for a fool, Rosamond sent the maidservant a narrow-eyed look. 'How do you send news to my mother?'

The hint of a smile on her lips, Melka did not bother to deny that she'd been reporting Rosamond's activities to Eleanor Pendennis. 'Jacob.'

'Jacob Littleton? Sir Walter's man?'

Melka nodded.

Rosamond sagged against the bolster, weak with relief. Perhaps matters were not as hopeless as she had feared. 'That is excellent news. You must go to him at once and tell him to fetch Sir Walter. Impress upon him the urgency of the matter. My stepfather must come to me without delay.' She'd tell him everything. He would know what to do.

'Gone,' Melka said.

Rosamond blinked at her. 'What do you mean? Who is gone?'

'Jacob. Gone to Cornwall two days since.'

Rosamond cursed under her breath. 'Is anyone else living in Sir Walter's lodgings in Blackfriars? Someone you'd trust with a message?'

Melka was shaking her head even before Rosamond finished asking the question. 'Only Molly.'

'The housekeeper.'

'Lazy slut,' Melka said, not quite under her breath.

Not for the first time, Rosamond wondered if Melka and Jacob were lovers. Had her maidservant reason to be jealous of Molly, a woman Rosamond remembered as plump and efficient but with a face as plain as pudding? It scarce mattered, except to Melka.

Now that the ache in her head was in abeyance, Rosamond willed herself to recall the scene in the Wardrobe of Robes. She saw again the dead man's face and what appeared to her to be clear signs of poisoning.

She knew far more than she wished to about the number of poisonous plants that grew in every housewife's garden. More than one of them might have produced gastric distress, bluish skin, enlarged pupils, and a quick death.

Closing her eyes, Rosamond heard again Potter's whisper, telling her he'd been attacked. She was certain that meant he'd been murdered. Spies often met with unfortunate ends. The real question was whether or not Griffith Potter's death had anything to do with Lady Mary and the negotiations with Muscovy. Potter might have been killed for some reason unrelated to his employment as an intelligence gatherer – by a jealous husband, mayhap, or because of a quarrel over a wager.

Rosamond sighed. Did it matter? A life had been taken. Someone would get away with murder unless she spoke up.

Once again she found herself standing in front of the window with its distant view of London. Since Sir Walter Pendennis was out of reach, she would have to ask Master Baldwin for help. He had not been her first choice for the simple reason that he'd refused to give her the name of Potter's master. In Kent, Baldwin was a justice of the peace with an obligation to punish wrongdoers. The more Rosamond thought about it, the more sense it made to send word to him. He could take her information directly to the mysterious but powerful man who had placed her at Chelsea Manor. That individual, Sir Francis Walsingham or someone else, would surely have the influence necessary to catch and punish Griffith Potter's murderer.

'Fetch paper, pen, and ink,' she ordered without turning around.

Behind her, Melka's footfalls were heavy as she crossed the room. The snap of the catch being released on Rosamond's capcase sounded loud as pistol fire and was followed by noisy thumps and rustlings as the maidservant rifled though the contents of the small bag.

Rosamond turned. 'You disapprove. Why?'

Melka replied in Polish. The gist of it was that putting anything in writing was a bad idea.

'You make me regret telling you of Master Baldwin's warning,' Rosamond complained.

Still, the reminder was timely. She dared not put what she suspected in a letter. Considering the matter, she took the writing materials from Melka. Baldwin was a merchant who imported all manner of goods. He sent ships to Muscovy and traded with the Low Countries and France. She would write to him asking to purchase some expensive bauble. He'd realize something was amiss as soon as he received her letter, even if he had not heard that Potter was dead. He'd deliver whatever she ordered in person, but what should she ask for?

It should be red. That went without saying. Silk, she decided. A bolt of the finest imported variety.

Twelve

'Red silk?'

Nick Baldwin stared at the words, bemused and alarmed at the same time.

'When did this arrive?' he demanded. 'Why was it not sent on to Whitethorn Manor?'

Startled by his employer's harsh tone of voice, Arthur Saunders flinched. Nick lifted one hand in a gesture of apology. He was not usually so short with servants, especially faithful, long-time retainers like Saunders, but if Rosamond was using the 'code' she'd spoken of devising – and he had the sinking feeling that she was – then time was of the essence.

'I had no notion it was urgent, sir. But it came only yesterday morning, when you were already on your way back to London from Kent. Any messenger I sent would have missed you on the road.'

Nick acknowledged his point with a nod. Although he customarily broke the two-days' journey with a stop for the night at a favorite inn in Rochester, he might as easily have returned to London by way of Maidstone, or even stopped for a day or two at his town house there.

'Have we any red silk in the warehouse?'

Saunders looked doubtful. Silk of any color was not a commodity in which Nick usually traded, despite the potential for high profits. In his experience, it was far too prone to damage during long sea voyages. Besides, the Italian merchants in London held what amounted to a monopoly on the importation of this luxury item.

'Send someone out to purchase a bolt of the stuff,' Nick ordered, 'and if any other communications arrive sealed with this device, make sure I see them at once.'

Saunders scurried away, confused but obedient. Nick saw no need to explain that both Sir Robert Appleton's widow and his daughter sealed their letters with the same crest. Indeed, it might be best to let people think all communications bearing that emblem came from Lady Appleton, Rosamond's foster mother. She did write to him on occasion. They had been friends – and more than friends – for twenty years.

None of the other paperwork that had accumulated during his absence had any bearing on Rosamond's request for silk, but Nick could not get her message out of his mind. Red silk was readily available in the queen's Wardrobe of Robes and Rosamond had been told to send all messages through Griffith Potter. That she had written to him instead worried him more with each passing hour.

Nick left the warehouse and walked to the headquarters of Walsingham's intelligence gatherers in Seething Lane. He was not surprised to find Sir Francis absent. The great man had heavy responsibilities and spent much of his time at court. The minion in charge was a scrawny beanpole of a man with knobby knees and a prominent Adam's apple, an officious fellow who appeared to think most highly of himself and did not deign to tell Nick anything, not even his name.

'I cannot help you, Master Baldwin,' he insisted. 'I have never heard of this fellow Potter.'

A young subordinate had been sorting papers at one of the many tables in the long narrow room that had once served as the great hall. He looked up at the mention of Potter's name, a guileless expression on his clean-shaven face. 'Oh, but sir, he's the one—'

The older man cut him off with a glare that did not bode well for the lad's future in espionage. The incautious words having given the lie to his denial, he went on the offensive. 'How did you learn of Potter's death?' he demanded.

Nick cursed softly. No wonder Rosamond had not been able to send a message by way of the clerk of the wardrobe. 'From you, sirrah. Just now. When did he die and of what cause?'

Walsingham's minion looked as if he'd just taken a bite out of a sour persimmon. 'You have no need to know the details.'

'Ah, a suspicious death, then?'

'That is none of your concern.' His shifty-eyed look confirmed Nick's guess as surely as a written confession.

'What arrangements have been made to assign his duties elsewhere?' he asked. 'Who has replaced him?'

'That is none of your concern, I tell you, and now I must ask you to leave. We have important matters to attend to here. Confidential matters.'

Nick resisted the urge to reach up, seize the taller man by the collar, and shake him until he coughed up additional information. 'If you will not talk to me, then I will go direct to Mr Secretary Walsingham. He knows the reason for my concern about Potter as, clearly, you do not.'

The threat provoked a sneer. 'The queen's principal secretary is too busy with affairs of state to have time for the likes of you.'

Again, Nick checked his temper, although his hands did curl into fists at his sides.

When he left the house in Seething Lane, it was to seek out his old friend George Barne, a man he'd known since the earliest days of the Muscovy Company. Barne, about to serve his second term as the company's governor, was a haberdasher by trade with a thriving business in London. He was also, since his late sister had been Sir Francis Walsingham's first wife, brother-in-law to the man Nick sought. He ran Barne to ground at Muscovy House, where he kept a small office similar to the one Nick worked in.

'I need to talk to Walsingham,' Nick said without preamble. Explanations were unnecessary. It had been Barne who had brought Nick together with the principal secretary, at Walsingham's request, so that he might act as a conduit to Rosamond.

Barne gave a short, humorless bark of laughter. 'Good luck to you.'

'Where is he?'

'I cannot say for certain, but judging by the message he sent me on behalf of the Privy Council, he is at court.'

'Where is the court?' Nick asked. The queen was wont to move from palace to castle to wealthy courtier's house as the whim moved her.

'At Windsor, but if you can wait until Monday next, I warrant he will be at Greenwich. That is when Pissemsky and his translator are to meet with several members of the Muscovy Company and sundry representatives of the Crown.'

'I have need to know his present whereabouts.'

'Have you tried the house at Barn Elms?'

'I am attempting to avoid racing about like a chicken with its head cut off.'

This time Barne's laugh was genuine. The accompanying smile altered his features in a dramatic way. His cheeks, slightly concave above a bushy beard and thick mustache, colored warmly. His eyes, although so deep set as to appear sunken beneath thick, dark eyebrows, sparkled with lively appreciation.

'Sit down, Baldwin.' He gestured toward the window seat and produced a bottle and two goblets from a sideboard. 'Most likely, Francis is still at Windsor and you will not be able to get close to him there. The Privy Council has more to deal with than Muscovy. I hear they are much exercised about the Great Conjunction.'

Nick grimaced. 'I have little patience with astrologers, especially those who claim they can use the stars to predict the future.' But he sat and accepted Barne's offering of imported Rhenish wine.

'I share your disdain for such figure-flingers, but it has been difficult not to hear what they have been saying these last few months. All London is talking about the Apocalypse heralded by the coming conjunction of Jupiter and Saturn.'

'Two planets are slowly closing in on one another,' Nick scoffed. 'What of it? I am no student of the skies, but even I know that something of the kind happens every twenty years or so.'

'But this time they will pass each other near the boundary between Cancer and Leo. That has only happened six times in the history of mankind and on each of those occasions a great disaster followed. One of them, if the stories are to be believed, was Noah's flood.'

'Floods, earthquakes and the like are acts of God. They are not written in the stars.' Nick was not an overtly religious man, but he did believe that much.

'Think what you will, but Walsingham has been consulting with John Dee on the subject.'

Nick respected Dr John Dee, the Royal Astrologer. He had done much to aid advancements in exploration and discovery and was currently involved in a scheme to send an expedition to seek a northwest passage to the Indies. But some of Dee's beliefs were extreme. There were even rumors that he had tried to conjure the spirits of the dead.

'Speaking of Dee,' Barne said, 'I hear that the Privy Council has asked him to submit a proposal for calendar reform.'

'More foolishness.'

'Perhaps so, but Spain and France have already adopted Pope Gregory's new calendar. Other Catholic countries will soon follow suit, if they have not done so already.'

'All good Englishmen stopped obeying Papist commands long ago.' Nick took another swallow of wine. Somewhere around the time he'd been born, Queen Elizabeth's father had put an end to the Pope's influence in England by breaking with the Church of

Rome. In order that he might set aside his first wife and marry Elizabeth's mother, King Henry had established the Church of England with himself at its head.

'Ten days gone overnight.' Barne shook his head as he leaned back in his chair. 'Only think of the confusion! Go from England to France and the date is ten days later than it was before you crossed the Narrow Seas. And the day of the week is different, too. As a merchant, surely you can appreciate the difficulties involved in using two different calendars.'

'I see no reason for England to change a system that has worked perfectly well since the days of Julius Caesar, and just at present I am more concerned about a much different matter.' He set aside the empty goblet and leaned forward. 'Have you heard anything about the death of a man named Griffith Potter?'

An hour later, little wiser than he had been when he'd left, Nick returned to Billingsgate. His concern for Rosamond's safety had increased tenfold. Collecting the red silk Saunders had procured, he set out for Chelsea.

En route, he came to the conclusion that it would not be wise to arrive as a messenger delivering goods from a merchant. That would oblige him to meet Rosamond in a place where there were other people about. He did not want to risk being overheard. Instead, he presented himself as Mistress Jaffrey's steward and claimed to be bringing possessions she had forgotten to pack when she left Bermondsey. The well-wrapped bolt of silk, a large, bulky parcel, gave credence to the lie.

He was shown to a small room adjacent to the chapel. In the old days, priests likely stored their elaborate vestments there. Now a plain black gown hung on a peg on one wall and the only furniture was a bench and an old, scarred table with one wobbly leg.

Accompanied by her maid, Rosamond joined him after a quarter of an hour. 'What took you so long?' she demanded. 'Did I not send for *red* silk?'

The haughtiness she'd inherited from her father was once more at the fore, but it was tinged with something else. Agitation? Fear? Her shoulders were stiff with tension. Her neck, too, to judge by the way she lifted one hand to massage the back of it.

'I was in Kent when your orders arrived, Mistress Jaffrey. I came as soon as I could.'

'*Mistress Jaffrey?* Why do you call me that? What are you playing at? Lady Mary's page said my steward had arrived with items I forgot to pack. I nearly blurted out that I had not sent for anything before I realized that it must be you.'

'Sit down and I will explain.' He gestured toward the bench.

'I do not wish to sit!'

Nick was hard put to keep his own temper in check. 'You are no longer a young child whose tantrums can be indulged or ignored. I only hope you have managed your own affairs these last two years with more self-control than you show now.'

She glared, but she sat. When she had arranged her skirts with exaggerated care, she looked up at him with an expectant expression on her face.

A wry, reluctant smile of appreciation tugged at the corners of Nick's mouth. In her younger years, he'd been as guilty as everyone else of spoiling her. And why not? She was probably the closest thing to a daughter he'd ever have.

Nick straddled the other end of the bench. As he did so, his gaze fell upon the maidservant standing patiently in the corner. It was the first time he'd had a good view of her face. He frowned when he realized that her features had a foreign cast but before he could puzzle out her origins, Rosamond poked him in the chest. She'd shifted her position so that she was facing him, one knee drawn up on the bench in front of her in a most unladylike way.

'Why did you not come as yourself?'

'As merchant with ties to the Muscovy Company? I thought better of it.' He explained his reasoning and expanded upon the theme. 'Moreover,' he concluded, 'what if someone recognized me as the man who accompanied you here when you first arrived? Better to let them think I am in your employ.'

'And am I now to call you by some other name?'

'Baldwin will do. It is common enough.'

Rosamond sighed. 'I wish I had known you could bring me more than the silk. I could have sent you to Bermondsey in truth.'

'What items are you lacking?' Remembering the boxes and trunks she had brought with her, he found it hard to believe she had left anything behind.

She stared down at her tightly clasped hands. 'A second warm cloak would not be amiss, but what I need most is my copy of *A Cautionary Herbal*.'

Nick bit back an oath. The book in question had been written many years before by Rosamond's foster mother, Susanna Appleton, as a warning to housewives and cooks. Its intent had been to help them distinguish plants that were poisonous from those that were benign. 'Why?'

'Griffith Potter is dead.'

'So I learned only this morning. Of poison?'

'That is what I believe.'

Nick braced himself. 'Start at the beginning and tell me everything.'

Thirteen

When Rosamond finished telling Nick Baldwin how she'd come to discover a dying man and her conclusions concerning his death, she looked to him for answers. 'Who would attack Griffith Potter? Why would someone want him dead?'

'You are certain the word he whispered was "attack?"'

Nodding vigorously, she leaned forward until she was so close to Baldwin that she could see the tiny wrinkles in the skin beneath his eyes. 'He recognized me, despite the pain he must have been enduring, and he wanted me to know that his death was not an accident. He did not choke on a piece of meat, as Master Gargrave would have it.'

'Do you accuse this fellow, Gargrave, of trying to cover up a crime?' Baldwin asked.

Rosamond thought carefully before she answered, although this was not the first time she had considered the possibility. 'I do not believe Gargrave meant to do more than spare me embarrassment.'

'But he saw the same things you did? The enlarged pupils? The blue-tinged skin?'

'He must have. Mayhap he did not know what they meant.'

'Rosamond, did you not just tell me that Ralph Gargrave's job is to test for poisons?'

'That does not mean he has ever seen a man die from that cause! And this was not a poisonous substance smeared on clothing. The poison must have been in something Potter swallowed. You know as well as I do how many possibilities there are.'

'I do know, but think a moment. If some deadly substance was the weapon, why did Potter not say so? "Poison" would have been as easy to whisper as "attack". There is another problem, too. How would he know he had been poisoned rather than taken ill?'

Rosamond frowned. She had not realized until that moment how much she had counted on Master Baldwin to believe her without question. His lack of faith in her powers of observation stung, especially as he was the one responsible for her being in this situation in the first place.

'He did not choke to death.' Her voice was firm, even haughty, and she held herself stiffly. 'If he had been choking, he would not have been able to speak at all. I am not mistaken in this.'

'Did you look for injuries? Applied to a man's skull, a cudgel can cause fatal damage without leaving any sign of a blow. Potter was losing his hair at the front, but it was thick at the back.'

'Do you not think that occurred to me? But I also thought it possible his assailant was still in the room. Then I noticed his coloring and, as I have already told you, went to fetch help.'

He was right. She should have turned Potter over to look for wounds. He was of slight build. She could have managed it.

'How long did it take you to fetch Gargrave?' Baldwin asked.

'A few minutes. No more than that.'

Although he took her through the events of that afternoon once again, nothing new emerged. His face grew more grave with every word she uttered. Rosamond felt her spirits lift at the sight, for she took it for proof that he believed her at last. He would help her find justice for Griffith Potter, help her discover if Potter's death was connected in any way to the negotiations with Muscovy and with Lady Mary.

'Was there an inquest?' she asked. 'Has his death been ruled an accident?'

'For all I know, the body was simply carted away and buried.' Baldwin's grimace spoke volumes. 'Such things are possible when someone important enough wishes to keep embarrassing questions from being raised.'

'The man Potter worked for,' Rosamond murmured. 'But it is not right to let murder go unpunished.' To her horror, she felt tears well up in her eyes. From frustration, she told herself. Not weakness.

Baldwin hesitated, then reached along the length of the bench to take one of her gloved hands in his and give it an encouraging squeeze.

She sent him a watery smile. 'The murderer was in the Wardrobe of Robes that day. If it was one of Lady Mary's party, then she is in danger, too.'

'As are you, if you pursue this matter.'

'I cannot help but feel it is all of a piece, and if that is true, it is to my own advantage to discover the truth.' When he said nothing, she added, 'You brought me into this. Help me now.'

Help Rob, she added silently, for if she was in danger, so was he.

'You and I would both be wise not to meddle,' Baldwin warned her, but she could see that he was weakening. The fond, indulgent look on his face was one she'd seen before, when he was about to give in to some ultimatum issued by her foster mother.

'I need your help, Master Baldwin.' It was the stark truth and they both recognized it. Lowering as it was to admit that she could not do everything herself, she was obliged to face facts.

He sighed and capitulated. His grip on her hand slackened and she slipped free of it.

'Tell me about the other gentlewomen who were there that day. What are their names?'

'The waiting gentlewomen are Margaret Ellerker, Elizabeth Farnham, and Anne Morgan. Lady Mary's tiring maid, Ticey Unton, was also with us.' He mouthed each name as she spoke it, committing them to memory.

'And what persons did you encounter while you were trying to locate Potter?'

'Artisans. Clerks. I do not know any of their names except for Ralph Gargrave. One of them told me Potter had been speaking with Gargrave earlier. That is why I sought him out. Another fellow suggested Potter was in the storeroom. I fear I do not remember what either one looked like. I was not paying attention.'

Baldwin had her repeat her account of what she had found in the storage room. She did so, in minute detail, but with the same lack of results.

Weary of being questioned, she left her perch on the bench and went to inspect the garment hanging on the wall. One of Augustus Treadwell's spare gowns, she supposed. Unadorned black wool was much favored by evangelical clergymen.

'The poison must have been in the ale,' Rosamond said.

'If there was a poison.'

She glared at him.

'Did you see anyone else while you were in the Wardrobe of Robes, before or after you found Potter?'

'There was a courtier present when we first arrived.' She frowned, feeling her forehead crease in the attempt to remember his name. 'Sir Jeremy? Sir Geoffrey? No – Sir Jerome. I cannot recall his surname. He made a great effort to impress Lady Mary and was attentive to all of us, annoyingly so. Brown hair and beard,' she added after a moment. 'Richly dressed. His bonnet was such a remarkable creation that I paid more attention to it than I did to his face.'

Baldwin heaved himself off the bench. 'I will make what inquiries I can. In the meantime, promise me you will keep your suspicions to yourself and speak of Potter's death to no one. I would not have you place yourself in danger.' He hesitated, then added, 'You are free to leave here at any time, Rosamond. No one expects you to risk your life to gather information.'

She bristled. 'I gave my word to gather intelligence in the hope of keeping my husband alive. How can I go when he may still be in danger?'

'As you wish.' Pride shone in his eyes and for just a moment she allowed herself to bask in that silent approval.

He turned to go.

'Wait!' She hurried after him. 'Have you had any word from Rob?'

'None, but I did not expect to. Letters are few and far between and often cross on the annual trading voyages, so that the answer to a letter written a year or more earlier arrives after the recipient has already written with more recent news.' He gave a rueful laugh. 'It is a miracle negotiations progress at all.'

'Is there no overland route?'

'A long and arduous one. It could take five or six months for news from Moscow to make its way across the whole of Europe to England.'

'Then, for all you know, our efforts here are in vain. Tsar Ivan may already have massacred every foreigner in Muscovy.'

'Unlikely.'

But possible, she thought. Distressed, she stared, unseeing, at the still-closed door until Baldwin took a step closer, wrapped his arms around her, and gave her a hug. There was no awkwardness in the embrace. He had held her in just this way when she was younger and had needed comforting. Of a sudden, she felt weepy again, but she refused to let tears fall. She cleared her throat.

'I would be glad of it to learn Potter was murdered for some other cause, but I fear these matters are all tied together.'

'I will do my best to find out more,' he promised, releasing her.

For an instant she felt bereft, a reaction that left her disconcerted. She did not like being dependent upon anyone but herself, not even an old friend of the family like Nick Baldwin. That thought reminded her of another difficulty.

'How am I to send reports now that Potter is dead? And to whom? Who controls this network of intelligence gatherers? I have a right to know,' she added when he hesitated to answer.

'Yes, you do. It is Sir Francis Walsingham.'

'Hah! I thought so.'

'I am glad you are pleased,' he said in a dry voice. His gaze shifted to the corner where Melka stood. 'Now answer one more question for me.'

Rosamond's tiring maid had been there all along, silent as a statue. From experience, Rosamond knew Melka would have memorized every word of their conversation. Wary of what Baldwin meant to ask, she temporized. 'If I can.'

'Oh, you can. And I fear you must. That is Melka, is it not? The girl your mother brought back to England with her after Pendennis's stint as ambassador to Poland?'

'It is.' Rosamond sent him a defiant look, daring him to question her choice of a servant. The Polish woman had not been much older than Rosamond was now when she'd left her homeland a dozen years before.

Nick swore under his breath, then asked, 'Do you trust her?'

Melka stopped pretending to be part of the paneling and moved closer, her consternation evident in her small, wide-spaced eyes.

Rosamond managed an encouraging smile, but at the same time she saw her tiring maid as Nick Baldwin must. Melka wore clothing typical of all maidservants, plain and dark, but the garments alone were not enough to make her look like the others. Her features, the shape of her face, were . . . different. Even her skin was a shade darker than was common in England.

'I have known Melka more than half my life,' Rosamond said.

'That is not what I asked you. Do you trust her?'

'She would not be here with me if I did not.'

Baldwin addressed Melka directly. 'How much do you know about Poland's war with Muscovy?'

'Enough,' Melka said.

He turned his head far enough to slant a questioning look at Rosamond. 'And you?'

'I have less interest in Poland than I do in Russia. You will remember that my mother and stepfather went there when I was still a young child, leaving me behind. Years passed before they returned to England.' She'd resented being abandoned, even though she'd loved living at Leigh Abbey with Lady Appleton.

'I can scarce forget.' A fond smile appeared on Baldwin's face but he was quick to banish it.

Although they shared good memories, those were not enough to convince Baldwin that Melka was trustworthy. The truth would have to serve. 'Melka came to me from Cornwall two years ago,' Rosamond said. 'She was sent by my mother to spy on me.'

Baldwin did not look surprised. 'Do you still report to Lady Pendennis?' he asked Melka.

Her answer was brief and unequivocal: 'No.'

'Are you loyal to Mistress Jaffrey?'

Melka nodded, her expression earnest.

'There!' Rosamond declared. 'Now cease badgering her.'

'She is Polish born,' Baldwin said.

'What of it?' Rosamond felt genuine puzzlement.

'Poland has seen considerable upheaval these last few years. Her loyalties may be in conflict with England's interests.'

'No conflict,' Melka said.

'There. You see.' Rosamond grabbed Baldwin's sleeve and tugged until he stopped glaring at her maid. 'It is the present that matters, not the past.'

'News from Poland last year,' Melka said.

Baldwin swung toward the maid, suspicion writ large upon his countenance. 'You know of the delegation?'

'What delegation?' Rosamond demanded. 'And why should Melka not know of one if it was made up of her countrymen?'

'The ambassador of Polonia – Poland – left England in September. Years of careful planning are about to culminate in a treaty by which Poland will protect England's source of supplies in the Baltic.'

This meant nothing to Rosamond, although she had a vague notion that Muscovy also bordered on that body of water. 'Will that anger the tsar?'

'Likely it will. The Polish king, Stephen Báthory, invaded Russia last year. In January, a Papal representative negotiated a truce between the two nations. To save himself, Ivan was forced to agree to it.'

'If Muscovy and Poland are no longer at war, I do not see how Melka's presence can cause any difficulties. In any case, Ambassador Pissemsky is unlikely to discover that I have a Polish maidservant. I do much doubt he will be aware of anyone in this household save Lady Mary.'

'I'd not be so certain of that. Unless he is an utter fool, Pissemsky employs spies of his own.'

'If you are about to suggest that I send Melka back to Bermondsey, you can save your breath. I will have no other servant.' Rosamond went to stand beside her maid.

Baldwin seemed amused by this show of solidarity. 'I know when to retreat. And when a battle is not worth fighting. But remember what I said about keeping your suspicions to yourself.' Once again, he strode toward the door.

'What about the herbal?'

On the threshold, he turned to face her. 'I will bring it to you only if you promise not to let anyone see you reading it.'

'I am not so addle-pated as you seem to think.'

'Addle-pated? Never that.' She thought he was fighting a smile. 'But you are, at times, a trifle over-confident.'

'Only a trifle.' There – a twinkle in his eyes. Her spirits lifted. 'Have no fear on that account. No one here suspects I am more than I seem and I mean to keep it that way.' She let the hint of a smile appear on her own face. 'In truth, there is only one matter that will appear to trouble me in the coming days.'

His hand on the door latch, he hesitated. A look of resignation came over his features. 'What matter is that?'

She sent him a cheeky grin. 'Why, the question of what to have made from this lovely red silk. What else could possibly be of more importance to a silly young gentlewoman?'

Fourteen

Rosamond did not have long to wait before she could consult her copy of *A Cautionary Herbal*. Nick Baldwin delivered it the following day, along with her spare cloak. He left both items, well wrapped, with one of Lady Huntingdon's servants. Rosamond was not surprised that no message accompanied them. She did not suppose he'd had time to learn any more about Griffith Potter's death.

In the privacy of her bedchamber, Rosamond poured over the little book her foster mother had compiled. She was looking for the symptoms she had observed in the dying man. Unfortunately, the volume was arranged by the names of the herbs, not the consequences of misusing them, making it necessary for her to read every entry. More than one poisonous plant could cause dilated pupils and discolored skin, but most of them also produced other effects, many of them unpleasant and some violent. In the end, Rosamond was unable to identify with certainty any one poison that might have been added to Potter's food or drink.

Frustrated, she tucked the herbal out of sight among her sleeves. In spite of her lack of success, she did not waver in her conviction that Potter had been murdered but, although she trusted Master Baldwin to relay her observations to Sir Francis Walsingham, she was not as confident that Walsingham would investigate. As Baldwin had pointed out, the spy master had secrets of his own to keep. If he was loath to admit that Potter had been one of his intelligencers, he might do nothing to solve the crime.

The arrival of the earl of Leicester at Chelsea to escort Lady Mary and her entourage to Windsor distracted Rosamond from her own efforts to unravel the mystery surrounding Griffith Potter's death. It was early morning when Leicester swept into the gallery where his sister, Lady Mary, and all their ladies were gathered.

Rosamond stared. She had seen his portrait once, one that showed him in the prime of life. He'd been a slender, handsome fellow with a dark, pointed beard and a bright, intelligent, if somewhat wary, gaze. Now only his eyes seemed the same.

Passing into one's fourth decade was said to herald the first part of a man's old age. The earl of Leicester was nearing his fiftieth year. It showed in his hair and bushy beard, both gone almost entirely white, and in the jowly face beneath. His body verged on portly and lacked the firmness it had once possessed. It came as a shock to Rosamond to realize that her father, who had died when she was a small child, would have aged in much the same fashion.

Despite his years, there was a smile on the earl's face and a jauntiness in his step. 'Gillions and I stand ready to serve you,' he announced once he'd kissed his sister in greeting.

'Who is Gillions?' Rosamond whispered to Nan.

'His bargeman,' she whispered back. 'Roger Gillions. He has served the earl for many years.'

The extra watercraft was welcome, since Lady Mary and Lady Huntingdon were to be accompanied by their waiting gentlewomen and tiring maids and all the trunks and boxes needed to hold their clothing, jewelry and other necessary stuff.

Curious to observe the earl close-up, Rosamond found a spot for herself on Leicester's barge. His gaze passed over her without pause. If he noticed any of her father's features in her face, he gave no sign of it. In truth, he paid scant attention to anyone besides his sister. He did not even seem much interested in Lady Mary.

Once they were out on the Thames and being rowed rapidly upriver on an incoming tide, Rosamond crept a little closer to Leicester and Lady Huntingdon. If she tilted her head just so and stretched her ears, she could overhear most of what they said to one another.

At first they talked of inconsequential matters – family news of little interest to Rosamond. She knew already that Lady Sidney was their sister and that their brother Ambrose was the earl of Warwick. She had almost given up hope of hearing anything significant when Leicester said, in a casual voice, 'I met with Pissemsky'.

That name made Rosamond's heart beat a little faster. Perhaps now, at long last, she would learn something useful.

'Did he raise the matter of the tsar's marriage?' Lady Huntingdon asked.

'He did not. I have no doubt the ambassador will wait to discuss the matter until his private meeting with the queen. Nor did he broach the tsar's request for asylum in England, should he be forced to flee his own realm.'

Frowning, Rosamond leaned a little closer. If these subjects had not yet been discussed, then how did Leicester know of them? She answered her own question almost as soon as she thought it: he employed spies.

The great men of England all kept intelligencers. Some even had paid informers at other courts in Europe. One way to stay in favor with the queen was to provide her with accurate information. Rosamond had heard her stepfather refer to the struggle for power among courtiers as a game, one with exceeding high stakes. His lip had curled in distaste when he'd spoken of the way they used espionage to attain their goals.

'What *did* Pissemsky discuss with you?' the countess asked.

'He asked for everything we expected him to request – arms, nitre, copper, zinc, and lead.'

'Materials for war.' Although the countess spent much of her time occupied with domestic concerns, she had been exposed to military matters from an early age. Her husband, based in York, was charged by the queen to keep peace along the border with Scotland, as well as to rout out potential traitors among the recusants who regularly broke the laws of England. These recusants refused to attend services of the Church of England because the Pope in Rome had forbidden it.

'The tsar wants an alliance against our common enemies – the king of Lithuania, the Pope, and the Roman emperor.'

Rosamond shared the confusion she saw on Lady Huntingdon's face.

'Lithuania?' Lady Huntingdon asked. 'Not Polonia?'

'Pissemsky uses the place names Polonia, Poland, Lithuania, and Livonia interchangeably. All are ruled by Stephen Báthory and it is Báthory upon whom the tsar wishes to make war. Despite the truce that the two rulers were persuaded to sign by a mediator supplied by Pope Gregory, Ivan has neither forgotten nor forgiven all their years of conflict. Báthory's success in invading Russia grates on the tsar. It was clear from my meeting with Pissemsky that he hopes to use England's resources to take his revenge.'

Lady Huntingdon looked thoughtful. 'The Roman emperor – that must be Rudolf the Second. I have heard that his court is full of wonders.'

Leicester retorted with some heat. 'No more so than Elizabeth's.'

'As I well know.' She responded to his defensive attitude with an indulgent, sisterly smile but it was quick to fade. 'The Pope is our common enemy, even if the others are not. Will the queen agree to this alliance? And will it be sealed with a wedding?'

Mollified by her ready admission of English superiority, Leicester answered with an honesty that surprised Rosamond. 'In truth, I do not know. Her Majesty is never enthusiastic when it comes to agreeing to a subject's marriage.' He lowered his voice. 'Certainly not mine.'

When a servant offering refreshments interrupted brother and sister, Rosamond slipped away, finding a quiet spot from which to watch the passing shoreline and consider what she had heard. Did Leicester mean that the marriage of Lady Mary to the tsar might never come to pass? Did Lady Mary realize that? Did Walsingham? And what would happen when Ivan found out he'd been denied his chosen bride?

A gust of wind made her shiver. Worse, it brought with it a storm of doubts. Was she wasting her time? She had learned so little since joining Lady Mary's household. Today was the first time anyone had so much as mentioned the tsar. And then there was the matter of Griffith Potter's death. Were her instincts wrong when they told her that the death of Walsingham's agent was somehow linked to negotiations with Muscovy?

Negative thoughts threatened to overwhelm her. She found herself wishing she could abandon her mission and return to the life she had made for herself in Bermondsey. Then she remembered Rob, and Baldwin's insistence that her presence in Lady Mary's household would keep him alive. She had to believe that was true. She knew she would never forgive herself if her husband died and she had not done all she could to prevent it.

Rosamond took a deep, calming breath. She told herself that it must be the biting cold on the river that caused her to despair. Her toes were so near to frozen that they scarce had any feeling left. She wrapped herself more tightly in her cloak and retreated from the rail, squeezing in between Nan and Madge to get as close as possible to one of the charcoal braziers that warmed the center of the barge. Surely, as soon as she was warm again, all her doubts would vanish. She thrust her hands toward the glowing coals, welcoming the warmth that rose up from them, and at once felt her accustomed self-confidence begin to return. She was not wrong. And once they were settled at court, she would find the connection she sought. She was certain of it.

Fifteen

Until she experienced Windsor Castle in mid-December, Rosamond had not truly appreciated how foreign the world of the royal court would be. She'd expected the festive air and gorgeous clothing. She'd also anticipated a chance to indulge in rich food, but in that hope she was disappointed. Until Christmas Day, the end of the four weeks of Advent, fasting was strictly observed. If there were meat, cheese or eggs to be had, Rosamond saw no trace of them.

'I thought there would be constant celebrations,' she complained to Nan.

Her companion chuckled. 'Be glad we broke with Rome. My grandmother told me that in the old days, back in King Henry's time, there would be three masses sung on Christmas Day, the first of them well before dawn. The choristers of the Chapel Royal would chant the genealogy of Christ while every person in attendance, even the old king, stood with head bowed and holding a lighted taper.'

'That must have been a lovely sight,' Rosamond mused.

Churchgoing, in her experience, consisted of long hours in uncomfortable surroundings that had been stripped of all the trappings of the old religion. Music, stained glass windows, lighting candles for anything except illumination and colorful vestments for the priest had all gone the way of reliquaries, the observation of canonical hours, and praying to saints. At Windsor, they attended services in St George's Chapel. It was most grand, but the service was exactly the same and the sermons equally dull.

'Grandmother also said that the sound of growling stomachs was sometimes loud enough to drown out the choir,' Nan added with another laugh, 'and that after the service, everyone went and stuffed themselves with food, since that was the first meal since Advent Sunday at which they'd been allowed to eat whatever they wanted and as much of it as they could hold.'

'We can still follow that tradition.' Rosamond had every intention of filling her belly until it hurt.

At first, her activities at court were much as they had been at Chelsea. Once Lady Mary was dressed for the day, she and her ladies sat and wrought or took bracing walks in the upper ward of the castle, a bare, open space that ran between the guest lodgings where Lady Mary had been installed and the royal apartments occupied by the queen.

For the most part, Lady Mary ignored her newest waiting gentlewoman as thoroughly at Windsor Castle as she had at Chelsea. Rosamond did not know whether to be grateful her mistress paid so little attention to her, thus allowing her to eavesdrop on her conversations with impunity, or to resent that the noblewoman took no more notice of her than she would a fly on the wall or a three-legged stool.

If Lady Mary considered herself superior to those who waited upon her, Queen Elizabeth, in her turn, ignored her cousin. The queen went hunting every day. Lady Mary did not. For her own part, Rosamond was happy to forego that bloodthirsty pastime. She disliked killing for sport. She would have enjoyed playing cards or dicing, but the earl of Huntingdon's disapproval still held sway in Lady Mary's lodgings.

Excitement reigned when Lady Mary announced they were to watch a tennis match and that, for the occasion, they were to have new gowns . . . identical gowns. Rich and colorful as these garments were, they amounted to livery.

Rosamond toyed with the idea of spilling red wine on the pale yellow brocade. She might have done it, had she not realized that would only result in being left behind in Lady Mary's lodgings while the other waiting gentlewomen enjoyed watching toothsome young men work up a sweat. The gentlemen wore nothing but silk drawers and lawn shirts when they played tennis.

The tennis play was a rectangular building that had been purpose-built for the queen's father. Henry the Eighth had been surpassing fond of the sport and in his younger years had often competed. Lady Mary and her attendants found seats on a cushioned bench in an upper gallery. The screened window in front of them overlooked the court. A match was already in progress and a small white ball flew back and forth across the fringed cord that separated the players.

'How is this game scored?' Rosamond asked.

'Does it matter?' Nan ogled the way shirts, damp with perspiration, clung to the broad, masculine chests.

Madge's full lips were not designed for pursing into a thin, disapproving line, but somehow she managed it. At the same time, her eyes strayed repeatedly to the near player's bare legs. He had a well-turned calf and a grace of movement that Rosamond could not help but admire.

'Points are scored when one player fails to return the ball,' Bess said. 'How many depends upon how far from the center cord the ball comes to rest.'

More courtiers crowded into the gallery, forcing Lady Mary's waiting gentlewomen to give up their seats and move to the back. No longer able to see the action on the court, Rosamond soon grew bored. When, with growing urgency, she felt the need to relieve herself, she went in search of the nearest privy. Mission accomplished, she lingered in the fresh air, even though the late December afternoon was passing cold. The chill in the air gave her a new appreciation of the yellow gown, which was well-lined and trimmed with cony fur.

She had just turned back toward the tennis play when, out of the corner of her eye, she caught the flash of a familiar color on the far side of the ward. Startled, she stopped and squinted in that direction. The woman's pale yellow gown was the twin of her own. Bess? Nan? Madge? The distance was too great and the shadows where the woman stood were too concealing, but it was most assuredly one of them.

Intrigued, Rosamond stared harder. Whoever the woman was, she was engaged in an intense conversation with a man. Her hand was on his arm. His head was bent close to hers in a way that spoke of intimate acquaintance. The man seemed familiar, too, although a voluminous cloak and a low brimmed hat hid both form and face. She toyed with the idea of sidling closer but the cold had begun to seep through the soles of her boots. Instead, she scurried back to the warmth of the tennis play.

The crowd had grown larger in her absence, and less inclined to let anyone pass. It was some time before she was able to rejoin Lady Mary's waiting gentlewomen . . . all of them.

Madge sent her a reproving look. 'You were gone a long time.'

'I had to fight my way back,' Rosamond said. 'This is a popular place.'

'You should have taken the stair.' Bess pointed out a narrow doorway nearly hidden by a wall hanging. If Rosamond had not been looking right at it, she doubted she'd have realized it was there.

'I suppose you have all been in and out a dozen times.'

Bess laughed. 'Only once apiece, since it is uncommon close in here.'

Just then another spectator jostled Rosamond, nearly knocking her off her feet and demonstrating why those brief respites had been necessary.

'Is there a reason you ask about our comings and goings in your absence?' Nan asked.

It might have been any of them she'd seen, Rosamond thought. Or someone else entirely. That shade of yellow could not be unique. 'No reason at all,' she temporized.

The next day they awoke to a world covered in snow, the first of the season. Bess was smiling broadly when she sat down to break her fast with the others.

'Why do you look so pleased with yourself?' Madge's eyes narrowed, as if she suspected the other woman had been with a lover.

Rosamond wondered, too. Had it been Bess she'd seen the previous day in such close conversation with a mysterious man?

'I dreamed I saw a swallow nesting in the eaves,' Bess announced. 'That is a sure sign that this will be a lucky day for me.'

'Superstitious nonsense.' Madge bit into a wedge of cheese with such force that her teeth came together with a loud click.

'What sign would foreshadow ill luck?' Nan asked.

Bess was ready with a prompt reply: 'Seeing a cow in the garden.'

'I doubt you will find one here,' Rosamond said.

'I hope not,' Bess said. 'Such a sighting oft times foretells a death.'

Nan laughed. 'If someone died every time they saw a cow, there would be not a soul left alive in all of England.'

Bess took no offense and Lady Mary's four waiting gentlewomen were in charity with one another when they set out, warmly booted and wrapped up in furs, to walk in the new-fallen snow. It crunched underfoot in a most agreeable fashion and they had not gone far when masculine shouts and laughter drew their attention to the far side of the ward. Several of the younger court gentlemen were flinging snowballs at targets and their delight in the activity proved infectious.

Rosamond scooped up a goodly quantity of snow in both leather-gloved hands and packed it together until it was of a suitable size to lob. It was of ideal consistency to make snowballs.

Bess followed suit. Madge held herself aloof, but Nan readily joined in the fun.

Rosamond shaped a second snowball, attempting to make it into a perfect sphere. She thought it a great pity she could not keep it as a decoration, but it had already started to melt. With an evil chuckle, she whirled and sent her perfect snowball winging toward Nan. It landed on her friend's shoulder. With a squeal and a laugh, Nan retaliated. Her missile struck Rosamond square in the chest and sent wet, cold snow spattering upward into her face.

Attracted by the noise, the young gentlemen began to throw a few snowballs in their direction. Rosamond fired back, gaining in accuracy with each attempt. In the free-for-all that ensued, she lost track of who hurled what. She was too busy sending clumps of hard-packed snow winging toward all and sundry and ducking for cover in between throws. Breathless with laughter, feeling more alive than she had in days, she popped up, reared back, and aimed at a young man in an orange-tawny doublet.

At the same instant, sharp pain exploded at the side of her head. With a curious sense of detachment, she felt her fingers loosen. Her snowball fell to the ground as the edges of her vision darkened. Stars winked. Or was that just sunlight on snow? Before she could decide, everything went black.

Sixteen

Someone whispered Rosamond's name.

'She's bleeding.' This voice was male, but Rosamond did not recognize it.

'What fool put a rock in the center of his snowball?' demanded a different gentleman.

No one answered him.

'An accident, surely,' said the female supporting Rosamond's shoulders. That was Nan.

Cautiously, Rosamond opened her eyes. The sunlight seemed twice as intense as it had been. She squeezed them shut again, but she could still see a red haze on the backs of her eyelids.

'She's conscious.' That was Bess, off to her left and a short distance away.

The side of Rosamond's head throbbed. The rest of her was numb with cold and no wonder – she was lying in the snow. With an effort, she lifted her right hand, feeling the tender spot with gloved fingers. The icy particles clinging to the leather felt good against her abraded skin but when she pressed down too hard, another explosion of pain caused her to cry out and nearly sent her tumbling back into oblivion.

'Stop that,' Nan ordered. 'You will make the injury worse.'

Rosamond did not contradict her, but neither did she remove her hand. If she was careful, the cold would numb the pain.

'Are you going to lie there all day?' Madge's impatient question came from somewhere off to Rosamond's right.

'Help me to stand before I turn into an icicle.'

Two of the young gentlemen rushed forward to assist her. Once she was upright, she was too dizzy to be properly appreciative. Their disjointed apologies made no sense to her until much later, when she was safely abed, the better for a sleeping potion and an herbal poultice pressed to the gash on her head.

The snowball she'd been struck by had contained a rock.

Rosamond's eyes shot open. She stared at the canopy over her head. It was possible a stone had been scooped up by accident, along with the snow. But most of what one found loose in the castle's courtyards were mere pebbles, and how could anyone have been so careless, or so wrapped up in the game, that he . . . or she . . . failed to notice the added heft? The snowball that had struck her must have weighed far more than one that had no rock inside it.

The conclusion was inescapable. Her accident had not been an accident at all. Someone had deliberately set out to injure her. Injure? Or kill? A hard blow to the head could do more than render someone unconscious.

Nonsense, Rosamond told herself. She was imagining things. No one had any reason to harm her and no one save Sir Francis Walsingham and Master Nicholas Baldwin knew why she had joined Lady Mary's household. *Just an accident* was her last thought as the potion she'd been given took effect and she drifted into sleep.

In the morning, she woke up believing it and, save for a slight, recurring headache, her life in Lady Mary's household resumed its normal course. She felt fully recovered two days later when Lady Mary announced that the queen was about to make a public appearance.

'We must all attend,' Lady Mary decreed.

'Her ladyship is impatient to get on with things,' Nan whispered in Rosamond's ear as they made their way toward St George's Hall. Once again they all wore their pale yellow 'livery'. 'She'd have preferred a private audience with the queen, but no summons has been forthcoming.'

The noise of the crowd assaulted Rosamond's ears long before they reached their destination. Lady Mary blanched at her first glimpse of so many people all in one place, even one so large as this one. The two liveried menservants accompanying them did not seem to know what to do next, either, but when an overweight woman, grandly dressed but stinking of musky perfume, shoved Rosamond aside and managed, with single-minded determination, to penetrate to the heart of the assembly, Rosamond followed her example. By poking and prodding those around her, she forged a path for the others to follow, ending up in a prime position.

Pleased, Lady Mary so far unbent as to give Rosamond a nod of approval.

The lengthy wait that followed undermined Rosamond's sense of accomplishment. Queen Elizabeth took her time about making her entrance.

'My feet hurt,' Madge complained, shifting her weight.

There was no place to sit. In truth, one was not permitted to sit in the queen's presence. To Rosamond's mind, that was just one more argument against taking a post at court. She did not understand why so many otherwise sensible people wanted to dance attendance on royalty. From all she'd heard, the rewards were few. More often, courtiers went into debt providing the queen with lavish entertainments and costly gifts.

At last Her Majesty appeared, gloriously dressed, her jewels so abundant and so dazzling that they succeeded in deflecting attention from the age of the woman who wore them. The queen, like her favorite, the earl of Leicester, was nearing her fiftieth year. The thick layer of paint on her face could barely conceal the wrinkles beneath.

The queen paused briefly to acknowledge her kinswoman. Lady Mary sank into a deep obeisance and kissed the ring her royal cousin wore on the outside of one of her gloved hands. Although Rosamond stood just behind her mistress, Her Majesty did not spare her so much as a glance, making Rosamond feel as insignificant as the tiniest mouse in the walls of the massive royal kitchens.

A few minutes later, no one noticed when she slipped away from the rest of the party. Once the press of courtiers obscured them from view, she applied elbows where they would do the most good to clear a path. She had no particular destination in mind. She simply could not bear staying in one place any longer. Recognizing Sir Jerome – the gentleman from the Wardrobe of Robes – she avoided him. Then she caught sight of the earl of Leicester, deep in conversation with a man dressed almost entirely in black. A small white ruff no more than two inches wide set off the stranger's *pic-à-devant* beard and called attention to the sour expression on his sallow face. He did not much care, Rosamond surmised, for what the earl was saying to him. She moved closer, curious to discover what that was.

'—a successful ploy.' Leicester sounded annoyed.

'I have the matter well in hand,' the other man said. 'Do not interfere.'

'Do you dare give me orders?'

'For the good of England, I dare much more than that.'

'Have a care how far you presume. She calls me her eyes and I am watching you.' With that thinly veiled threat, Leicester abandoned his companion and set off around the perimeter of the hall, his shoulders stiff and his pace rapid.

Rosamond was about to follow him when a hand clamped down on her arm, forcing her to halt rather more abruptly than was comfortable. She turned her best glare on the dark-bearded man who had been quarreling with the earl of Leicester. It had no effect. He tightened his grip, hauling her through the press of people just as the queen mounted a dais and a great cheer went up.

With all the noise, bustle and confusion around them, screaming for help would have been a waste of breath. Rosamond's attempts to extricate herself from her captor's shackle-like hold were an exercise in futility. Heart slamming against her ribs, breath coming in short gasps, she was close to panic by the time he dragged her out of the hall and into the great watching chamber used by the queen's guards. To her dismay, the yeomen of the guard not only recognized the bearded man, they were unwilling to challenge him. Not one of them came to her aid as he hustled her into a small antechamber.

Cold anger cleared Rosamond's mind of fear. She was not helpless. The second this arrogant fellow let go of her arm, freeing the hand she needed to reach the knife concealed in her boot, she would seize the advantage.

It was a good plan, but instead of releasing her, he spun her around to face him, grabbed her by the shoulders, and gave her a shake that rattled her teeth. 'What do you think you are doing, Mistress Jaffrey?' he demanded. 'I did not send you to Lady Mary to spy on *me!*'

'How do you know my name? Who are you?'

His smile put her in mind of a wolf. 'They told me you were clever. Have I been deceived?'

'*You* sent me to Lady Mary?' Appalled, Rosamond stared at her captor. *This* was Mr Secretary Walsingham?

He had a long, lean face dominated by a large nose and dark eyes that burned with a disconcerting intensity. Close to him as she was, she could not help but notice that his hairline formed a widow's peak, but that did not make him seem any more approachable.

When he finally let go of her arm, she did not even consider running away. Although his scowl was formidable, outrage at the way he'd treated her prevented her from cowering. Her voice was coldly furious. 'I'd have known to avoid you if you had taken the trouble to recruit me in person.'

At her retort, his eyes narrowed. Rosamond did not suppose he was accustomed to being criticized, least of all by a woman. He expected her to be terrified of him.

'Have you caught Griffith Potter's murderer?' she demanded.

He blinked, as if taken aback by her question. 'Potter choked on a piece of meat.'

'He did no such thing!' Hands fisted on her hips and eyes blazing, she faced the queen's principal secretary. 'As he lay dying, he told me he had been attacked. Does that mean nothing to you? The man was in your service.'

For an instant, she thought he might strike her for her insolence. Instead, he sent her a stern look. 'While I look into the matter, the rest of the world must continue to believe that his death was an accident.'

'But what have you learned so far? Who do you suspect of killing him?'

'That is none of your concern.'

'But I—'

'Enough!' He cut her off with a slicing motion. 'I sent you to Lady Mary for one purpose and one purpose only, to gather information. You are not to exceed your commission. Is that understood?'

'But—'

He leaned closer, his expression so fierce that she backed up a step. 'Is that understood?' He bit off each word and spat it at her. The sheer menace in his voice kept her from arguing further.

'It is.'

'Good. Remember this: knowledge is never too dear. If you follow instructions and do not embroider upon them, the cost to you will be small. Deviate from your task at your own risk.'

With that final warning, he strode out of the tiny anteroom. Rosamond was left awash in uncertainty. Did he intend to hunt down Griffith Potter's killer or not? Not, she felt certain, if investigating the murder would expose secrets he wished to keep.

Why had he tried to frighten her? Calm reason would have served him better. She had no doubt that he could be ruthless, but what call had he to threaten her? She had her own reasons to help his cause, and more resources than he was willing to credit.

She was not to embroider upon her instructions? She would if she could. Rosamond's thoughts grew more and more rebellious as she made her way back through the watching chamber to the crowded hall.

A slim young man in a strawberry-colored doublet bumped against her in the press of people. 'Your pardon, mistress.' He was gone just as suddenly, slipping between two larger men and vanishing.

Rosamond stared at the spot where he had been, struck by an idea. The fellow had been about her size. His voice had been only a bit lower than her own. If she were to dress herself in male attire, glue on facial hair, and create a more manly appearance with bulges in the appropriate places, she could move much more freely both at court and elsewhere. She could ask questions that would be unsuitable coming from a woman, and get answers, too.

A small, secretive smile playing about her lips, Rosamond rejoined Lady Mary. As soon as she could manage it, she would obtain doublet, hose, and codpiece and keep that disguise near at hand. Let Sir Francis Walsingham make what he would of that!

Seventeen

Three men, Nick Baldwin among them, gathered near the hearth at Muscovy House, enjoying the pleasant scent and welcome warmth of burning apple wood. During the last week, Nick had been a regular visitor to the headquarters of the Muscovy Company, giving others who frequented the place a chance to grow accustomed to his presence. He'd held off asking questions lest he arouse unwelcome suspicion.

Tonight that would change. He was after specific information and the best source for it was seated beside him on a settle drawn up close to the fire. Robert Jacobi, physician to the queen until she'd sent him to Muscovy to assume similar duties with the tsar, had returned to England in the entourage of Feodor Andreevich Pissemsky and was currently acting as the ambassador's translator.

'Personable fellow' was how George Barne had characterized Jacobi when he'd first pointed him out to Nick. That had been three days ago.

'Talkative?' Nick had asked.

'He can be,' Barne had replied.

After Nick had delivered Rosamond's copy of *A Cautionary Herbal* to Chelsea, he had met briefly with Sir Francis Walsingham to relay her information to the principal secretary. Walsingham had been even more close-mouthed than usual. Although he had implied that he was already looking into the death of Griffith Potter, he had promised nothing. Worse, he had refused Nick's request for authorization to visit the Wardrobe of Robes and talk to Ralph Gargrave. Instead, Walsingham had repeated the advice he'd given Nick once before: retreat to one of his country estates and stay there.

For the first time in his life, Nick wished he had influential friends at court. He'd served in Kent as a justice of the peace, but his neighbors there were no more courtiers than he was. Only among London merchants did he have any clout, and it was in their company that he still had hopes of learning something useful.

'I have met your man Wharton,' Jacobi said, giving Nick the opening he'd been hoping for. 'Met him at England House.'

'Do you visit there often?' Nick asked.

'As often as possible.' Jacobi was a small, compact man, dark-haired and dark-eyed. He had been quaffing ale at a steady rate for the last hour. 'Where else in Moscow can I go to hear men speak in my native language?'

Nick was about to ask a more direct question when they were joined by a gentleman wearing a tall, plumed hat and a richly embroidered cloak. In a haughty manner, he handed the latter to an underling and then stared hard at the three men by the fire, each in turn.

'Sir Jerome Bowes,' Barne muttered under his breath. A fine high ruff framed the newcomer's pointed beard, light brown with a hint of ginger in color. What little of his close-cropped hair showed beneath his bonnet was the same shade.

'Here you are at last, Jacobi,' Bowes said. 'The ambassador did not seem to know where to find you.'

'There are times when I prefer the company of Englishmen,' Jacobi replied. 'Sit down, Sir Jerome, and have a cup of ale.'

Bowes snagged a stool and complied. He nodded at Barne in a way that indicated he'd met the governor of the Muscovy Company before, but he leveled a suspicious look at Nick.

'This is Nicholas Baldwin, Sir Jerome,' Barne said. 'He went to Muscovy with the first wave of English merchants and helped open trade between the two nations.'

'I did little of note,' Nick protested. 'I was a mere stipendiary in those days. Anthony Jenkinson was the leader of the expedition. He was the one who dealt with the tsar.'

'Then no doubt he was also the first Englishman to suggest a treaty sealed with a marriage.' Jacobi chuckled.

Bowes looked surprised. 'The idea goes that far back?'

'Indeed, it does.' Jacobi turned to Nick. 'Who did Jenkinson propose as a suitable bride?'

'I do not believe he made any specific suggestion.' In truth, Nick doubted that Jenkinson had mentioned the possibility of an English bride at all. Back then the tsar had been married to his much loved first wife. Some said it was her death that had caused him to go mad.

Jacobi took another swallow of ale. 'Bomelius proposed that Ivan wed the queen.'

'Bomelius?' Bowes leaned closer, as if the name evoked a morbid fascination.

It rang a distant bell in Nick's memory, too, although he could not think why.

'That thrice-damned fool lied about our gracious majesty's age,' Jacobi said. 'He led the tsar to believe that Elizabeth Tudor was just a slip of a girl who'd be willing to come to Muscovy to wed him and would thereafter permit him to rule both kingdoms.'

'I trust you disabused him of such a notion.' Bowes sounded angry.

Nick studied the courtier over the rim of his cup, suddenly struck by a thought. Could this Sir Jerome be the Sir Jerome Rosamond had met in the Wardrobe of Robes? The more he considered the possibility, the more likely it seemed. Bowes wore clothes that were costly enough to fit her description.

Jacobi drank again before he answered. 'I told the tsar the truth. By then he already knew how untrustworthy Bomelius was. It was not easy for me, being there as that fellow's replacement.' He shook his head, as if to clear away unpleasant thoughts. 'For the first few months, I feared that at any moment I, too, might be charged with conspiring against the state and tortured.'

'Is that what happened to this Bomelius?' Nick asked. 'His history is unfamiliar to me.'

With only minimal coaxing, Jacobi was persuaded to tell the whole appalling story.

'Was he guilty?' Nick asked when the tale was done and their cups had been refilled.

'Of plotting against the tsar?' Jacobi shook his head. 'I do much doubt it. More likely he was trying to send money back to England. There were English ships in port.'

'But the port was controlled by Poland?'

'Aye, and because he had disguised himself as his servant and gone there in person, the tsar assumed he was a spy making his report to his Polish masters.'

It occurred to Nick that Bomelius might indeed have been sent to Muscovy to gather intelligence, but not for the Poles. He'd have been in a position to gather a great deal of information useful to England during his time at the tsar's court. As was Jacobi. It took no great leap of imagination to believe both men had likely been recruited to spy for Queen Elizabeth.

'Does the tsar still wish to marry an Englishwoman?' he asked, pretending ignorance of the proposal currently in play.

'He does.' The more ale Jacobi quaffed, the more his tongue loosened. 'One of the queen's own cousins, no less.'

'Which one?' Bowes asked.

Something in the courtier's expression made Nick certain Bowes already knew the answer, just as Nick himself did. They were all liars here, some more skillful than others.

'Lady Mary Hastings.'

'Why her?' Bowes's lips thinned. 'The queen has other kinswomen far more fair to look upon.'

'But Lady Mary is the earl of Huntingdon's sister,' Jacobi said, 'and Huntingdon is the nobleman most likely to succeed to England's throne should aught happen to Her Majesty.'

'Pray God the queen has no need of a successor for many years to come!' Barne murmured.

They all drank to that sentiment.

Conversation became general then, and aside from learning that Bowes hoped to be named English ambassador to Muscovy, Nick heard little else of note. After a time, an earlier remark began to prey on his mind. When Jacobi announced he must return to Pissemsky and the rest of the delegation, Nick offered to accompany him.

'It is unwise to venture into London's streets after dark on your own,' he added, 'and we are going the same way.'

This last was a lie. Nick had no idea where the ambassador and his entourage resided in London, although he was fairly certain it was nowhere near Billingsgate.

Jacobi had no objection. They set off together through the quiet, ill-lit streets. At the first opportunity, Nick hired a link boy to light their way.

'I remember Bomelius slightly from his time in London,' Nick remarked. 'He married while he was here.'

'Did he? I never met the man myself. He was a quack and a charlatan, more fortune teller than physician. From all I have heard of him, I am not surprised he came to a bad end.'

Nick let that pass. 'The girl he married – did she go with him to Muscovy?'

Jacobi belched. 'Oh, aye. She's still there. The tsar won't let her return to England. He believes that a man's entire family should suffer for his sins.'

Although he'd half expected to hear something of the kind, Nick's heart ached. 'Never tell me she's in prison?'

'I do not know where she is, but she was forbidden to leave Moscow on pain of death.' Jacobi turned down a narrow alley and gestured toward a tall stone house with a courtyard entrance. 'That's where we're lodged. Pitiful poor place for an embassy in my opinion, but it was the best to be had.'

It appeared to be a fine, fair residence to Nick. From the look of it, the place boasted its own stables and a garden. He bade his companion a friendly farewell and when Jacobi had disappeared inside, turned back the way they had come.

Following the link boy with his flaming torch, he walked home in a perturbed frame of mind. Why had he bothered to ask after Jane Bomelius? He hadn't given the girl a single thought for nearly twenty years. It had been longer than that since he'd last seen her.

Jane Richards of St Stephen Walbrook had been a pretty young thing in the old days – fifteen or sixteen years old and immensely curious about the world beyond London. Every time he'd gone to visit her father, she'd plagued him with questions about his time in Muscovy.

He wished with all his heart that he could do something to help her, but he had no illusions about the fate of those who angered Tsar Ivan. Even if he were in Muscovy, he'd be powerless to come to her aid. Until Ivan tired of playing cat and mouse with Jane Bomelius, a man would have to be a great fool to interfere in the game.

Eighteen

'The Yule log.'

Rob Jaffrey's voice was filled with longing. He pictured his father leading the revelers who dragged the enormous length of tree trunk back to the manor house from the nearby wood. He could almost hear the laughter and shouts of joy, nearly smell the pine needles.

'We lived in London,' Jane said. 'We did not bring home a Yule log, but we did decorate the entire house and we had a great feast on Christmas Day and another on Twelfth Night. On New Year's Day, we exchanged gifts, just as the great folk do.'

'In the country, all work but the most necessary – cooking and caring for animals – ceases until Plough Monday.' Rob shook off melancholy and lifted his cup in a salute to his hostess, sipping the fine wine he himself had brought.

During the last month, he had paid frequent visits to Mistress Jane Bomelius. If he could have afforded to pay for better lodgings, he would have urged her to move into them, but he'd had to content himself with sharing a few of the luxuries that came his way. For her part, she'd tried at first to refuse his gifts, but he'd soon won her over. She was starved for simple comforts. Even his small kindnesses had garnered visible results. Renewed hope and nourishing food had rejuvenated her.

Jane was far younger than Rob had first supposed. She had married her physician husband when she was only sixteen. That was the same age, he confided to her, at which he had so foolishly wed Rosamond Appleton.

Forget Rosamond, he ordered himself. He did not wish his estranged wife to cast a pall over his enjoyment of Jane's company.

'All the spinning wheels have flowers twined through them,' he said, 'so that none of the women will be tempted to work.'

Jane laughed. The delight in her eyes took additional years off her age. 'An unnecessary precaution, I assume.'

'Did you have hogglers in London?' Rob asked, remembering another country custom.

She shook her head. The firelight glinted on golden streaks in her long hair. She wore it unbound in the intimacy of her own home, her usual kerchief discarded. For a moment, Rob forgot what he'd been about to say. Jane Bomelius was still a beautiful woman, the more so in his eyes for all that she had endured.

'What are these hogglers?' she inquired in her soft, sweet voice.

Rosamond would not have asked. She'd have demanded.

Turning to stare into the hearth fire, Rob swore he could see his wife's face in the flames. When he blinked, the image vanished. He told himself it was relief he was feeling, not longing.

'It's an old word – hogglers – and I doubt anyone living today knows what it means. Our hogglers are men of the village of Eastwold in Kent. They go from house to house to collect alms for the church at Yuletide. They sing as they go. At Leigh Abbey, Lady Appleton always presents them with a small velvet pouch full of coins – for the betterment of the Parish of St Cuthburga.'

'I have never heard of such a thing,' Jane said. 'What other strange rites do you practice in the country?'

Seated atop his cloak on the hard-packed floor before the fire, Rob brought his legs up to his chest and wrapped his arms around them, resting his chin on his knees. He wondered, thinking of the previous Christmas with his family, what had possessed him to leave home. At first, travel had been exciting. He'd enjoyed seeing and experiencing new things. But he'd been stuck in Moscow too long. He could only imagine how difficult Jane's exile had been.

'Lady Appleton uses a charred piece of the previous year's Yule log to light the new one. Once that is done, everyone partakes of a bowl of spiced wine.'

'Is it as potent as this one?' Jane asked, taking another sip from her cup.

'More so.'

Rob had not thought the wine he'd brought was strong at all, and it had not occurred to him to dilute it. Jane, more accustomed to barley water, had begun to feel its effects. She watched him with eyes that did not quite focus, but she did not seem to mind being tipsy. Watching her, he felt a trifle lightheaded himself.

'What do you do on Christmas Day?' she asked.

'The whole community gathers at Leigh Abbey. We feast on minced pies and brawn with mustard, and bread and cheese, and fruit and nuts.'

'And more spiced wine?'

He chuckled. 'That goes without saying.'

'Here in Moscow, Christmas marks the end of one of the Russian church's four annual periods of fasting.' Jane took another sip of wine. 'They are great ones for fasting, the Russians. Every Wednesday and Friday all year long, and they do not just eschew meat, but all food. This Yuletide fast ends with the appearance of the first star on Christmas Eve. They call it holy supper when they finally eat again, for it contains twelve foods in honor of the twelve apostles.'

'Including meat?'

'Alas, no. The main dish is a sort of porridge called *kutya*, made with honey and poppy seeds, and there is a bread called *babal'ki*. There is mushroom soup, too, and other dishes I cannot now recall. And red wine. Always there is red wine.' She smiled a little crookedly and took another sip from the earthenware cup in her hand.

'The people of Muscovy feast, as do the English,' Rob said. 'Only the foods are different. Do they go to church on Christmas Eve, as we do?'

'Oh, yes. After they break their fast with this holy supper, they exchange gifts and then they go to a worship service that lasts until two or three o'clock in the morning.'

Rob sent her a curious look. 'Is the Russian faith really so different?' It seemed to him that there was more pageantry, but that the basic tenets of the two religions were similar. They were both Christian churches. It was not as if the tsar was an infidel or a heathen.

Jane's reaction was unexpectedly passionate. 'It is not the *English* church!' She came up off her stool to kneel beside him on the floor, her expression as earnest as he had ever seen it. 'To convert to the Russian Orthodox church would be as bad as becoming a Papist.'

In an effort to calm her, he placed one hand on her upper arm and held her gaze. 'No one can force you to abandon your faith, Jane.'

It was the most natural thing in the world for his arm to slide upward and drape itself casually over her shoulders. She needed comforting, he told himself. When her head drifted down to rest against his chest, that felt right, too.

'Tell me more about Leigh Abbey,' she murmured sleepily.

'On New Year's Day, we wassail the apple orchard.'

'I do not know what that is.' She snuggled closer, as if she intended to use him as a pillow.

It was the wine, Rob thought. It had made him sleepy, too.

He cleared his throat. 'Wassailing the apple orchard is a tradition that ensures the next year's crop will be good for cider. Like everyone else, we exchange gifts earlier in the day, but in the evening of New Year's Day, all the townspeople and all those who live at Leigh Abbey gather beneath the oldest apple tree in the orchard. The ceremony begins shortly after sundown and is always performed by a young girl. It is a great honor to be chosen.'

Both of his sisters had taken their turns. So had Rosamond. Rob hastily took another swallow of his wine, draining the cup. He did not want to think about Rosamond. Those memories, especially the sweet ones, brought nothing but pain.

'The girl wears a wreath of greenery on her head, like a crown. She fishes a crust of bread out of the bottom of a large wooden wassail bowl and climbs a short ladder so that she can place this gift in the crook of the tree. Then everyone sings.' He reproduced a bit of the carol for Jane's benefit: 'Old apple tree we wassail thee, hoping thou will bear.'

'You have a most pleasant singing voice,' Jane murmured, turning her face up to his.

He meant to tell her more about the singing, and how the villagers drank of the wassail as torchlight lit the apple orchard. The words never materialized. Instead, he found himself kissing Jane Bomelius.

Nineteen

'Did you hear?' Nan asked, her face aglow with excitement. 'The earl of Leicester's New Year's gift to the queen was a magnificent necklace. It has twenty pieces, all of them letters, and contains a cipher in the midst of them.'

'They say every piece is set with diamonds and that there are two pearls between each letter,' Madge put in.

'Someone told me that there are diamonds hanging from every one of them, too,' Bess contributed.

With nothing to add, Rosamond kept silent. Whether or not their description was accurate, the earl's extravagance overshadowed every other gift Her Majesty had received.

Rosamond had presented Lady Mary with a ruff and Lady Huntingdon with a little rose-scented pomander ball. In return, she had received a pair of gloves from Lady Mary and a tortoiseshell comb from Lady Huntingdon. She and her fellow waiting gentlewomen exchanged embroidered handkerchiefs. Each of them chose an emblem to use like a signature in one corner. Rosamond picked her family crest, the apple pierced by an arrow, although her apple looked more like a tennis ball than a piece of fruit. Bess used a single flower, a rose, and Madge a tiny bird. Nan's device was the most elaborate. She embroidered a miniature heart, resembling the emblem used on playing cards, crowned with a circlet of flowers. The whole was so tiny, meant to show off Nan's skill as a needle-woman, that it was difficult to make out the details.

The four of them had Lady Mary's lodgings to themselves that afternoon while Lady Mary was in attendance on the queen. Madge passed around a box of ginger candy, a gift from an admirer. Rosamond leaned back against a nest of pillows piled on the floor and sighed with contentment. It was pleasant to have friends. At times like this, she could almost forget that one of them might be involved in Griffith Potter's death.

Bess and Nan brought out a chessboard – one of the few games of which everyone approved – and half-heartedly began moving pieces around the board. Madge, throwing caution to the winds,

sank down onto a floor cushion with her legs folded beneath her
to play with the kitten given to Lady Mary by Frances Howard.

'Leicester might have done better to let Lady Mary's offering
outshine his,' Rosamond mused, 'if he truly wants her suit to succeed
with the queen.'

'What suit?' Madge teased the kitten with a length of yarn,
laughing when it leapt for the strand, missed, and tumbled off the
edge of the pillow.

Rosamond smiled to herself. 'She must have some reason for
coming to court. Everyone else does.'

'Perhaps she is looking for a husband?' Bess suggested.

'I am surprised she is not already wed. She must have a respectable marriage portion, being a noblewoman and all.'

Nan abandoned the chessboard and joined Rosamond and Madge
on the floor. 'She was to have been betrothed to the earl of Oxford,
but he married someone else.'

'What a pity!' Madge exclaimed. 'If she'd married him, she'd be
a countess now.'

Nan snickered.

'What?' Rosamond demanded.

'Nothing.'

Rosamond's eyes narrowed. The expression on Nan's face
reminded her of Watling when he'd tipped over a bowl of cream
and managed to lap it all up before anyone noticed. 'You know
something.'

Nan refused to say more, but Rosamond remembered that she'd
once said Lady Mary was 'impatient to get on with things'. At the
time she'd thought Nan was referring to an audience with the queen,
but now she wondered if she'd meant marriage to the tsar. Did Nan
know about that? And if she did, how *long* she had known? And
why were the others ignorant of what was going on?

A few minutes later, when both Madge and Bess were fully
occupied with the kitten, Rosamond leaned closer to Nan. 'You
know what is in the wind.'

'I may have heard that Lady Mary has a greater title than countess
in her future.'

'What title?' Rosamond kept her voice as low as Nan's had been.

'Empress of Muscovy,' Nan whispered back.

'M-m-muscovy?' Rosamond stumbled over the place name, trying
to make it seem as if she'd never heard it before. 'Where is that?'

'A great distance from England.' A faraway look came into Nan's eyes. 'It is a land of riches beyond imagining, the place where sables come from.'

'And Lady Mary is to wed its king?' Rosamond grasped Nan's arm. 'How do you know this? Has Lady Mary taken you into her confidence?'

Nan scoffed. 'She is better at keeping her plans close than anyone I know. It was by accident that I overheard Lady Huntingdon inform her sister-in-law that the emperor of Muscovy wished to marry her and that the earl of Huntingdon approved of the alliance.'

Rosamond wondered how long ago that had been. She'd been under the impression that Lady Mary's name had only lately been put forward to be the tsar's bride. 'What more do you know of this plan?'

Nan grinned. 'I know that I want to be one of the empress's ladies.'

'You'd willingly go so far away from England? Never see family or friends again?'

'I left my family a long time ago. I have no reason not to leave England, too, and from all I've learned, Muscovy has much to recommend it.'

There are not enough riches in all the lands of the tsar, Rosamond thought, *to tempt me to abandon my homeland and live in such a barbarous place.*

'What have *you* heard about Lady Mary's future?' Nan asked.

'I know far less than you. I guessed that something was afoot, but I did not know what it was. Will you tell me if you find out more?'

'You will be the first to know,' Nan promised, 'so long as you swear you will not try to usurp my place.'

Rosamond could not repress a shudder. 'You need have no fear of that!'

Twenty

Playgoing, like card playing, was frowned upon by the earl of Huntingdon and therefore discouraged as an entertainment for his womenfolk. They had not been in the audience when Lord Strange's Men presented *A History of Love and Fortune* at court. Uncertain if Lady Mary could be persuaded to attend the production of *A History of Ferrara* on Twelfth Night, two days hence, Rosamond contrived to escape her duties for an afternoon by pleading a debilitating headache. She'd suffered several real ones since she'd been hit with that snowball, but this time the excuse was simply a convenient lie.

She slipped unseen into the hall where carpenters were busy erecting a stage at one end of the cavernous room and, facing it, tiers of seating on temporary scaffolding. Most of the seating was already partitioned into boxes. The queen's chair, on a dais, occupied the box directly in front of the stage.

Moving silently as a mouse, trying not to cough from inhaling the sawdust that filled the air, she crept closer to the spot where members of the Earl of Sussex's Men had congregated. She had seen them perform before, in an inn yard, and recognized one or two of them. She stretched her ears to hear what they were saying, hoping to discover that they were rehearsing.

They were not.

'I wonder that it is worth the trouble when we are to be paid but ten pounds,' one player grumbled. 'That is less than a good night's earnings at the Curtain or the Theatre.'

A second member of the company rounded on him. 'Cease your naysaying! It is an honor to play before the queen.'

Rosamond recognized the speaker as Richard Tarleton, the company's leading clown. He was renowned for his comic facial expressions and his jests. The latter had made him even more famous than his counterpart in Lord Howard's Men.

The other man's reply was obscene but creative. Rosamond bit back a laugh. She did not know the fellow's name, but he did have a way with words. Mayhap he was the one who wrote the company's plays.

'Any news of the earl?' a third man asked.

'Nothing good,' Tarleton said. 'He is still dying.'

Rosamond's amusement vanished. They spoke of their patron, the earl of Sussex. They were right to be concerned. As a nobleman's retainers, a company of players gained a legal status that permitted them to leave their homes and travel anywhere in England to perform. Without a patron, they had no protection from England's law against vagabonds. If local authorities objected to their presence, they could be thrown in gaol.

Although she could sympathize with the players' plight, Rosamond knew she would be a great hypocrite if she were to pray for the earl to recover his health. Freed of her nursing duties, the countess of Sussex would come to court. If that happened, she would be sure to unmask Rosamond as an imposter. Lady Sussex had never recommended her young neighbor to Lady Mary Hastings as a waiting gentlewoman. Rosamond's claim to have been part of the Sussex household in Bermondsey would also be revealed as false.

Lost in contemplation of how disastrous such exposure would be, Rosamond stifled a startled squeak when a young man suddenly appeared right in front of her. A moment earlier, he had been sitting on a barrel listening to the other players argue.

'Is there aught I can do for you, mistress?'

She did not recognize him, but a glance told her the most likely reason why he looked unfamiliar to her. He was slender and clean shaven, making him a good candidate to take the women's parts in the company's plays. Heavily made up, wigged, and buried under elaborate costumes, he would look completely different than he did now.

She cocked her head. She sensed nothing unfriendly or threatening about him. A quick glance at the other players reassured her that none of them were paying the least bit of attention to her.

'You can satisfy my curiosity,' she said.

He essayed a gallant bow, even going so far as to doff his cap. 'Henry Leveson at your service, mistress. What would you like to know.'

'I am Mistress Jaffrey, waiting gentlewoman to Lady Mary Hastings.'

'Well met, Mistress Jaffrey.' His enthusiasm made her wonder if he knew she was wealthy. 'What is your question?'

'Why have you chosen to present a history play? Comedies are so much more entertaining.'

'*A History of Ferrara* was the queen's choice.' Leveson shrugged, as if to say that it would not have been his preference, either.

'I saw your company act in *The Red Knight*. A most excellent play.'

Leveson looked pleased. 'I played three separate women's roles in that one, but it is a pity you did not see me in *The Cruelty of a Stepmother* or *Murderous Michael*, where I took even more parts.'

'Tragedies?' She wrinkled her nose in distaste. 'There are enough sad stories in real life. I do not care to see them enacted on the stage.'

'Tragedies of blackest hue can depress the spirit, for all that they have moral value.' Leveson pulled an unhappy face. 'It is for that reason that we rarely present one at court. In truth, most courtiers share your preference for comedies. Besides, it is never a good idea to make the queen sad. Mistress Jaffrey, I—'

A bellow from the stage cut off whatever he had been about to say. 'Leveson! Get your lazy arse down here!' It was the player whose curses had so impressed her.

'He sounds impatient,' Rosamond observed.

'John Adams, the leader of our company.' He sent her a regret-filled look as he abandoned her. 'He must be obeyed.'

'Who's that there?' Adams shouted. 'No spectators!'

Rather than be escorted out of the hall, Rosamond fled, returning to her bed and her pretense of a headache. She spent the rest of the afternoon thinking of ways to convince Lady Mary to attend the performance on Twelfth Night and bring her waiting gentlewomen with her.

Twenty-One

Twelfth Night found Rosamond and the other waiting gentle-women gathered outside Lady Mary's bedchamber. Within, Ticey was dressing their mistress in all her finery, a process that could not be rushed. Good-natured banter filled the air while they waited. Even Madge, who claimed to disapprove of plays and players, was bright eyed with anticipation.

Quietly pleased with the success of her campaign to convince Lady Mary to attend *A History of Ferrara*, Rosamond listened to the others chatter excitedly about the coming performance. For herself, she looked forward to seeing Henry Leveson on stage. She'd always thought it a great pity that females were not permitted to act in public, but if men had to take the women's parts, she appreciated those who were convincing in their roles.

A shriek from the inner chamber shattered Rosamond's reverie. The screaming started an instant later.

Shocked into silence, at first no one moved. Then Rosamond wrenched open the door. The sight that met her eyes brought her to an abrupt halt just inside the bedchamber. A moment later, Nan plowed into her back, forcing her to move forward again.

Lady Mary was on the floor, thrashing about amid the rushes. Pitiful mewling sounds came from her throat as she pawed in a frantic fashion at her face. What little Rosamond could see of it appeared to have turned an ugly red.

The wailing continued, diverting Rosamond's attention. Lady Mary's tiring maid was the source of the racket. Ticey stood near her mistress, her eyes fixed on Lady Mary and an expression of horror on her pale face. Tears streamed down her cheeks.

Her inaction was no help to anyone. Rosamond stalked up to her and slapped her hard. The noise ceased.

'Help me,' she ordered, and turned her attention to Lady Mary.

Nan was ahead of her. She'd already reached the writhing noble-woman and knelt beside her, seizing her hands to stop her from doing further damage to herself. 'You must not dig at your face, my lady. You will leave scars.'

The other two waiting gentlewomen had followed them into the bedchamber. Madge leaned down, blocking Rosamond's view. She reared back as soon as she got a good look at Lady Mary. 'God save us! It is the pox!'

Both Madge and Bess edged away. Even Nan let go of Lady Mary's hands and put her own behind her back.

With a sound of pain and distress, the noblewoman rolled onto her side, once again hiding her ravaged features.

'It is a death sentence,' Bess hissed, careful to keep well away from the afflicted woman.

Rosamond glared at her. 'It is no such thing. Many people survive smallpox. Some even escape being scarred by it.'

'You have the right of it,' Nan agreed, but she rose to her feet and put a little more distance between herself and the woman on the floor. 'The queen herself is proof of that.'

'Fetch Lady Huntingdon.' Rosamond directed the order at Bess, since she was closest to the door. Then, with a scowl for Nan, she took her turn to kneel beside their stricken mistress.

Gently, Rosamond rolled Lady Mary toward her and pulled the noblewoman's hands away from her face. Angry pustules were already forming. The sight was so ugly it made Rosamond gag, but she did not retreat.

This was not the pox.

It was far worse.

Ticey hovered nearby. Arms wrapped around herself, she was trembling but no longer hysterical. Seeming more afraid of Rosamond's ire than of infection, she whispered, 'What can I do, Mistress Jaffrey?'

'Take the box Lady Mary's sleeves were packed in and fill it with snow. Bring as much as you can carry. Hurry!'

'What good will snow do?' Nan demanded. 'You waste your time.'

'It will give her ease. Cold numbs pain.'

'Then we must thank God that it is winter,' said Madge.

Rosamond did not respond to this pious sentiment. She was too busy examining Lady Mary for other symptoms. She reached for the noblewoman's right hand, lying limp beside her body. Like her face, it was red and blistered.

She shifted her attention to her surroundings. A stool lay on its side a few feet away, as if it had been flung there with considerable force. It was not the only thing out of place in the bedchamber. Lady Mary's looking glass had been overturned and her washbasin and pitcher had tumbled to the floor. A large wet patch indicated that one or the other, perhaps both, had been nearly full of water.

Lady Mary's gloves lay on the table, next to the spot where the pitcher and washbasin must have stood before they were knocked over. They all wore similar thin leather gloves most of the time, especially in winter. Lady Mary had taken them off to wash her face.

Before Rosamond could speculate further, Ticey returned with the box full of snow. Following Rosamond's directions, she knelt on Lady Mary's other side. The first handful of snow landed awkwardly on the noblewoman's cheek. Shocked, Lady Mary tried to roll away, but Ticey, emboldened by Rosamond's example, held her in place. Although the mistress flailed weakly at the maid, she lacked any real strength.

With sure, steady strokes, Rosamond also applied cold, wet snow to Lady Mary's face. It melted the moment it touched her hot skin. She was burning up, but not with fever.

Rosamond did not have a great deal of experience with nursing, or with smallpox, either, but she was certain that what she saw in front of her was not the result of illness. Lady Mary's face was mottled with burns and even pitted here and there . . . as if some caustic substance had been applied with a heavy hand.

With a little sigh, Lady Mary lost consciousness.

Working rapidly, Rosamond washed every bit of visible skin. Even though she was wearing gloves, her fingertips tingled. They felt as if they had come in contact with stinging nettles.

'Send someone for more snow,' she called out to Madge, who was still keeping her distance. 'And for fresh clean water.'

'How will that help? Have a care, Rosamond. The pox is horribly contagious. You must send for a physician. And pray.'

'You may do both, *after* you follow my instructions.'

'I will go.' Nan dashed for the door when Madge continued to dither.

Rosamond turned her attention to Lady Mary's hands. She applied snow to the right one and instructed Ticey to do the same to the left.

Madge inched closer to the exit. When she reached it, she hesitated only a moment before scurrying away.

Left alone with Ticey and the unconscious Lady Mary, Rosamond addressed the tiring maid in a low voice. 'What happened here?'

'It weren't my fault.'

Rosamond applied more snow and shifted uncomfortably in her sodden skirts. She was kneeling in a puddle of melted snow. Lady Mary's clothing was likewise soaked, but although the noblewoman's body twitched now and again, she was otherwise limp and unresponsive, as oblivious to the wetness as she was to the pain.

'Tell me what Lady Mary was doing just before she knocked over the looking glass and fell to the floor.'

'Washing her face and hands.'

'What was she using?'

'Water, mistress.' Ticey grimaced. 'Mistress Jaffrey, my hands burn.'

Rosamond grabbed Ticey's wrist to stop her from touching Lady Mary's skin again. The girl's bare hand had turned a bright, fearsome red. It might have been from the cold, but Rosamond did not think so.

'What's amiss?' Lady Huntingdon swept into the bedchamber as if she expected her mere presence to put everything to rights. She gasped when she caught sight of her sister-in-law.

Two servants bringing more snow and two pitchers of cold water arrived close on her heels. Rosamond saw no sign of Nan or Bess or Madge.

'A moment, my lady,' Rosamond said to the countess. She turned to Ticey and instructed the tiring maid to use water from one of the pitchers to wash her hands. 'Do a thorough job,' she added.

Afraid of what she would find, Rosamond stripped off her own sodden gloves. There were no blisters on her skin and only a hint of red discolored her fingers and palms. Since it was likely safe to touch Lady Mary bare-handed after all the washing they had done, she turned the noblewoman's care over to Lady Huntingdon's women.

The moment she stood up and stepped back, Lady Huntingdon approached Lady Mary. 'Lord be merciful! Smallpox.'

Rosamond said nothing, but she was certain only one thing could account for Lady Mary's symptoms. It was not disease. A caustic substance had been added to the washing water. When it had come in contact with the noblewoman's bare skin, it had caused a terrible reaction.

She had no idea what the poison might have been. She could only pray that washing it away had prevented further damage. Some poisons could seep through the skin and into the vital organs. If this was one of them, then nothing anyone could do would save Lady Mary's life. Her own life, and Ticey's, might be forfeit as well.

'I must go and change into dry clothing,' Rosamond murmured.

Lady Huntingdon paid her no mind. Her horrified gaze never left her kinswoman as servants lifted Lady Mary from the floor and carried her to her bed. There Ticey took on the task of divesting her unconscious mistress of her dripping clothing.

That the countess did not ask why Rosamond, Ticey, and Lady Mary were so wet surprised Rosamond, but she was glad to escape without being questioned. On her way out, she stooped to pick up the bowl and pitcher. No one noticed that she took them with her, or that she took great care not to let her skin come in contact with the interior of either vessel.

Safe in her own small chamber, Rosamond emptied a small traveling chest of clothing, wrapped both pieces of crockery in cloth, and hid them at the bottom. She was not certain that preserving the bowl and pitcher served any purpose, but if she was right about poison, there might be some way, at a later date, to test residue.

Melka appeared just as she was closing the lid on the chest. She had, by some means known only to servants, heard that Lady Mary had fallen ill. 'Smallpox?' she asked.

'I do much doubt it.' Rosamond considered what to do next as Melka helped her out of her wet clothing and into simpler garments suitable for tending the sick. 'Walsingham will be attending the play. Do you know him by sight?'

She was not surprised when Melka nodded.

'Good. You must seek him out and press a note into his hand.' She went straight to her capcase for a quill, ink, and a tiny scrap of paper upon which she wrote two words: not smallpox. After entrusting this message to her maidservant, she returned to Lady Mary's bedchamber.

The next hours passed with interminable slowness. It was a long time before Lady Mary regained consciousness. When she did, she was in terrible pain. Tears streamed down her ravaged face, making the burns and lesions sting all the more.

The physician Lady Huntingdon had sent for arrived near midnight. Typical of his kind, he scarce looked at his patient before declaring that she suffered from the pox. Then he hurried away, lest he become infected. Lady Mary's care was left to her servants and her sister-in-law.

'What will happen now?' Rosamond asked.

'When there is an outbreak of an infectious disease at court,' Lady

Huntingdon answered, 'be it smallpox or the plague, queen and courtiers alike are wont to flee, leaving the sick behind to live or die as God pleases.'

No easy task in winter, Rosamond thought. If Walsingham had received her message, and believed it, surely he would advise the queen not to bother. There was no need for a wholesale evacuation of Windsor Castle.

Before another hour passed, a message arrived from Queen Elizabeth. Lady Huntingdon frowned when she read it. 'We are ordered to take Lady Mary back to Chelsea without delay,' she told the gentle-women huddled in the outer chamber. 'We are to be quarantined there.' Sounding puzzled, she ordered them to make the necessary preparations.

Rosamond wondered what devious game Her Majesty was playing. Melka had delivered Rosamond's message to Sir Francis Walsingham. The queen knew by now that her cousin was not suffering from a contagious disease. For some reason, she did not want it known that someone had tried to kill Lady Mary. In that case, Rosamond supposed, the quarantine made sense. Lady Mary would be protected from another attempt on her life . . . unless the first one had been made by a member of her own household.

Needing to question Ticey without delay, Rosamond took advantage of the chaos of everyone rushing about, making hurried preparations for the journey down the Thames, to take the tiring maid aside.

'Let me see your hands,' Rosamond ordered, and examined them closely. Ticey's fingers and palms looked as if they had been scalded with boiling water. She kept hold of the girl's fingers until Ticey met her eyes. 'Tell me of Lady Mary's washing water. Was there anything special about it?'

Ticey chewed on her lower lip, a worried expression on her face.

'Whatever happened is not your fault, Ticey. What is important now is that I learn everything I can about the few minutes before Lady Mary cried out and fell to the floor.'

'My lady liked scented water.' Ticey blurted out the admission in the same tone another woman would have confessed to a deadly sin. Given the fervor for reform in the household, Rosamond was not surprised.

'Did she add perfume to the washing water?'

Ticey nodded. 'A new one. A New Year's gift.'

'Who gave it to her?'

'I do not know, mistress. Nor did Lady Mary. She said it came from a secret admirer.'

At Rosamond's urging, Ticey retrieved the small bottle that had contained the scent. Its shape confirmed Rosamond's suspicion. She could only be grateful that Lady Mary had known nothing about the way apothecaries packaged their medicines. This potion should have been swallowed, not diluted in washing water. Lady Mary's mistake had undoubtedly saved her life. If she had drunk even a small portion of the caustic liquid, she would surely be dead.

Taking great care, Rosamond removed the stopper from the bottle and sniffed. The scent was pleasant but unfamiliar. Sweet smelling ingredients had been added to mask the odor of the poison, and likely its taste, too. Rosamond slipped the empty bottle into her pocket for safekeeping. At the first opportunity, she entrusted this new evidence to Melka, telling her to store it in the chest with the bowl and pitcher.

The time-honored way to test for poison, although Rosamond deplored the cruelty of it, was to give some to an animal and observe the consequences. She refused to sacrifice a dog or cat or – terrible thought! – the kitten Frances Howard had given to Lady Mary. She would wait until she could procure a rat.

Finalizing their preparations to leave Windsor did not take long. At first light, before most of the courtiers had risen from their beds, Lady Mary was carried out of the castle on a litter and onto a waiting barge. Her retinue followed, their own servants in tow.

Rosamond hung back, sheltering in a gateway on the pretext of adjusting the hood of her cloak against the early morning chill. Her real purpose was to watch the others as they passed by. She regarded each one in turn with suspicion, especially the other waiting gentle-women who had been her close companions for so many weeks. Lady Mary's 'secret admirer' could have been anyone, but the members of her own household were still the most likely suspects, especially those who had also been at the Wardrobe of Robes when Griffith Potter was murdered.

'Mistress Jaffrey,' a soft voice called. 'A word?'

She turned to find the young player, Henry Leveson, lurking behind a bush.

'I have no time for banter.' At the moment, amusing herself was the last thing on Rosamond's mind. She hurried after the others, suddenly fearful of being left behind if she delayed too long.

Leveson came after her, catching hold of her forearm to stop her progress. She opened her mouth to protest but the objection never reached her lips. In the pale morning sun, Leveson's face looked a decade older. More startling still, there was an intensity in his gaze that had been absent, or well hidden, at their first meeting.

'Who are you?' she whispered.

'Someone able to pass on any message you wish to send to the one who employs us both.'

He was Walsingham's man? Why had no one told her? And did she dare take his word? Uncertain, Rosamond fell back on facetiousness. 'You do not speak, I presume, of the earl of Sussex.'

His grin was fleeting. 'Was it poison?'

If he could ask that question, did it follow that he knew of the note she had sent to Sir Francis Walsingham? Rosamond hesitated only a moment longer before following her instincts.

'Tell him it was,' she said, 'and that I suspect it was the same poison that was used to kill Griffith Potter.'

Twenty-Two

Once they were back at Chelsea, Lady Mary was installed in her own bedchamber with Ticey to look after her. Rosamond also remained at her bedside, until Lady Huntingdon summoned her to the small parlor where she did the household accounts.

'Are you not afraid of the pox?' she asked. Seated before a small writing table, she had been composing a letter. To her husband in York, Rosamond supposed.

Rosamond was tempted to tell the countess of her conviction that Lady Mary's 'pockmarks' were the result of poison, not disease. They were terrible to look upon, but not contagious. She caught herself in time. They would be quarantined at Chelsea for some time to come, waiting to see if anyone else fell ill. No one outside the household would be able to come close enough to Lady Mary to harm her, but that would not protect the noblewoman if the villain was a member of her own staff. If Rosamond was to keep Lady Mary safe, she had to continue to pretend ignorance. Then, too, in a case of attempted murder, no one was above suspicion, not even Lady Huntingdon.

'I had the disease as a small child,' she lied. 'No one ever catches smallpox twice.'

'If common belief is true,' the countess said slowly, 'those who survive one bout with this deadly illness cannot be brought low by it a second time. I pray it is so, for I have seen the terrible results of selfless service to a stricken mistress. My only sister nursed the queen when Her Majesty fell ill of smallpox, then caught the disease herself. The queen recovered both her health and her looks, but my sister's face is so badly scarred that she refuses to let anyone see it unveiled, even her own much beloved husband.'

'I will gladly take the risk,' Rosamond said, 'but I must have help.'

What she could not say aloud was that Lady Mary needed guarding. Events at Windsor had changed everything. No matter what her orders, Rosamond could no longer think of herself as an intelligence gatherer and naught else. It was her duty to protect Lady Mary against any further attempts on her life. Moreover, she had an obligation to discover what person had been responsible for the first attack.

'The queen lay close to death,' Lady Huntingdon said, her thoughts centered on her disfigured sister, Lady Sidney. 'Even her physicians had given up hope. And yet, within a week of the day she first fell ill, she had recovered fully. We must pray that Lady Mary's ordeal has a similarly happy conclusion.'

Prayer? Rosamond thought. *Practical assistance would be better.*

'Someone to help me?' she reminded Lady Huntingdon. 'Let me have my own tiring maid, and Lady Mary's Ticey, since she has already been exposed, and one other. Then we will each be able to rest between periods of watching over our patient.'

'Whatever you need,' Lady Huntingdon promised, rising from her chair and leading the way to the door. 'I place my dear kinswoman in your hands, Mistress Jaffrey.'

The more fool you, Rosamond thought. *For all you know, I could be the one who wants her dead!*

She followed the countess into her outer chamber and heard her ask for a volunteer from among the other waiting gentlewomen. After a moment's hesitation, Nan stepped forward. 'I will help nurse my lady.'

'Excellent.' The matter settled, Lady Huntingdon led the rest of the company off to the chapel, where Augustus Treadwell was waiting to lead them in prayer.

'Have you already had the pox, as I have?' Rosamond asked.

'Does it matter? It is God's will who is stricken and who is not, and I have a duty to our mistress. If you are brave enough to stay at her side, then so am I.' Nan nervously clasped and unclasped her hands but the determined look in her eyes convinced Rosamond that she would stay the course.

Your courage is the greater, she thought. Like everyone else, Nan believed that Lady Mary was suffering from a contagious disease, yet she was willing to risk her life – and if not her life, her looks. She was either exceeding devoted or excessive foolish.

They adjourned to the sickroom, where Ticey had been watching over the ailing woman. The maidservant looked up at their entrance, unshed tears shining in her eyes.

'Is she sleeping?' Nan asked.

'She was in such pain that Lady Huntingdon bade me to give her poppy syrup.'

Lady Mary lay so still that Rosamond had to look closely to see the rise and fall of her chest. She wished she'd listened more closely to her foster mother's lectures on the properties of herbs and the compounding of cures. She had no idea if unconsciousness was the best treatment but at least, in this state, Lady Mary would not be scratching her inflamed skin and making the damage worse.

Nan's thoughts ran in the same vein. 'Some of her scars may well be permanent.'

'I am more concerned with preserving her life than with saving her appearance.'

She tried to think of more she could do. She could almost hear Susanna Appleton telling her to 'use common sense'.

'Strips of soft fabric,' she said aloud.

Nan sent her a questioning look.

'We must wrap her hands to keep her from digging her fingernails into the rash. But first, I think, we should apply a soothing poultice.' She dug deep into her memories, searching for the lessons of school-room and stillroom. 'Borage will ease the itching, burning sensation, especially if it is mixed with chamomile flowers.'

She dispatched Melka to fetch the ingredients she needed. Both were readily available. Every good housewife, even a countess, oversaw the planting of herb and kitchen gardens and kept a stillroom, if only to distill rosewater and other perfumes.

I must be bold, Rosamond thought. *Nothing I do is likely to make matters worse.*

When Rosamond applied the mixture of borage and chamomile, she was pleased to see the hands already looked less angry. She left wrapping her in the cloths Melka had brought to Nan and Ticey and turned her mind to recalling more of her lessons at Leigh Abbey.

Water parsnips could be used to make a cream to remove freckles. That tidbit was useless! Burdock root helped all skin disorders, but would it ease the burning and blistering Lady Mary had suffered? She considered and discarded a half dozen more cures as the long, watchful hours passed.

After a time, she turned from ruminating on cures to consider causes. The poison had most likely come from a plant. Plants were easier to obtain than metals or mineral salts, and less expensive than theriacs concocted of dozens of ingredients.

She had a quiet word with Melka, instructing her maidservant to get hold of the earl's rat catcher and procure a live rodent. She would test the dregs left in the bottle Lady Mary had received as a gift. She was certain they were lethal, but the way the rat died might reveal something useful.

In the meantime, while Nan dozed, Rosamond once again questioned Ticey. The girl could add nothing more to what she had already said and insisted that Lady Mary herself had chosen the bottle and poured its contents into her wash basin.

During the endless day that followed, Rosamond brooded. Had there been anything she could have done to prevent what had happened to Lady Mary? Should she have recognized Potter's death as a warning to her to be on her guard against an attack on the noblewoman?

She wondered, too, whether she should have been so hasty to take Henry Leveson at his word. *Was* he Walsingham's man, or did he serve some other courtier, mayhap one who did not want negotiations with Muscovy to succeed? Leveson had shown her no proof that he came from the principal secretary. If he had been designated to take Griffith Potter's place as a conduit for messages, then why had he not told her so on the day she first met him?

They had been interrupted, she remembered. He'd been about to say something when a shout from the leader of the company of players had called him away. That was no excuse! It would have taken no more than a single word, Walsingham's name.

Late the next night, when Rosamond sat alone with her feverish charge, Lady Mary suddenly awoke. Her pain-filled eyes needed a moment to focus. She stared hard at her waiting gentlewoman and then, through cracked lips, whispered Rosamond's name.

'I am here, Lady Mary.' She poured a goblet of barley water and helped the noblewoman swallow a goodly portion of it, one tiny sip at a time.

'Why are my hands bandaged?' Lady Mary asked.

'It is for your own protection, my lady. If you scratch the eruptions on your face, they will leave permanent scars.'

Lady Mary's breath quickened. Fear made her eyes go wide. 'Am I going to die?'

'I do much doubt it, since you have survived this long. Are you in pain?'

'The skin of my face feels strange. Tight.'

'Does it itch?'

Lady Mary took a moment to consider her answer. 'Not intolerably, no.'

'That is a good sign.' In truth, Rosamond did not know if it was or not, but she thought it must be better than what had come before. Another thought occurred to her when Lady Mary blinked several times in succession. 'Can you see me clearly? Did any of the wash water splash into your eyes?'

The eyes in question abruptly narrowed. 'What was wrong with my wash water?'

Rosamond hesitated.

'I command you to tell me. If you do not, I will dismiss you from my household.'

The return of her haughty manner was the best reassurance Rosamond could have had that Lady Mary was on the road to recovery. 'You added a foreign substance to that water, my lady. Something in that bottle caused your . . . condition.'

'Impossible!'

'Would you rather be diagnosed with the pox?'

'The perfume was a gift. I receive many gifts, especially of late.' With a smug, superior air, she added, 'I cannot speak of it, but great plans have been made for my future.'

'But you must survive to enjoy it. It has been given out that you have the pox, but in truth whatever was in that scent caused your face to burn and blister. If the disfigurement does not fully heal, I wonder if those grand plans will still go forward.'

'You talk nonsense.' There was a note of uncertainty in her voice.

'Do I? You know something of the rival factions at court. Is it so impossible that someone might wish to harm you, thus preventing your betrothal to . . . a certain foreign prince?'

'Why do you hesitate to speak his name?'

'Because you do, my lady. The matter seems to be a great secret, even in your own household.'

'How do you know of it, then?'

'I have ears.'

The sound Lady Mary made might have been a weak attempt at a laugh. 'His name is Ivan. When I marry him, I will be empress of Muscovy.'

Lady Mary closed her eyes but Rosamond was not fooled into thinking she had drifted into sleep.

How much more should she tell the noblewoman? The bottle *had* contained a poison meant to kill her. The rat Rosamond had tested it on had died, but too quickly to tell if its symptoms resembled Griffith Potter's death throes. Rosamond knew better than to mention Potter to Lady Mary or anyone else. Any revelation about his death would inevitably lead to questions that would end with the discovery that she had entered the household under false pretenses. Even if she was not sent away, her usefulness would be compromised.

'My lady?'

Lady Mary's eyelids lifted to leave the merest slit for her to look through.

'Who gave you that gift?'

'I do not know. I found it in my bedchamber when I returned from a walk.'

'When? What day?'

'I do not remember.'

'What made you use the contents to wash with?'

'I liked the scent.'

'Did someone *tell* you it was an additive for washing water?' When the question was answered with sullen silence, Rosamond came to a decision. Lady Mary could not protect herself if she did not know she was in danger. 'The truth is, my lady, that a bottle of that shape customarily holds a potion meant to be swallowed.'

'How was I to know? It did not have a label reading "drink me".' She sounded petulant again. 'My face hurts. My hands, too.'

'I will give you more poppy juice for the pain, but first you must answer one more question. Did you empty the bottle into the basin or did Ticey?'

'I did.'

Rosamond nodded, glad to have confirmation that the tiring maid had told her the truth. She helped Lady Mary to sit up far enough to swallow a spoonful of the opiate.

'I splashed the water onto my face with my hands,' Lady Mary murmured. 'I thought the coolness would be refreshing. I had been dancing.' The drug acted quickly. She already sounded cup-shot.

'Dancing? Alone in your chamber?' The admission startled Rosamond.

'I was happy.' Lady Mary's words slurred. 'Going to a play. Talk to the queen.'

'Did the pain begin at once?'

Tears leaked out from Lady Mary's closed eyes. 'I do not want to remember.'

That meant it had, Rosamond thought. Mayhap it had been a good thing. Lady Mary had reacted by knocking the washbasin aside, thus preventing any more of the caustic liquid from coming in contact with her skin.

She sat at Lady Mary's bedside, watching over the noblewoman as she slept. Rosamond's body was still, but her mind spun with unanswered questions. She did not dwell on Lady Mary's surprising admission that she'd been looking forward to attending a play or the even more astonishing confession that she'd been dancing. The much more important question was who could have left that poison in Lady Mary's bedchamber?

It must have been someone at court and, further, someone who could reach Lady Mary's bedchamber unchallenged . . . or sneak in when it was unoccupied. Try as she might, she was unable to narrow down the possibilities. She had the best of reasons to know how easy it was to slip into or out of a room without being noticed.

She had no proof that the same person, or the same poison, had killed Griffith Potter, but the more she considered that possibility, the more likely it seemed. When Potter had gasped out that single word – attack – mayhap he had not meant that *he* had been attacked. Mayhap he had meant to warn her of a coming attack on someone else.

Rising, Rosamond paced, circling around the idea as she made a circuit of the bedchamber. Did her theory narrow the field of suspects or widen it? During their visit to the Wardrobe of Robes, she had absented herself, unnoticed, from the others. Another member of Lady Mary's entourage could have done the same.

This was not a new thought, but she had spent hours on end with the other gentlewomen and found nothing untoward in their behavior. She had grown fond of Nan and Bess and learned to tolerate Madge. She liked young Ticey, too.

There is no room for emotion here, she warned herself. What persons had been in the Wardrobe of Robes and also at Windsor Castle? The list was short: Ticey, Bess, Madge, and Nan. Any one of them might have met with Griffith Potter before Rosamond herself crept away to look for him.

The more difficult question was *why* one of them would kill him. Had he posed a threat to the plan to kill Lady Mary? Mayhap he had, but how would the killer have known that? Walsingham's information gatherers were not in the habit of announcing themselves to all and sundry. They barely admitted who they were to those who *needed* to know.

Rosamond plunked herself down on the seat built into a window alcove. Although the window itself was shuttered tight against the icy January night, a cold draft touched her neck and made her shiver.

Lady Mary's proposed marriage to the tsar had to have been the reason for the attack. As Rosamond had suggested, there were rival factions at court. But even if that was the case, someone much closer at hand had to be involved. Constant vigilance must be her watchword from now on. If a member of her own household had already harmed Lady Mary, there must be no second attempt.

Ticey seemed unlikely. She had been in a position to tell Lady Mary that the bottle contained a drink and had not done so. Not Nan, either. Nan believed she would find wealth and happiness in Muscovy. She wanted Lady Mary to wed the tsar. If the reason behind poisoning Lady Mary was to thwart the efforts of the queen and the Muscovy Company, Nan was not the culprit.

That left Madge and Bess, but Rosamond could not think of a single reason for either of them to harm their mistress. Head in her hands, Rosamond closed her eyes. This was hopeless! She had no answers, only more questions. If Potter had been attempting to warn her of an attack on Lady Mary, why did he not just say so? If he could manage only one word, the name of the poisoner would have been much more helpful than 'attack'. Or, as Master Baldwin had suggested, 'poison'. The specific poison would have been even more useful.

Rosamond's eyes flew open. She came to her feet in a rush. Potter *had* said something else. When she'd first found him, he'd looked up at her and said 'you'.

Could it be that simple?

Could she have heard 'you' when what he'd really said was 'yew'?

Twenty-Three

'Yew,' Rosamond read in Lady Appleton's *A Cautionary Herbal*, 'has no place in medicine, although some claim it can be used to make an antidote against poisoning by monkshood. Bark, leaves, seeds, needles and fruit, both fresh and dried, all parts are poisonous to man and beast. Some few who have eaten of the red berries have survived by the Grace of God, but if you use the decorative boughs of yew at Yuletide, do not let children near them.'

She consulted the list of symptoms. Lady Appleton had gathered them not from watching victims die of the poison but from reading accounts in texts both ancient and new. A large dose of the poison, she wrote, could cause sudden death. If the victim lingered, he might hallucinate.

Rosamond frowned. Potter had not shown any sign that his mind was affected. She read on.

Dilated pupils. He'd had those. Cold sweat. Yes. Face tinged with blue. He had also vomited. And it seemed that the time it took yew to kill varied a good deal. In one case, the onset of acute symptoms had been rapid indeed. A man had appeared healthy one moment, gasped the next, and within ten minutes was dead. In another instance, two cows had eaten of yew branches. One had died almost at once. The other had lingered a few hours.

Rosamond had been warned, in her days in the stillroom, that some people, and some animals, were more susceptible to an acute reaction than others. That was all the more reason to take great care what herbs one used in distilling medicines or perfumes and in seasoning food. There were other factors, too – the age of the victim, how much poison had been consumed, whether the poison had been diluted or given full strength.

'Although some find the smell unpleasant and it has a bitter taste,' the entry continued, 'horses and cattle are often found dead beside it. Because false rumor holds that yew possesses magical powers, having been worshipped by the Druids of old, some foolish souls harvest its berries and leaves for luck. Oil of yew is an irritant that causes inflammation of the skin. Although formerly much used in the treatment of painful swelling of the joints, it can make the condition worse if too much is used. The wood does make fine bows, but for any other purpose yew is best avoided.'

Rosamond closed the book and sat quietly for a long time. Oil of yew was an irritant to the skin. That could explain the damage to Lady Mary's face and hands. Applied, however briefly, to her skin, it had burned and caused a painful rash. The damage had begun to heal but it was impossible as yet to tell if there would be scars.

One question remained. How had Griffith Potter *known* he'd been poisoned by yew? Rosamond considered the matter and decided that mayhap he had not. What he'd known was that yew was the intended weapon in the attack on Lady Mary.

That supposed that he'd known his killer and that he had somehow coaxed the information out of a villainous murderer before being slain himself. Mayhap Potter had been a little too clever, Rosamond thought. He had believed himself to be the victor in the game of espionage but had ended up as just another victim.

'Let that be a warning to you, Rosamond Jaffrey,' she whispered in the privacy of her bedchamber. 'Trust no one and be careful what you eat and drink.'

Twenty-Four

Over the next few days, Lady Mary's health improved. Since no one else had fallen ill, life at Chelsea soon returned to its normal routine.

Rosamond alone remained alert to danger. She feared that someone in the household at Chelsea, having failed to kill Lady Mary the first time, was only waiting for the right moment to attempt a second attack. Much as she disliked the idea, the most likely culprit remained one of the four women who had been with Lady Mary in the Wardrobe of Robes and at court.

Leaving Lady Mary in the company of her sister-in-law, Ticey, and Nan, reasoning that she'd be safe enough when there were three of them with her, Rosamond went in search of Madge and Bess. She found them in the gallery, where the light streaming in through the tall windows was good for sewing. There was room between them on the long, low settle. Rosamond pulled a plain cloth shirt out of a sewing basket and began to hem the garment to give to the poor. Madge and Bess were similarly occupied.

'Have you ever considered,' she asked, 'that somewhere in London there must be hundreds of men wearing new shirts and nothing else? It stands to reason that there are, since I have never heard of anyone sewing hose or breeches to give away.'

'You should not jest about acts of Christian charity.' Lips pursed in a prim line, shoulders stiff, Madge radiated disapproval.

'Or set foot outside unless your conscience is clear,' Bess added in a low voice. She winked at Rosamond when Madge wasn't looking.

'Why? Has some new danger arisen while we've been locked away? A Spanish invasion? A plague of locusts?'

'Neither, but Doctor Treadwell brought us news of a lesser catastrophe in Paris Garden. Some of the scaffold seating collapsed during a bear baiting. Eight people were killed and many more injured.'

Madge sniffed. 'It serves them right for indulging in such an ungodly activity on the Sabbath.'

'Death seems a harsh penalty for having a little fun.' Rosamond had never attended a bear baiting herself, but she knew people who had. They were no better or worse than anyone else.

'Sundays are for prayer and contemplation,' Madge insisted. 'Why else should all good Englishmen and women be required by law to attend church?'

'And after church services, we are bidden to do no work,' Rosamond countered, 'the Sabbath being a day of rest. That seems to me to give us license to amuse ourselves. Are those who play at bowls or tennis or go for a sail on the Thames also to suffer death?'

'That is as God wills. Wondrous are the works of the Lord. What happened at Paris Garden is a sign that all such amusements should be banned.' Madge jabbed needle into cloth with unnecessary force. 'Bull and bear baitings. Cockfights. Plays. They are all abominations.'

Religious fervor had never impressed Rosamond, especially when it simply parroted back the sentiments of a preacher. As chaplain, Augustus Treadwell had much to answer for. 'I suppose that next you will say we are due for an apocalypse.'

Bess's head was bowed over her stitches, hiding her expression, but Rosamond thought she sounded worried when she said, 'There have been portents. What of Lady Mary's illness? How could she be stricken and no one else?'

'That, too, was God's will.' Madge's face wore a smug little smile. 'Lady Mary must have done something to provoke the Lord's wrath.'

'What nonsense!' Rosamond gave Madge her best glare. She'd gained a new respect for their mistress during Lady Mary's recovery. The noblewoman was not so prideful as she had been, and she had been almost pathetically grateful for the relief Rosamond's poultices and potions had given her.

'Everyone has dark secrets,' Madge insisted. 'Lady Mary has been keeping something from us. Have you not sensed it?'

'Her secret is not dark at all,' Rosamond said. 'Lady Mary is to wed the tsar of Muscovy.'

Bess dropped her sewing. Madge's eyes grew big as gold sovereigns. Both reactions seemed exaggerated to Rosamond. Was one false? Were both?

'Did you not guess? Why else do you think the queen favored her with the gift of a gown?'

They peppered her with questions, most of which she could not answer. Neither doubted for a moment that she spoke the truth, which made Rosamond even more suspicious of the two of them.

'Mayhap her illness was a sign she should not go.' Bess was a great believer in signs and portents, seeing them in everything from cows in gardens to dogs howling in the nighttime.

'Say rather that it was divine intervention to discourage her from contemplating such a thing.' Madge lowered her voice. 'They are all heathens in Muscovy.'

'No,' Rosamond said, remembering Master Baldwin's stories from long ago. 'They are Christians. Their church is similar to the church in Rome, only different.'

'That is just as bad! Marry him and she'd have to convert to his faith. It is not to be thought of!'

'The marriage seals a treaty. It is important to England. I have no doubt but that Queen Elizabeth, as head of the Church of England, can grant Lady Mary a dispensation for . . . compromising her faith.'

Outrage left Madge's face devoid of prettiness. 'Such a thing is not to be thought of! She will condemn herself to eternal damnation by such an act.'

The queen? Or Lady Mary? Before Rosamond could ask, Madge was on her feet and hurrying away. 'Where is she going in such a rush?'

'The chapel. Where else?'

'To pray for guidance?'

'Or for a lighting bolt to strike Lady Mary down before she can commit a heinous sin.'

Rosamond said no more. She picked up her sewing and smoothed out the hem. Her uneven stitches marched across the fabric, mute testimony to her failings as a waiting gentlewoman. But as a spy? In that role she might have begun to have better success. Madge's religious zeal was becoming more extreme, even for this household, and a zealot might well be capable of poisoning two innocent people in the misguided belief that she was saving their souls.

Twenty-Five

The cell door creaked open, bringing Rob Jaffrey out of a state halfway between sleep and unconsciousness. The small, noisome chamber was in pitch darkness. He sat on an ice-cold stone floor, his back propped against an equally cold stone wall, his arms held at an unnatural angle above his head by shackles attached to a metal ring. He turned his head toward the sound, a movement that made his neck scream in agony. Most of the rest of him was too numb to feel anything at all. He closed his eyes as the light of a single torch blinded him. If his hands had been free, he'd have used them to shield his face.

'Jaffrey?'

The incredulous voice belonged to Egidius Crew. Shuffling feet came closer.

Rob tried to ask, 'Are you a prisoner, too?' but the words came out as an unintelligible croak. It had been a long time since anything liquid had moistened his throat and longer still since he'd been given food to sustain him.

Crew spoke in rapid Russian, barking commands. Someone used a key to release Rob from the heavy metal cuffs. He was so weak that his arms flopped limply to the floor. He heard his hands strike stone with a sickening thump before the rest of his body slumped and slowly toppled sideways.

Strong hands seized his shoulders and hauled him upright. Swatting ineffectually at the man who held him, he tried again to speak. The hands shifted, supporting him as someone else lifted a cup to his dry, cracked lips and dribbled small beer into his mouth. He swallowed, not without pain, but the reward made the effort worthwhile.

'Not too much at first or you'll make yourself sick.' That was Crew again, from behind him.

Slowly, he opened his eyes. The light still made him wince, but he could see. It was Harry Vaughan who held the cup, coaxing him to swallow just a bit more before he took it away.

'Do you think you can stand?' Crew asked.

Rob tried to shake his head and nearly howled with pain. Just a stiff neck, he told himself. Nothing was broken. Anything wrong with him could be mended once he was out of this place. He needed warmth and food and sleep. He had never valued those simple pleasures enough.

The two men helped him to his feet, one of them on each side, and maneuvered him out of the cell. Crew spoke again to the guard, words Rob did not understand but which were obeyed. For a few more minutes, he believed that he was being set free. Then they stopped walking. A door opened and another prison cell yawned before him.

It was better than the last. There was a bed with a mattress and it had a chamber pot beneath it. Crew eased him down onto the padded surface while Vaughan used the torch to light a branch of candles on a table. There was a chair, too. And a window through which pale sunlight entered . . . along with the January cold.

Crew must have read the despair in his eyes. He sent Rob an apologetic look. 'This was the best we could manage for now, but you must not give up hope. You're to have a charcoal brazier for heat and your traveling chest with clean clothes. You're to be supplied with washing water, too.' He managed a faint smile. 'You smell rank, my friend.'

They did not attempt further conversation until servants had brought in the promised luxuries and Rob's friends had helped him remove his fouled garments. He was of little help with the process. He felt weak as a newborn kitten. Only when he was clean, garbed in fresh clothing, and lying on the bed beneath a warm blanket and a fur coverlet, did Crew speak again.

'This will do for now. Negotiations are ongoing for your release.'

'Why am I being held?' This time, thanks to more small beer and a little cold soup, his words could be understood.

'You do not know?' Vaughan looked at him askance.

'No one has told me anything.'

'They say you were associating with a known traitor. A woman. We supposed that meant Mistress Bomelius.'

Rob tried to sit up, only to fall back onto the bed, his head swimming. 'Jane – has she been harmed?'

His friends exchanged a speaking glance.

'As far as anyone knows,' Crew said after an interminable silence, 'she continues as she was.'

'We did warn you,' Vaughan muttered.

'She has done nothing. Nor have I.' He'd have been more convincing were he on his feet, but there was nothing to be done about that. At least his voice was stronger with every word.

'Guilt or innocence has naught to do with it.' Crew clapped him on the shoulder. 'Stop worrying about the woman and concentrate on your own well being. I will arrange for you to have a servant to nurse you back to health.'

'So that they can execute me?'

'I do not think it will come to that.'

Rob heard the doubt in Crew's voice but tried not to dwell on it. As long as he was alive, there was a chance that he would stay that way.

'We have to leave you now,' Crew said, 'but be of good cheer. We will do all we can to get you out of here. With luck, the tsar's desire for a new treaty with England will sway him in your favor.'

Crew's footsteps receded as he left the cell. A moment later, Rob heard him speaking Russian to a guard.

Sensing that Vaughan was still nearby, he made a weak attempt at a jest. 'Have you any words of encouragement for me, Harry? Or, if not, mayhap you could leave your pistol with me when you go. I will return it as soon as I can persuade the guards to release me.'

Rob expected a laugh. His friends at Muscovy House knew full well how much he disliked firearms.

The sound Harry Vaughan made was closer to a snarl. 'I would only give you a weapon if I could be certain you would use it on yourself.'

'Are matters so dismal that I must consider self murder?'

'Better death by your own hand than to let the tsar's torturer have his way with you.'

'It will not come to that.' Rob tried and failed to inject confidence into the words.

'If it does, remember to keep your mouth shut about the rest of us. There is no reason we should suffer just because you could not stay away from that whore.'

'She is not—'

'You've tupped her. Do not bother to deny it. We all saw that well-satisfied look on your face every time you returned from your rambles around the city. You're likely to end up the same way her husband did, with the fire licking at your boots.'

In a rush, Rob remembered his arrest. The tsar's guards had been waiting for him when he left Jane's house. He supposed he'd brought it on himself. He had been warned. But he did not understand why Vaughan was so angry. That he and Crew had been allowed to visit the prison argued that only Rob was to suffer for associating with Doctor Bomelius's widow.

The solid door closed behind Harry Vaughan with an ominous thud. The sound of a key turning in the lock reinforced Rob's knowledge that he was in serious trouble.

Exhausted, his mind drifted as the cold slowly seeped out of his bones and was replaced by warmth and drowsiness. He wondered, as he had once before, if Vaughan would feel the same if his beloved queen of hearts should find herself in Jane Bomelius's predicament. Then his wayward thoughts shifted to Rosamond as he'd last seen her, splendid in her anger. They had not parted on the best of terms, although he could not now remember why it was that they had quarreled.

Would his wife enjoy being a widow? He imagined that she would. Widows assumed complete control of their lives and fortunes. Even though Rosamond had already claimed similar rights and privileges for herself, she'd be glad to be freed from the burden of a living husband.

He took consolation in the knowledge that she would not remarry. She'd never take the risk of losing all she'd gained by his death. As he drifted into a dreamless and restful sleep, a tiny smile curved his lips upward at the thought.

Twenty-Six

'Are you certain we can be private here?' Nick Baldwin asked.

'As near as matters.' They were in the stables at Chelsea Manor. Rosamond resumed running one gloved hand over the flank of a gentle gray mare. There were hedgehog-skin brushes available to groom the horses, but she preferred this less abrasive means.

She'd had a horse of her own when she was a girl – a roan gelding named Courtier. She'd taken him to Derbyshire with her when she'd been sent there to be trained as a gentlewoman. After Courtier fell ill and died, she had vowed never to allow herself to grow so attached to an animal again. She had succeeded admirably in keeping this promise to herself . . . until she acquired Watling.

'Have you something to tell me?' she asked.

A sound of frustration escaped him. 'I must ask the same of you.'

It had been nearly six weeks since they'd last met. Rosamond had left court a fortnight earlier. For most of that time she had tried, unsuccessfully, to discover who had been behind the attack on Lady Mary. Rosamond could understand why Master Baldwin, a mere merchant, had not been able to meet with her at court, but once she'd returned to Chelsea he might have made the short journey from Billingsgate at any time. He had gone to some trouble to establish himself as her steward. There had been no need to hide such a visit.

The cheerful sound of whistling alerted her to the approach of a stable boy. It was not yet time to lead the horses outside and water them, although Rosamond knew that this was done several times a day. Most likely he was coming to muck out the stalls.

One of Baldwin's gloved hands snaked out to catch her arm. 'We cannot risk being overheard.'

The footsteps grew louder each time hobnailed boots struck the wooden floor. In mere seconds, the lad would round a corner and see them.

Rosamond's objections died on her lips when she caught sight of the expression on Baldwin's face. Without a word, she left the mare munching contentedly on peas and beans that had been dried and crushed and mixed with the chaff and motioned for him to follow her to the tack room.

After he made a slow circuit of the room, making Rosamond wonder if he expected to find a spy sheltering beneath a pile of spare horse blankets, he took up a position in front of the only door. So long as he stood there, it could not be opened.

Rosamond upended a leather bucket to use as a footrest and then seated herself on a bench with her back braced against the wall. She crossed her arms beneath her breasts and fixed him with a hard stare. 'What news have you brought?'

'First I must ask you a question. Did Lady Mary truly contract the pox?'

Rosamond frowned. Had Walsingham failed to share the information she'd sent him with Nick Baldwin? 'She was poisoned.'

'I feared as much.'

'You should have been told.' When he narrowed his eyes at her, she recounted her brief conversation with Henry Leveson as she'd been leaving Windsor. 'He claimed to be the principal secretary's man, but I have not seen him since, nor can I think of any reason why am I likely to. Did he tell me the truth? Is he in Walsingham's pay?'

'Players are often used as spies.'

'Oh, I do not doubt he works for someone, but is it Walsingham or some other?'

Baldwin shifted his weight, clearly uncomfortable with her question. 'I am not in Sir Francis's confidence.'

'Will he agree to see you if you request an audience?'

'If I have something of importance to report, I will make sure the information reaches him.'

Rosamond's eyes narrowed. Did he have access to Walsingham or not? It scarce mattered, she supposed, since he was the only person available to carry news of her discovery to the principal secretary.

'The poison used was yew.' In as succinct a manner as possible, she explained how she had reached that conclusion.

'You are certain that someone in this household was responsible? Anyone could obtain yew, and make use of it again.'

Rosamond stood, kicking the bucket out of her way. It was not in her nature to sit still for long. 'Not just one of the servants. One of her *women*. Ticey, Nan, Madge, and Bess were with her in the

Wardrobe of Robes and at Windsor. I favor Margaret Ellerker, but I have found not a shred of evidence to condemn her.'

'Have a care, Rosamond,' Baldwin said when she had expounded upon Madge's extreme religious views. 'If you have the right of it and she realizes that you suspect her, your own life may be in danger.'

'I am far more clever than she is.' Rosamond did not consider this boasting. Noticing she was trailing strands of hay, she bent to brush them from her skirt. She tried to sound casual as she asked, 'If Lady Mary had died, what would have happened to the treaty?'

'Perhaps nothing.'

Rosamond's eyes narrowed. 'What do you mean?'

Baldwin looked uncomfortable. 'The queen met with Pissemsky in a private audience four days ago. Doctor Robert Jacobi served as translator. Fortunately, Jacobi is also a friend of the Muscovy Company. According to him, the prospect of an English bride for Ivan was broached, but when Pissemsky mentioned Lady Mary's name, Her Grace remarked that Lady Mary was not likely to please the tsar.'

'Because she is disfigured?' Rosamond strove to remain calm, but her mind was racing, remembering what Baldwin had told her about the tsar's violent reaction to being thwarted.

'According to Jacobi, Queen Elizabeth said Lady Mary's beauty was negligible. She praised her virtue but called that her only ornamentation. When the Russian ambassador insisted that the tsar was set upon Lady Mary and no other as his bride, the queen informed him that she had recently been ill with smallpox. Her Grace insisted that Pissemsky postpone meeting her until she completes her recovery.'

'Does Queen Elizabeth want Lady Mary to go to Muscovy as the tsar's bride or not?'

Baldwin gave a rueful shake of his head. 'It is impossible to know. Her Majesty never shows her hand. And yet, even if she does not intend to permit the marriage, I have no doubt that she will pretend to favor the union of Ivan with an English princess. Queen Elizabeth is well aware that to do otherwise would place every English person resident in Russia in danger. If she must, in return for trade concessions, I am certain the queen will eventually agree to sell her cousin to the tsar.'

'And if Lady Mary had died?' Rosamond asked again.

Baldwin looked thoughtful. 'No doubt a substitute would have been found. The queen has other cousins. I have heard that some are far more fair than Lady Mary.' In a bemused voice, he added, 'Someone told me so only recently, but I cannot remember who it was.'

Rosamond realized she was pacing and forced herself to stop when she reached the far side of the tack room. She turned to look back at Master Baldwin. 'If there are factions at court opposed to a treaty with Muscovy, could there not also be factions in favor of one, but opposed to an alliance that would give the earl of Huntingdon greater influence?'

'There cannot be all that many eligible women, and even fewer who would be so anxious to marry the tsar that she would sanction the murder of her rival.'

'Well may you scoff at such an idea, but consider this – women are mere pawns in the games played by powerful men. Tell Walsingham to look hard at those of the queen's kinsmen who have most to gain from bartering a sister or a daughter for advancement at court.'

'Walsingham does not take orders, Rosamond. He gives them.'

'Convince him.' Exasperation had her curling her hands into fists and wishing she could pound on something to vent her frustration. 'There must be something we can do to protect Lady Mary.'

Baldwin said nothing. He did not seem to be listening. Leaning against the door, he had a faraway look in his eyes. Rosamond was about to demand his attention when he abruptly came to life.

'You believe that someone in the Wardrobe of Robes that day poisoned Potter, someone who was at court for Yuletide.'

'Have I not said so? One of Lady Mary's women.'

He shook his head. 'There was another person present that day at Whitehall. You mentioned a Sir Jerome. Was his surname Bowes?'

Frowning, Rosamond nodded. 'I saw him at Windsor, too. Who is he?'

'A far more likely villain than any of your companions. Bowes hopes to be named English Ambassador to Muscovy. Logic would suggest he'd want Lady Mary to prosper so that he can escort her to Moscow himself, but he is the very man who spoke of royal cousins more beautiful than she is. I believe you have the right of it, Rosamond. Bowes has another bride in mind for the tsar, one more likely than Lady Mary Hastings to dance to his tune.'

Twenty-Seven

Although he did not linger at Chelsea Manor, Nick took the time to set up a better means of communication between them before he left. Rosamond could only dispatch an order for a bolt of silk to the warehouse in Billingsgate once without arousing suspicion, especially since Sir Jerome Bowes knew of Nick's ties to Muscovy. Although the risk that Bowes would find out was slight, Nick preferred to take no chances with Rosamond's safety.

'Send word to me at Willow House,' he instructed. 'You can have Melka hail a wherry and pay the boatman to deliver a letter.'

'You would have me put something in writing?' Rosamond could not quite hide her sarcasm.

'Nothing of importance. It is the receipt of the letter that will signal that you have news, or are in need of my assistance. But you must think of a way to order your servants to fetch me without delay when you do write.'

'Charles can do it.'

'Charles?' The name was unfamiliar. 'Can he be trusted to keep quiet your business to himself?'

'Oh, yes.' Her smile held more than a hint of mischief. 'He is a mute.' Removing her right glove, she tugged off one of her rings, a distinctive piece of jewelry made in the shape of a rose with a single colored stone at the center. 'Show him this. He knows it is mine. Then explain what it is he must do.'

An hour later, Nick was back in London. Early the next day, he took the ferry across the Thames from Billingsgate. At Willow House, he showed Rosamond's ring to Charles and gave him his instructions. The fellow grasped the situation at once, which relieved Nick's mind, but he also wanted a favor to secure his good will.

The cat, Watling, missed Rosamond most terribly. He had been making his unhappiness known in a variety of unpleasant ways. The cook was threatening to leave and the other servants had taken to stuffing wool in their ears when they went to bed because Watling yowled so loudly all through the night.

Charles might be mute, but he was not deaf, and he made his

wishes abundantly clear. Nick was to take the cat away with him and keep him until Mistress Jaffrey returned home.

Watling allowed Nick to pick him up and stroke him, but he fought tooth and claw against being stuffed into a large basket and carried to the ferry. It was that evening in Billingsgate before he stopped hissing every time anyone came close to him.

His lap full of purring, well fed feline, Nick considered what to do next. He was worried about Rosamond. As long as she was convinced that there was a poisoner in the household, she would not be content to wait and watch. She would ask questions and so risk becoming the killer's next target.

He needed to keep a closer eye on her, but he dared not go to Chelsea again unless she sent for him. Too many visits from her 'steward' and people would wonder why Rosamond needed to keep such a close eye on him. Stewards were supposed to take charge of estates during the owner's absence.

Had one of Lady Mary's waiting gentlewomen been involved in Potter's murder? Rosamond had given him a few salient facts about each of them. Margaret Ellerker, from Yorkshire, was pretty and pious and unforgiving of sinners. A Herefordshire native, Anne Morgan was brave, ambitious, and excited by the prospect of traveling to Muscovy. Elizabeth Farnham hailed from Leicestershire. She was the superstitious one, seeing signs and portents of doom every time she turned around. Many of these came to pass, in Rosamond's opinion, because the young woman was also afflicted with an appalling degree of clumsiness.

Nick speculated about Mistress Farnham's belief in the supernatural. It suggested a way to send a message to Rosamond without attracting undue attention. There were drawbacks to the plan, but not enough to make him abandon it. The next morning, as a precaution, he would set certain events in motion.

In his other endeavor, Nick was less successful. Sir Francis Walsingham was at court. So was Sir Jerome Bowes. Nearly two weeks passed before Nick managed to meet with the queen's principal secretary at Barn Elms.

'Be brief, I pray you,' Walsingham greeted him. 'Queen Elizabeth arrives here in five days' time and I have many matters left to attend to.'

'Give thanks that Her Gracious Majesty only plans to dine and will not stay the night.' In spite of the grave matters on his mind,

Nick could not quite hide his amusement. The entire manor was in a state of chaos and he'd never seen Walsingham so flustered. Even his collar – the plain white linen band he preferred to a ruff – was askew.

'How would you know? You have been spared a royal visit altogether.'

'There was that incident some years ago,' Nick reminded him, 'when the queen proposed to honor my neighbor at Leigh Abbey. The preparations started weeks in advance. Had they come to fruition, the queen's harbingers would have arrived ahead of Her Grace with the royal bed and other furnishings to displace the usual occupants of the chambers Queen Elizabeth was to use and all their possessions. You will be spared that inconvenience and saved the expense of cleaning up after members of the court have made free with your house and their horses and the carts carrying their baggage have left your land rutted and despoiled.'

'There is still the expense of providing entertainment for Her Grace after the meal.' Walsingham waved Nick into a chair. 'The queen is not one to be content with a juggler and a band of minstrels.'

'May I suggest a play? I hear good things about a young fellow with the Earl of Sussex's Men, one Henry Leveson. And he is already your man, is he not? That is what he claimed to Mistress Jaffrey just before she left Windsor.'

'He is.' Walsingham looked at him through narrowed eyes, as if he did not like admitting to anything, even the obvious.

'And did he relay to you Mistress Jaffrey's message concerning poison?'

'He did. Your young friend waxes fanciful. Lady Mary was stricken with the pox, from which she has now recovered.'

Nick had to struggle to keep his voice level. It would do him no good to shout at the queen's principal secretary. 'I am sorry to have to contradict you, Sir Francis, but the truth is otherwise. Mistress Jaffrey may not have her foster mother's expertise with poisons, but neither is she the sort who indulges in foolish fancies.'

In brief, he sketched out Rosamond's reasoning and the conclusion she had reached.

'Yew?' Walsingham repeated.

'Yew.' Nick's voice was firm. 'Easy to obtain. Easy to administer. It is possible the poisoner is someone with access to the household, someone present in the Wardrobe of Robes when Potter was killed and also at court at Yuletide. That would be the other waiting gentlewomen and Sir Jerome Bowes.'

A frown increased the depth of the lines etched in Walsingham's forehead. 'I will look into the matter.'

'And Mistress Jaffrey? She has heard not a word from your man Leveson since leaving court and I do much doubt that the Earl of Sussex's Men will perform at Chelsea in the near future. The household is not known to encourage players. How is she to send you word should she discover more?'

'Your Mistress Jaffrey appears to manage.' Walsingham's dry tone hinted at disapproval. 'Her assignment was to observe, not investigate.'

'That pigeon is already out of its coop, and you have left her without any means to send for help should the need arise.'

Nick could almost hear the thoughts tumbling around in the other man's head. 'No doubt *you* have a way to communicate with her.'

'If needs must.'

Accurately reading an opponent was one of Walsingham's skills. 'What do you want?'

'The results of your investigation. Pissemsky cannot leave England until spring. Time aplenty for another attack on Lady Mary. Do you think Rosamond Jaffrey will stand idly by if that happens? She'd risk her own life to protect another, and could well lose it.'

Walsingham ended the staring match by rising from behind his work table and striding to a window that looked out over the gardens. One hand came up to rest against the side of the casement. 'I have a daughter,' he said after a moment. 'I understand your concern. But for reasons I have no intention of explaining, the world must continue to believe Lady Mary was ill, not poisoned.' There was a look of wry amusement in Walsingham's eyes when he turned to look at Nick again, a sight far more alarming than his ire. 'I will send word to you if my agents discover anything you should know, and you may share that intelligence with Mistress Jaffrey. Until then, Master Baldwin, our business is at an end.'

Twenty-Eight

'Can you see anything?' Bess tipped her head back so far that she was in danger of falling over and landing in a welter of skirts.

Rosamond glanced upward. She had been told that the stars formed patterns, but she'd never been able to pick them out. An archer? A scorpion? A crab? As far as she could see, there were only bright points of light sprinkled at random through the blackness above.

'Are you warm enough, my lady?' Ever solicitous, Nan stood close beside Lady Mary as if ready to catch her should she become dizzy.

The precaution was unnecessary. Lady Mary had been growing stronger every day. She had resumed walking for exercise, although it was unusual for her to be out of doors after dark. On this particular evening, she and her three waiting gentlewomen had ventured into the gardens out of curiosity, intrigued by Bess's claim that they would be able to see the approach of the Great Conjunction in the sky overhead.

The Great-Lot-of-Nonsense, Rosamond thought. She'd leafed through a book Bess was reading on the subject. It claimed that the alignment of the planets foretold a disaster of Biblical proportions. Only the gullible believed such tales, but Bess was as credulous as a child when it came to seeing omens in ordinary things. It did not surprise Rosamond that she had worked herself into a frenzy of excitement over such a spectacular portent.

Small signs of things to come or a grand foreshadowing, worry about the future seemed to Rosamond to be a waste of time. It was the present that needed tending to. She continued to be vigilant in watching over Lady Mary and kept a close eye on her waiting gentle-women, Madge in particular. So far, no one had put a foot wrong.

'I have forgotten my snoskyn!' Lady Mary exclaimed, belatedly noticing the empty plaquette on the velvet belt she wore. A half dozen other trinkets hung from it, everything from a small pair of scissors to a miniature portrait of her favorite brother. 'Fetch it for me, Rosamond. My hands grow cold.'

Rosamond hesitated, but she told herself there was safety in numbers. No one was likely to harm Lady Mary before witnesses.

Still, she chafed at the delay when it took longer than she expected to find the small hand warmer in Lady Mary's bedchamber. By the time she chanced upon the snoskyn at the back of a cupboard, nearly a quarter of an hour had passed. A glance out the window at the top of the stairwell showed her four distinct shapes lit by starlight.

Although it was not her fault that the hand warmer had been difficult to find, guilt lent speed to Rosamond's steps. Lady Mary's hands would be well nigh frozen by now. She took the narrow, winding flight of stone steps at a run. Halfway down, rounding a bend, she hit a slick patch and her feet flew out from under her. She was moving so fast that she could not catch herself. She bounced off one wall, then another.

Instinct had her throwing her arms over her head, but she had no way to protect the rest of her body. She tumbled headlong, out of control, bouncing off every step on the way to the bottom. She landed on her right side and lay there, shaken, her mind as rattled as her bones.

After a moment, she felt rational enough to assess her injuries. Her back and buttocks and elbows all throbbed. Slowly, she flexed one leg, then the other. Her arms worked, too. Nothing seemed to be broken, although she knew she must be bruised from head to toe. She gave silent thanks for the layers of clothing she wore. Without all that padding, she'd have suffered far worse damage.

Getting to her feet was painful, but not excruciatingly so. When she was upright and had retrieved Lady Mary's snoskyn from the corner where it had landed, she made a halfhearted attempt to brush herself off, then decided it was not worth the effort. Nothing was torn. The cloak she wore over her other garments would hide any streaks of dirt when she went back out into the darkness. Later, Melka would know something had happened – she'd be the one who'd have to clean and mend Rosamond's kirtle – but no one else needed to find out that she had been so clumsy as to tumble down a flight of stairs.

As Rosamond repaired the damage to her coif and adjusted her hood, she looked back up the stairwell. She had already taken overlong to perform a simple task and no one had come looking for her. A few more minutes could scarce make any difference.

Gingerly, painfully aware of every movement, Rosamond ascended to the point where she had lost her footing. Slipping off her gloves, she felt the surface of one stone step, then the next. She was not certain what she was looking for. This close to an outside wall, it would not have surprised her to come upon a patch of ice. Then, too, the stone itself dipped a little in the middle, worn down by constant traffic.

She moved on to the next step and gasped when her searching fingers came in contact with a smooth substance that was neither stone nor ice. It spread across the entire step in a long, thin line. Rosamond scratched at it with her fingernail. Lifting her fingertips to her nose, she sniffed. She had not been mistaken. It was candlewax.

Had a servant been careless? It was possible. Wax dripping from candles was by no means uncommon. It puddled and hardened where it fell.

She ran her hand over the spill on the stone step. If someone gestured with the hand that held a candle . . . .

Frowning, she used the knife she kept in her boot to scrape the step clean. She did not want anyone else to slip and fall. All the while she told herself that no one in this house meant her any harm. No one knew of her mission here. She had been circumspect in watching over Lady Mary. Furthermore, anyone who came this way might have slipped on the wax. There could have been no certainty that she would be the one to fall.

She told herself that repeatedly all the way back to the garden with Lady Mary's snoskyn.

Bess claimed to have located the planet Jupiter in the sky above and was chattering excitedly about Saturn and Cancer and Leo. Her enthusiasm appeared to have infected the others. Lady Mary, staring in rapt attention at the heavens, accepted the snoskyn without rebuking Rosamond for the delay in fetching it. Nan's benign smile suggested she shared Rosamond's skepticism but she, too, kept her eyes on the firmament. Even Madge, who was wont to deride Bess for her superstitious beliefs, stole furtive looks at the stars, as if she could not quite keep herself from wondering what purpose God had in mind with the Great Conjunction.

Rosamond stared at the other woman. Could Madge have crept back into the house under cover of darkness and drizzled wax on the stair?

Preposterous!

Rosamond put the possibility out of her mind. A fall was much too chancy as a means of killing someone. Therefore it must have been an accident.

Twenty-Nine

A fortnight after Nick's meeting with Walsingham at Barn Elms, the principal secretary's officious protégé from the house in Seething Lane paid a visit to the warehouse in Billingsgate.

'Has he kept his promise?' Nick asked. 'Did he look into Sir Jerome Bowes's associates and Mistress Ellerker's background?'

The secretary's secretary looked affronted by the suggestion that there had ever been any doubt about the matter. 'We also delved into the histories of Anne Morgan, Elizabeth Farnham, and Beatrice Unton.'

The fellow was stiff-necked and pinch-faced, but he had brought information. Nick sent Mistress Saunders for cakes and ale and invited Walsingham's man into the room Nick's late mother had liked to call her parlor. The best chair, well padded with cushions stuffed with wool from his own flocks in Northamptonshire, was already occupied. Watling opened one green eye long enough to cause the messenger to blanch. The cat curled his lip, showing the tip of one sharp tooth, but made no objection when Nick resettled him in his lap.

Walsingham's minion remained standing, his pale blue eyes darting from the chased-silver clock to a delicate green glass vase filled with an arrangement of dried flowers.

'Souvenirs of my travels,' Nick said.

They were also proof of his success as a trader, as were the carved figures on the mantel over the fireplace and the huge *mappa mundi* hanging on one wall. Tables covered with Turkey carpets might have become more common in recent years, but few were used as background to display such fine treasures.

'Bring the chair by the wall over here,' Nick instructed when one of his apprentices appeared with the refreshments Mistress Saunders had prepared.

The lad did not wear livery, as the servant in a great house might, but he was neatly dressed in a plain linen shirt and dark fustian breeches and coat. After he'd placed the tray on the table at Nick's elbow he followed orders and then departed as silently as he'd materialized.

Nick gestured for his visitor to sit. He poured ale from a Dutch-made pitcher into two finely crafted cups. Although he was nowhere near as patient as he wished to seem, he waited until the other man was seated and provided with both food and drink before sending him an expectant look. There was more to be gained by cultivating the fellow than by alienating him.

Nick's guest ate two of the little seed cakes Mistress Saunders had provided, drank deep, and refilled his cup from the pitcher before he made any attempt to satisfy Nick's curiosity. Smacking his thin lips, he offered what passed for a smile. 'Nothing untoward has been uncovered about any of them, unless you count Sir Jerome's too-hasty temper.'

'Mayhap I should decide for myself.' With an effort, Nick managed to keep his voice mild and unthreatening.

Looking bored, the minion recounted the basic facts about Sir Jerome Bowes. Born in Staffordshire. To France with the earl of Lincoln as a young man. One of the queen's gentlemen. Knighted by the earl of Sussex in the year following the rising of the northern earls. Abroad in the embassy of Sir Philip Sidney to the court of Rudolf the Second. Briefly banished from Queen Elizabeth's court after a quarrel with the earl of Leicester. Resident in Paris for the last few years until the December just past. Upon his return, he had received a grant of lands from the Crown worth £100 per annum.

Nick frowned. In Paris in December? It had been mid-December when Griffith Potter died. Bowes must have gone to the Wardrobe of Robes immediately after his return to England. Had he known Lady Mary would be there?

Then another thought occurred to him. 'Is Bowes one of Walsingham's spies?'

The minion had just opened his mouth. It snapped shut and pursed into a thin, hard line.

Nick made a sound of disgust. 'I see. I have no need to know. Go on, then. What else can you tell me?'

'None of the women poses any threat to Lady Mary Hastings.'

Nick let his silence speak for him. He had a long wait before the other man heaved a world-weary sigh and resumed his report.

'Mistress Margaret Ellerker is the only child of a minor Yorkshire gentleman. In his will, Ellerker asked that Lady Huntingdon take his daughter into her household. Her ladyship has trained a great many young gentlewomen over the years, although she herself is childless. Most of her wards have been heiresses. Margaret Ellerker is one of the least of them – no marriage portion to speak of. When her education was complete and there was no acceptable gentleman willing to marry her without a larger dowry, Lady Huntingdon sent her to Lady Mary as a waiting gentlewomen.'

'Trained where? Sent where? I was under the impression that Lady Mary and Lady Huntingdon shared a household.'

'The earl and his countess occupy the King's Manor in the city of York when not at court. Lady Mary, for the most part, has lived at the Huntingdon family seat, Ashby-de-la-Zouch in Leicestershire. Only recent events have required the countess's presence at the side of her sister-in-law. Huntingdon took a short-term lease on Chelsea Manor, that they might be housed at a convenient distance from the queen's principal residences.'

'Has Margaret Ellerker any other family?' Nick asked.

'None, nor any friends outside the Huntingdon circle. She is renowned for her piety, even in that set.'

Nick had always been a trifle suspicious of those who announced their evangelical leanings to the world, but he kept that opinion to himself. 'Nothing suspicious about Mistress Ellerker, then?'

He could not say he was surprised. The more time that passed without a message from Rosamond, the more likely it seemed to Nick that Bowes, rather than a member of Lady Mary's household, was the one responsible for the poisonings.

'Nothing.' The minion cleared his throat. 'To continue. Anne Morgan's grandmother was at court in the queen's father's day, but her parents are of little consequence. Their holdings are situated close to a manor owned by Lady Hunsdon and that noblewoman stood as one of Mistress Morgan's godmothers. That is why, when she was of an age for it, the young woman was placed in the house-hold of Lady Howard of Effingham to be trained for service. Lady Howard is Lady Hunsdon's daughter.'

He paused in his recital to help himself to another seed cake and quaff more ale.

'Why did Nan Morgan leave Lady Howard's service for Lady Mary's?' Nick asked.

Annoyance left a deep crease in the fellow's forehead. 'No doubt some new, younger gentlewomen arrived to be trained and there was no more room for her. One household can hold only so many women.'

In other words, he did not know the answer. Nick gestured for him to continue.

'Elizabeth Farnham came straight to Lady Mary from Loughborough in Leicestershire.'

'What family has she?'

'A brother only. Her parents are dead. The last name you asked about, Beatrice Unton, had an even worse time of it.'

'Lady Mary's tiring maid?' She went by Ticey, he recalled. He'd nearly left her name out of his request for information, so inconsequential was her place in the household.

Walsingham's protégé nodded. 'She's from Berkshire, near Faringdon, distant kin to Sir Edward Unton. Possibly his own illegitimate daughter, although no one will confirm that. She was in service to Unton's wife before being rescued and sent to Lady Mary.'

'Rescued?' Nick tried to remember what he knew of the Unton family. 'Sir Edward died a few months ago. Does that signify?'

The minion chuckled. 'It led to his widow being put in their son's custody. It seems she has suffered bouts of insanity for many years. Young Beatrice did well to escape from her service.'

'Who helped her?'

'Does it matter? The Untons have no other ties to Lady Mary Hastings or to this current business.'

All in all, Nick thought the information Walsingham's spies had uncovered was useless. It neither condemned nor exonerated anyone, but mayhap Rosamond could make more of it than he had.

Thirty

The crone wore an academic gown shiny with age. The hood concealed most of her face, leaving only her mouth visible. It pursed, blew out a breath, and muttered, '*Vidi, vidi, vidi.*'

'I saw. I saw. I saw,' Rosamond translated. 'What is that supposed to mean?'

'You understood her?' Lady Mary asked.

Rosamond could feel the old woman's gaze upon her, sharp as a poniard, but at the moment it was the noblewoman's suspicious tone of voice that caused her greater concern. In the awkward silence that followed the question, she debated how much she dared admit. That she had a facility for languages was no sin, but Latin was not generally taught to girls. No more than Russian or Polish were. She forced a laugh.

'I have a few words only, my lady. It is no great matter.' Lady Mary continued to look skeptical. 'It is part of a famous quotation taught to schoolboys: I came, I saw, I conquered. It seemed strange to me that the soothsayer repeated only part of it.'

'It does not seem strange to me,' Bess interrupted. 'She is here to *see* into our future.'

Everyone's attention shifted back to the visitor in the black gown. As if such a sound was expected of her, the old woman cackled.

Rosamond repressed the derisive comment that hovered on her lips. Her hands lightly clasped in front of her, she assumed an attentive attitude.

It was Bess who had first heard of the soothsayer, from her brother. He claimed the old woman's predictions were infallible. Rosamond wondered if Farnham was as superstitious as his sister. Did he see portents in burnt porridge and omens in overturned baskets, too? With all the fuss of late about the Great Conjunction, even those who would not ordinarily be taken in by charlatans had begun to believe their fate was written in the stars.

Dame Starkey had been well paid to come to Chelsea. She'd balked at first, claiming that she did not like to travel any farther

from her home than Westminster or Southwark. Offering her double
her usual fee had changed her mind.

Under Rosamond's critical gaze, the hired prognosticator
arranged a number of items on a table in the small chamber she
had requested for the reading. First came a small wooden bowl,
then a flask, and then a deck of cards with odd-looking figures
painted on them. Several rolls of parchment tied with velvet ribbons
emerged next from the depths of a leather bag. Last of all, she
produced a burned-down candle in a black candlestick. With great
solemnity, she relit the taper.

'Be seated,' she said in a low voice, and settled her own bulk in
the best chair in Lady Mary's apartments, the one padded with
sheep's wool and trimmed with elegant gold fringe.

On the opposite side of the table, Lady Mary subsided into a
Glastonbury chair while the rest of them − Rosamond, Nan, Bess,
and a sour-faced Madge, took their places on plain wooden stools.
A long silence followed, during which the fortune teller did nothing
more exciting than stare into the candle flame.

Rosamond fidgeted. The single charcoal brazier placed close to
Dame Starkey provided insufficient warmth for the rest of them on
this cold afternoon in late February. Outside the windows, a winter
wind gusted, rattling the shutters and sending icy drafts straight
through every chink in the casements.

At last the soothsayer spoke: 'I see a long journey.'

'To what place?' Lady Mary demanded.

'A distant land. A foreign place where the weather is even colder
than it is here and everyone perforce wears fur.'

'Muscovy,' Lady Mary breathed, although none of her waiting
gentlewomen were supposed to know aught of the plan to wed her
to Tsar Ivan.

'I have cast a horoscope for each of you.' The old woman placed
the stubby fingers of one hand atop the rolled-up charts.

The announcement startled Rosamond. 'How is that possible?
You would need to know when we were born.'

'I was provided with the time and date of your nativity, Mistress
Jaffrey, and those of the others here gathered. Come and see.'

'I will have my horoscope first,' Lady Mary interrupted.

The hooded head nodded in acquiescence. 'As you wish.' Her
hand hovered over the rolls of parchment before selecting one and
offering it to the woman who had paid her fee.

Rosamond frowned. There were no markings on the outside of the rolls. How did Dame Starkey know which belonged to Lady Mary? The obvious answer was that it did not matter.

Lady Mary unrolled her chart and held it close to the candle to read it. Even a brief glimpse of the page was enough to tell Rosamond that it was typical of its kind. The signs of the zodiac were all present. The relative positions of these astrological houses were supposed to signify what influence the planets would have on Lady Mary's future.

'I do not understand what any of this means,' the lady in question wailed.

'The stars are favorable,' Dame Starkey intoned in a solemn voice.

'But what does that *mean*? Am I to wed? Will I be empress of Russia?'

'That is one possible future. You will travel, of that you may be certain.'

Speaking in a low murmur, she continued making predictions for Lady Mary. Rosamond did not bother to listen. It was nonsense, all of it!

When Dame Starkey finished with the noblewoman, she picked up another chart, claiming it was Nan's. It was as unreadable as the first, giving the fortune teller leave to interpret it as she willed.

'Do you see a long journey for me, too?' Nan asked. 'Will I go with Lady Mary to Muscovy?'

Dame Starkey lifted her hand, one stubby finger pointed. 'You, Mistress Morgan, will travel far.'

She repeated her performance, including the vague mumbling, and then moved on to Bess and Madge. She left Rosamond until last.

'Travel? A tall, dark stranger? Wealth?' Rosamond did not bother to unroll the chart Dame Starkey handed her.

'All those. Or mayhap none. The stars do not lie, but neither do they always show the future clearly. Many interpretations are possible.'

'But I am certain that you have some means to narrow down the possibilities, especially if you are well paid to do so.'

Dame Starkey ignored the offensive remark and busied herself pouring water from the flask into the bowl. 'Will you try your luck as a scryer, Mistress Jaffrey?'

Intrigued, and perhaps a bit envious, the other women edged closer to the table.

'What must she do?' Lady Mary asked.

'Look deep into the water. Stare at the way the candle flame is reflected in the liquid. Think of the questions you wish to ask and in the patterns that form you will find your answers.'

To refuse would be churlish, but Rosamond was determined not to give the soothsayer any satisfaction. She glanced into the water. 'I see nothing.'

'Look again.'

Rosamond sighed and did so, blinking in surprise when a face – Rob's face – seemed to swim up out of the depths. It was gone a moment later.

Imagination, she told herself.

'If one means does not avail you, another will.' Dame Starkey removed the bowl of water and began to shuffle the deck of cards. Her motions were slow and methodical. By the time her hands stilled, every eye was fixed on them, even Rosamond's.

She placed the cards in a pattern, muttering to herself as she did so. Rosamond could discern no rhyme nor reason in any of it, but the fortune teller made a great show of interpreting what she saw. Yes, Rosamond would travel. Yes, there would be wealth. And there was a man with mole-colored hair.

Rosamond swallowed hard at that last pronouncement. Because of his distinctive hair color, Rob had answered to the name Mole throughout their childhood.

'No,' Dame Starkey corrected herself. 'I was wrong. You will not gain wealth. You will acquire *more* wealth.'

'Are you already a rich woman, Rosamond?' Nan sounded a trifle put out not to have known this already.

Rosamond was spared having to answer because the fortune teller was still droning on, repeating a variation of the same things she had already told each of the others. As she pretended to see Rosamond's future in the cards, the monotonous litany of predictions wove a spell, one that required an effort of will to break. Rosamond shook herself free only by rising abruptly to her feet. Her stool tipped over with a clatter that made the others jump.

'I can see no more.' Without further ado, Dame Starkey scooped up the tools of her trade and stuffed them back into her leather bag.

'Dame Starkey?' Bess ventured in a small, anxious voice. 'You have not spoken of the Great Conjunction. It will be upon us in less than a month. Will we survive it?'

'Do not trouble yourself about the doings of planets, child. Only the stars determine what will be. Besides, it is as likely that those two heavenly bodies will meet in the watery sign of Pisces as in one of the fiery signs of the trigon. I predict that the conjunction will occur close to the border of Aries.'

More nonsense, Rosamond thought as she righted her stool. 'Excellent,' she said aloud. 'That means we have no reason to live in fear and dread.'

'None at all,' Dame Starkey agreed.

'And yet,' Rosamond said, unable to resist baiting the old woman, 'learned men have written books about a coming apocalypse. At least a half dozen of them have been published in the last year to warn of what will happen after the Great Conjunction. Some say the world will end in November.' Others, for no good reason that Rosamond had been able to discern, had chosen 1588 as the year when disaster would strike England.

Before Dame Starkey could answer, Madge spoke up. 'Such speculation is not only wrong, it is sinful. The Great Conjunction predicts the coming of the third age of the angel Gabriel, when God will punish the neglect of his truth.'

'Those who think that are as deluded as the rest,' Nan objected.

The debate became heated, as it did every time the subject of the Great Conjunction was raised. Sensing that her opinion was no longer required, Dame Starkey finished packing the items she'd brought with her and moved away from the table.

'By your leave, my lady,' she said to Lady Mary, 'I will borrow this gentlewoman to help me to the water stairs.'

She thrust her bundle into Rosamond's arms and hobbled out of the room without giving either Lady Mary or Rosamond a chance to object.

Dame Starkey's limp disappeared a few steps beyond the door. She proceeded on her way with long, sure strides, confident that Rosamond would follow her. Halfway down the tree-lined path between house and river, she confounded Rosamond yet again by whirling around, seizing her arm and tugging her into the concealment of the evergreens. There snow still blanketed the ground. Rosamond's shoulder brushed against the branches, dislodging needles and releasing their pungent scent.

'I have something further to tell you, young Rosamond,' Dame Starkey said.

Suddenly wary, Rosamond froze. The woman might be old and

stout, but she was sturdily build. Rosamond's fingers twitched, aching to reach for her knife, but before she could suit action to thought, Dame Starkey flung back her hood.

For the first time, her features were visible. Rosamond blinked. There was something familiar about the dark eyes, and about the chin, too. 'Who are you? Who sent you?'

Ignoring the first question, the crone answered the second. 'I come to you from a merchant pretending to be a steward.'

Rosamond sent her an incredulous look. 'Master Baldwin?'

The old woman chuckled. 'Is that so difficult to believe?'

'It is if you have ever heard him rail against prognosticators. He calls your kind fig—'

'Figure-flingers. Yes, I know. But he makes an exception for that arch-conjurer, Doctor John Dee, and he has conceded that, for the most part, I do no harm.'

Although it seemed the soothsayer did know Master Baldwin, Rosamond remained wary. 'How could he be the one who sent you here? It was Bess who—'

'Was told my name and reputation by her brother? The same brother who sent her a book on the Great Conjunction? The brother, in truth, who has no idea he has been so obliging?'

Rosamond no longer doubted Dame Starkey's word. 'All your knowledge of the future – that came from Master Baldwin. He told you about Muscovy.'

'He did.' The old woman returned the hood to its former position, once again hiding her face.

'Have you a message for me?'

She nodded. 'I have been entrusted with a good deal more than that. Do not interrupt.'

A meek nod was all Rosamond had time for before Dame Starkey launched into a fast-paced summary of a report Baldwin had received. She did not say from whom, but Rosamond could guess. She already knew some of what she was hearing. None of the rest suggested any motive for murder.

Throughout Dame Starkey's recitation, the crone kept one eye on their surroundings, especially the path still visible through the trees. Rosamond cocked an ear, alert for approaching footsteps, but the only sounds in the winter silence were distant shouts from watermen on the Thames and the screech of a jay far overhead.

'If you have questions,' Dame Starkey said, 'I cannot answer them.

I have repeated everything he told me.' She took her pack from Rosamond and was already turning away when Rosamond spoke.

'You can answer one question. Given your profession, why is Master Baldwin willing to trust you?'

The old woman eyed the path but made no further move toward it. 'Ten years past, Nick Baldwin came looking for a fortune teller he believed was extorting money from his mother. Did you know her? Winifred Baldwin?'

Rosamond nodded. Mistress Baldwin had been a terrible and terrifying old woman, but she'd died nearly a decade ago. By Rosamond's reckoning, that would have been shortly after her son's meeting with Dame Starkey.

'She was my mother, too. Nick Baldwin is my half brother.'

Rosamond's mouth dropped open in astonishment. With the hood in place, she could no longer see Dame Starkey's eyes or chin, but now she knew why they had seemed familiar, and why Master Baldwin trusted her. Family members, even estranged family members, shared a bond one had to go to great lengths to sever.

This time it was the old woman who hesitated when Rosamond would have resumed their walk to the water stairs. 'Have you any message for me to take back to Nick?'

'I have learned nothing new.'

'Are you certain of that?' Before Rosamond could answer, Dame Starkey added, 'I am not a seer, but I have eyes that see. You have the remnants of a nasty bruise on your wrist. I saw it when you reached for your horoscope.'

'It is nothing. A tumble down the stairs.'

'Were you pushed?'

'Do you think I would hide it if I had been? I slipped. It was an accident.' Rosamond managed a laugh, but then she found herself telling Dame Starkey the whole story. 'For just a moment,' she added, 'I did wonder if someone had deliberately spread wax on the stair, but I was only being fanciful. No one has any cause to hurt me.'

'Are you certain of that? Think, child. Have you had any other accidents? Any other injuries? Has there been any other time when you . . . wondered?' Her sharp eyes caught Rosamond's twitch. 'Tell me.'

'It is *nothing*.'

'Tell me anyway.'

She sighed. 'We engaged in a battle with snowballs at court. A game. Only someone scooped up a rock along with the snow and it struck me in the head.'

'An accident?'

Dame Starkey's skepticism was contagious. Was it possible, Rosamond wondered, that she had been attacked? Twice?

'Think,' Dame Starkey bade her once again. 'Did anything happen just before either incident that would make someone afraid of what you might know?'

Of a sudden, Rosamond felt like the greatest fool in Christendom. How could she have been so blind to what was right in front of her? 'Shortly before I was struck with the snowball, I saw one of Lady Mary's waiting gentlewomen with a man. He seemed familiar, but I could not, and still cannot, put a name to him.'

'Which gentlewoman?'

'I cannot put a name to her, either. We were all dressed alike that day.'

'If you saw them, they could have seen you. What happened just before your fall down the stairs?'

'I may have shown too plainly my concern for leaving Lady Mary unguarded, but no more than that, and we have all been anxious that she not overexert herself.'

'Which of them could have followed you inside and set a trap?'

'Any of them. It was night. If the others were looking up at the sky, one might have slipped away for a few minutes under cover of darkness.'

'This attempt to harm you, like the first, appears to have been conceived on the spur of the moment. You must be ever vigilant. It is impossible to predict the actions of someone given to acting on impulse.'

Lady Mary's poisoning had been planned, Rosamond thought, but Griffith Potter's murder might have been yet another case of the killer taking advantage of an unexpected opportunity. Her mind beset by possibilities, Rosamond followed Dame Starkey back to the path. As she watched the old woman scramble down the water stairs and climb into the boat waiting to take her back to London, she had to fight the impulse to leave with her.

Thirty-One

After hearing what Dame Starkey had to say, Rosamond tried harder to delve into the lives of her companions at Chelsea Manor. The normal ebb and flow of conversation around the embroidery frame had given her some insights, but idle chatter was discouraged even there.

As always, Nan was the most willing to share information, especially if that allowed her an opportunity to boast a bit. So it was that Rosamond learned the identity of Lady Howard's mother, whose family were neighbors of Nan's in Herefordshire. She was Lady Hunsdon, wife of one of the queen's cousins, but on the Boleyn rather than the royal side. In consequence, Lady Howard had no claim to the throne and her daughters were unlikely to be considered as brides for the tsar.

'I am Lady Hunsdon's goddaughter and share the name she was born with.' Pride glowed in Nan's eyes, but she kept her voice low.

She and Rosamond shared a window seat. Lady Mary, Bess, and Madge occupied a settle a few feet away. Lady Huntingdon's chaplain stood facing them, his back to Nan and Rosamond. Doctor Treadwell read aloud from one of the 'improving' books the countess and her husband were so fond of. Today's selection was a pamphlet titled 'Doctor Fulke's answers to the Roman Testament.'

The text was a slight improvement over John Calvin's *Exposition of Job*. Treadwell had spent two full weeks working his way through that one. Rosamond much preferred the sort of books her foster mother read to her household. She'd never imagined she would wax nostalgic about Sir Thomas Hoby's translation of *The Courtier of Count Baldessar*, but listening to all four volumes of that tome in succession would be preferable to day after day of sermons and theological philosophizing.

Just as Rosamond bent her head close to Nan's to ask another question, Treadwell spun on his heel and bore down on them. A thin man, he was not physically imposing in the ordinary sense, but he knew how to look down that hawk nose of his with eyes that burned with religious fervor. His long, reddish-brown hair flared out beneath his black cap as he moved. What should have looked faintly ridiculous somehow became fearsome. A dragon breathing fire would not have been a more daunting sight. Instead of belching flames, Treadwell spewed out the threat of hell fire and damnation.

'Female idleness is the devil's playing field!'

Rosamond's fingers itched to slap that sanctimonious expression off the chaplain's face. A subtle pinch from Nan brought her to her senses. Drawing in a deep breath, she squeezed her eyes shut and fought for calm.

Nan stepped into the breech. 'Your pardon, sir. It was necessary to confer about which silks we should use next in our needlework.'

She gestured at the embroidery frame. The design of the small wall hanging was a colorful scene of King Solomon handing down judgment. Seeing this, Treadwell mellowed, although he did not look entirely convinced that Nan had told him the truth.

'Silence is a virtue,' he intoned. 'Speak only when you must and avoid idle chatter.' He started to turn away, then swung toward them again. 'Should any member of this household wish further instruction in the proper behavior of a good Christian woman, she has only to ask.'

'You are most generous with your time,' Lady Mary murmured. 'Should some of my women wish to avail themselves of your offer, they may do so with my blessing.'

I would rather walk barefoot over hot coals, Rosamond thought.

The chaplain's rule against casual conversation made it difficult for Rosamond to ask questions. The following day, just as she thought she might be about to worm confidences out of Bess Farnham, Treadwell came upon them. His accusing gaze went straight to the needle stuck in a section of the linen cloth Rosamond was supposed to be stitching.

'Idle hands! Idle chatter!'

'Are we never permitted to speak to each other?' Rosamond demanded.

Her boldness made him livid. He shook a long, bony finger at her, waggling it right under her nose. 'You must learn your place, mistress. As penance, you will read the preface to Thomas Underdowne's *Theseus and Ariadne*, which warns women against spending too much time with their gossips. That, Master Underdowne and I agree, is the cause of all manner of vice.'

'Doubtless you are correct,' Rosamond said through gritted teeth. 'I will endeavor to mend my ways.'

She managed to hold her tongue while he harangued her. Another five minutes passed before he continued on his way. The moment he was safely out of earshot, she turned to Bess.

'A lowly female should never be idle!' She jabbed her finger at the end of the other woman's nose, making her start and cross her eyes. With a twist, Rosamond turned it into a rude gesture she had observed at the Horse's Head Inn.

Bess clapped both hands over her mouth to contain her mirth, but her entire face was alight with amusement. 'It is a good thing Madge did not see that,' she said when she could manage speech. 'She'd be convinced you'd damned yourself for all eternity by showing such disrespect.'

'Is that not your opinion, too?'

'Oh, no. I will only warn you that a proper gentlewoman would never behave so.'

A few days later, they were in the brew house listening to a lecture on an improved method of cleaning the fermenting vats when Rosamond created an opportunity to take Madge aside.

'I have heard all this before,' she whispered, leaning close to the other woman, 'and the fumes are making my head ache.'

'I feel dizzy, too,' Madge admitted.

No one objected when they sought fresh air. No one noticed when Rosamond replaced the stopper in the small bottle she'd brought with her. She'd had to hold her breath while making sure Madge got a good whiff of it. Solicitous, she led her fellow waiting gentlewoman to a garden bench.

'It is too cold to sit,' Madge objected.

'I'd have thought you'd be accustomed to the cold. You come from the north, do you not?'

'York,' Madge agreed.

'Do you still have family there?'

Madge shook her head and suddenly her eyes were swimming with unshed tears. 'I became a ward of the earl of Huntingdon when my father died. The countess raised me. This is my home. They are my family. My only family.' A tear dropped onto the hands folded in her lap.

Rosamond did not let pity sway her. Madge might be pretty and gently born but, according to Dame Starkey, she was also poor. That made it most unusual that a nobleman would provide for her. 'Are you kin in truth?' she asked.

'I only wish I were. Mayhap then the earl would provide me with a dowry.'

Rosamond tried to think of a way to dig deeper but she had to be careful not to ask too many questions. She did not want to provoke an inquisition in return.

Madge swiped at her eyes and sniffed. 'I am an ungrateful sinner to complain about my lot in life. In truth, I thank the good Lord every day that I am part of so godly a household.' With that, she stood and marched purposefully back into the brew house.

Rosamond followed at a snail's pace. She did not know what to make of Madge. Her piety seemed genuine, if annoying. In Madge's shoes, she'd resent the earl and his countess, and mayhap Lady Mary, too.

'Here you are,' Nan said, startling Rosamond. 'Madge said you were feeling ill.'

'I am recovered. I was woolgathering.'

Linking her arm through Rosamond's, Nan drew her toward the brew house. 'Whither did your thoughts fly?'

'To dowries and the lack of them.'

Nan laughed. 'But you are already married.'

'And you know a gentleman presently on the Continent to make his fortune. Will he seek you out in Muscovy, do you think, if you travel there with Lady Mary?'

'Never doubt it. He would follow me to the ends of the earth if I desired it.' Nan's eyes sparkled.

Horse-faced she might be, but animation made her more than comely. Rosamond believed her when she said she could entice a man to do her bidding. 'I perceive he is more than a mere friend.'

Nan grinned. 'Harry? Mayhap he is, for all that he is a Welshman and a bit of a pirate, too.'

Herefordshire, where Nan had been born, bordered the Welsh counties. 'Have you known him a long time?'

'Since we were children. He is the only person I have ever met who is as ambitious as I am.'

'There are worse qualities to have in common,' Rosamond said.

As the next days passed, she learned more about both Nan and Madge, but always in tiny bits. Bess's history remained elusive. She was friendly enough in the stolen moments when Augustus Treadwell was not staring down his hawk-like nose at them, waiting to catch them in a misstep, but she was reluctant to talk about herself.

On the next occasion when they were alone together, one morning as they broke their fast, Rosamond tried asking Bess about Ticey instead. 'You were already in Lady Mary's service when Ticey arrived, were you not? What do you know about her?'

'It is a sad story.' Bess sipped barley water and nibbled a bit of cheese. 'Her former mistress was quite mad. She had strange fancies, one of them that Ticey was her husband's bastard. She took it out on the girl by boxing her ears and giving her privy nips.'

Rosamond's heart went out to the victim of such treatment. Most women did resent their husband's merrybegots. Lady Appleton had been a notable exception. Rosamond, the child her husband had fathered, had never been treated with anything but affection.

For a moment, feelings of guilt threatened to overwhelm her. She'd repaid all those years of love and devotion by creating a rift between them so wide and deep that it might never be mended. She must try, Rosamond told herself. When she was free of Lady Mary and all her responsibilities here, she would put her faith in the true meaning of family and—

'The earl of Leicester.'

Rosamond's attention snapped back to her companion. She'd missed most of what Bess had said. 'What has Leicester to do with Lady Unton?'

Bess looked startled by the sharpness of Rosamond's question, but she answered readily enough. 'She is not Lady Unton. Sir Edward Unton's widow, Ticey's former mistress, calls herself Lady Warwick because her first husband was the earl of Warwick, the elder brother of the present earl.'

'Then this Lady Warwick is the sister-in-law of the earl of Leicester?'

Bess nodded, her mouth full of bread. When she had swallowed she sighed. 'Lady Warwick's father was executed for treason on orders from her husband's father, the duke of Northumberland, and then he, the duke, was executed, too, and Lady Warwick's husband died soon after his release from the Tower of London. I would pity her, were it not for poor Ticey. She was like a timid little mouse when she first arrived at Ashby-de-la-Zouch, afraid of her own shadow.'

Rosamond ate her bread and cheese, all the while trying to recall what she knew about the duke of Northumberland. Her father, her stepfather, and Lady Appleton had been raised in his household, but that had been long before Rosamond's birth.

It scarce mattered. The bastard daughter of the second husband of a noblewoman, no matter who Lady Warwick might claim as kin, was not related to royalty. Ticey Unton had not tried to kill Lady Mary in order to pave her own way to the Russian throne.

Later, when an opportunity presented itself, Rosamond tried asking Ticey about Bess.

'Mistress Farnham's brother George is a toothsome gentleman,' Ticey confided. 'He, too, was taken into service in a noble household.'

'Which one?' Rosamond asked.

'It was not my place to ask, mistress.'

She did resemble a mouse, Rosamond thought, and could not find it in her heart to badger such a timid, self-effacing creature. It was not until Ticey returned to her duties that Rosamond remembered Melka's assessment of her. Haughty, she'd said. Could Ticey be both shy and proud? Rosamond could not answer that question any more than she could say with certainty who had murdered Griffith Potter and tried to kill Lady Mary.

Thirty-Two

'This is not a good time,' objected Walsingham's secretary, the same thin-lipped, spindle-shanked, officious fellow who had delivered Walsingham's report to Billingsgate.

'Get out of my way, sirrah.' Nick's voice was low and threatening and he added a shove for good measure.

Nothing short of a dagger in the back would have stopped him. He'd been trying for days to speak with the queen's principal secretary. He refused to be put off any longer.

Tenacious as a deerhound scenting its prey, the minion dogged Nick's heels all the way to Walsingham's study. Like the corresponding chamber at Barn Elms, the one in the house in Seething Lane contained a surfeit of paperwork. Much of it was sorted into a series of chests. One bore the label 'navy, havens & sea causes' while the contents of another were identified as 'religion and matters ecclesiastical'. The latter, Nick presumed, contained lists of recusants and the examinations of papists and priests.

The great man looked up from behind an enormous black desk. He scowled at the intruders but then motioned Nick forward and signaled for his man to leave.

'I suppose you have heard the latest news from Moscow,' Walsingham said when they were alone.

The mention of Muscovy took the wind out of Nick's sails. He braced for the worst. 'What news?'

'Tsar Ivan's current wife gave birth to a son. The boy was born the eighteenth day of October.'

Nick was not surprised that it had taken until now, nearly the middle of March, for word to reach England. Such were the perils of overland travel.

'That is not why I am here. I've come because of Mistress Jaffrey. I have left more than one message for you concerning the attempts on her life.'

'Ah, yes. Hit by a snowball, was it not? And slipped on the stairs? Your Mistress Jaffrey appears to be prone to accidents as well as subject to fancies.'

'That snowball had a rock embedded in it.'

Walsingham resumed his study of one of the maps in the county survey compiled by Christopher Saxton. Nick had recently acquired his own copy of the book and could understand why the principal secretary was fascinated by it, but he'd be damned if he'd let Walsingham dismiss Rosamond's concerns so casually.

Nick had to admit that his own first reaction had also been to discount both incidents as accidents, but his sister had convinced him there was reason for concern. She was a sharp old bird, accustomed to noticing small details about those who consulted her, details that helped her impress them when she pretended she could see into the future. Unfortunately, in this case, she had detected nothing to allow her to single out one of the other women at Chelsea Manor as a suspect. Despite that, she was convinced that Rosamond was in danger so long as she remained in Lady Mary's household.

'Have you at least found a way to send the Earl of Sussex's Men to Chelsea Manor?' Nick asked. If the place were more like most country houses, a company of players could spend as much as a week in residence without raising any eyebrows. Given the earl of Huntingon's evangelical leanings, such a visit was problematic.

Walsingham favored him with a narrow-eyed look. 'Sussex's Men are to be disbanded. The earl is dying. He has no further need of their services.'

Nick waited. Walsingham would not let a trained intelligencer like Henry Leveson go to waste. The only question was whether or not the fellow could be of further service to Rosamond.

'Do you know what this is?'

The question was rhetorical. Walsingham held the paper he plucked from the stacks of correspondence that littered the top of his desk in such a way as to prevent Nick from glimpsing so much as a single word written upon it.

'I have been ordered, along with my other duties, to put an end to one of the petty rivalries among noble courtiers. They try to outdo one another when it comes to their clothing, their retainers, and the New Year's gifts they present to the queen. Those noblemen who sponsor companies of players are particularly antagonistic towards one another. This past Yuletide the queen passed over Leicester's Men and the earl of Oxford's players to ask those wearing the livery of Lord Strange and the earl of Sussex to entertain the court. In spite of that, there were . . . incidents. Her Majesty has now devised a new solution to the problem, the creation of a company to be known as the Queen's Men. I have the unenviable task of telling Leicester, Oxford, and the rest that they must surrender their most talented players to the queen.'

'Will Sussex's men go to the new company?'

'Two will, Richard Tarleton and John Adams.'

'And Leveson?'

'It may be possible for him to join the Earl of Leicester's Men. Leicester will need replacements. He is about to lose four of his players to the queen.'

Leicester's Men might reasonably be invited to entertain at Chelsea Manor, since Leicester was the countess's brother. Good, but not good enough. Nick cleared his throat. 'If the Russian ambassador and Lady Mary are to meet, the danger to Lady Mary may escalate. The poisoner—'

'I am not convinced that there *is* a poisoner. We have only the opinion of a young and inexperienced gentlewoman to support such a claim.'

Walsingham was charged with dealing with a multitude of issues, everything from thwarting new schemes on behalf of the queen's imprisoned cousin, Mary of Scotland, to reading reports on what the French king ate for his supper. But his scheming had placed Rosamond Jaffrey in jeopardy and Nick was determined to make him take action to reduce the threat to that young woman.

'With all due respect, Sir Francis, if you do not see the sense in Mistress Jaffrey's conclusions, it is because you are wilfully blind to the truth of them.'

Walsingham's expression was closed. 'Your faith in Rosamond Jaffrey's abilities does you credit, Baldwin, and I have no doubt that she will deal in an efficient manner with any crisis that arises.'

'She entered into this enterprise to help ensure her husband's safety in Muscovy,' Nick reminded him, 'not to risk her life!'

'She knew there were dangers inherent in her task. She is not ignorant of the nature of the work her father and stepfather once did.'

And with that, Walsingham dismissed him.

Thirty-Three

'It is warm enough to walk in the garden,' Lady Mary declared, looking out a window on a sunny March morning. 'I wish to see if any flowers have yet poked their heads above the ground. Primroses come early, and some of the plants imported from Holland may have sprouted. This was a royal manor once. Mayhap the old king ordered his gardeners to plant tulips here, as he did at Whitehall. Nan, fetch my cloak.' She looked around, bemused. 'Where is Nan?'

'Abed with the pain of the first day of her monthly courses,' Rosamond said.

As this was a regular occurrence, Lady Mary did not question it. 'Go you, instead,' she ordered Rosamond.

'By your leave, my lady, may I retrieve cloaks for myself and Madge?' Receiving nodded permission, Bess scurried alongside Rosamond toward the narrow staircase leading to the upper rooms.

Rosamond bade her ascend first and was reassured by her lack of hesitation as they trudged up the steps in single file. She reminded herself to watch her footing on the way back down, although just at present she was more concerned about leaving Lady Mary alone with Madge Ellerker. It was not likely that Madge would attack their mistress in broad daylight, but Rosamond did not like giving her the opportunity.

'A walk in the garden on the Ides of March,' Bess muttered under her breath. 'Even if it were not so cold out of doors, this is a most unlucky day.'

Rosamond ignored her grumbling.

'What if Lady Mary should take a chill and fall ill again?'

'She is in excellent health.' Rosamond bit off the words, letting her irritation show. 'I do wish everyone would stop fussing over her. Even the marks on her face have faded to almost nothing.' What remained could easily be covered with cosmetics.

At the top of the stairs, Bess turned to face her, blocking the way. 'Why are you so wroth with me? What have I done to earn your displeasure?'

Rosamond could not see the other woman's expression in the

dimly-lit stairwell, but Bess sounded as if she thought herself ill-used. 'I beg your pardon, my friend. I am out of sorts with the whole world today.'

'Your monthly flowers?'

Rosamond laughed. 'I have not that excuse. Not yet.' Although, now that she thought about it, she realized that all the women in the household did seem to require cloths to contain the bleeding within a week of one another. 'No doubt it is just this changeable weather.'

Bess moved out of the way to allow Rosamond to join her. An icy eddy of air from a window had her hugging herself against the cold. They both lengthened their strides.

'I hate cold weather,' Bess said.

'Then you had best not go to Muscovy with Lady Mary. They say it is winter half the year in that clime.'

'What choice have I?'

You might arrange matters so that Lady Mary cannot go, Rosamond thought. But would Bess want her mistress dead when that meant she would lose her position? She had no family save her brother to take her in. Unless he had inherited a house somewhere, his sister had no place to take refuge.

Aloud, she said only, 'Will you fetch my cloak, too?'

Assuring Rosamond that she would, Bess continued on toward the small rooms occupied by Lady Mary's four waiting gentlewomen while Rosamond entered Lady Mary's privy chamber, passing rapidly through this empty outer room to reach the noblewoman's bedchamber.

Lady Mary owned a half dozen cloaks, all kept in a standing clothes press so large a person could squeeze inside it, even when it was filled with clothing and accessories. Rosamond smiled, as she always did when that thought crossed her mind. It was a perfect spot for a lover to hide, but what lover would dare invade precincts prayed over by Augustus Treadwell?

She'd just reached for the knob on the door to the clothes press when, without warning, it flew open of its own accord. The solid oak panel connected with Rosamond's forehead, knocking her aside with stunning force.

Unable to catch herself as she fell, she landed flat on her back. She did not lose consciousness, but neither did she get a good look at her attacker. Vision blurry, head throbbing, and the wind knocked out of her, she saw only a blur of motion as someone fled through the door to the privy chamber. Man or woman, young or old, she could not tell.

Rosamond rose as far as her knees before a wave of dizziness stopped her. She closed her eyes, struggling to gather her wits and the strength to stand. An intruder had been in Lady Mary's bedchamber. She and Bess had not been quiet on their approach. She was wearing sturdy boots. Her footfalls on the tiled floor of the privy chamber alone would have been loud enough to give warning of her approach. There had been time for someone to hide in the standing clothes press. Had Rosamond not been looking for a cloak, she might have come and gone without ever realizing that anyone was there.

Taking a deep breath and a firm grip on the edge of the cupboard door, Rosamond hauled herself to her feet. She stood still for a moment, waiting for another wave of wooziness to pass. Feeling gingerly of her forehead, she found a lump had already begun to rise.

As soon as she could manage it, she examined the entire bedchamber, looking for anything out of place. Nothing seemed to have been disturbed. Apparently, she'd arrived on the scene in time to prevent any mischief.

But who had the intruder been? And what had been her . . . or his . . . intent?

Not Madge, she thought. Madge could not have left Lady Mary's side, not when she was the only waiting gentlewoman in attendance. Even if she'd felt an urgent call of nature, she'd have been obliged to wait until Bess or Rosamond returned to excuse herself.

Not Bess, either, unless she could be in two places at once.

Had Bess seen anyone? Not likely, Rosamond decided. She'd have sounded the alarm and come into the bedchamber to look for Rosamond, too.

Ticey? That made no sense either. The tiring maid would have no reason to hide. She had an excuse to be in Lady Mary's bedchamber at this or any other hour of the day.

That left only Nan, bedridden in her chamber. Although this answer seemed just as preposterous, Rosamond unsheathed the knife in her boot and hurried back the way she had come. Bess had already been and gone by the time she reached the waiting gentlewomen's chambers. Like the monks' cells of old, the tiny rooms were all in a row.

With her free hand, Rosamond lifted the latch to Nan's quarters and slipped quietly inside. Soft, even breathing greeted her. Nan lay on her back with the covers drawn up to her neck. By the dim light filtering in through the single window, Rosamond could just make out the shape of a small brown bottle lying on its side on the table beside the bed.

She crept closer to pick it up and squint at the label. She'd always had good night vision and her eyes adjusted quickly to the semi-darkness. In an apothecary's crabbed but legible handwriting, the contents were identified as crushed angelica, marjoram, and rosewater. Nan had taken a common nostrum to relieve cramping. When the pain had eased sufficient to allow it, she had apparently drifted into sleep.

Rosamond surveyed the rest of the room. The furniture was identical to that in her own chamber, right down to the traveling chest beneath the window. Rosamond had once caught a glimpse of its contents, an extraordinary number of small but expensive baubles. Gifts from her family, Nan had said. Although she wanted no part of them, they kept trying to bribe her to let them back into her life. Rosamond wished her estranged family would make such overtures. She'd agree to a reconciliation in a heartbeat.

A low moan issued from the bed. As Rosamond watched, Nan's face contorted with pain before relaxing again into drugged slumber.

As silently as she had entered, Rosamond departed, glad her own courses never affected her so badly. The lump on her head was likely to cause her more trouble, both in pain and inconvenience. There would be no hiding it, or the bruising that was sure to follow.

For just a moment, she considered telling the truth about what had happened to her. Then Lady Mary would be warned of her danger. But what if no one believed her? She'd thought her questions to the noblewoman, shortly after she'd been burned by the poison, would convince Lady Mary that her life was in danger. What Rosamond had failed to take into account was that dosing a person with poppy syrup affected the memory. Lady Mary remembered nothing of what Rosamond had said to her. Moreover, like everyone else in the household, she accepted the diagnosis of the queen's physician – she had been struck down by that dreaded disease, the pox. That she'd recovered and no one else had fallen ill were attributed to the power of prayer.

Reluctantly, Rosamond abandoned any thought of explaining the true situation at this late date. She had no proof that anyone had been hiding in the clothes press, let alone that they'd intended harm to Lady Mary. Without revealing her reasons for being so suspicious and confessing all that had gone before, she'd just be shouting into the wind.

She'd have to claim she'd had an accident. She'd say she tripped over her own feet, fallen, and struck her head on a stool. No one had doubted that story a few weeks earlier when Bess had told it. Then again, in Bess's case, it had been the truth.

Rosamond returned to Lady Mary's bedchamber and selected a cloak at random, a handsome item made of dark blue brocade trimmed with lynx fur. Knowing her mistress well by now, Rosamond collected the matching snoskyn, too.

With extreme caution, she made her way down the narrow stairs. All the while, she kept trying to make sense of what had just happened to her. She'd caught someone in Lady Mary's bedchamber, someone who'd had no business being there. But who?

No common thief, that was certain! Nor had it been Master Baldwin's favorite suspect, Sir Jerome Bowes. Madge, Bess, and Nan were all accounted for. Ticey seemed unlikely. But any one of them might have recruited an accomplice.

That thought was more chilling than the temperature in Chelsea Manor's gardens.

Thirty-Four

The news Nick Baldwin had for Rosamond on a day in late March could not be sent in a letter, nor could it be delivered by a fortune teller or a mute manservant. He went in person to Chelsea Manor, once again in the guise of Mistress Jaffrey's steward. This time they met in the gardens, for the afternoon was fair, if breezy.

Daisies and yellow daffodils had put in their first appearance of the year, and in the orchard the peach and cornelian trees had blossomed. With Rosamond at his side, Nick walked away from the house, moving steadily eastward without speaking. After a gradual climb uphill, they reached ground high enough to give them a view of the church spires of London some two and a half miles distant and the gently rolling, rapidly greening countryside closer to hand. From this vantage point they could also see if anyone was approaching in ample time to guard their tongues.

Rosamond turned to him eagerly, rushing into speech before he could utter a single word. 'I nearly caught a prowler in Lady Mary's chamber.'

Nick bit back a curse. 'Who was it?'

'I do not know. I was caught off guard and did not see.' She pointed to a spot on her forehead.

She had applied some sort of paint to cover a bruise, but now that he knew where to look, it stood out plain in the sunlight. 'What happened?'

'The intruder was hiding in a large clothes press. When I went to open it, he shoved the door outward so that it struck me. I did not lose consciousness, but the blow prevented me from getting a good look at him or giving chase.'

'Him?'

She sighed. 'I cannot be certain of that, either, but Madge, Bess and Nan were all accounted for and Ticey would have no reason to hide.'

'An accomplice?'

'I fear so. Whoever it was could have been trying to taint something, but I have taken pains ever since the incident to examine every article in Lady Mary's possession, especially items of clothing.'

'At risk of being poisoned yourself?' There were poisons that could be imbedded in fabric and enter the body through the skin of the wearer. The thought turned his innards to ice. 'That is not why you were sent here.'

'Am I to let the villain succeed? Besides, I am careful.'

'It would take a small army to circumvent every possible danger. No one expects you to stand guard day and night.'

'Then let Walsingham send reinforcements.'

'The most he is willing to do is dispatch Leveson. The player is now a member of the Earl of Leicester's Men.'

He gave her a concise summary of the creation of the new Queen's Men and the dissolution of the earl of Sussex's company. All the while, he was trying to think of some way to ease into the subject that had brought him to Chelsea in the first place.

Rosamond listened, her eyes on the distant city. When he paused, she turned to face him. 'What is it you are not telling me, Master Baldwin?'

With no help for it, Nick spoke bluntly. 'I have troubling news from Muscovy. Rob was taken into custody by the tsar's guards sometime in January. Two days ago, George Barne, governor of the Muscovy Company here in London, received word of his arrest.'

'January?' Rosamond whispered.

'The report was dispatched as soon as the incident occurred, but it takes months for any message to travel so far. In truth, the letter arrived with remarkable swiftness.'

Rosamond stood stock-still on the hilltop, staring at nothing. Her face wore as blank an expression as Nick had ever seen upon it, but she did not look as if she was about to faint or weep or otherwise lose control of herself. After a moment, she asked, 'Why was he seized?'

'He had been . . . associating with an enemy of the tsar.'

'And was this enemy also arrested?'

Nick grimaced. 'Not as far as I know.'

Rosamond sent him a sidelong look. 'Explain, if you please.'

It did not please him at all, but he did not see that he had any choice in the matter. 'He came to the aid of a poor widow, an Englishwoman living in Moscow.'

'A . . . woman?' Although her voice remained even, Nick sensed some strong emotion at work beneath Rosamond's surface calm.

'Her name is Jane Bomelius. She was Jane Richards before her marriage. I knew her slightly when she was a girl in London. She wed a physician who went to Muscovy to serve the tsar. His employment ended badly. Bomelius was accused of treason and died in prison. You do not need to hear the details. Jane was left to fend for herself in Moscow.'

'How long has she been there on her own?'

Nick had to calculate, and even then he was uncertain he was correct. 'Five or six years.'

'That is disgraceful! Why did no one try to help her long before this? At the least, the Muscovy Company should have paid her passage back to England.'

'As I understand it, they were not given any opportunity to offer assistance. The tsar forbade her departure from Moscow. Rob is fortunate he was not summarily executed.'

'He is not dead. I would know it if he were.' Rosamond spoke forcefully, holding her hands clasped tightly in front of her.

Nick had never doubted she had feelings for her husband, but he had likened them to the love one bore a favorite cousin. The two young people had been close friends for many years. Although Rob had adored Rosamond all his life, Nick had always thought she'd married him for convenience. She'd seemed to care more for her independence than for her spouse. Now he reconsidered.

'What is being done to secure his release?' Rosamond asked in a low voice.

'The Muscovy Company's agent in Moscow will have been attempting to negotiate with the tsar, but Tsar Ivan does not grant many audiences to foreigners. Indeed, the only Englishman he seems to trust is Doctor Robert Jacobi, and Jacobi came to England with Ambassador Pissemsky to serve as the ambassador's translator.'

'Can the matter of Rob's release be raised as an amendment to the treaty?'

Nick hated to dash her hopes, but he had to be honest. 'That is most unlikely, Rosamond. Rob Jaffrey is of no importance to either queen or tsar.'

With an inarticulate sound, she swung away from him, but not before he glimpsed the glitter of unshed tears in her eyes. Her voice was choked and bitter as gall. 'I understand. To ask for Rob's release would give Pissemsky an opening to ask for concessions in other areas.'

Arms wrapped around herself, she slowly circled the top of the rise, stopping her restless movements only after she returned to the spot where Nick stood.

'What if I appeal to the queen directly? Surely, if Her Majesty wrote to the tsar, requesting that one of her subjects be released, he would be inclined to grant that favor.'

'She might be persuaded to do so, but who is to approach her with that proposal? I do not have entrée at court, nor do you.'

'Walsingham?'

Nick shook his head. 'You cannot count on his help. He has nothing to gain by it.'

'Then I will offer one of the queen's ladies in waiting a generous bribe to persuade Her Grace to take an interest in Rob's fate.'

'How are you to make your offer to someone at court? The queen is at Richmond Palace and you cannot leave Chelsea.'

'It is no great distance to travel.' She gestured westward along the Thames. 'Even if I cannot haunt the queen's presence chamber myself, I can write letters. What of the tsar? How can he be persuaded?'

'Gifts are always welcome, the more exotic the better.' He hesitated. 'My presence in Muscovy might help persuade Ivan to free Rob, but such a journey is not something to be undertaken lightly.'

'How soon can we leave?'

'We? Oh, no.' He shook his head. 'And there is no sense in departing in any case until the Muscovy Company fleet sets sail. An overland journey takes five or six months. Ships leaving England in May or June will reach Russia more quickly. In good weather, the voyage takes only four or five weeks.'

'Terrible things could happen to Rob in the meantime!' As Rosamond's self-control slipped, Nick heard the anguish in her voice and read the desperation in her dark brown eyes.

'I will go to Muscovy,' he heard himself promise. 'I will find a way to free Rob and bring him safely home.'

'Let me—'

'No!' He placed one hand on each of her shoulders and gave her a little shake. 'Although it pains me to say it, Rosamond, you would only be a hindrance if you made the journey with me. You serve Rob best by staying here and petitioning the queen's ladies.'

'Is there nothing else I can do?'

'You can pray.'

Thirty-Five

In the days following Baldwin's visit to Chelsea Manor, Rosamond did pray most earnestly for Rob's safety, but she did not trust to blind faith. She also bombarded the queen's ladies in waiting with expensive gifts, accompanying these tokens with requests for their help.

None replied.

As March turned into April, she repressed her fears as best she could and threw herself with renewed vigor into guarding Lady Mary. She stayed close to the noblewoman and firm in her resolve to trust no one at Chelsea Manor.

A ray of hope presented itself early in the month when the queen at long last approved the painting of a likeness 'in small' of Lady Mary, a miniature portrait that Ambassador Pissemsky was to present to Tsar Ivan when he returned to Muscovy. The sooner it was completed, the sooner Pissemsky would take possession of it and the sooner he, and the entire Muscovy Fleet, would sail, and with it Master Baldwin, bound for Moscow to free Rob Jaffrey from prison.

The identity of the artist the queen had selected had been a matter for much speculation in the days preceding his arrival. Would it be Nicholas Hilliard? George Gower? Mayhap Cornelius Ketel? Or Marcus Gheeraerts? Quentin Metsys the Younger was another possibility. He had recently completed a new portrait of Queen Elizabeth.

It was much in fashion to send portraits as tokens to family and friends, and to lovers, too, but Lady Mary had never had her likeness made, nor had any of her attendants. They were gathered in the gallery when the chosen one arrived, a servant trailing after him to carry his easel, brushes, and pots of paint.

Lady Mary let out a little sound of dismay when she saw him. Rosamond felt her own jaw go slack. The fellow did not look a day over twenty.

He bowed deeply and rose smiling. 'Good day to you, my lady. I am Marcus Gheeraerts the Younger.'

Disappointment had the noblewoman pursing her lips, but she was well aware she had no choice but to accept the painter the queen had chosen. She bade him begin work and sat where he directed her, leaving her waiting gentlewomen to their own devices.

Rosamond lingered close at hand, both to look out for Lady Mary's safety and because she was curious about the process of capturing a person's appearance. Gheeraerts sketched in chalk first, creating a likeness of his subject with a few deft strokes.

Rosamond frowned. Lady Mary was a plain-looking woman, but not *that* plain. She sidled closer and closer until at last Gheeraerts looked up and scowled. She mumbled an apology and backed away.

When the session concluded, Lady Mary bade Rosamond remain with Master Gheeraerts, lest he lose his way en route to the river stairs. Calling Ticey to her side, she swept out of the gallery, declaring that she wished to change into more comfortable clothing. For the sitting, she had worn full court dress with a farthingale so wide she could scarce pass through the doorway. A huge, stiff ruff tightly encircled her throat.

'Does she think I mean to steal the plate?' The portrait painter sounded more amused than insulted.

'I am the one she meant to rebuke. I have been hovering.'

Gheeraerts chuckled. While his servant cleaned brushes, he took up his chalk again, this time using several colors on a square of specially prepared pink paper. In a matter of minutes, he had produced a likeness of Rosamond that exactly resembled what she saw in her looking glass.

'This is most wonderful!'

He sketched a bow in acceptance of her praise.

'But if you can draw this accurately, why does Lady Mary's portrait look so unlike her?'

Gheeraerts went still, only his fingers moving as they curled into a fist. 'I was instructed to make her look plain as a bowl of pottage.'

It was on the tip of Rosamond's tongue to ask who had given the order, but she bit back the question. She knew the answer already. The queen had sent him. The queen, or her principal secretary, had instructed the artist in his duties. Her Majesty did not want her cousin to appeal to the tsar.

'It is a tribute to your talent,' Rosamond said after a moment. 'For a man who paints well to paint poorly must present a great challenge to his skill.'

'You are kind to say so.'

'Only honest.'

He held out the sketch. 'A gift.'

Although Rosamond did not hesitate to take the portrait, it disconcerted her that her first thought was to send the sketch to Rob.

Thirty-Six

As ordered, Rosamond accompanied Master Gheeraerts and his servant to the river stairs, but instead of returning to the house after a wherry had carried them out of sight, she chose to walk in the gardens. Her thoughts still centered on her husband, she felt the need to be alone with the jumble of emotions coursing through her.

Her husband had been imprisoned because of a woman. That fact had nagged at her from the moment Baldwin revealed it.

Rosamond wondered what she was like, this Jane Bomelius. Surely she must be too old to be considered a rival for Rob's affections. Then again, women could be married off to much older men when they were no more than girls. Jane Richards might have been as young as twelve when she accompanied her husband to Muscovy. If that were so, she could still be in her early twenties.

It did not matter, Rosamond told herself. However deeply Rob had involved himself in the Widow Bomelius's life, he was still *Rosamond's* husband. She would do all she could to extract him from his difficulties abroad. She would write more letters, send more expensive tokens to ladies close to the queen. She had made a list of which ones to try next. And she could solicit the help of noblemen as well as ladies-in-waiting. Her mind leapt first to the earl of Leicester.

But there the task she had undertaken for Sir Francis Walsingham and the promise she had made to herself to protect Lady Mary came in conflict with her desire to help Rob. The moment she admitted to Leicester that her absent spouse was in Muscovy, her reasons for joining Lady Mary's household would be suspect. To remain, she'd be obliged to reveal that Walsingham had sent her and that she'd lied about having come from Lady Sussex. Her deceitfulness would anger both the earl and the countess, and she had no reason to think they would believe her if she tried to tell them that Lady Mary was in danger. She'd be dismissed, leaving Lady Mary at the mercy of her enemies.

It was a quandary indeed.

Better, she thought, to avoid the earl of Leicester altogether and find some other favorite at court to beg the queen's assistance. It was not as if she did not have the wherewithal to offer generous recompense for the service. The difficulty lay in getting her request past a bevy of retainers. Every man of influence had scores of them to protect himself from being imposed upon by the common rabble. She'd have to work her way up, level by level, bribe by bribe, until she reached someone who had the queen's ear.

A snatch of birdsong recalled Rosamond to her surroundings. The gardeners had been busy. The gravel paths she'd been following without noticing wound between raised flower beds and areas of grass and had brought her into a tunnel arbor. In another month, ferns would make the interior lush and green while roses, both red and white, climbed the trellises. At present, she could still see the sky overhead. The prevalent scent in the garden was that of lilacs.

When Rosamond turned to retrace her steps, she realized that she was still carrying the sketch Master Gheeraerts had given her. She stopped to admire it again, studying her own narrow face, dark eyes, dark hair, and high forehead. The artist had also managed to capture a certain air of stubbornness about the jaw. Rosamond frowned. The woman Gheeraerts had sketched wanted her own way and usually got it.

Was that how everyone saw her? Stubborn translated far too easily into willful. Was that why Rob had put so much distance between them, to be free of her domineering ways?

She told herself it did not matter if that had been his reason. She still owed him her loyalty and every effort she could make on his behalf. They were bound to each other for life, no matter how many miles might separate them. When he was safely back in England—

Think of something else, she ordered herself, and once again set off in the direction of the manor house.

A flash of color beneath an arbor caught her eye, not bright blossoms but shimmering fabric. A gown of peacock blue and another of dusky rose flanked flat black wool as the three people seated on a bench bent their heads close together, so deep in conversation that none of them noticed Rosamond. One was Augustus Treadwell. The others were Madge Ellerker and Nan Morgan.

Rosamond started to back away, but she'd gone no more than a few steps before she sensed that there was also someone behind her. She whirled around to find Bess Farnham standing a few feet away. She beckoned to Rosamond and led the way into the manor house.

'What are they up to?' Rosamond whispered as soon as the door was closed behind them. 'I can understand that Madge might have asked for additional religious instruction, but Nan?'

Bess snorted. 'I heard a rumor that Treadwell is to be named to a living in a wealthy parish near London.'

'Never tell me that Nan sees him as a marriage prospect.' Side by side they made their way back toward the chambers allotted to Lady Mary and her servants.

'No, but Madge does. Mayhap Nan is trying to make her jealous.'

Rosamond frowned. 'If Nan and Madge are in the garden and you and I are here, who is attending Lady Mary?'

Bess sent her a puzzled look. 'Ticey is with her. Lady Mary sent the rest of us away. After sitting for so long in one pose for Master Gheeraerts, she is resting. For myself, I am glad of the respite. It is also tiring to be at her beck and call every hour of the day.'

Although Bess's sentiments echoed her own, Rosamond did not feel easy in her mind until she had slipped into Lady Mary's chamber to see for herself that the noblewoman was safely asleep in her bed. Ticey, needle and thread in hand, sat by the window mending a tear in a chemise. She looked up when Rosamond peeped in and lifted a finger to her lips. Rosamond crept away as quietly as she had come.

She went back to wondering what subject had so engrossed Treadwell, Madge *and* Nan. It seemed to her that there had been something furtive about the three of them. If anyone but Nan had been involved, she might have suspected a conspiracy to convince Lady Mary to refuse the tsar's offer of marriage, but Nan wanted to travel to Ivan the Terrible's 'heathen' country.

Deciding upon a direct approach, Rosamond seized the first opportunity to present itself, when she and Nan met in the passageway on their way to chapel for Sunday services. 'What were you and Madge and the chaplain talking about so earnestly in the garden?' she asked. 'And do not try to convince me you have of a sudden turned pious.'

Nan smirked. 'No fear of that. Madge asked me to serve as chaperone, lest tongues wag over the excessive amount of time she spends in private religious instruction of late. Our Madge has set her cap for Augustus Treadwell, Rosamond. Never doubt it.'

'Madge may want to marry the chaplain, but does he see her as a prospective bride? She has no dowry, as she has told us many times.'

'And that is why her conscience suddenly demanded she avoid being alone with him. She is afraid she will be tempted to lure him into her bed, knowing full well that if he got her with child, there would be a marriage, with or without a portion.'

Rosamond tried to imagine Augustus Treadwell as a lover and felt her features contort into a grimace.

Nan choked back a laugh, since they were about to enter the chapel. 'He is not to my taste, or to yours,' she whispered, 'but he will do well enough for Madge.'

Thirty-Seven

Lady Mary sat for Master Gheeraerts several more times before her portrait was ready for the queen's approval. Lady Mary herself had no say, nor did she see the finished painting.

A week after her last sitting, a small package arrived at Chelsea Manor. It bore Rosamond's name and inside was her own likeness in small, painted in oils on vellum stuck to a playing card, ready to be fitted into a case. In common with the original chalk drawing, it showed a young woman with an abundance of character and strength of will.

On the same day Rosamond received her portrait, a messenger delivered a letter to Lady Mary from the queen. With the possible exception of her sister-in-law, she told no one what it said, but she became remarkably cheerful and did not seem to mind in the least being left behind when the countess of Huntingdon left Chelsea Manor to spend several days in London. During that time, Lady Huntingdon was to attend the wedding of Elizabeth Howard, eldest daughter of Lord Howard of Effingham. Queen Elizabeth would also be among the wedding guests, since the bride had lately been one of her maids of honor.

'I wish Lady Mary had been invited,' Nan muttered. 'Then I could have gone, too.'

'That is not why you are out of sorts,' Madge taunted her. 'You expected your own invitation, but if you thought the Howard sisters your friends, you were guilty of the sin of pride. You were a servant in that household, no more.'

Nan's face flamed. 'I knew my place!'

Bess and Rosamond murmured sympathetic words, but Nan was not to be consoled. She jabbed her needle into her embroidery with such force that it went clean through the fabric and into the skirt beneath.

For once, Rosamond was glad to see Augustus Treadwell appear. Madge forgot all about lecturing Nan. She seized the chaplain's forearm to draw him aside.

He gave a start at her forwardness but then went willingly enough.

He was so bemused by Madge's behavior that he did not even take the time to bid good day to Lady Mary.

The noblewoman stood alone at one of the tall, mullioned windows, gazing out into the distance. Rosamond wondered if she was dreaming of her future as empress of Muscovy or simply wool-gathering, but she did not speculate long. Madge's low-voiced conversation with the preacher was much more intriguing.

She had him cornered in an alcove. Rosamond wished she were closer to the pair but she was anchored in place with Nan on one side of her and Bess on the other. 'What has Madge so agitated?' she asked.

'It must be the players,' Bess said. 'The Earl of Leicester's Men are to visit Chelsea Manor. I have no doubt that offends the holier-than-thou Mistress Madge, but if she thinks either she or the chaplain can talk Lady Mary out of hosting them, she is much mistaken. Lady Huntingdon approved the entertainment before she left for London.'

Rosamond was delighted by this news. Leicester's company was one of the best in the land, famous for the excellence of their repertoire. She hoped they would perform one of the comedies, something with a plum role for Henry Leveson.

That she would contrive to speak with him was the sugar on her almonds. She wondered if Leveson would have a message for her. She had not heard from Master Baldwin for nearly three weeks, not since he'd brought word of Rob's arrest.

Nan had nothing to say about the players. She was still bemoaning the fact that she would not be attending Elizabeth Howard's wedding. 'The Howards think they are better than the rest of the world,' she grumbled. Then she sighed. 'Well, and so they are.'

'How do you mean?' Rosamond asked as she stitched in a desultory manner. Once she left Chelsea, she silently vowed, she would never pick up a needle again.

'Do you not know the story of King Henry the Eighth and Queen Anne's sister, Mary Boleyn?'

When Rosamond admitted that she did not, Nan took it upon herself to remedy the lack. Rosamond's stitches grew increasingly uneven as she listened to the tale. She had known that Lady Howard's father, Lord Hunsdon, was the queen's cousin, but she had dismissed the importance of that information because the connection was on the Boleyn side.

'King Henry was Lord Hunsdon's real father?'

Nan laughed, but her expression was earnest. 'Not only that, but the Howards have as much royal blood in their veins as the Tudors do. I cannot remember what king they are descended from, but their line is every bit as pure as the earl of Huntingdon's.'

There was food for thought! Even though Lord Howard's eldest daughter was about to wed an Englishman, the energetic and nubile Mistress Frances was also a cousin to the queen – twice over, if Nan was to be believed – and therefore a viable candidate to offer to the tsar as a replacement for Lady Mary Hastings.

Rosamond slanted a look at Nan. Nan was fond of Frances, but would she have murdered a man and tried to kill Lady Mary on the slim chance that the younger, more attractive woman would be chosen to replace her? Nan might reason that she could travel to Muscovy as Frances's lady-in-waiting, but she had already secured that post with Lady Mary.

It was as well that Augustus Treadwell began to read to them from Lady Bacon's translation of John Jewel's *Apologie of the Church of England*. Otherwise Rosamond might have asked Nan outright. *Think first*, she admonished herself as the chaplain droned on. It would be rash to speak too soon. She must give herself time to consider whether this new theory made sense.

By the next day, she had decided that it did not, but she still had questions for Nan. Her friend squirreled away knowledge about the rich and powerful and Rosamond wished to learn more about the various factions at court. To her frustration, no opportunity presented itself for a word in private.

The day of the wedding came and went. The day the players were to perform drew nigh. And then, unexpectedly, Lady Huntingdon returned early to Chelsea Manor. Rosamond had scarce heard of her arrival from Bess before she was summoned to the countess's privy chamber.

When the noblewoman sent her waiting gentlewomen away, Rosamond's puzzlement turned to alarm. Lady Huntingdon was quietly furious. Her entire body shook with it. Hectic color rouged her cheeks. She held her hands so tightly clenched at the front of her stomacher that her knuckles had gone white. 'You have practiced deceit, Mistress Jaffrey.'

'My lady?'

'Do not play the innocent with me. I paid a visit to the earl and countess of Sussex after the wedding. It was most illuminating. Lady

Sussex had no notion who you were and she most certainly did not recommend you to me.'

Rosamond's thoughts scrambled. Unable to think what to say, she said nothing.

'What kind of woman takes advantage of the wife of a dying man in such a way? It is reprehensible. More, it is criminal.'

'My lady—'

Lady Huntingdon did not want to hear excuses or explanations. Her voice rose, drowning out every feeble protest Rosamond attempted. 'I have ordered your tiring maid to pack your belongings. You will be escorted to a waiting barge. You will not speak to anyone before you leave. Consider yourself fortunate that I do not have you arrested and imprisoned for what you have done.'

At a signal, two of her manservants seized Rosamond, one by each arm. Belatedly, she realized that they had been in the chamber all along, lurking in the shadows. They were big and burly and her feet scarce touched the ground as they hauled her out of the house and down to the water stairs.

Farther along the path, Rosamond caught sight of yet another Huntingdon henchman shoving Melka ahead of him. When they reached the waiting watercraft, he pushed her again, this time with sufficient force to cost the older woman her balance. Arms rotating like windmills, Melka narrowly avoided falling into the river. The bundles she'd been carrying were not so fortunate. They flew every which way, half of them splashing into the Thames to disappear beneath the murky water.

One of the men with Rosamond laughed.

'Dirty foreigner,' the other sneered.

Rosamond took great pleasure in giving the first man a hard kick in the privates and shoving the second into the Thames. She hopped onto the small, hired row barge. 'Pepper Alley Stairs,' she told the watermen, 'and I suggest you cast off with as much haste as you can manage.'

With a fine sense of self-preservation, he followed her suggestion. They were well out onto the river before either of the countess's retainers was in a position to retaliate. They shook their fists and shouted curses. Rosamond smiled and waved.

Once they were out of sight of Chelsea Manor, her smile vanished. It was in a somber and dispirited state of mind that Rosamond Jaffrey returned to Willow House.

Thirty-Eight

Rosamond kicked a stool halfway across the gallery of her house in Bermondsey. Then she righted it, sat down, and removed one of the slippers she was wearing instead of her accustomed boots, having been given no time to change her footwear before she was ejected from Chelsea Manor. As she massaged her sore toes she barked an order at Charles: 'Go at once to Billingsgate and fetch Watling. He should never have been taken there without my permission.'

As she should have expected, Master Baldwin returned with the cat. He listened with annoying patience to her tale of woe, commenting only when she finally ran out of words.

'You did what you could. No one can ask more of you than that. For myself, I am relieved to have you safe at home again.'

'I did not do enough!' She sprang to her feet, unable to sit still and listen to platitudes. 'Rob is still a prisoner in Muscovy. Lady Mary's life remains at risk. And I am no closer to discovering who killed Griffith Potter than I was on the day he died.'

'Rosamond—'

'Do not try to dissuade me. I must find a way to regain my place in that household.'

'Now that Lady Huntingdon knows you lied to her? I do much doubt anything or anyone can change her mind.' He shifted to settle himself more comfortably on the same window seat where he'd waited for her on the day he'd recruited her and, as he had then, ran gentle hands over the cat ensconced on his lap.

'She did not give me a chance to explain.'

'What would you have said? You could not have told her about Walsingham.' The look on her face must have convinced him otherwise because he started to shake his head. 'No. No, you cannot think to—'

'It is hardly a secret that Walsingham is a spy master. I've no doubt every nobleman at court employs similar intelligence gatherers.'

'Rosamond, think – how would telling Lady Huntingdon the truth better her opinion of you?'

'I do not care what she thinks of me, so long as I can convince her that Lady Mary is in danger.'

'You have no proof that she is.'

'I tested the dregs of the scented liquid Lady Mary added to her wash water on a rat. The rat died.'

He continued to shake his head. 'Since you and Melka were the only ones to observe that result, you will not be believed.'

Rosamond seized a plump pillow from another of the window seats and flung it at his head. He ducked and it fell to the floor, startling Watling into abandoning his perch but otherwise doing no harm.

With an effort, she brought her temper under control. There had to be a way to get back into favor at Chelsea Manor. 'The reason Walsingham arranged for me to become Lady Mary's waiting gentlewoman was to eavesdrop on conversations that might take place in the Russian language. Now more than ever, he needs me to do that. The time is fast approaching when Lady Mary will meet with the ambassador from Muscovy.'

'Walsingham will have to manage without your help. Your part in this is done. Be glad of it. Think of it this way. Now you will have more time to petition the ladies of the queen's privy chamber to intercede with Her Grace on Rob's behalf.'

Annoyed as she was, Rosamond managed to sheath her sharp tongue. Was she supposed to feel pleased that he was worried about her safety? His overprotective attitude was almost as infuriating as her failure to win any support from influential courtiers.

She forced a smile and let him think she would heed his advice, but as soon as he left she sent Charles to purchase boy's clothing that would fit her, fulfilling a promise she had made to herself at Yuletide.

He brought back a shirt of fine Holland cloth, knitted stocks to cover her lower limbs, and a doublet of blue camlet. Breeches and sleeves with turned-back cuffs fastened to the doublet with linen points, and to complete the ensemble there were a black coat and a black cap with a silver badge.

Delighted with the look and feel of these new garments, Rosamond took herself off to the Horse's Head that same afternoon to test out the effectiveness of her disguise. This time she stood with the crowd in front of the makeshift stage. It was much less pleasant there than in the gallery – ripe smells rising from the bodies of her fellow playgoers had her wishing for a pomander ball filled with orris root or ambergris – but the freedom of movement was wonderful.

She reveled in every part of her new outfit, although she'd had to bind her breasts to keep them from giving her gender away. Worn over the shirt, the doublet, with its back lined with stiff canvas and its close-set buttons to fasten the front, nipped in at her waist and then hung down nearly to mid-thigh, coming to a V-shaped point at the center. Now that bulging codpieces had gone out of style, what the doublet did not conceal, the breeches did, covering her from her waist down over her upper legs.

To walk unencumbered by chemise, petticoat, farthingale, kirtle, and gown was one of the most pleasurable sensations she had ever enjoyed. She could scarce keep the grin off her face when she mastered the 'manly' stride that went with her role. Speaking in a gruff voice, her long hair pinned tight against her head and concealed beneath a short wig and the hat, and her complexion darkened with a cosmetic to give her the appearance of someone who spent time out of doors – Melka had talked her out of trying to approximate the look of beard shadow – she encountered not a single person in the crowd who looked at her askance.

Her enthusiam knew no bounds when she realized that the players performing that afternoon were no other than Lord Leicester's Men. She recognized Henry Leveson at once, although he was resplendent in women's clothing. But to her dismay, when he chanced to look her way, his eyes widened in recognition, penetrating her disguise as easily as she had seen beneath his.

She considered leaving before the play was done, but that was a coward's way. She tarried until the player, back in his own garments, joined her in the inn yard.

'You left Chelsea House,' he said.

'Not by choice.' She gave him an abbreviated version of what had happened.

'A pity,' he said, 'but such things happen.'

'I wish to return.'

'Impossible now.'

She gave a rueful laugh and gestured at the boy's clothing she wore. 'Mayhap as a groom?'

He looked at her as if she had grown horns. 'You must not even jest about such a thing. Indeed, you must not play such games ever again. You could be arrested for dressing as a man.'

'You dress as a woman!'

'Only on stage. And you know what the reformers think of that!'

Although she had no intention of following his advice, Rosamond let the subject drop. 'What is Walsingham doing to protect Lady Mary?'

'I could not tell you that, even if I knew. You have met him, have you not? He's not one to share information.'

'He might fare better if he did,' Rosamond muttered. 'What about you, then? What vital intelligence does he expect you to gather at the Horse's Head?'

Leveson laughed. 'The temper of the masses, what else?'

'And no doubt Leicester's Men will tour in the country during the summer. Nothing ever happens there. What a waste of your talent.'

Praise had him puffing up like a peacock. 'I will have opportunities to ply my trade again before we leave London.'

He leaned back against the stage, his casualness all but begging Rosamond to ask for details. Willingly, she obliged.

'Have you ever heard the name Albertus Laski?'

'Never. Who is he?'

'Laski is a Polonian prince and palatine of Sieradz, as well as the nephew of a famous reformer. He tried to seize the Polish throne eight years ago, but since then he has been reconciled with the current king, Stephen Báthory.'

Rosamond frowned, remembering something Master Baldwin had told her. 'The same King Stephen who is the great enemy of Tsar Ivan?'

'The same. Some think Laski's real purpose for coming to England is to prevent the sale of arms to Muscovy.'

'Hence Walsingham's interest.'

Leveson just smiled.

'Will Lord Leicester's Men perform for this prince?'

'It seems likely. Laski is foreign royalty and, as such, must be well treated by Queen Elizabeth. He must be housed and fed and entertained with appropriate fanfare. Thus he is to be installed in Winchester House and his most frequent visitor, on the queen's behalf, will be the earl of Leicester.'

Although Rosamond gave no outward sign of her interest, her heart beat a little faster. Winchester House was a landmark of Southwark, only a short walk from her own abode. Hearing that the prince was in residence, she mused, it would be only natural for another Polonian to pay him a visit.

Thirty-Nine

'Laski a bad man,' Melka protested.

Rosamond stared at her tiring maid. 'What do you know about him?'

She burst into such rapid-fire Polish that Rosamond was hard put to translate. Laski was not to be trusted. He dabbled in alchemy. While in Paris some years ago, he had married a young Italian woman – a prostitute, to hear Melka tell it, although Rosamond thought it more likely she was simply a low-born female of ill-repute. The worst sin of all, Melka saved till last: Laski was a Catholic.

'None of that has any bearing on the present situation,' Rosamond said.

Melka glared at her.

'Besides, your reason for visiting Winchester House will be the hope of finding some of your countrymen among the servants. It would be presumptuous of you to expect the prince himself to receive you.' She took both of Melka's hands in hers. 'All you need do is make one friend among Laski's retainers. Learn when Leicester is expected. Convince your new friend to allow your mistress to lie in wait for the earl inside the house. Will you do it, Melka?'

Melka muttered something in Polish that Rosamond did not try to translate, but she nodded.

As soon as Laski and his party were installed in Winchester House, Melka made her first foray. She returned two hours later with a foolish grin on her face. Rosamond had no difficulty coaxing details out of her. Upon hearing that a Polish woman had come to his door, Laski himself had insisted upon meeting her. To hear Melka tell it, the prince was a fine specimen of manhood. He was handsome, with an 'English' complexion and a magnificent white beard so long that he had to tuck it into his belt to keep it out of his way.

'Mayhap he should consider trimming it,' Rosamond said.

Melka looked appalled and insisted that the beard was a thing of beauty, as were Laski's clothes. He dressed all in red, except for a pair of yellow boots with toes that curled upward.

This sounded pretentious to Rosamond, but her opinion scarce mattered. 'Did you find out anything about Leicester?'

Melka had done better than that. She had secured an invitation for Rosamond to have dinner with the prince, a meal that was to be shared with Laski's new friend Robert Dudley, earl of Leicester.

Rosamond did not question such phenomenal good luck. With Melka's help, she made certain she looked her best and arrived at the appointed hour in high good spirits. She bantered with her host and his guest through a meal she barely tasted, giving the impression of lightheartedness and gaiety. Jugglers performed. Then singers. There was no dancing, since Rosamond was the only female present. When Laski, from a surfeit of food and drink, lapsed into sleep sitting upright in his carved and gilded chair, Rosamond gratefully accepted the earl's offer to escort her home.

'It is near enough to walk,' she told him.

Leicester laughed. 'I came by coach.' Even as he spoke, it appeared from the stable yard in the back of Winchester House.

As they were jounced over the cobblestones en route to Willow House, Rosamond drew in a strengthening breath. Here was the privacy she needed to plead her case. She could not afford to waste a moment of the short journey.

'My lord, Lady Mary Hastings is in grave danger.'

From the facing seat, Leicester watched her with hooded eyes. 'I wondered when you would come to the point, Mistress Jaffrey. I am aware that my sister dismissed you when she learned you lied when you said you'd been sent to her by Lady Sussex, but I also know you are Sir Robert Appleton's daughter. The resemblance to your father is remarkable.'

'It was not my lie. Sir Francis Walsingham insisted I tell Lady Huntingdon that story.'

Leicester sat up straighter, the movement accompanied by an odd creaking sound that made Rosamond wonder if he wore a body-stitchet to keep his girth in check. 'Go on.'

She gave him an edited version of how she'd come to join the household at Chelsea Manor, leaving out the part Master Baldwin had played. It did not trouble her at all to betray the confidence of the queen's principal secretary. Walsingham had failed her from the start. At the least he might have asked permission from Lady Sussex to use her name. Properly approached, she might well have given it.

'Go on,' he said again. 'Why do you believe Lady Mary is at risk?'

Lest her theories be thought fanciful, Rosamond recounted only what she knew to be true. She described Potter's symptoms and repeated his dying words and then explained why she was so certain Lady Mary had been the poisoner's next victim.

'The rat died,' Leicester repeated, his expression grim.

'It did, my lord. Most horribly.' Skipping over her own injuries, she told him how she had surprised an intruder in Lady Mary's bedchamber. 'Only five individuals were in the Wardrobe of Robes when Griffith Potter died and also at court when Lady Mary received that anonymous gift,' she added. 'Lady Mary's waiting gentlewomen – Margaret Ellerker, Elizabeth Farnham and Anne Morgan – and her tiring maid, Beatrice Unton. Sir Jerome Bowes seems an unlikely suspect, but he was also there.'

'Bowes has a temper,' Leicester mused, 'and he is no friend of mine, but he has more to gain by befriending Lady Mary than by killing her. He hopes to be appointed ambassador to Muscovy.'

Rosamond reached across the space between the seats to touch his arm. 'You are certain Lady Mary is well?'

'I would have told you if she was not, but I admit that your story troubles me.'

The coach passed through the gate and into Rosamond's courtyard and came to a stop. She heard her groom of the stable hail the driver but when he would have opened the door and let down the steps, the earl waved him away.

'I have no doubt that my rivals at court would delight in seeing me and mine pushed aside for a royal cousin of their choosing.' He flexed his fingers on one knee, as if imagining what he would do to anyone who opposed him.

Rosamond waited, growing more uneasy with every passing moment. She twitched when he spat out a name. ·

'Farnham! It has to be.'

'One of Lady Mary's waiting gentlewomen is Elizabeth Farnham,' she whispered, 'but why do you think she is the guilty party?'

'Has she a brother named George?' When Rosamond nodded, Leicester sent her a wolfish grin. 'There's your villain, then. George Farnham is a retainer of the earl of Shrewsbury and Shrewsbury's countess has a granddaughter who is also cousin to the queen.'

Was it possible? Had Bess murdered Griffith Potter and tried to kill Lady Mary? 'There is no proof,' she reminded the earl.

'You would be amazed what a man . . . or a woman . . . will confess to under the right sort of questioning.'

He meant torture. Rosamond's stomach tightened painfully at the thought.

'What if you are wrong, my lord? The poisoner will still be there, and she will know that her earlier crimes have been uncovered. Lady Mary will be in even greater danger than before. If you believe what I have told you, convince your sister to take me back. Let me stay close to Lady Mary to guard her from harm.'

She felt his gaze boring into her, taking her measure, judging her.

'What better case can be made for one of the others?' he asked.

Rosamond had to swallow before she could speak. 'Ticey could be acting on your former sister-in-law's behalf. Lady Unton, or whatever she calls herself, is said to be a madwoman.'

'She calls herself Lady Warwick,' Leicester said through gritted teeth. After a moment's consideration, he shook his head. 'A tiring maid is capable of doing much harm, I agree, but having freed young Ticey from her mistress's clutches myself, I can assure you that the girl would never again do her bidding.'

'Madge Ellerker, then. She opposes the marriage to the tsar for religious reasons. Why, even Nan Morgan might be behind the attacks, acting on behalf of one of Lord Howard's daughters.'

Leicester reached for the door latch. 'I will tell my sister to get rid of the lot of them, and there's an end to the matter.'

Rosamond caught his arm. 'What if I am wrong? What if the poisoner is someone else in the household? Help me to return, my lord. Let me unmask the person behind all these troubles.'

He sat back, regarding her with renewed suspicion. 'What advantage is there to you in serving as a guard dog? You have no need to make your way in the world. You have your father's fortune. And do not try to convince me that you are acting out of affection for Lady Mary. She's as prickly as a nettle and always has been.'

'You know that I have a husband.'

Leicester's nod was wary.

'He is at present in Moscow.' Her voice shook, but Rosamond soldiered on. 'He is in one of the tsar's prisons, but even if he were not, every Englishman in Muscovy is in danger should negotiations with Ambassador Pissemsky fall through. You have the queen's ear, my lord. You—'

'I knew there would be something.'

Rosamond held her breath, fearing that he was about to refuse to help her.

'You want me to speak to the queen on your husband's behalf.' The wolfish smile returned. 'I agree. But hear me well, Mistress Jaffrey. If I do so, and convince my sister to take you back, I will hold you responsible for Lady Mary's safety. If aught happens to her while you are in her service, your husband will not be the only one to live out his days in a dank, cold prison cell.'

Forty

Rosamond returned to Lady Mary's household in early May after nearly a month away. Nothing appeared to have changed. The routine of prayer, needlework and improving books continued, unaffected by political machinations, crazed killers, or the absence of one insignificant waiting gentlewomen.

'Lady Huntingdon told us you had a family emergency,' Bess said when they, along with Madge and Nan, were seated in their accustomed places around the large, free-standing embroidery frame. Augustus Treadwell had not yet appeared to read to them and Lady Mary was closeted with her sister-in-law.

Lady Huntingdon had not been pleased to learn the truth behind Rosamond's deceit, but once she knew everything she saw the sense in using one of Lady Mary's own women to protect her. Male guards would be of no use if the killer struck from within Lady Mary's bedchamber. The countess balked, however, at Rosamond's suggestion that Lady Mary be informed of the attempt to poison her. She was to remain in ignorance of her danger.

'There was a death in my husband's family.' Rosamond kept her head bowed over her stitches to hide her face. 'There was no time for the news to reach him. That is why it fell to me to settle the estate. Did anything of note happen here while I was away?'

'That courtier we met in the Wardrobe of Robes visited a time or two.' Madge sounded disapproving.

Bess laughed aloud. 'Say rather that he has been here a half dozen times. He is a most pleasant fellow. He brings us gifts, sweets and trinkets, but those are nothing compared to the expensive baubles he presents to Lady Mary.'

'Do you mean Sir Jerome Bowes?'

'I see you remember him, too,' Nan said with a sly smile.

Rosamond wondered if the earl of Leicester knew about Sir Jerome's visits to Chelsea Manor. Both Leicester and Master Baldwin had told her that Bowes hoped to be named England's ambassador to Muscovy, but Lady Mary had no say in that appointment. Had Baldwin been right to suspect Bowes was the poisoner?

'Sir Jerome gave Lady Mary a linnet in a cage,' Nan said. 'It sings most sweetly.'

'A monkey would have made a better pet,' said Bess.

'Mayhap he will present her with one of those next.' Madge grimaced. 'Nasty, dirty little beasts. Better to keep a dog or a cat.'

'Such gifts are the sort a suitor might bring to his beloved,' Rosamond mused, 'but Sir Jerome must know that Lady Mary is all but betrothed to another.'

'She is too far above him in any case,' Nan said. 'More likely he hopes to have her support *after* she is married. He makes no secret of his quest for the ambassadorship.'

'Thus he has a *reason* to court Lady Mary, but he would have us believe that he spends time with each of us for the pleasure of our company alone.' Madge's critical tone softened as she spoke and Rosamond caught a quick exchange of smiles between the other two women.

'On one visit, Sir Jerome brought his lute,' Nan said. 'He played a song just for Madge.'

Her pretty face pinker than usual, Madge tried to make light of the incident. 'He played many songs that day.' She took two quick stitches in her embroidery before directing a scathing glance at Nan. 'You are the one he walked with in the garden. Twice.'

'Jealous?' Nan asked, a mischievous glint in her eyes.

Bess shook her head at their squabbling and turned to Rosamond. 'He paid flattering attention to each of us. Once he sat and talked with me about poetry for a quarter of an hour and another time he picked a flower in the gardens and tucked it into my hair.'

'Men like that only want one thing from a woman.' Madge's lips flattened into a thin, disapproving line.

Bowes was up to something, Rosamond thought. He would bear watching if he came to Chelsea Manor again.

'Has there been any more news about the marriage treaty?' she asked aloud.

Bess and Nan exchanged another speaking glance. Madge brightened and looked smug.

'We are not supposed to know about it yet,' Nan said, 'but Madge overheard Lady Huntingdon and Lady Mary talking. The meeting between Lady Mary and the ambassador from Muscovy is to take place in York House.'

'That is the Lord Chancellor's residence,' Bess added. 'We expect Lady Mary will be summoned any day now, and all of us with her.'

Torn between elation and dread, Rosamond continued to ply her needle as if she had not a care in the world. Soon the waiting would be over. One way or another, the negotiations for the treaty would end, the matter of Lady Mary's marriage would be settled, the ambassador would sail for home, and Rob, God willing, would be freed.

Forty-One

Rosamond wondered if professional players felt this nervous before the start of a performance. Hidden at the far end of one of the long, vine-covered tunnel arbors, their small party waited for the pre-arranged signal to begin strolling through Lord Chancellor Bromley's garden at York House. Ambassador Pissemsky's meeting with Lady Mary was to appear to be a casual, chance encounter. In truth, the staging had been carefully planned and well-rehearsed. The first act opened with the Lord Chancellor greeting the ambassador and escorting him to a banqueting house purpose-built at the exact center of the garden, where refreshments awaited them.

The choice of setting was no more random than the meeting itself. The land between the mansion called York House and the river contained an elaborate plantation. Graveled paths ran between mulberry trees, trellised herbers with turf-topped benches and rampant lions and dragons fashioned from shrubbery. Herbacious borders filled the air with sweet smells while stone benches tucked away in odd corners offered a place to rest for the weary.

Rosamond willed herself to be calm. She closed her eyes and inhaled slowly, savoring the fragrant air. The middle of May was too early for red and white roses and honeysuckle, a combination that produced a heady early-morning scent she'd always found pleasing, but hyssop and germander had been used as edging plants for the borders of a nearby bed filled with aromatic herbs. Lavender, sage, savory, and wild marjoram had been planted there to attract bees and butterflies but the combination of smells had the happy side effect of making humans mellow.

Just ahead of Rosamond and the other waiting gentlewomen, Lady Mary stood between Lady Huntingdon and Lady Bromley. At the first distant sound of male voices, all three tensed. The ambassador and the Lord Chancellor were about to step on stage.

Footsteps approached and then Lord Chancellor Bromley, in a hearty voice, spoke the words they'd been told to expect: 'It is but a modest repast, I assure you.'

Lady Mary drew in a shaky breath and stepped out of

concealment, closely followed by the other women. All around them flowers bloomed in a profusion of colors and shapes, everything from golden broom and red peonies to purple flag. Lady Mary and her entourage made a pretty contrast. She was dressed in purest white while Lady Huntingdon and Lady Bromley wore black. The rest of the party were attired in their yellow livery.

Their orders were to feign ignorance of the presence of anyone else in the garden until they came face-to-face with the ambassador, his interpreter, and the Lord Chancellor. As planned, Lady Huntingdon remarked upon the fine embroidery on Lady Bromley's sleeves and that good lady launched into a litany of praise for the skill of her needlewomen. This meaningless chatter served to bring them closer to Feodor Andreevitch Pissemsky.

Lady Mary, as instructed, acknowledged Pissemsky with a regal nod.

'Look your fill,' Bromley said.

Pissemsky stared at Lady Mary.

She stared back.

For several long minutes, no one said a word. Then Pissemsky spoke in his own language.

Rosamond had been primed for this moment. To her relief, she had no difficulty understanding his words. In the next instant, the ambassador's translator, the man Rosamond knew must be Doctor Robert Jacobi, confirmed their meaning: 'It is enough.'

Lady Mary and her entourage resumed their stroll through the garden. Servants scurried forth with more food and drink. Rosamond was not surprised to see Melka among them. To impress the ambassador, everyone had been pressed into service.

A short time later, as had also been arranged in advance, the ambassador's party left the banqueting house to admire the flowers. The two groups meandered past each other at intervals. Rosamond, ears stretched, managed to overhear bits and pieces of what Pissemsky said. He seemed to be complaining that he had not yet received the promised portrait of Lady Mary.

As soon as the ambassador departed, Lady Huntingdon and Lady Bromley went in search of the Lord Chancellor. Lady Mary collapsed onto the nearest bench. 'He seems so . . . foreign,' she whispered.

'He *is* foreign,' Madge said, 'and a heathen, as well.'

As if he had only been waiting for his cue to step onto the stage, Augustus Treadwell appeared from behind a flowering shrub. 'She speaks the truth, my lady, and I have more distressing news to impart to you.'

Rosamond had to move aside to allow the chaplain close to Lady Mary. At her nod of permission, Treadwell sat beside her on the bench and took her hand in his. 'One of the requirements of this marriage is that you and all your attendants be baptized in the Orthodox religion.'

Lady Mary's eyes widened in alarm. 'I must give up my faith?'

'I fear the tsar insists upon it.'

'Is there no remedy?'

The chaplain allowed himself a small smile. 'My lady, if you would save your immortal soul, you must refuse the match. Write to the queen and beg to be excused.'

'But it is my duty to marry where I am told.'

'Your duty to God is greater and the queen, as God's anointed, will not force you to go against your conscience once you make plain to her *why* you cannot wed.'

'If the tsar's demand that we convert is not enough to sway you,' Nan said, stepping closer to the bench, 'then consider this. He is called Ivan the Terrible and he earned his name. Not only has he tortured and executed many of his noblemen, he also killed his own son in a fit of rage.'

'He ordered the massacre of foreign merchants,' Treadwell interjected.

Rosamond felt her blood run cold. In that instant, fear for Rob's safety blocked out everything else. She could not hear, could not see, could not think.

Dizzy, she leaned against a nearby trellis and tried to focus her mind. She hated this feeling of helplessness and fought not to give in to it. It took an effort, but she forced her concern for Rob to the back of her mind. The best thing she could do – the *only* thing she could do – was keep her ears open and her wits about her. There was no telling what tidbit of information she gathered might make all the difference.

'Tsar Ivan's guards inflict terror on innocents,' Treadwell said.

'He already has a wife, but he means to put her aside to wed you, my lady.' Nan leaned closer and lowered her voice, 'and yet he will not give up his mistresses. It is said that he is attended at all times by a retinue of a hundred concubines.'

Rosamond blinked. Surely that charge was an exaggeration.

And why was Nan suddenly so anxious to convince Lady Mary to give up her plans. What had happened to change her mind? Nan was the one who had claimed all along to want to go to Muscovy.

Rosamond's gaze shifted to Augustus Treadwell, waxing prolific on the folly of embracing the Orthodox faith. She remembered the day she'd seen Nan with Madge and the chaplain in the garden at Chelsea Manor. She'd thought then that they were plotting something, until Nan had convinced her otherwise.

A glance at Bess told Rosamond that she was also puzzled by Nan's change of heart.

Abruptly, Lady Mary held up a hand for silence. 'Say no more. I am convinced. I will petition the queen to relieve me of this burden. I will decline the honor of becoming Empress of Muscovy on the grounds that I cannot, in good conscience, betray the faith in which I was raised.'

Rosamond could not fault the woman for refusing to be tied for life to a devil like Ivan the Terrible, but the cat-lapped-up-the-cream smile on Nan's face troubled her.

Forty-Two

The Lord Chancellor, thinking to please Lady Huntingdon, had arranged for the earl of Leicester's company of players to perform after supper that evening. Before the night was over, Rosamond meant to speak with Henry Leveson. She lost one opportunity because her maid broke one point after another as she helped Rosamond change into more elaborate clothing.

As soon as they were the only two people left in the dormitory-style lodgings Lady Mary's gentlewomen were obliged to share during their stay at York House, Melka left off fussing over a sleeve. When she closed and locked the door, Rosamond belatedly realized something was troubling the older woman.

'What is wrong, Melka?'

Melka's answer was to close her eyes and speak in an approximation of a deep male voice . . . in Russian. Using her uncanny but useful ability to parrot back entire conversations word for word, she repeated a conversation she had overheard earlier in the day. Rosamond had her do it twice more before she was satisfied that she understood it all. Not only was the dialogue in a foreign tongue, but Ambassador Pissemsky had difficulty with common English names. He pronounced Hastings 'Hantis' and referred to Lady Mary as 'the princess of Hountinski', his version of Huntingdon, and called Lady Mary's brother the earl an 'appendage prince'.

Speaking to his English interpreter, Doctor Jacobi, Pissemsky had ordered him to write down the details the tsar had asked for – Lady Mary's height, complexion, and measurements and whether she possessed 'dorodna,' a word that meant stately appearance.

It was the last part of what Melka had overheard while serving refreshments in the banqueting house that gave Rosamond most cause for concern. Pissemsky had referred to a 'waiting gentlewoman', although Rosamond could not tell from the context whether he was speaking in general terms or meant one of Lady Mary's waiting gentlewomen in particular. She was still pondering this question when the play began and Henry Leveson came on stage in one of his women's roles. At the same moment, Rosamond saw Nan slip out of the candle-lit hall.

Less suspicious souls would have assumed that she needed to visit the privy. Rosamond thought the other woman's manner far too stealthy for that. Before she could think better of the impulse, Rosamond followed her.

In the screens passage, the sound of scurrying footsteps gave her a direction. Moving swiftly, she was in time to see a door close. She eased it open again and stepped outside.

Darkness engulfed her. She blinked, willing her eyes to adjust to the diminution of light. The scrape of flint against steel off to her left gave her a moment's warning before the lantern Nan was lighting flared. Rosamond cursed her full skirts and the vivid popinjay blue of her gown as she pressed herself against the wall and tried to make herself as small and inconspicuous as possible.

There had been no time for Rosamond find a cloak to cover her finery, but Nan did not have one either. Even the faint glow of her lantern – the candle had been lit but the slats were closed to a sliver – reflected the shimmer of her willow-green gown and cream-colored sleeves, making her easy to keep in sight. Neither of them was appropriately dressed for a nocturnal excursion through the narrow streets and narrower alleys of the city of Westminster.

Nan walked briskly, keeping to the shadows, circling York House to exit the grounds by way of a side gate that avoided the main thoroughfare at Charing Cross. She seemed to know where she was going, even though the houses crowding close together all looked the same to Rosamond. When they passed close to an alehouse, a wave of boisterous laughter rolled out, startling her, but the streets themselves seemed empty of everyone but herself and Nan.

There was no moon and although householders were supposed to hang lanterns by their doors, few did so. Rosamond stumbled more than once but dogged determination drove her on.

Without warning, Nan turned aside. Rosamond skidded to a stop. Another few steps and she would have been seen. She could hear Nan clearly as the other woman greeted the person she'd come to meet. The deeper rumble of a male voice answered her.

An innocent assignation? Or something more sinister?

Creeping forward, step by slow step, Rosamond peered into what she now recognized as a small, overgrown garden at the back of a tenement. It was enclosed by a stone wall, except for the gaping hole where the gate had once been. Nan stood in the shadow of a tree. Her back was to Rosamond and one hand rested on the arm of the cloaked figure beside her. She'd placed her lantern on the ground. Its pale, narrow beam fell far short of illuminating the man's face.

A steady murmur of conversation continued. Rosamond bent low and followed the wall, one hand on the rough stone for guidance, until she reckoned she was level with the tree. Holding her breath, careful to make no sound, she rose up and peered over the top of the wall.

In the darkness, nothing moved. Even the voices had ceased. Had it not been for the faint glow from Nan's lantern, Rosamond would have thought her quarry had departed.

A low, throaty laugh drifted toward her. One shadow in the blackness separated into two.

'Enough,' Nan said. 'I have no time for dalliance.'

They were no more than a foot away from her. Rosamond went still. Then the man spoke and even her breath stopped. She knew that voice. Nan's companion was Ralph Gargrave, yeoman of the robes, employed in the Wardrobe of Robes to examine the queen's garments for poison.

Her thoughts in chaos, Rosamond eased lower until she was sitting on the ground, heedless of the damage she was doing to the expensive fabric of her gown. In need of the support, she rested her back against the wall. Only then did she dare draw in a shaky breath.

A stray comment Madge had made months earlier came back to her, something about a bald man who had visited Nan – courting her, Madge had implied – when Lady Mary and her waiting gentle-women were still at Ashby-de-la-Zouch. Gargrave? If he and Nan had been lovers all this time, it was no great leap to conclude that it must have been Nan and Gargrave she'd seen at Windsor Castle.

But if Gargrave was Nan's lover, why keep his courtship secret? Why sneak out of York House to meet him tonight? All her senses alert, as cautious as a mouse approaching a cat, Rosamond got to her knees and inched upward again until she could hear what Nan was saying.

'I wish I had realized sooner how easy it would be to dissuade Lady Mary. Who would have believed that any woman would let religious scruples keep her from becoming an empress?'

Gargrave's harsh voice was anything but loverlike. 'I'd not have blood on my hands if you had.' In the lantern's glow, he stood with head bowed, twisting his cap in his hands.

'I did not ask you to kill anyone.' Nan's tone could have frozen the embers in a brazier.

'I did it to protect you, my heart.'

'You did it to protect yourself.'

Rosamond stifled a gasp. *Gargrave* had killed Griffith Potter? For *Nan*?

Tears stung the backs of her eyes. She had liked Nan Morgan. Nan had been the first to befriend her when she joined Lady Mary's household. She had bravely nursed—

With a sick wrench of the stomach, Rosamond realized the truth. If Ralph Gargrave killed Griffith Potter to protect Nan, then it followed that Nan had been the one who had tried to kill Lady Mary. Nan had not been brave when she offered to help nurse her mistress. She'd known Lady Mary was not contagious.

Questions bombarded Rosamond as she strained to hear more of the exchange on the other side of the wall. How had Griffith Potter found out about the plan to use yew to kill Lady Mary? How had Gargrave known what Potter suspected? Had he *meant* to commit murder on the same day as Lady Mary's visit to the Wardrobe of Robes? Had Nan's presence that day somehow precipitated Potter's death?

No answers were forthcoming. Nan soothed Gargrave with meaningless platitudes. She allowed him a few more minutes of kissing and fondling and then pushed him away, telling him she had to return to York House before she was missed.

Rosamond stayed in concealment until she was certain both Nan and Gargrave were well away, but although her body remained motionless, her thoughts continued to move apace. By the time she rose and dusted off her skirts, she knew what she had to do.

Walking back to York House was a slow business, fraught with danger. She had to avoid hazards both seen and unseen, including broken cobbles underfoot and a band of drunken revelers wending their way homeward from an alehouse. She had no idea how late it was when she reached the Lord Chancellor's residence.

Her heart sank when she entered the great hall of York House and found it deserted. The players had packed up their props and painted sets and departed.

Earlier that evening, she had meant to give Henry Leveson a

message for Sir Francis Walsingham, warning him of Lady Mary's change of heart. The discovery she had just made was even more important. Was Walsingham at court? At Barn Elms? Or at his headquarters in Seething Lane? Grimly determined to report what she knew, as well as what she suspected, she squared her shoulders. She had no idea how she would manage it, but somehow she had to locate the queen's spy master without delay.

Forty-Three

Steps dragging, Rosamond left the hall. She would find Melka and change into clothing more suitable for a river journey at night. Seething Lane was closest. She would start her search there.

A voice spoke her name, causing her to start and cry out in alarm, but when Henry Leveson stepped out of the shadows the sensation of relief was so powerful that she swayed. Leveson caught her arm to steady her.

Rosamond despised showing weakness and hated that her next words came out sounding breathless. 'I thought you had gone.'

'I should have. The rest of Lord Leicester's Men are halfway back to London by now.'

'And the spectators?'

Leveson grinned. 'They separated into two groups. The Bromleys and some of their less pious guests intend to gamble the night away in an upstairs chamber. Those ladies who must live up to the standards of the earl of Huntingdon have adjourned to the chapel.'

For once, she blessed Augustus Treadwell's habit of long-winded evening prayers. Tonight the excessive piety of the household would serve her in good stead. No one would notice when she left York House in Leveson's company.

'Let me carry your messages to Seething Lane,' the player begged when she told him what she wanted him to do. 'No respectable woman is out and about at this hour of the night. It will be difficult enough to find a boat to take me to London. I may have to walk the length of the Strand and then wait outside the city gate until it is opened on the morrow.'

'Nonsense. Just promise the boatman a fat fee. I will gladly pay whatever he asks.'

'The watch keeps an eye on landing places. Those abroad after dark are subject to arrest. I do not mean to insult you, Mistress Jaffrey, but they will take you for a wh— That is, some might mistake your reason for being abroad so late.'

Rosamond waved his objections aside with a fine disregard for logic. 'My information is too important to let petty concerns prevent me from delivering it in person to the principal secretary. Tell the boatman to land just above London Bridge. From there it is but a short walk to Sir Francis's house in Seething Lane. You are certain he will be there and not at court?'

Leveson leapt on this excuse. 'He may have gone away again. You should stay here until I can ascertain his whereabouts.'

'If he is not there, then you will escort me to Master Baldwin's warehouse in Billingsgate. Enough argument.' She made a shooing motion. 'Look for a boat while I change into less conspicuous clothing. I will meet you at the water stairs in a quarter of an hour. And do not even think of going on without me,' she called after him. 'I will follow on my own if I must.'

Convinced she was doing the right thing, Rosamond went in search of her tiring maid. While Melka helped her out of one set of garments and into another, Rosamond outlined her plans. Melka voiced the same objections Leveson had and with an equal lack of success. Rosamond could not be talked out of going to London, not even when Melka reminded her that Sir Francis Walsingham was likely wroth with her for telling the earl of Leicester how she'd come to join Lady Mary's household.

'Fetch my dark blue wool cloak,' she ordered.

It would ward off the chill from the river and help hide the fact that she was a woman. She toyed with the idea of assuming her boys' clothing. At times like this it was damnably inconvenient to be female, but being caught in that disguise would have even worse consequences. Besides, she'd be better off facing Walsingham garbed as a proper gentlewoman.

'I will return at first light,' she told her maid. 'Go you and sleep in my bed, the covers over your face. In the morning, with any luck at all, I will be able to convince the others that I felt ill and retired early.'

She could always lie and say that her monthly courses had come upon her. Thinking back, she'd wager that was what Nan had done in the hope of an opportunity to spend time, unobserved, in Lady Mary's bedchamber.

The boat Leveson had found was old, cramped, and smelled of fish. The man at the oars, seen by the light of the lantern hung on a pole in the stern, was even older. His pale face was deeply-lined, especially around the eyes and mouth, and his chin sported random patches of gray stubble instead of a proper beard.

The creak of the oars and the sound they made when they swept through the water were not the only noises on the river, but few people traveled this late and most of those who did were up to no good. Rosamond shivered, although the night air was not especially cold. She was remembering some of the more graphic tales she'd heard of criminal activities. There was even one legendary story about a murder. Two foreign merchants had been slain in a boat at night in the middle of the Thames between Southwark and London.

She glanced at Leveson. He looked uneasy, as well he might, but he *was* Walsingham's man. Baldwin had assured her of that. She presumed he knew how to defend himself and protect her, too. Just in case he did not, she shifted position to give her right hand more space to move. She had taken the time to assume the boots with the concealed knife. She wished now that she had chosen to wear the cloak that contained the second blade.

After what seemed like hours but was well less than one, the small watercraft arrived at Old Swan Stairs.

'Let me take you direct to Master Baldwin,' Leveson pleaded. 'In the morning, he can escort you to—'

'The information I have will not wait.' Rosamond thrust a sovereign into the boatman's hand and disembarked unassisted.

She had always had an excellent sense of direction and she'd taken the time, after learning from Master Baldwin that Walsingham's house was located in Seething Lane, to discover for herself just where in London to find that street. Leveson trotted along beside her as she strode purposefully along Thames Street in the direction of London Bridge and the Tower.

Gracechurch Street, called Gracious by most Londoners, became New Fish Street as it swept southward to the bridge. As in Westminster, the lanterns that were supposed to be lit and hung before each door were conspicuous by their absence, leaving most streets and alleys in darkness. The main thoroughfare and the bridge were exceptions. Since they were also more likely to be patrolled by the watch, Rosamond crossed the wide expanse of New Fish Street at an even more rapid pace.

No one challenged her.

As she glided silently through each intersection she ticked off the names in her head. First came Pudding Lane, then St Botolph Lane. Long Lane, which was sometimes called Love Lane – she had not troubled to ask why – was followed by St Mary, Church, Hart, and

Water Lanes. When the Custom House rose up ahead, she knew she needed to bear left instead of proceeding straight ahead. The way broadened in front of her and several narrow streets branched off at odd angles.

'There,' she whispered, pointing north. 'Seething Lane.' Beneath her feet, she felt the start of a gentle rise. If they continued eastward, they'd find themselves climbing Tower Hill to the place of execution. 'Which house is it?'

Resigned to his fate, Leveson guided her to a side entrance at Walsingham's headquarters. At his knock – three quick raps followed by two slower ones separated by a count of five – it was flung open by a tall, gangly man with a prominent Adam's apple. He took immediate exception to Rosamond's presence and he and Leveson stepped aside to huddle together and argue in whispers.

After a few minutes another man, this one slender with dark yellow hair and a beard several shades lighter, joined in the debate. Their voices were too muffled for Rosamond to overhear what they were saying but whatever Leveson said on her behalf eventually convinced the gatekeeper to let her enter. After a short wait in a small, unfurnished anteroom, she was escorted to Walsingham's private study.

The principal secretary sat behind an enormous desk piled high with papers and looking as alert as if it was the middle of the day instead of the middle of the night. He was not pleased to see her.

'You would have done better to stay away from Chelsea Manor once your deception was discovered.'

'If I had, I would not have learned who killed Griffith Potter. Or who tried to poison Lady Mary. Or that she has decided that she no longer wishes to wed the tsar,' she added as an afterthought.

Walsingham's hard, unblinking stare would have disconcerted a lesser woman. Rosamond stared back. He looked tired, she thought, and felt a moment's sympathy for him. Then she hardened her heart and went on the offensive.

'You are angry with me for revealing to the earl of Leicester that you were the one who sent me to his sister, but you have only yourself to blame for that. You wished me to gather intelligence and then you dismissed what I discovered because I had no proof. Unlike you, Sir Francis, I could not ignore my suspicions. I had to go back, and it is as well that I did.'

'Have you proof now?'

'Decide for yourself.'

She told her story without elaboration, repeating word-for-word what she had overheard Nan and Gargrave say to each other.

Walsingham's face wore a stoic expression but Rosamond thought she glimpsed a spark of admiration in his eyes. 'Your information is most useful, Mistress Jaffrey. I thank you for bringing it to me. Keep your ears open upon your return but pretend you know nothing of Mistress Morgan's activities.'

Rosamond's clenched fingers bit into her hands as she tried to contain her frustration, but she'd never been good at keeping her temper when her sense of injustice was aroused. 'You cannot let murder go unpunished! It is unconscionable. And even if you value the life of one of your own men so lightly, what Nan and Gargrave have done is also treason.'

'I do not need you to teach me my duty, Mistress Jaffrey.'

She refused to back down. 'But you do, Sir Francis, if it is your intention to do nothing.'

His response was an odd snorting sound. She stared at him. Could that possibly have been a laugh?

'Mistress Jaffrey, you must learn to trust your elders. Go back to York House.'

'Not until you assure me that *some* action will be taken. From what I overheard, it is clear to me that there is no longer any danger to Lady Mary but Nan must have been suspicious of me. Who else could have arranged those accidents?'

'Do you fear for your own safety?'

In all honesty, she had to admit she did not. 'But I do not understand why you cannot order Nan's arrest, and Gargrave's, too. What I overheard is proof of their guilt.'

'I am not accustomed to explaining myself, Mistress Jaffrey.'

'And I am not accustomed to following orders unless I have good reason to.'

His reply was curt. 'Pissemsky.'

She blinked at him. 'You want the ambassador to return to Russia believing the marriage to Lady Mary will go forward. I understand that. But what—?'

'Any change in Lady Mary's household will alert his spies. This is not the time to raise questions.' Walsingham sent her a withering look. 'There is more at stake here than one woman's crimes. I will deal with Mistress Morgan after the ambassador is safely on his way back to Muscovy.'

Grudgingly, Rosamond accepted his logic, although she was not certain she agreed with him. It seemed neither she nor Nan could leave Lady Mary's service. Not yet.

'What about Ralph Gargrave? He is the one who murdered Griffith Potter. I heard him confess to doing so to protect his lady love. Will you ignore that, too?'

Walsingham's face told her nothing, but after a moment he rose and strode toward the door. 'Wait here,' he ordered.

Forty-Four

Left alone in Sir Francis Walsingham's study, Rosamond was tempted to take a closer look at his papers but she resisted the urge. Instead, she curled up in a chair. Well before Walsingham returned, she had nodded off.

He shook her by the shoulder to wake her.

Still half asleep, she blinked up at him.

'Gargrave is in custody.'

His words brought Rosamond instantly awake. She sat up, wincing as her cramped muscles protested the sudden movement.

'I had him brought here rather than to the Tower,' Walsingham continued. 'It occurs to me, Mistress Jaffrey, that confronting him with you might be more effective than torture.'

Unsure whether to be flattered or insulted, Rosamond followed the queen's principal secretary and spy master into another room in the house in Seething Lane. The yellow-haired man was already there, as was Ralph Gargrave. The latter had not been handled gently. One eye was swollen almost shut and blood stained his face and shirt. His sleeve looked as if it had been slashed. He was tied to a chair, his arms pulled back at an unnatural and undoubtedly painful angle.

Tamping back a rush of pity, Rosamond hardened her heart and stepped closer to the prisoner. 'Do you remember me, Master Gargrave?'

His undamaged eye widened as he recognized her.

'You were so kind to me that day, assuring me you would look after my reputation and take care of all the nasty details associated with Master Potter's sudden, *accidental* death.' Acid dripped from her words, making him wince.

She was considering whether or not it would be beneficial to strike him when he began to babble. In astonishment, she listened as a confession poured out of him.

'I cannot live any longer with the guilt,' Gargrave wailed. 'It is a terrible sin to kill a man.'

'Why did you do it, then?'

'He knew too much. He found the letter.'

'What letter?'

'From her. From the queen of my heart.'

'Do you mean Nan Morgan, Lady Mary's waiting gentlewoman?' Rosamond glanced at the man with the yellow hair and beard. He sat quietly in a corner, taking down every word Gargrave said. A small pair of spectacles perched halfway down his nose, making him look more like a clerk than a spy.

Gargrave began to sob. 'She is innocent in all this. I had to protect her.'

Interrogating a man whose self-control crumbled like a chunk of stale bread challenged Rosamond's patience, but Walsingham, standing at the back of the room, seemed desirous that she continue what she'd begun.

'Innocent?' Her tone mocking, Rosamond walked in a circle around the bound man. 'Innocent? She tried twice to kill me, Master Gargrave.'

'No. She would not.'

'She would. I saw you with her at Windsor Castle. The next morning, I was struck in the head by a rock. I escaped without permanent harm, but such a blow might as easily have killed me.'

His one good eye pleaded with her for forgiveness. 'I did not think you recognized me, for all that I saw your face plain enough, but I warned Nan that you might have seen us and I called you by name. When she demanded to know how I knew you, it all tumbled out – that I'd killed Potter for her sake. She knew nothing of his death till then. I swear it. But she . . . she said I had done well. And then she rushed back into the tennis play by a side door, hoping to make it appear as if she'd never left the company of the others.'

'She tried again to kill me,' Rosamond said, 'by spilling wax on the stairs in a place I was sure to step. I fell all the way to the bottom, Master Gargrave. Hardier souls than I have met their deaths from such a fall.'

'No,' he moaned.

She leaned in, until their faces were mere inches apart, waiting until he met her eyes to speak in a low, threatening tone of voice. 'Yes. And now you are going to tell me the rest of the story. Why did you help her? How did you help her? Why did you kill Griffith Potter?'

At times incoherent, Gargrave unburdened himself. Rosamond once again felt pity, if only for a brief instant, as she pieced the fragments together. He had met Nan during her days in Lady Howard's service, when she had visited the Wardrobe of Robes in that noblewoman's company. He had fallen in love with her and she had encouraged his feelings, even claimed to return them.

'You visited her at Ashby-de-la-Zouch.' Rosamond circled him again. It took little imagination to guess what had happened next. A suitor traditionally gave gifts to his beloved. He'd have wanted to send Nan tokens of his esteem and if he could not afford to buy expensive things, why then he had his pick of all the items courtiers had given to the queen.

'How many of the articles of clothing you examined for poison did you send to her once you were certain they contained no toxic substances?'

'I am no thief!'

'Liar!' She cuffed him lightly on the side of the head. 'You sent her sleeves and ruffs and jewelry.' All those baubles Nan had claimed came from her estranged family in Herefordshire must have been gifts from Ralph Gargrave. 'What did you get in return?'

'She promised to marry me.'

Rosamond could not help herself. She laughed. 'She lied. Her whole purpose in this has been to leave England. Or did she invite you to accompany her to Muscovy?'

Color rose in his face. Embarrassment? Anger?

Stopping in front of him, Rosamond pointed an accusing finger. 'Did you procure poison for her?'

'Only something to put down a sick horse.' A greenish tinge overtook the red in his cheeks, as if he had, at last, fully comprehended how badly he had been used.

'A *horse*?' The man had been besotted indeed to believe such a tale. Nan did not own a horse. Even if she did, she'd not be the one charged with ending its life. 'How did she communicate this request to you? Did you visit Chelsea Manor?'

'In a letter,' he blurted. '*The* letter. The one he saw.'

'Potter?'

Tears streamed down Gargrave's cheeks. 'He saw the letter. He pretended he had not read it, but I knew better. In it she asked me to have a vial of poison ready for her when she visited the Wardrobe of Robes with Lady Mary. Potter was waiting to see which waiting gentlewoman approached me. Then he would have reported both of us to the yeomen of the guard.'

Rosamond stopped him with a hand on his shoulder. He jolted in pain but she held on. 'Which waiting gentlewoman? Do you mean to say that Potter did not know the letter came from Nan?'

'She never signs her love letters.' Gargrave bit back a sob. 'She draws a heart with a little crown upon it to signify that she is the queen of my heart.'

Rosamond could envision it perfectly. It was the same emblem Nan had embroidered on the handkerchiefs she'd given as New Year's gifts.

'I had to protect her,' Gargrave whispered.

'You used the poison you had prepared for her to kill Griffith Potter.'

A broken man, Gargrave nodded.

In a low voice, Walsingham said, 'That is enough to hang them both.' He gestured for Rosamond to leave the room.

'I am not finished.' The dazed look on Gargrave's face was not encouraging. Rosamond slapped him hard enough to leave a red palm print on his cheek and make her hand sting. 'How did Potter know it was yew you'd given him?'

Sniffling, Gargrave mumbled something. Another slap, lighter this time, produced a more coherent answer. 'I told him! He was already a dead man. There was nothing that could save him and I wanted him to know what he'd forced me to do. After he collapsed, I went back to my post and I pretended nothing had happened.'

'And then I came along,' Rosamond murmured. 'That must have given you a shock, hearing me ask for the man you'd just murdered.'

'It was not the way I meant for him to be found, but by then he was already dead. I thought I had persuaded you to let me handle the matter.' He was all but pouting when he added, 'What proper gentlewoman would *want* to become involved in the investigation of a murder?'

'Potter was not dead. Not quite. He had enough life in him to warn me that something was wrong.'

Her brow furrowed as she remembered the scene. Was it possible he'd meant no more than that *he* had been poisoned with yew? Or had he tried to warn her that Lady Mary was in danger? She did not suppose she would ever know now and she did not suppose it mattered. The result had been the same.

'Did you meet with Nan afterward?' she asked.

'Only long enough to tell her that I no longer had the poison to give her. She was most displeased. I promised to procure more and bring it to her at my first opportunity.'

'At Windsor,' Rosamond said slowly, 'after which she used it to try to kill Lady Mary.'

Walsingham stepped in to take Rosamond's arm and end the interrogation. 'Dawn is nigh, Mistress Jaffrey. If you are to have any hope of concealing your absence, you must return to York House at once.'

Reluctantly, Rosamond let him lead her away but, at the door, she turned back. The yellow-haired man had produced shackles. Gargrave would be taken to the Tower of London. He'd suffer more intensive questioning there, and possibly torture. Rosamond found she did not much care what happened to him, but she did care deeply about what was to be done with someone else.

'Do you still mean to allow Nan her freedom? The real blame for Griffith Potter's death belongs to her and she did try to kill Lady Mary.'

'And your good self, as well,' Walsingham agreed. 'Therefore I advise against provoking her. I have already explained why it is necessary to keep Lady Mary's household intact for the nonce. I will deal with Mistress Morgan after the ambassador sails for Muscovy.'

Rosamond was far from satisfied and it struck her suddenly that although she would be wise to comply with the principal secretary's orders, she did not have to do so with meek obedience. What could he do if she refused? Arrest her? That would not accomplish his purpose.

'If I return to York House,' she said, 'and accompany Lady Mary back to Chelsea Manor and pretend to know nothing of Nan's guilt or Gargrave's arrest, there is something I must have in return.'

Walsingham sent her a look that had her blood running cold. 'What is it that you want from me?'

'Your promise that you will join with the earl of Leicester in asking the queen to demand my husband's release from the tsar's prison.'

For just a moment, his stern countenance softened with what might have been amusement. 'I have already done so, Mistress Jaffrey, on behalf of our mutual friend Nick Baldwin. And on his behalf also, I have implored the queen to request the return to England of Mistress Jane Bomelius.'

Forty-Five

Being with Nan day after day, never able to let down her guard, always needing to behave as if she knew nothing of what Nan had done, was one of the hardest tasks Rosamond had ever undertaken. Each night she fell into bed exhausted by the strain of playing her part.

The queen did not acknowledge Lady Mary's petition to be free of the tsar's unwanted courtship for some time, although the earl of Leicester did send word to his sister that no one was to speak to outsiders of Lady Mary's feelings in the matter. Thus Lady Mary had to bear with equanimity the teasing of those friends from court who wrote to her or visited Chelsea Manor. They took to calling her the empress of Muscovy, laughing at her blushes, unaware of the terrible fears she harbored now that her chaplain had broken his silence and warned her of Tsar Ivan's evil reputation.

On the tenth of June, Sir Jerome Bowes paid a formal visit in his role as English ambassador to Muscovy, having been named to that post a few days earlier. Lady Mary deigned to walk with him in the gardens, accompanied by Nan and Rosamond.

The roses and honeysuckle were in bloom, scenting the air with their pleasant combination of fragrances. Rosamond drew in a deep, soothing breath. Nan smiled and pointed to a butterfly. It seemed an ordinary day, except that every word she and Nan said to one another was a lie.

'You may speak freely in front of my attendants,' Lady Mary said.

Sir Jerome looked doubtful but complied with her wishes. 'I have orders, direct from Queen Elizabeth, to discourage the match between your ladyship and the tsar.'

Lady Mary swayed and clung to Sir Jerome's arm until she recovered herself. 'I am most gratified to hear it.'

'The matter must be handled with great diplomacy.' He preened a bit. 'I am not authorized to take Ambassador Pissemsky into my confidence and it will be many weeks yet before I am admitted to Tsar Ivan's presence and can broach the matter of his marriage. At that time, I will hint that your family is loath to have you live so far away from them and reveal that you were recently ill and are still far from well.'

Lady Mary frowned at that. 'I am wholly recovered.'

'Do you wish to change your mind and marry him?' A hint of sarcasm laced his words.

At her side, Rosamond felt Nan stiffen.

'I do not,' said Lady Mary, 'but neither do I wish to have lies told about me.'

'Revealing the truth is not possible. Her Majesty wishes to maintain trade relations with Muscovy. The tsar must continue to believe in the possibility of a marriage alliance with the princess of his choice. He will accept delay but not outright refusal.'

'Do you mean to tell him that I may yet be persuaded to accept him?' Alarm had Lady Mary's voice rising to a shrillness that made Rosamond wince.

'Have no fear of that, my lady. Rather I will suggest to him that others of the queen's cousins may suit him better.'

To judge by the sour expression on her face, this plan pleased Lady Mary even less, especially when Bowes refused to tell her what ladies he had in mind.

Rosamond glanced at Nan and was unsurprised to find her smiling. Nan must have hoped all along that another royal cousin would be substituted for Lady Mary. Her actions made sense only if she was convinced that Lord Howard of Effingham's daughter Frances would be next in line to be offered to the tsar.

'Your portrait will be delivered to the ambassador in a day or two,' Bowes continued. They had reached the high ground at the end of the garden with its distant view of London's church spires. 'Pissemsky will also receive a corrected copy of the English proposals for the treaty. Once he has both in hand, he will be escorted to Gravesend and given the honor of reviewing the Muscovy fleet before it embarks to escort him back to his homeland.'

'I will be greatly relieved when he has gone,' Lady Mary said.

'He will depart soon, I promise you. And now, I must return to London. I have much to do before I set sail.' He indicated the peascod-bellied, popinjay-green doublet he wore. 'I cannot represent England at the tsar's court looking like a beggar.'

Lady Mary wished him God speed and a successful embassy. He had already left the garden when Nan noticed that the oversized peacock feather he wore tucked into the band of his tall hat, had fallen to the graveled path.

'Sir Jerome will be bereft without it,' she said as she scooped it up.

Lady Mary shaded her eyes. 'It will never do to deprive him of his plumage. If you hurry, you can overtake him at the water stairs.'

Rosamond watched Nan run after the new-made ambassador with a deep sense of uneasiness, then chided herself for imagining new schemes where none existed. Nan believed herself safe. She had only to be patient until Lady Mary's replacement was named and she would gain her heart's desire.

Less than a week later, Nan was gone.

Her possessions, including the chest full of gifts, were also missing.

Rosamond was about to send word to Sir Francis Walsingham when a messenger arrived at Chelsea Manor to tell Lady Mary that Ambassador Pissemsky had left London for Gravesend. That meant, Rosamond realized, that she, too, was free to leave. Accompanied by Melka, she returned to Willow House.

She slept poorly her first night back in her own bed. The thought that Nan might escape punishment for her crimes grated on her. Had she returned to her family in Herefordshire? If so, Walsingham's agents would find and arrest her. But what if she had fled farther afield, or lost herself in the crowds of London? Rosamond racked her brain to think of some way she could help in the search. She did not intend to let Nan elude justice.

The next morning, the seventeenth day of June, she sent word of Nan's disappearance to both Sir Francis Walsingham and Master Nicholas Baldwin. She was not surprised when Baldwin called on her that same afternoon.

She was the image of a proper gentlewoman when she received him, dressed in layers of stifling fabric, needlework in hand, seated near a window in the gallery, but she scarce waited for him to greet her before she rushed into speech.

'I will scour the length and breadth of England for Nan Morgan if need be,' she vowed. If nothing else, the quest would distract her from worrying about Rob.

'Leave that to Walsingham,' he advised, 'and let me depart for Gravesend with an easy mind.'

'You know me better than that.'

He sighed. 'I do. Will you at least promise to be careful?'

'I will. Do you sail in one of your own ships?'

He nodded. 'The *Winifred*. Sir Jerome Bowes will be aboard the *Dolphin*. He carries the queen's request that Rob be released, but I take with me sufficient funds to bribe every official in Muscovy. One way or the other, he will be freed.'

If he is still in prison, Rosamond thought. *If he is still alive.*

He *had* to be. Surely she would know if he was dead.

'When do you sail?'

'Within the week. The wind and the tide make that decision. Is there a message you wish me to give to Rob when I see him?'

There was a great deal she wanted to say to Rob, Rosamond thought, but it needed to be said in person. And yet, there was something Master Baldwin could deliver to him. 'Wait here,' she told him.

Hastening to her bedchamber, she fetched the plain leather case that contained the portrait in miniature Master Gheeraerts had given her. She wanted Rob to remember what his wife looked like. His young wife. His legal wife . . . as opposed to any mistress he might have acquired.

'Bring him back to me,' she said when she entrusted the token to Master Baldwin. She waved him away when the catch in her voice brought a look of pity into his eyes.

That night she dreamed of Rob, a troubled, nightmarish vision of an emaciated man she scarce recognized, chained to a wall in a dank prison cell. That image was still in her mind the next morning when a stranger arrived at her door.

By his dress he was a prosperous merchant. He introduced himself as George Barne, governor of the Muscovy Company. 'I have brought you a letter from your husband,' he announced. 'It was smuggled out of Moscow at the end of January, hidden in the false bottom of a bottle of aqua vitae.'

Rosamond's hand shook a little as she took it. Rob's handwriting was tiny, since he'd had but one sheet of paper. When he'd filled the page in one direction, he'd turned it upside down and written between the lines. He'd covered both sides that way.

Her consternation grew as she read. His mind must have been affected by his imprisonment. He wrote without coherence, rambling on about the size of his cell – smaller than the converted storeroom allotted to Parker scholars at Cambridge – and then stating baldly that he was terrified of dying so far from home. Was he ill? There was a feverish quality to the disconnected thoughts.

Tears came into her eyes as she read that he'd never stopped loving her. But the next sentence was, 'I beg you to pray for me, and be kinder to my mother.'

How typical of Rob! She scrubbed at her damp cheeks, sniffled, and read on, reaching the bottom of the page and turning over the much folded paper. He wrote that the Muscovy Company's agents in Moscow had done all they could for him. She blinked away more tears. Rob mentioned Toby Wharton, Master Baldwin's man, and someone named Egidius Crew. Then he wrote, 'I no longer count on Vaughan's help.'

A few lines later, the name appeared again. 'Vaughan calls his love in England his queen of hearts and claims she is a paragon among women,' Rob wrote, 'but none can compare to you, my dearest Rosamond.'

Even as the sentiment warmed her, Rosamond's hand clenched on the page. Queen of hearts? Was it possible?

She answered her own question. It was more than possible. It could not be coincidence that Ralph Gargrave called Nan the queen of his heart or that she signed herself with that emblem. This fellow Vaughan must be the friend Nan had spoken of, the man who had gone abroad to make his fortune. She had never said where he was, but once she had called him by his Christian name. Rosamond searched her memory, then turned to George Barne.

'Have you a Harry Vaughan in your employ in Muscovy?'

Forty-Six

Traveling to Gravesend from Billingsgate was a simple matter of paying twopence for a place on the Long Ferry, the tilt-boat that made the journey downriver at every ebb of the tide. For a quarter of an hour beforehand, the ringing of a bell warned passengers that departure was imminent. Rosamond paid for Melka and Charles to accompany her, Charles to carry her traveling chest, since she intended that they stay in the port town until the Muscovy fleet set sail.

Despite the protests of her maid, Rosamond made the trip wearing her boys' clothing. Henry Leveson might have seen through her disguise, but no one else had, and she chose to disregard his warning that she could be arrested for pretending to be a man. She felt certain a lad could get more answers than a woman could, since 'he' could ask questions in places she could not go.

Three dozen passengers huddled under the 'tilt' to shelter from the rain, but the awning did nothing to protect them from the gusting wind. Since an early morning fog obscured much of the shore during the first few miles on the river, Rosamond studied the people around her. She thought it unlikely Nan would be among them, but she'd be foolish not to look for her.

One fellow passenger, by the smell of his clothes, was a fishmonger. Another, by the finery she wore, was a whore. Both no doubt hoped to profit by what they found at the end of their journey. Of Nan Morgan there was no sign.

As they neared Gravesend, Rosamond smelled the sea . . . and the mudflats. Despite the poor visibility, she could make out the beacons, one on each side of the Thames, ready to be lighted to warn of invasion, and caught a glimpse of white from the steep chalk ridge rising up from the waterside.

She had visited Gravesend only once before, but remembered it as a village that climbed upward from the shore until it met the London road on its far side. All outbound ships were required to anchor in this port at the mouth of the Thames until they'd been searched by customs officials and received clearance to depart.

All English subjects were required to have a license to travel abroad.

Gravesend was where ships' crews loaded the last items of cargo and took on provisions, as well as where passengers waited, sometimes for weeks, for a favorable wind. The town was always full of travelers, seamen, whores, thieves and dockside astrologers selling prognostications for the voyage. In consequence, Gravesend boasted several fine inns. Rosamond bespoke a room at the best of them.

Nan would come here. Rosamond felt certain of it. She must know that Walsingham's men were searching for her. That being the case, her best hope was to flee the country, and if Harry Vaughan was indeed the man Nan had known since childhood, then it made sense that she would try to reach Moscow.

Once in Muscovy, Nan would be safe from English justice. She could live out the rest of her life in comfort. She might even end up serving the empress of Muscovy, if Frances Howard was sent in Lady Mary's stead.

Was Nan disguised as a boy, as Rosamond was? Or had she obtained a forged passport and persuaded one of the captains to let her book passage to Muscovy? It would be unusual for a woman to travel with the merchant fleet, but such a thing was not unheard of. How else had Mistress Bomelius made the journey?

Rosamond went first to the Customs House, but the fussy little man who was Gravesend's customer waved her away, telling her to come back after the fleet had sailed. Thwarted, Rosamond went in search of Master Baldwin's ship, the *Winifred*.

The sun had at last driven the fog away, although the clouds scudding across the pale blue sky were dark, wispy things rather than the puffy white shapes Rosamond preferred. She had just reached the waterfront when a company of men in stammel red cloaks caught her eye. A grizzled old mariner in the boisterous dockside crowd told her that the cloaks were livery. Sir Jerome Bowes was taking thirty such fellows to Muscovy.

He pointed to the ship that would transport Bowes and his entourage. 'Thirty cart loads of personal possessions he's had loaded aboard, too, and his horses.'

Shielding her eyes, Rosamond studied the *Dolphin*. She picked out the *Winifred* next and then the *Solomon*, the *Thomas Allen* and the *Prudence*. There were five or six more ships in the fleet, but she could not make out their names. When her gaze moved back to the *Dolphin*, she saw two figures at the rail. Sir Jerome Bowes was unmistakable in his fine, tall hat. At his side was a richly dressed woman. For a moment Rosamond thought she must be one of the whores. Then she blinked and looked again. The long, narrow face above the finery was distinctive. Nan Morgan smiled up at her companion, placing one hand on his sleeve as she laughed at something he'd said. When a freshening breeze stirred the feather on his hat, she gave it a playful flick with her fingers.

Rosamond's hands curled into fists. Nan must have spent more time in Sir Jerome's company during his visits to Chelsea Manor than she'd realized.

As she continued to watch the *Dolphin*, Nan left the rail, climbed a set of steps to a higher deck, and passed through a door. A cabin? Rosamond had never been aboard any vessel larger than the earl of Leicester's barge, but it made sense that such an august personage as the English ambassador would have a private cabin and that Nan, who would not hesitate to share his bed if it kept him sweet, would occupy it with him.

When Bowes went to another part of the ship to speak with some of his men, a plan came into Rosamond's mind, fully formed and splendid in its simplicity. The distance to the spot where the *Dolphin* rode at anchor was not great. She had only to make her way on board, catch Nan by surprise, and persuade her to leave without making a fuss. A sharp blade pressed against vulnerable skin should do the trick.

Rosamond found a lad willing to row her out to the *Dolphin* for a farthing. As he cast off, she thought she heard Melka's voice calling her, but she kept her eyes on her goal. She'd have to climb those shallow shelves that were the boarding steps the way she would a ladder.

Her boys' garb had deep pockets. She fished out another coin and dropped it into the lad's outstretched hand. 'Wait for me,' she ordered in a gruff voice, and began the ascent.

The deck was in utter confusion. Several barefoot seamen wearing only coarse white linen trousers worked a large, mechanical winch. More seamen swarmed aloft, bent on doing something complicated with the sails. She did not know what was going on, but she was grateful for the commotion. No one noticed when she slithered over the rail.

She caught a glimpse of a great square sail of blackened gray as she scurried toward the stairs Nan had climbed and scrambled up them. Moments later, she slipped inside a small, strangely shaped room. Sunlight streamed in through latticed windows, illuminating white walls that slanted inward and low black beams. A lantern hung from one of them, the candle inside curiously fastened on a base with two thin wood props on either side.

Rosamond reached for the knife in her boot, but before she could draw the weapon from its hidden sheath, she saw that she would not need it. Nan lay on a bench built into the wall, equipped with pad and bolster to make it into a bed. Both hands clutched her abdomen, her face was a ghastly shade of green, and a vile smell rose from the latrine bucket beside her.

'Get up,' Rosamond ordered. 'We are going ashore.'

Nan stared at her, glassy-eyed. 'I am too ill to stand.'

Rosamond's stomach was steady, but she felt the motion of the ship. Even at anchor, it rocked and lurched. She reached for Nan's arm. 'You will feel better once we are on dry land.'

Nan evaded her to bend over the latrine bucket.

Rosamond retreated, trying not to breathe too deeply. The worse Nan felt, the easier it would be to convince her to return to shore. Once there, she'd find a constable to take Nan into custody.

The sound of retching was pitiful to hear, but Rosamond hardened her heart. As soon as it stopped, she hauled Nan to her feet, but a sudden movement of the ship sent them both sprawling. Rosamond nearly lost her footing a second time when the *Dolphin* pitched sideways. She took a step toward Nan, but a small table leapt into her path, dealing a painful blow to her lower limbs. She caught herself on the sea chest beneath the window and, for the first time since coming aboard, looked out.

Her view encompassed two other vessels, one with white sails and one with brown. Behind them, the houses and shops on shore grew steadily smaller. The width of the water increased. The rolling motion of the ship intensified, accompanied by the sounds of creaking timbers and water smacking against the sides.

With slowly dawning horror, Rosamond realized that the *Dolphin* had sailed. She was not going to be able to take Nan ashore, nor could she disembark herself.

Why had there been no warning? There should have been bells. Whistles. Too late, she remembered the seamen she'd seen high above her head, releasing that huge sail. And those others – they must have been raising the anchor. She'd been so intent on reaching Nan that she'd missed the obvious signs of imminent departure.

A low moan came from the bed. 'Am I going to die?'

'You are seasick. You will only wish you were dead.'

Rosamond felt a trifle queasy herself as the ship moved out into open water. Until they made landfall, she was trapped here with the woman she'd hoped to send to prison.

Forty-Seven

Rob Jaffrey was dreaming of England and Rosamond when he was rudely shaken from sleep. One hard hand grasped his shoulder. Another covered his mouth.

He choked back a muffled expletive when he recognized the man crouching beside his pallet. Pitch darkness made the smell the clove Toby Wharton had stuck in his cheek more pungent than ever. Rob stilled, waiting, certain that Nick Baldwin's man meant him no harm.

Shifting one hand beneath Rob's elbow, Wharton helped him to his feet and urged him toward the cell door. Whatever he intended, it was to be done with stealth. Rob picked up his boots from their accustomed place by the bed. He slept fully dressed, using his cloak for additional warmth. It might be summer outside, but within these thick stone prison walls there was a pervasive chill.

He spared a moment's regret that he had to leave his few possessions behind, but he could sense Wharton's urgency. If he was being spirited out of prison in the middle of the night, there was a good reason for it.

Wharton's route appeared to have been worked out in advance. No guards materialized to challenge them. Doors had been left unbarred. There was even enough light from distant torches to move without danger of tripping and sounding an alarm. Even so, it seemed to take eons before they passed through the last gate and emerged from the fortified building where Rob had been held for so many months.

They were not yet safe. They were still in the city and the tsar's rule extended into every nook and cranny. But it was a pleasant summer night. Stars shone above. Smells of kitchen and stable tickled Rob's nose. Locked away from them, he'd forgotten how pleasant they were. Even the stink of the midden was welcome proof that he had escaped his prison.

He'd hoped to be freed by legal means. Was he an outlaw now? Rob shoved his feet into his boots. There would be time to ask questions when they were safely out of Moscow.

It was nearly dawn before they stopped on the outskirts of the city near a wood. Wharton whistled two notes, high and low, and a hay cart appeared from among the trees.

'In there.' Toby gestured toward the back. 'Burrow in deep and stay quiet.'

Rob did as he was told. He had no idea how many hours passed before the cart halted. He held his breath. Friend or foe? A zealous soldier with a sword . . . or a pitchfork . . . would put a quick end to his freedom. Then he heard that most welcome sound, his own name spoken in a whisper. He sat up, sending hay spilling in all directions.

Wharton's grin and the smell of cloves greeted him as he emerged from hiding. 'Good lad.'

Rob hopped down from the cart, staggering a little as he landed. The two men embraced. Rob looked around him as he brushed himself off. They stood in the middle of a deserted road somewhere in the countryside. Hitched to a nearby birch tree were two horses, saddled and waiting. Wharton jerked his head in that direction.

'I've food in the saddlebags. If you're able to ride, we need to be on our way. They were not inclined to let you out, lad. We had to resort to bribery. Be glad Baldwin has deep pockets.'

Rob disliked being in debt to anyone, but he could scarce argue when the alternative was continued imprisonment . . . or worse. 'Why was the tsar so determined to hold me?'

'Pure cussedness is my guess.' Wharton's look of disgust spoke volumes. 'Or, more likely, he gave the order to arrest you and then forgot you existed. Best to get you out of Muscovy before he remembers.'

It was a long journey, overland first and then by water, and Rob's first glimpse of the anchorage at St Nicholas, early in the morning of the twenty-fifth day of July, filled him with despair. Only a few small vessels were in sight. If the fleet had already sailed for England, he would be stranded in Muscovy for another full year.

Wharton hid him in a warehouse and went in search of news, but when he returned an hour later, he was beaming. 'Good tidings, lad. The ships have not yet arrived from England. They are expected any day now. We'll be on our way home before you know it.'

'Thank God.'

Wharton opened the bag he carried and began to divide bread and cheese with which to break their fast. 'In the meantime, it seems I have a small matter of business to attend to. I could use your help.'

'Anything.' Rob owed the other man more than he could ever repay.

'Good lad,' Wharton said, slapping him on the back. 'You'll not be surprised to hear that Harry Vaughan has been up to no good.'

'I supposed he was trading on his own.' Rob helped himself to more cheese and some of the ale Wharton had brought to wash down the food.

'He has been stealing from the Muscovy Company, and he is here in St Nicholas with a cache of sables. I have been authorized to confiscate them and take Vaughan into custody.'

Rob munched slowly on his bread, considering. 'Could Vaughan have been behind my arrest?'

'Only if you saw something you shouldn't have at England House.'

'Mayhap he believes I did.' Rob recounted Vaughan's odd behavior that day in prison. 'It was as if he feared my arrest could prompt his, but at the same time, he seemed glad to have me safely locked away.'

'You said nothing of this when I spoke to you in your cell. The first time,' he clarified, and bit into a thick slice of bread topped with an even thicker wedge of the cheese.

Wharton had brought medical supplies a few days after Rob had moved into the larger cell.

'I was ill. Feverish.' He frowned. 'I think I wrote something about Vaughan to Rosamond when I was still half crazed and confused.' Had the letter reached her? Had she cared?

'You did give me a letter, but I dispatched it overland to England without reading it. Well, we will discover the truth, never fear. We will have all of the long voyage home to persuade Vaughan to answer our questions.'

The location of the warehouse where Harry Vaughan was storing his ill-gotten gains was not difficult to discover. The English settlement of St Nicholas was located on an island too small for keeping secrets. Accompanied by Rob and four Muscovy Company men, Wharton led the raid.

The men Vaughan had hired as guards fled at the first sign of trouble, leaving him to be caught red-handed with the sables. Bellowing curses, he rose from behind the table where he had been taking inventory. Anger and frustration distorted his face into an ugly mask.

'Surrender,' Wharton shouted. 'You cannot hope to escape.'

He wore a sword but did not draw it. The three men behind him carried cudgels. With the fourth man, similarly armed, Rob entered through a side door. He saw what Toby Wharton could not, that Vaughan's wheel-lock pistol lay within his reach. When Wharton moved closer, Vaughan grabbed for it.

Rob had no doubt that the weapon was primed and ready to fire. If Vaughan pressed the trigger to release the wheel lock, he could scarce miss hitting Wharton. With his friend's life in danger, Rob acted without thinking. He flung himself at Vaughan, seizing the hand that held the gun.

The other man was stronger than he looked, and despite improved conditions, Rob had lost flesh while in prison. With excruciating slowness Vaughan turned the pistol in Rob's direction.

'Drop it, Vaughan,' Rob gasped. 'What point is there in killing me?'

Vaughan's pale blue eyes held a look of desperation as his finger tightened on the trigger.

In the second before the priming power ignited, a shower of sparks flared in the minuscule space between them. Instead of firing, the pistol exploded, flinging the two men apart.

Rob's ears rang. A haze of smoke filled his vision and the stench of gunpowder clogged his throat. Then none of that mattered. Excruciating pain overwhelmed everything else.

It was a blessing when blackness descended.

Forty-Eight

Rosamond looked down at herself. The disguise she'd thought so clever no longer gave her an advantage. As a boy, she'd be expected to live rough with the seamen, assuming they did not throw her overboard for being on the *Dolphin* without a passport. There was no help for it. She would have to present herself as a woman and hope she'd be allowed to share this cabin with Nan.

A search of Nan's belongings yielded clothing that would fit well enough. She chose the oldest and plainest garments and fashioned a kerchief out of a length of cloth. She'd barely completed her disguise when the cabin door opened and Sir Jerome Bowes strode in.

He stopped short at the sight of her. 'Who are you?'

Head bowed, Rosamond whispered her answer: 'Mistress Morgan's maid, sir.'

Men like Bowes never noticed servants, but it was likely he'd think it nothing out of the ordinary for Nan to have brought one with her. She needn't have worried. He lost interest in her the moment he smelled the overflowing latrine bucket.

Sir Jerome Bowes displayed an excellent command of invective. He'd expected to enjoy Nan's favors throughout a long, dull voyage in return for sharing the captain's cabin with her. His anger was so intense that for a moment Rosamond feared he meant to turn them both out, to find what shelter they could elsewhere on the *Dolphin*, but in the end he left them in possession.

'Rosamond Jaffrey,' Nan whispered. Hatred flashed in her eyes, but only until the ship gave a violent lurch. Then she groaned and clutched her belly.

'I know a remedy for seasickness,' Rosamond said. 'I will obtain the ingredients from the ship's doctor if you promise not to tell Sir Jerome who I am.'

Once Nan agreed, Rosamond ventured forth from the cabin. Although the ship tossed and rolled without ceasing, the weather was fine. It did not take her long to master the trick of walking without falling and a helpful seaman took her to the ship's doctor, in truth only an apothecary, who did indeed have a plentiful supply of ginger and rose water. No one questioned her claim to be Nan's servant.

In quiet seas, in cramped quarters, the two women spent the first week pretending they were still friends. The cabin offered a number of amenities. The dishes, tankards, and spoons were all of pewter. The food was plentiful and well prepared, since it was safe to have a fire for cooking. That the ship's cook had a tendency to flavor everything with peppercorns could be forgiven.

By the second week at sea, Nan felt well enough to complain of the stink.

'I have emptied the latrine bucket and washed it out with sea water, so it must be pine tar you smell,' Rosamond said. 'Console yourself with the thought that it could be much worse. One of the seamen told me that this vessel customarily carries wine and spices. He said that if the regular cargo had been fish, that would be *all* we'd smell.'

Nan watched her through heavy-lidded eyes. 'How did you get here, Rosamond?'

'I climbed aboard and hid myself until the ship sailed.' Since she had no intention of telling Nan the truth, she had prepared a lie and told it with a glib tongue. 'You know my husband went abroad. I learned only lately that he traveled to Muscovy. I mean to confront him there and demand that he come back to England. I am tired of fending for myself.'

Nan seemed to accept the fabrication. Rosamond hoped to lull her into a false sense of security. They had a long voyage ahead of them, plenty of time to get at the truth, but she could not resist asking one question. 'Why did you run away from Chelsea?'

'I thought I could persuade Sir Jerome to take me to Muscovy with him. As you can see, I succeeded.'

'But why?'

Swallowing the last bite of their meal, Nan looked up and met Rosamond's eyes. 'Like your husband, my friend Harry is also in Muscovy. He has been all along.'

Harry Vaughan. Rosamond had not needed confirmation, having already ascertained from George Barne that the Vaughan employed by the Muscovy Company in Moscow bore the Christian name Henry, but it was gratifying to receive it all the same. 'Is this Harry the reason you wanted to accompany Lady Mary to Muscovy?'

Nan chuckled. Her eyes glittered in the lantern light. 'Shall I tell you a secret?'

Rosamond hid her eagerness. 'If you wish.'

'I knew even before I went to Ashby-de-la-Zouch that the tsar would ask for Lady Mary's hand in marriage. It was Tsar Ivan's English physician who suggested her name to him and he boasted of it to his fellow Englishmen at English House, the headquarters of the Muscovy Company in Moscow. Harry wrote to me at once and, since I had realized by then that I would never be among the gentlewomen Lady Howard took to court with her, I cozened her into recommending me to Lady Huntingdon for Lady Mary's service.'

'How clever of you,' Rosamond murmured, thinking that Doctor Robert Jacobi was not the only one given to boasting, 'but if that was your plan, why did you tell her such terrible tales about the tsar? You and Madge and the chaplain frightened her into refusing the match.'

Nan made a disgruntled sound and left the table to return to the bed and burrow into her blankets. Every day they sailed farther northward and into a colder climate. 'It did not take me long to realize that Lady Mary would never succeed as empress of Muscovy. The tsar would despise her on sight. He's put aside other wives. He'd be even quicker to dispose of Lady Mary, treaty or no.'

'So you tried to save her?'

'I tried,' Nan said in an exasperated tone of voice, 'to kill her, so that another royal cousin could take her place, one sure to be pleasing to the tsar, one I could influence.' She turned her head to skewer Rosamond with a narrow-eyed look. 'I doubt that shocks you. You had your suspicions ere now.'

'I admire determination,' Rosamond lied, 'although murder is perhaps a bit too ruthless for my taste.'

Did Nan guess she'd been sent to Chelsea Manor as a spy? Despite the accidents Nan had staged to protect herself and her plans, it seemed unlikely. She'd been afraid that Rosamond would say the wrong thing to the wrong person at the wrong time, no more. Best not to mention those incidents, Rosamond decided. She would pretend to have no suspicion that the rock in the snowball and the wax on the stair had been deliberate attempts to injure her.

'I wish you had taken me into your confidence sooner,' she said instead. 'We might have worked together toward a common goal.'

Nan said nothing.

'I suppose it is Frances Howard you want to marry to the tsar.'

'And why not?' After a long silence, Nan added, 'You suspected there was poison in Lady Mary's wash water, yet you said nothing.'

Let her think so, Rosamond cautioned herself. 'I could prove nothing. Was she supposed to drink it?'

'Yes. Stupid cow.'

'And that time in her bedchamber? Were you the one hiding in the standing wardrobe?'

Again, Nan laughed. 'I suppose I must beg your pardon for striking you with the door. I'd gone there to sprinkle a new poison onto one of Lady Mary's chemises. It was supposed to enter through her skin and kill her, but I never got the chance to apply it. I hid when I heard you coming.'

'You claimed to be ill that day, suffering from cramps.'

'A convenient lie. That was not the first time I'd told it. It is pleasant to have a day or two in bed every month.' Her restless movements told Rosamond she'd found it far less pleasant to be confined for weeks on end to a tiny cabin at sea.

'What happened to the poison?'

'When you came to my room, I scarce had time to thrust the vial into a box and get under the covers. After you'd gone, I discovered that the vial had broken. I had to dispose of it, and the box, lest I be poisoned myself.'

Rosamond had more questions, but to ask them would reveal that she knew more than she was supposed to. She was tempted to demand answers anyway, but before she could abandon caution the motion of the ship changed. Nan squeezed her eyes shut and whimpered.

At first there was just a steady rolling from side to side but then, without warning, it seemed as if the ship was about to turn upside down. Rosamond held her breath and clung to the side of the bed. The *Dolphin* shifted and rolled back with equal violence, sending even those items she'd thought were secure flying through the air.

The storm raged for days. A time or two, Rosamond went flying, too. One of the heavy chests bounced with so much force that it broke open, scattering its contents. Nan, sick as a dog, was no help at all. In the end, Rosamond resorted to tying them both to the bunk with heavy ropes.

Nan became convinced that she was about to die and Rosamond took ruthless advantage of the other woman's terrified state. She had kept several doses of poppy syrup in reserve. Now she withheld the oblivion Nan sought until she answered Rosamond's remaining questions. Often the replies were no more than an anguished yes or no, but by the time they reached calm seas once more, Rosamond had confirmed almost every guess she'd made about Griffith Potter's death and the attempts on Lady Mary and herself. Reluctantly, she had to accept that Nan had not known of Potter's murder until well after he was dead.

'You know too much.' The hatred was back in Nan's eyes.

'I know enough to be sure you will keep my secret until I am safely ashore in Muscovy. In return, I will not betray your sins.'

Nan did not look as if she believed her. Rosamond pinched Nan's nose, forcing her to open her mouth, and administered the opiate. When it took effect, she went to sit in the cabin's only chair, wrapped in blankets against the increasingly frigid temperature. The sea was still too rough to allow for lights or heat or cooking. Everything in the cabin was wet, including the blankets and the clothes she wore. There was no way to dry anything. Worse, Rosamond was uncomfortably aware that she had developed salt water blisters in unfortunate places.

All that she could survive. She was not so certain about her fate once the fleet reached St Nicholas. Nan would do nothing until then, not when Rosamond was the only one on board willing to nurse her through another bout of seasickness. But once they made landfall? With Nan sedated, Rosamond had time to wonder and worry about the future. Too much time.

Fears for her own safety were not the only thoughts that occupied her mind. Concern about Rob returned to plague her. She prayed he was alive and well, but what would she say to him when they met again? What would he say to her?

She had many regrets. Day after day, they all conspired to add to her misery. She found herself reliving mistakes she'd made two years ago and more. When she returned to England – *if* she returned to England – she vowed to make amends. But Rob? One minute she wanted them to have a real marriage, even children. The next she convinced herself that she'd be a fool to give up her independence for any man, even Rob Jaffrey.

Then she remembered that the point might be moot.

The nearer they came to their destination, the more concerned Rosamond became about Nan's enmity. Once or twice, Nan felt well enough to invite Sir Jerome to share her bed. On those occasions,

Rosamond was banished from the cabin. She watched Sir Jerome's face when he left, searching for any sign that Nan had betrayed her. She was not reassured when he continued to ignore her.

Sooner or later, Rosamond knew Nan would attempt to dispose of the only threat to her plans for a new life in Muscovy. To be safe, Rosamond devised a way to disembark as soon as the *Dolphin* made landfall at St Nicholas. She would have to be quick about it. Nan, by herself, was dangerous enough. If she persuaded Sir Jerome to help her, Rosamond's danger would increase tenfold.

Forty-Nine

Long before the *Dolphin* reached the mouth of the Dvina and the port on the White Sea used by the Muscovy Company in Russia, Rosamond had grown heartily sick of shipboard life. The smell of festering bilges, the discomfort of wet bedding, and the sheer boredom of day after day of the same monotonous routine were made worse by a deteriorating diet.

At first food had been plentiful if uninspired – stock fish, smoked pork, salt beef, cheese, even fresh plums, washed down with beer of middling quality. Early on, Rosamond had wrinkled her nose at buttered peas, salted eggs and bacon, and had much disliked the bag pudding made of raisins and currants, but she'd have offered up all the money in her purse to sample such delights after five weeks at sea.

Watery oatmeal pottage with parsnips was the best of what was left. Neat's tongues stored in bran and ship's biscuit turned even Rosamond's strong stomach. To make matters worse, she recognized the signs of scurvy in her aching joints, her painful gums, and a feeling of general lassitude. The ship's apothecary reluctantly agreed to let her have some of the lemon juice mixed with saltpeter and nutmeg that he gave to the crew as a cure.

At the first sighting of St Nicholas, Rosamond changed into the disguise she'd arrived in. Her boys' clothing was as damp as everything else in the cabin, but it smelled better than what she'd been wearing and she could move more freely in breeches than in skirts.

Nan watched her through narrowed eyes. Although she kept one hand pressed to her stomach, she seemed better able to tolerate the ship's constant rocking than she had been. 'Help me to wash,' she ordered.

Silently, Rosamond obeyed. By the time Nan was garbed in garments less foul, her hair free of snarls and covered with a cap, the noise from the deck – whistled commands, shouts, and the clanking of the anchor as it was dropped – told them that their journey was over at last.

'Shall I try to discover how soon we can go ashore?' Rosamond asked, already sidling toward the door.

'Dressed like that? No decent woman wears men's clothing.' Nan's eyes glittered with hatred as she lunged at Rosamond.

Nan had not been confined to bed for the entire voyage, but neither had she taken much exercise. She would have fallen if Rosamond had not caught her arms. Nan twisted in her grip, pushing her farther into the cabin. At the same time, she screamed for help at the top of her lungs.

By the time the door crashed open to admit rescuers, Rosamond's knife was in her hand. She realized her mistake the moment she saw the look on Sir Jerome's face. Nan flung herself into his arms while two other men seized Rosamond. One of them wrested the knife away from her.

'Who is this?' Sir Jerome demanded, staring at Rosamond over Nan's shoulder.

'She is a mistress of disguise,' Nan said in a tremulous whisper. 'She claimed to be a maidservant you'd hired for me. I fear she murdered my real tiring maid before we left England. I was too ill at first to question her, and then she threatened to kill me if I did not keep her wicked secret.'

'You are safe now, my little queen of hearts,' he murmured. His voice turned to ice when he barked orders at the men holding Rosamond prisoner. 'Take her to the hold and clap her in irons.'

Rosamond pretended to sag in defeat. As she shuffled toward the door, the grip one of the men had on her arm loosened a fraction. Now all she had to do was lull her other captor into thinking she did not intend to put up a fight. Once she was close enough to the rail she would pull free and fling herself overboard. She had learned to swim at an early age, having badgered Rob into teaching her. Once she escaped from the *Dolphin* she could swim to the *Winifred*.

But she had reckoned without Sir Jerome's temper. No sooner had she been hauled out of the cabin than he seized hold of her himself. Although she struggled, she was helpless against his greater strength. He dragged her toward the stairs and when she dug in her heels he slapped her so hard that her ears rang.

Rosamond went limp, but this time the feint fooled no one. Sir Jerome dragged her down from the half deck, cracking her shins against every step. 'You are a spy,' he hissed into her ear. 'My enemies sent you.'

Her heart in her throat, she tried to deny the charge, but he was not listening. She flailed with her left hand, reaching for the second knife, the one concealed in her cloak, but it remained just out of her grasp. An open hatch loomed ahead of her – the hold, even now being emptied of its cargo.

In a dark, dank corner, someone had installed a set of manacles. Rosamond managed to bite Sir Jerome's hand and kick one of his men in the privates before they had her secured. For her trouble, she was struck a second time, leaving her with an aching jaw and the taste of blood in her mouth. Sir Jerome ordered her searched, a command his men followed with far too much enthusiasm for Rosamond's comfort.

When he had possession of the second knife and her purse, he sent the others away. He opened the latter and gave a low whistle when he saw how much money it contained. 'Why were you aboard the *Dolphin*? Who sent you to spy on me?'

Rosamond's only answer was a glare.

He leaned closer. 'You carry no passport. No papers of any kind. And no one in Muscovy knows you are aboard this ship. Think about that. When I return, I want answers.'

Left alone in the dark, Rosamond yanked on the chains that held her. It was no use. She could not free herself and she doubted any of the crew would go against the new ambassador to rescue her. She shuddered as she remembered the feel of hands searching her and hoped none of them decided to pay her a visit with some other purpose in mind.

Her cheek stung where Sir Jerome had struck her the first time and she was still dizzy from the force of it. The second blow had loosened a tooth. She worried it with her tongue until a scurrying sound distracted her. She squinted into the blackness surrounding her but could see nothing. She was battened down below the hatches in the dark and damp with the rats. The constant motion of the *Dolphin*, even at anchor, made the dizziness worse.

This was not the way she had envisioned her first day in Muscovy!

Rosamond huffed out an exasperated breath. She would not cry. Nor would she feel sorry for herself. There had to be a way out of this predicament. She just couldn't think of one at the moment.

What she did think of was Rob. Was this what his imprisonment was like? Had he been in chains all these months. Her stomach twisted at the thought.

Despite her best effort to remain optimistic, Rosamond sank into despair. She tried to distract herself by listening to the sounds of the ship, trying to identify what was happening on deck. They'd be disembarking, unloading Sir Jerome's thirty cartloads of possessions, settling into whatever accommodations had been provided for them in St Nicholas. Ambassador Pissemsky's party had been on another ship. She supposed they'd set out for Moscow together before long, mayhap even on the morrow.

Sir Jerome had promised to come back. Would he let her go if she told him what he expected to hear? She could say Walsingham had sent her. It was almost true.

A snort of laughter escaped her. Say that and he'd likely kill her on the spot.

She tensed at a loud creaking sound. The hatch opened, letting in a shaft of daylight. She heard someone descend into the hold. Heavy footsteps came toward her, but all she could make out was the silhouette of a large man. When he lifted the lantern he'd brought with him, the glare momentarily blinded her. She was still blinking rapidly, trying to clear her vision, when he spoke.

'It is only by great good fortune that the *Winifred* was the last ship in the fleet to leave Gravesend. Otherwise I would never have guessed you could be this much of a fool.'

Rosamond sagged in relief. 'I am in your debt, Master Baldwin. I had begun to fear for my life.'

'As well you should.' He made short work of the shackles, having somehow procured a key to open them.

Baldwin lost no time helping her up to the deck and over the side, where he had a skiff waiting to take them ashore.

'How did you know where I was?' she asked as soon as she was seated.

'Melka saw you climb aboard the *Dolphin*. When the ship set sail, taking you with her, she commandeered a rowing boat and hailed the *Winifred*. She even had the foresight to bring your traveling chest, that I might deliver it to you here in St Nicholas. She'd have come with it, I suspect, had she not felt a greater obligation to return to Willow House and look after Watling. What were you thinking, Rosamond, to do such an irresponsible, dangerous thing?'

'Dress as a boy?' she asked, hoping to make him smile. 'Or try to take Nan into custody on my own?'

'Is that what you were about? Madness! I saw her come ashore. She has acquired a powerful protector.'

Rosamond leaned toward him, eager to tell him all she had learned, but he cut her off with an impatient gesture.

'Do you have any idea what you have put me through for all these weeks? I did not know if you were alive or dead. And when Nan Morgan disembarked and you did not, I feared the worst.'

She tried to apologize but he was not listening. A moment later, the small boat bumped against the landing.

'Guard your tongue,' he whispered, and then, in a louder voice, said, 'Welcome to Rose Island.'

Rosamond frowned. 'I thought this place was called St Nicholas.'

It was heaven to be on land again and inhale the mingled scent of roses and rosemary, both of which grew wild. The sound of birdsong and the sight of fir and birch trees off to one side and good green pasture beyond a few stark wooden buildings delighted her. Curiously, it seemed warmer here than in England.

'St Nicholas is the name of the monastery on the mainland opposite. We are at the mouth of a river. It is ten miles wide here, where it flows into the White Sea and several islands divide it into channels. When the first English explorers arrived, they found mooring at the mouth of the southernmost channel. That is where Muscovy Company headquarters remain to this day.'

Rosamond realized he was speaking as much for the benefit of passers-by as to educate her on the geography of the place. As soon as they entered one of the buildings, his false smile and jovial manner vanished as if they had never been.

'You have not asked me about your husband.'

'You did not give me a chance to, but now that I am here, I fully intend to go to Moscow with you and secure his freedom.'

'Too late for that.'

Rosamond stared at him. His grave tone of voice and bleak demeanor made her think the worst had happened. Her heart gave a great thud in her chest and seemed to stop. Her breath backed up in her throat. She took an unsteady step toward him.

'No. He cannot be dead. He—'

'Not dead.' Baldwin's manner softened a little when he saw her horrified expression. 'But he has been gravely injured. Come with me.'

They climbed a narrow staircase to the floor above and entered a small room. Two men were within, lying on pallets. Only one of them turned his head toward them as they came in. The other appeared to be unconscious.

Rosamond stared, shock holding her still. It was Rob who lay unmoving. She scarce recognized him. His face was paler and thinner than when she'd last seen it. Worse than that, it was pocked with livid burns. She could not see the rest of his body, but feared the damage was widespread. That one wrist was broken was clear enough. It was held immobile by splints.

She tried to say his name but only a choked whisper came out. She cleared her throat and tried again. 'Rob?'

His eyes opened, then widened in disbelief. 'Rosamond? Am I dreaming?'

She flung herself to her knees at his side, reaching out to him and then pulling back when she realized it would hurt him to clasp him to her and hug him the way she wanted to. 'You're free. You're alive.'

And she burst into tears.

Fifty

Rosamond was not much given to crying, but she sobbed uncontrollably until she saw how distressed Rob was by her display of emotion. Only then did she manage to choke back her tears. Still sniffling a little, she took the handkerchief Master Baldwin supplied and blotted her cheeks. Heat climbed into her face as she crushed the damp cloth in one fist. While she'd wept and clung to Rob's good hand, she'd been oblivious to the fact that she had an audience. With the return of her usual self possession came an acute awareness that others had witnessed her embarrassing loss of control.

She squared her shoulders and scowled fiercely at the cause of her lapse. 'Why are you not at Cambridge? You have put me to the great inconvenience of coming here to fetch you back to England.'

Rob, curse him, reared up and gave a shout of delighted laughter. 'There's my Rosamond!'

She would have been angry with him in truth had his face not suddenly gone white as bleached linen. He gasped in pain and fell back against his pillow.

'Lie still.'

With as much gentleness as she could manage, she peeled away the sheet, undid his bandages, and examined the burns that disfigured his arms, chest, and belly. They did not extend onto his upper arms or down into the lower regions of his torso, but they were extensive all the same. She winced at the sight of so many blisters.

Someone had cleaned each patch of damaged skin and anointed it with healing salve but Rosamond felt heat rising from Rob's body. Her breath caught. Baldwin had been right. Rob had been gravely injured. She could still lose him to a fever.

'Artemesia,' she murmured. 'Or centaury with water. He should drink as much liquid as possible. Any liquid.'

'He's been treated with oil of eggs,' said a voice from the other pallet. 'The sovereign cure for burns. And there's poppy juice for when the pain gets too bad.'

Rosamond belatedly recognized Master Baldwin's man, Toby Wharton. The faint smell of cloves tickled her nose. She twisted around so that she could see Baldwin himself, giving him her best glare.

'An oil made from plantain leaves is better, stamped together with daisy leaves, the green bark of elders, and green germanders.'

'I will send for the ingredients. You will no doubt want to care for Rob yourself, now that you are here.'

Rosamond said nothing as she reapplied the bandages and pulled the sheet up to Rob's neck. He seemed to have drifted into sleep . . . or unconsciousness . . . and she did not try to rouse him. Rest healed and the steady rise and fall of his chest gave her hope that he would recover, but it was worrying her that he had failed to remark upon the bruise on her face. Neither had he noticed that she was dressed as a boy.

'What happened to him?'

It was Wharton who answered. 'A pistol exploded, killing the man trying to fire it and injuring both your husband and me. The blast threw me against a wall, broke two of my ribs, and singed my beard so badly that I had to shave it off.'

'And Rob?'

'He was struggling with Vaughan for possession of the gun at the time.'

Rosamond sat back on her heels and stared at him. 'Harry Vaughan?'

Wharton nodded. 'The same. He was stealing furs from the Muscovy Company. We planned to take him back to England for trial. Instead we buried him here on Rose Island.'

'Did he ever speak to you of a woman he called his queen of hearts?'

'Now how could you know a thing like that?' Wharton marveled.

Rosamond made herself more comfortable on the edge of Rob's pallet and provided her listeners with a condensed version of the schemes Nan had hatched. 'I still hope to find a way to bring her to justice,' she added. 'Can an agent of the Muscovy Company take her into custody?'

'It would be unwise to challenge Sir Jerome Bowes,' Baldwin said. 'As ambassador, he has authority over all other Englishmen and women in Muscovy.'

Wharton made a derisive sound. 'He's powerless to do anything unless the tsar permits it. Did Doctor Jacobi return with Pissemsky?'

'He did.'

'Talk to him. See which way the wind blows.'

Baldwin returned an hour later, by which time Rosamond's traveling chest had been brought ashore from the *Winifred* and she once again looked like a proper English gentlewoman.

Rob was awake, but Rosamond could not tell how much he understood of the conversation going on around him. She kept one hand on an undamaged part of his arm as Baldwin recounted his meeting with Jacobi.

'It is as well I followed your advice without delay,' he told Wharton. 'On the morrow, Ambassador Pissemsky and his party leave for Moscow.'

'With Sir Jerome? Is there no way to delay him? If we keep Nan here, mayhap—'

He held up a hand to silence her. 'Sir Jerome Bowes has been ordered to remain on Rose Island until he is summoned by the tsar. That summons may be some time in coming, but Jacobi himself was entrusted with several commissions by the queen. One is to gently persuade the tsar to give up his quest for an English bride, since none will ever be forthcoming. The other is to present Ivan with a letter asking that Mistress Bomelius be allowed to leave Muscovy. By the time that request reaches the tsar, we will already be on our way back to England. She will have to sail home with next year's fleet.'

Rosamond glanced at Rob. Although his eyes were closed, she did not believe he was asleep. Was he afraid she would demand he explain why he'd tried to help Jane Bomelius? Rosamond had too much pride to ask, as well as a healthy sense of self-preservation. Why risk being hurt by his answer?

During the next two days, while Rob slept, Rosamond passed the time at the sickroom's single window watching cargo be loaded onto the ships. The fleet had arrived in St Nicholas nearly a month later than usual and would sail home as soon as possible, carrying everything from hemp to honey to an assortment of furs that ranged from lynx and white wolf to the skin of a great water rat that was said to smell naturally of musk.

More than once, Rosamond caught sight of Nan Morgan, walking arm-in-arm with Sir Jerome. As long as her quarry was still within reach, Rosamond continued to devise and discard plans that would separate Nan from Sir Jerome, spirit her aboard the *Winifred,* and imprison her there for the journey back to England. None had a prayer of success while Nan held Sir Jerome's interest.

On the third day, Rob's fever broke. He did not have much strength and still took frequent naps, but he was himself again. When she asked questions, he answered them, speaking of his time in Muscovy, his imprisonment, and his escape, but saying not a word about Jane Bomelius. Then it was Rosamond's turn. Two more days passed with talking and sleeping and talking again before she concluded her tale with Nan's plan to join forces with Harry Vaughan.

'She cannot be allowed to profit from her crimes,' Rosamond added, 'even if she does seem likely to escape punishment.'

'She did not kill anyone,' Rob observed. 'It was that fellow Gargrave who poisoned Potter.'

'Only because her attempts at murder failed. If she had succeeded, I would not be here.' She was settled, cross-legged, on the pallet Wharton no longer needed, her skirts billowing out around her. She was amused to realize that she did not know quite what to do with her hands. She had grown accustomed to the feel of a needle in one and a piece of embroidery in the other.

'It would have killed me to lose you,' Rob said.

The emotion behind the words disconcerted her. 'You very nearly died in any case.'

They both fell silent after that tart-tongued remark. Rosamond felt as if she'd just kicked a puppy, but she was unaccustomed to censoring her opinions when she was with Rob. Why deny the truth? He should never have come to Muscovy in the first place.

'If you do find a way to take Mistress Morgan back to England to face trial, she might well be pardoned,' Rob said after a while. 'Or those in power could choose to overlook her crimes, rather than have the whole story become public.'

'More likely Sir Francis Walsingham would lock her in an obscure cell in the Tower of London and forget she ever existed.'

Rob shuddered. 'That is not a fate I would wish on anyone.'

Another uncomfortable silence fell. Then Rob shifted on his pallet, angling himself so that he faced her. 'It is unlikely she knows Vaughan is dead. Will it devastate her when she learns of it?'

'She has scarcely been faithful to him. She played the whore with Ralph Gargrave and Sir Jerome.'

'And what will happen to her when Sir Jerome returns to England?'

Rosamond considered. 'She could go back with him. I doubt she knows that Sir Francis Walsingham is looking for her, and she believes I have been disposed of. But it seems more likely to me that she will remain behind, waiting for the arrival of the tsar's English bride.'

'If Doctor Jacobi is to be believed, that bride will never come.' He let that thought hang in the air between them for a moment before adding, 'I call that a fitting punishment. An Englishwoman alone in Moscow will not thrive.'

Rosamond wanted, very badly, to ask if Mistress Bomelius's situation was what made him so certain. She bit back the question and stared down at the hands she held clenched in her lap. He was right. If Nan stayed, she would get what she deserved, and if she should choose to return to England with Sir Jerome, Rosamond would be waiting for her.

It was enough.

It would have to be.

She stole a glance at Rob, expecting to find him watching her.

Instead, he was trying to reach beneath his pillow. He sucked in his breath when the movement aggravated his injuries. Rosamond leaned toward him, but he waved her back. In his hand was the miniature portrait Rosamond had asked Master Baldwin to give to him.

'Why did you send me this?'

'To remember me by. Why else? At the time I did not know we would be reunited here in Muscovy.' She tried to make light of the gift, but there was a tell-tale quaver in her voice.

'I could not forget you, Rosamond, even if I wanted to.'

The rueful expression on his face annoyed her enough to make her forget that she'd meant to exercise restraint when it came to certain subjects, at least until Rob was fully recovered. The accusation burst out of her. 'Were you thinking of me when you left the country without a word? You abandoned me!'

'Aband—! Rosamond, you had done everything in your power to drive me away.'

The pain in his voice made her ashamed. 'I meant for you to stay at Cambridge,' she muttered, 'not run off to Muscovy.'

With an abrupt movement, she rose to her feet. She was not ready to discuss the failure of their marriage. Not yet.

'It is time for you to rest. You must not overtire yourself if you are to recover properly.'

'Your wish is my command, wife.' He promptly closed his eyes.

Rosamond stood staring down at him, hands fisted on her hips. He was mocking her, the exasperating man!

'We have a long voyage home ahead of us,' he said, eyes still shut. 'Two months at sea, at the least, and given the crowded conditions aboard ship and the fact that we *are* married, we will doubtless share a cabin. We will talk of this again.'

She bent down to place one hand on his forehead, pleased to find it cool to the touch. When his eyes flew open, she held his gaze and murmured, in her sweetest voice, 'Just remember that I keep a knife in my boot.'

He grinned up at her and she could not help but smile back.

Their voyage home might be long, but it most certainly would not be dull.

A Note from the Author

For information on sixteenth-century seafaring I am indebted to James L. Nelson, who once sailed on the replica of the *Golden Hinde*. Any errors in this area are mine. I would also like to thank my husband Sandy, my agents, Meg Ruley and Christina Hogrebe, and fellow writers Kate Flora, Kelly McClymer, Barbara Ross and Lea Wait for their encouragement and support.

Although this is a work of fiction, it is based on real events. Readers who want to know more will find 'the real story' and a bibliography of my sources at KathyLynnEmerson.com.